WAVES OF
MURDER

J B Raphael

First published in the UK in January 2015 by MyVoice Publishing

Cover Design by James Welch

Published by: MyVoice Publishing
www.myvoicepublishing.co.uk

ISBN: 978-1-909359-48-2

With thanks to Lynn
for her continued hard work and support.

Thanks also to James Welch
for his technical expertise in the design of the cover.

Chapter one

The sun piercing through the gap in the curtains, woke Jonathan Weston, he blinked with sore eyes. The smell of bacon frying wafted into his bedsit from the next door room. The tenant had a cooked breakfast every morning. He had only seen his neighbour once or twice, he went to his office job well-dressed, dark suit, white shirt, shiny shoes and neat brief case. Jonathan guessed that he worked in a bank, oh well he thought, at least he had a job, I haven't. What will today bring on the dole, very little money, only his sister Vicky to help, which she did gladly. A successful private doctor who adored her brother, gave him money, loaned him her car and generally looked after him. She would have him move into her four bedroom house in Belsize Park, but her husband Peter, also a doctor said 'No, I would like to preserve our privacy.' Jonathan had a good education, but when he left school he allowed his mind to be addled by foolishness, girls, fashion, cars, booze, you name it. Everything except drugs, he loathed the thought of them, his friends tried to introduce him to cannabis, but he declined, just watching them act like idiots under the influence.

"Hi ya Vicks," he almost shouted, as he pressed the 'Entry' button at the side of the electric gates to her house, "it's Jono," he said.

"Hello darling," came the reply as the gates started to swing open. He walked up the gravel driveway to the front door which opened with a flood of light from the large hall. She threw her arms around his shoulders, hugging him tightly, "Come in, come in," she said enthusiastically, "You will stay to dinner won't you, it'll only be 15 minutes, it's home-made spag bol, your favourite!" she said with a huge smile. The dining room was beautifully furnished with only the best fabric and furniture, "Peter's up in Manchester at a Medical Council conference, so it's just the two of us, what's your news?" she asked.

"Nothing," he replied, "I've had a couple of job interviews, but I dont't hold out much hope. It's bloody hard out there," he added, " no job, no money, no hope," he lamented.

Vicky took his hand and said,"Money isn't a problem, how much do you need?" she asked.

"About a grand," he said.

"Okay," and reached for her handbag and produced her cheque book, "Why do you need it?" she questioned.

"I need clothes, my wardrobe is a joke," he answered and lifted his foot to reveal a hole in the sole of his shoe.

"Oh, darling," she said, "look, I'll make this out for £1500, there's bound to be other bits and pieces you'll need."

"Good morning, sir," the friendly, smiling face said, "how can I help you?"

"I'm in need of a new wardrobe," Jon replied, "suit, shirts, ties, shoes and underwear." After an hour and a half he left with his purchases and £600 lighter, but the clothes were good, from a good up-market men's store. Back at his flat, he un-packed a suit, sports jacket, three shirts, two pairs of slacks and a pair of good leather shoes etc. A nice shave and then a hair-cut, he thought. After visiting a unisex hairdressers in Earls Court, he caught sight of himself in a store window, I look good, bloody good! he thought. He picked up a free newspaper from a stand outside the Tube station, at the bottom of the front page was an advert 'Cruise to the sun' it shouted, 'Med, 12 nights all inclusive £699'. Mmm he thought, I quite fancy that, sun, sea and a bit of luxurious living, if only for 12 days. "It's holiday time," he shouted at the sky.

A middle-aged woman passer-by said, "Is it? can I come?"

Jon walked on thinking I'll need some more money, but I'll leave it a week or two. He walked into a local travel agent with the paper advert, "I'd like to book this trip please," he said to the most beautiful blue eyes he had ever seen.

"Would you like to sit down?" she said, pointing to a desk, purposely bending to display her rear as she pulled in a chair. "I'm afraid that offer has finished, fully booked, well it would be at that price wouldn't it?"

"Well, what's on offer now then?" he asked, looking at her cleavage which was well shown.

"Well, what do you fancy?" she asked, looking down at her chest, smiling.

"Oh, I still want to cruise, preferably the Med sunshine," he answered.

"Well, that offer was for an inside cabin on the Arcadia, you can have an outside stateroom with balcony for £1600 all inclusive, with £100 on board spend," she explained, looking into his eyes, smiling and fingering the top button on her blouse.

"Would you like to go out for a drink tonight?" Jon heard himself saying, "and we can seal the deal then."

"I'm not allowed to socialise with clients, but I won't tell anyone if you don't, and after all it would be a business meeting, perhaps I could claim overtime?" she said smiling, and accepting his invitation.

They met, as arranged, at the local wine bar at six, in the mean-time Jon had been to his sister for another £1000 and to borrow her car. She was more than happy to do this, and poo poo'd Jon when he swore that he would repay her as soon as possible. Lorna, the travel agent, looked terrific, and they chatted freely about their lives. She was 24 and single, had been in the travel business since leaving school. They decided to eat at the wine bar, the menu looked very good. Two hours later Jon settled the bill for a very good meal.

Outside, the white Audi Coupe looked amazing, and when Lorna saw it she said, "Wow, is that yours?"

"No," Jon said, "company car," he lied, "I sell them, they're great cars, this is 60 grands worth," he added as he opened the door for her.

A gentleman, she thought, she liked that. They drove out into the countryside and Jon stopped the car in a lay-by on a B road, "Oh I see," Lorna said, "it's passion time is it?"

"No," Jon started to speak, but her mouth was on his before he could say any more. Although a coupe, with the seats pushed forward there was a lot of room in the back. Their lovemaking was outrageous, and passing motorists only saw the car moving to a certain rhythm, with the windows opaque with hot air! They both sagged back into the luxuriant leather seats, gasping and laughing at the steamed up windows. "Can I take it that the stateroom on the cruise is available as a free upgrade?" Jon asked.

"Whoa tiger, you'll have to hit the spot more often!" she replied.

He laughed loudly, there was a knock on the window which

interrupted their conversation. Jon leant across Lorna and wiped the window with his hand to see a policeman's face, he lowered the window. As they were both fully dressed there was no problem, "Are you all right miss?" the officer asked.

"Yes, thank you," she answered, "we were just discussing holidays."

"Is this your car, sir?" he asked.

"No officer," Jon said, "it's a company car," he lied.

"I see, sir," said the policeman, " well, good night, drive safely," he said. As no offence had been committed, the officer left it there. He didn't fancy a load of paperwork towards the end of his shift.

Jon dropped Lorna off at a small block of flats just outside the town centre, they made a date for Saturday night.

Saturday night arrived, and Jon picked Lorna up at the block exactly on time, 7 o'clock. He leaned across to open the door and revealed a huge bunch of flowers on the seat, "Oh," she said, "you really are trying for that upgrade aren't you?" and handed him an envelope, "well, you've got it," she said, taking a sniff of the flowers.

Jon opened the package to find tickets for the cruise, stateroom etc., all for the lower bargain price. "How did you manage to swing this?" Jon asked.

"Let's say the guy at head office owed me a small favour," she replied.

"I see," he said with a knowing smile.

"I'd come with you if I could, but it's difficult to find a child carer for two weeks, that won't eat your purse," she said seriously.

Jon started the car and they were soon parking outside 'Maison Ricard', a very highly thought of French restaurant at the better end of the High Street. Over a very good, but expensive dinner, Jon thought about Lorna's suggestion, and said that as she had saved him a lot of money, he would gladly pay for a child minder if she would like to accompany him. Her smile was enormous, but at the same time, beautiful, "Well, that's it then, we're going on a cruising holiday !" Jon said. Dessert was sex, sex and more sex, once again in the back seat of the car, but no interruption from the Police. This time Jon had parked well off the main road, in some trees. At 2am they left their little love place and Jon drove Lorna home, they kissed outside her bijou block and Jon asked her to call him with her answer.

Jon's mobile rang, the voice said, "I'd like to accept your offer, I'd love to come with you," Lorna said.

"Good heavens! I only asked you an hour ago!" he replied.

"Well, there's no sense in hanging about," she responded, "I'll make all the arrangements."

Jon's mobile rang, "Darling, can I have my car back, ple-e-ez?" Vicky begged.

"Sorry Vicks, yes, I'm coming round tonight, 'bout 7 ish okay?"

"Bless you," she said, "see you then. I've got to go out, so you'll have to feed yourself, there's plenty in the fridge," she added, "if you like you can take our Golf runabout."

Jon arrived on time, pressing the gate electric remote at 7pm exactly. Light flooded from the main door as Vicky opened it. She looked gorgeous, obviously not visiting a patient, "Going somewhere special?" Jon asked, as he handed her the car keys.

"Yes, I'm having an affair, didn't you know? That bastard Peter's been having one for two years, what's good for the goose etc etc!" she said, as she donned her coat. "The Golf's round the back, you know where the key is, oh, don't forget to set the alarm when you leave, you know how don't you?" she added.

"Yes, yes," Jon said, "enjoy yourself." He immediately called Lorna and told her to grab a cab and gave her the address. She arrived at 8 o'clock looking 'wow' as he said, "I'll pay the cab."

"Done it," she said.

Jon gave her a £20 note, "That should cover it," he said.

"This is one super house," Lorna said, "is this where you live?"

"Yes," he lied, "it belongs to my sister, big time private doctor, but I do have a tiny flat down the road in Chalk Farm," he said, adding some truth to his story. He poured some wine in the kitchen that looked as if it had never been used. "Now, about our little holiday?" he asked.

"Well," she said, "how's August for two weeks, five star,

Med and North Africa, outside stateroom. Oh, have you got a tuxedo? there are four formal nights, very posh!" she said.

"No, but I'll get one. M & S have some nice ones, and all the accessories," he said.

When Jon came out of the fitting room, he looked fantastic in his DJ. Over 6 ft and slim, the suit was perfection, "You look absolutely terrific," Lorna said, "I'll take a dozen!" she laughed, " as long as you're inside them!" she laughed again.

They drove down to Southampton in Vicky's Golf, with free valet parking all they had to do was take their luggage into the terminal at gate 10, to join the cruise boat 'Ajaxia'. An enormous ship, eighty-five thousand tons of pure white majesty. After the embarkation controls they were told their luggage would be taken to their stateroom on deck B, B220. Jon opened the door with the key card, 'wow' they said in unison, it was really de-luxe, Lorna ran in and jumped on to the king-size bed, Jon followed just as a porter knocked on the door with their bags. Jon gave him a £5 note, he said, "Thank you sir," and disappeared.

"Did you see that guy's name badge, it was Elvis," Jon laughed, " he wasn't wearing blue suede shoes though!" he added, and they both roared with laughter.

Dinner was informal, they were shown to a circular table by a white-jacketed maitre'd, their name cards were on the table. Soon they were joined by three more couples, two middle-aged and one who were on honeymoon and were joined at the hip and even held hands while eating with the other hand! Jon struck up a conversation with Zak, a fine looking 60 year old with a wonderful head of silver hair. He'd been an air-line pilot, and had taken early retirement as he didn't like flying, everybody at the table laughed. The ice was broken, the other couple were very down-to-earth, from Sussex, a pharmacist in his 40's with an Asian wife. Jon introduced himself and Lorna, Zak and Sandra, David and Sangita smiled nicely but Jack and Collette just smiled weakly and went back to looking into each others eyes. Jon was waiting for Jack to stab his face with a fork whilst looking at his bride!

As soon as dinner was over Jack and Collette rushed back to their cabin, their excuse being tired after a long journey and day. The diners that were left smiled at each other and

Zak started singing 'Memories'! Jon and Lorna liked Zak and Sandra and he suggested they went through to the 'London Pub Bar' that was situated amid ships on the promenade deck. Zak related some very funny 'true' stories about his flying days around the world and admitted to being a member of the 'Mile High Club'. Sandra laughed and said, "It's all right, I know all about it, I was with him in the toilet!" They all laughed.

Zak and sandra said goodnight and left arm-in-arm. Jon had noticed a very attractive middle-aged woman looking at him and smiling the whole time they had been in the bar. Well coiffured, and dripping in expensive jewellery, a seed of an evil plan was germinating in his brain.

Jon laid awake for most of the night, resisting the advances from Lorna, saying that he was tired. At six in the morning he had the whole plan formulated, but what would he do about Lorna? No, he couldn't kill her, they were closely linked, could he tell her of his plan? May be. He laid the plan aside for a couple of days and enjoyed sun, sea and sex with Lorna. The attractive lady from the bar seemed to be everywhere, the sun deck in a bikini that revealed how well kept she was, Jon decided to tell Lorna what he intended. Her jaw dropped when he told her that he would seduce the woman, rob her and throw her body overboard.

"We will get home with thousands, and no-one will be any the wiser," he said.

"You're an evil bastard," she said, but she didn't shout, "I'm glad I don't have any diamonds," she added, "or I'd be swimming in the Med." She had noticed the woman, as women do when with a good-looking man, "Those diamonds she wears are amazing, that lady is asking for trouble," she said, taking Jon's hand and giving a silent 'go ahead' for the plan.

That night was a formal night, and Jon proudly wore his new dress suit, his plan was to separate from Lorna, as agreed, and go it alone. He sat, after a one course dinner, in the bar. Thirty minutes passed and then she walked in, paused slightly when she saw Jon alone sitting at the bar. She sat three spaces from him, smiled and said, "Good evening."

"Good evening," he heard himself say with a slightly dry mouth.

"Alone tonight?" she said with a smile.

"Er, yes," said Jon, "I'm really alone on the cruise, my sister has found a friend," he laughed.

"Oh, she's your sister?"

"Yes," he lied.

He found her mid-western accent attractive, and she said, "I love your British accent, what do you do?"

"I sell German cars," he lied.

"Oh, I have a German car, a Mercedes sporty convertible," she said. Jon couldn't take his gaze away from the diamonds, her necklace, her bracelet, her rings and the watch. She must have been wearing at least £200,000 worth. "You like my little trinkets, do you?" she asked, "they're a girl's best friend," she laughed, "I owe them all to my late husband, he left me 2,000 sq miles of wheat in Oklahoma, the world needs food. By the way, I'm Clarice van Houten," she offered her hand in introduction.

"I'm Jonathan Weston," he replied, taking her hand but regretting telling her his real name, but then thought that she will never be able to tell anyone, tonight would be her last. After two more drinks, Jon stuck to iced Perrier water, he needed a clear head for what was to come. Clarice suggested that they go to the casino, "Oh, I'm not a gambling man," he said.

"Oh, but I am!" she laughed, "c'mon it's fun!" she pouted. They walked into the small but luxuriant casino which was quite full. Ten o'clock seemed to be the gambling hour, they found two seats at the roulette table. Clarice opened her sequinned bag and pulled out $2000 in 100's, pushing forward $500, she said with the voice of authority and experience, "Chips please." She gave 100 to Jon, "There you go, honey, see what you can do with that." Jon was embarrassed but no one noticed, all too busy with their gaming. Jon did well, going red, black, evens, odds. After about half an hour he had amassed $1000, Clarice had done even better and had $10,000 in chips in front of her. She went on to win $20,000 before she cashed her chips. Jon had won another $500. "What a night," she said, as she gave him $5,000, "Don't worry it's not a gift, you're going to earn that back at my suite," she pouted, as she took his arm. They arrived at A200 ten minutes later, Clarice opened the mini bar and took out a bottle of Dom Perignon champagne, "Let's celebrate," she said to Jon, who was sitting on the luxurious sofa. She opened the bottle with a bang and poured out two flutes, "Cheers!" she almost shouted, chinked Jon's glass and sat beside him. Jon sipped two tiny sips and then put the glass down on to a small table. "I'll be back in a minute," she said, and went into the bedroom. Jon sat and thought deeply as to what was ahead. He had cold blooded murder on his mind and needed to go over the plan again in his brain. He noticed the balcony and walked over and opened the sliding door and looked down at the waves. Good, he thought, do the deed and over she goes, at about 3 o'clock in the morning. It was now one o'clock, two hours to go. The bedroom door opened to reveal a naked Clarice, apart from the diamonds which sparkled amazingly in the light. "So, what do you think?" she asked. Jon was completely aghast and speechless, she was beautiful, what a shame she only had 2 hours to live. She walked across to him and looking down, said [imitating Mae West with her hand on her hip] "is that a gun in your pocket, or are you just pleased to see me?" she laughed, Jon could only manage a smile. She gently lifted him to his feet, covering his mouth with hers and then turned and led him into the bedroom. What followed, Jon could until now, only fantasize about. For almost two hours they had sex in positions that Jon had never dreamed of. They lay side by side gasping and laughing at the same time. Clarice was still wearing her jewellery, Jon had felt the bracelet and watch chaffing his back as her orgasm moans reached crescendo. Jon suddenly saw his chance, he rolled over, grabbed her around the neck and pressed with his thumb on her windpipe, with all of his weight. She gasped her last breath with eyes bulging, beautiful eyes that didn't deserve to die, but his needs were great. Her arms and legs stopped thrashing and her face stilled, she just gazed at the ceiling, eyes wide open not blinking ...... she was dead!

Jon jumped out of bed, shaking. He'd done it, but how did he feel? Elated at the thought of the diamonds, but fearful of the horrendous deed he had just committed. He looked down at her beauty, she certainly didn't deserve to die. She still stared at the ceiling, he bent over and softly closed her eyes. Getting dressed, he now implemented his plan, stuffing all her cash into his pockets, he then started to remove her diamonds. Bracelet, necklace, watch and rings plus she wore a diamond anklet that he hadn't noticed. He removed it. At three o'clock he lifted her off of the bed, and fireman style, carried her into the lounge area, through to the balcony and tipped her body overboard. He watched as it fell to the sea with only a minimal splash, and immediately was gone with the speed of the ship.

With his ill-gotten gains stashed safely upon him, he opened the door slightly to see if there was anyone about, then alarm bells rang in his head, FINGER PRINTS. His were not on record, but what if they were taken and matched in her suite? He closed the door and started to wipe, with a damp tissue, everything he had touched. The glass, the door knobs, the surfaces of the bed, the flush handle on the toilet, the champagne bottle, he was in a frenzy of cleaning everything. The window handle, the balcony rail, in all he spent an hour and a half cleaning and wiping. As he left at 4.45am he wiped the door knobs, sweating, but was confident that he had done a good job. He knocked on the door of his stateroom, he was sure nobody, not even ship staff, had seen him make his getaway.

"Well," Lorna said, "is it all sorted?"

"Yes," Jon replied, "it's all done and dusted," he added, and started to empty his pockets on to the bed. Lorna's eyes bulged as she looked at the diamonds and cash.

"How much is there?" she asked.

"About a quarter of a million," Jon replied.

"Wow," she said, "good times, here we come."

"All we have to do now is to act normally, like a couple on a cruise, okay?"

"Yes," Lorna agreed.

"Now, I need to sleep," Jon said.

He got undressed and Lorna saw the chafe marks on his back, "A hard night?" she asked.

He ignored her remark and settled down to get some sleep, but sleep didn't come. He laid awake thinking of what he'd done, 'cold blooded murder' shouted in his brain, for what? Money. Eventually drowsiness overcame him and he drifted into a fitful sleep. Lorna heard him mumbling as she dressed. They left their stateroom at 10 o'clock, Jon took a 'do not disturb' sign with him to hang on the door of Clarice's suite, he carefully wrapped it in a tissue, no finger prints, not even on an insignificant sign.

Jon and Lorna sat in silence with only coffee and toast, they had no appetite for a full breakfast. Suddenly they were brought back to reality by Zak and Sandra, "Morning," they said in unison.

"Morning," J & L replied.

"How's it all going?" Zak asked.

"Not sure yet, couldn't sleep last night, strange bed and the movement of the ship, might have a bit of 'mal de mer'," Jon laughed, trying to be normal and cheer himself up.

"Well, I'm sorry to tell you this, but tonight we enter the Bay of Biscay," Zak said, " gets rough!"

"Oh well," Jon replied, "thanks for the warning, I'll get some sea-sickness pills from the pharmacy."

"Good idea!" Zak replied.

Jon had made a small package of the diamonds and deposited it in the ship's safety deposit box. Just a brown envelope with the gems wrapped in toilet tissue, he didn't want it to look too valuable. He even said this to the receptionist who gave him the pass key, "It's not much, I just don't want to carry it around. Oh, by the way, the safe in my cabin doesn't seem to work properly, but don't worry there's nothing in it now," he said over his shoulder, "thanks," he added. This made sure that if push came to shove, what he had said was on record.

On a cruise liner carrying about three thousand passengers, you very rarely see the same person twice, unless of course they sit at your designated dinner table. So Jon wasn't bothered about having been seen with Clarice. But Jon suddenly went cold, sweating at the same time, DNA on the bed sheets, his was on record after a skirmish outside a pub. He jumped up and almost ran to Clarice's cabin to remove the 'do not disturb' sign. Luckily the cleaner was down the deck hall, Jon could see his wagon and hear him singing. He snatched the sign, folded it as he almost ran away, and pocketed it, sighing with relief as he headed back to a very puzzled Lorna. He told her where he had been and why, she also looked relieved and took his hand as a comforter. The sight of all the diamonds and cash outweighed the fact that Jon had slept with another woman, she felt that she was now secure financially, pay off the credit cards, handbags, shoes and even a car were now on her imaginary shopping list.

The Bay of Biscay, as promised by Zak, was very rough and they both suffered from sea-sickness, as did 75% of the passengers. On the second day it became much calmer and life got back to normal on the ship. Their moods became better in their cabin, and they started to enjoy their holiday.

Gibraltar was the next port of call, but on the morning of the docking an envelope came under their door, it included a photograph of Clarice and asked 'Have you seen this woman?' Jon looked at Lorna and put his finger to his lips, "We know nothing, okay?"

"Yes," Lorna said.

As the 'Ajaxia' edged on to the quay, Jon looked down from his balcony and his heart sank. Two police cars, four uniformed English coppers and two plain clothes officers were waiting at the end of the gangway, watching every passenger as they disembarked. Jon thought, not to go ashore might look a little suspicious, so he decided that they should look like a happy couple going to do some shopping and sightseeing. They reached the bottom of the gangway after their names were checked off by security, and were supplied with wristbands as identification. As they stepped off, a plain clothes officer stepped forward and said, "Mr Weston, Jonothan Weston?"

Jon's heart went crazy, and his brain went into overdrive, "Yes," Jon said, "how can I help?"

"I'm Inspector Taylor of the British Gibraltan Police," he declared, at the same time showing him a photo of Clarice, "do you know this woman?"

"Yes," Jon said, "I had a drink with her in the English Pub bar, three days ago. She's American and tried to pick me up, well that's what I thought. But I told her that I was on the ship with my girl friend, she then lost interest. I saw her again later in the casino but that was only for ten minutes, I lost £20 and left. My girl friend was very tired and declined to come with me," he explained.

"Okay, sir, thank you very much," the Inspector said, smiling. He even doffed a non-existent hat to Lorna.

They sauntered through Gibraltar, it was like going back to

the sixties. They did a little shopping, but only a small amount, Jon didn't want to be seen flashing any big money about. No cameras, no jewellery, no electrical goods or booze which was all cheap and tax free. Back to the ship after an enjoyable day, the police were still at the quayside, but the plain clothes officers had gone, only the two police cars and four uniformed men were at the bottom of the gangway. They embarked and walked into the main reception area, the two CID men were at the main desk. "Keep walking," Jon said, " to the Crows Nest bar." In the Crows Nest they met Zak and Sandra and joined them, acting happy and carefree. They ordered a bottle of red wine, "The sun's over the yard arm isn't it?" Jon laughed, and poured wine for Zak and Sandra.

"I understand there's a woman missing from the ship, some American, probably in someone else's cabin!" Zak laughed, Jon and Sandra joined in the laughter. They finished the bottle and said they would see them at dinner.

At the dinner table, the honeymooners still only had eyes and hands for each other, and didn't join in the conversation, which was mainly about the missing woman. David, the pharmacist, said that she had probably got drunk and fallen overboard in the Bay of Biscay. "She'll probably surface, er, excuse the pun, and wonder what all the fuss is about in the morning," Jon said, looking at Lorna.

"Or, she found a toy boy who murdered her for her diamonds!" Sandra laughed, as did everybody. Jon, although laughing, went cold and hot at the same time. Lorna took his hand and squeezed it tightly under the table. The tannoy announced that the ship would be held over for another day as the police were still making enquiries into the disappearance of a passenger.

Lorna and Jon agreed to act normally and to take a leaf out of the honeymooners book, and show affection whenever possible. Lorna said," I know you're under pressure, but can we take this idea to our cabin as well?"

Jon smiled, and kissed her cheek, "Yes, I think we can!" he said. But at the back of his mind he was very worried about the extra day's investigation. His fears were buried when, the next morning, the tannoy announced that sailing time would be at 6pm. Jon's heart lifted and he started looking forward to the rest of the holiday. At 6pm, the Ajaxia moved away from the dock and sailed majestically into the blue Med, "Fantastic," Jon said. But he wondered how the Detective Inspector had picked him out by name as he came off of the gangway, but there had been no follow-up. "Thank ...," he stopped himself saying 'Thank God', that would have been grossly blasphemous and evil.

After all the trauma and drama, the ship settled down to normal cruising. Dinner every night, one formal night, when Lorna and Jon really put on a show of being the loving couple at the dinner table, in the bars and on the dance floor. Their table companions commented on their behaviour, "You kids are having a good time," Zak said, "how about joining us in the Crows Nest and we'll make a real night of it, what do you say?" he added.

"Yes," Jon agreed, "let's do just that." the evening went like a dream, and they finally said good night to Zak and Sandra at 1am. Sex was on the menu, Jon and Lorna didn't stop at any position that existed! At 3am they fell into a deep sleep.

The Med was beautiful, and very blue, next port of call was Casablanca, Morocco. What a culture shock, camels, Arabs selling trinkets, but Jon was looking for particular plaque, 'Ricks Bar Americain' from the Humphrey Bogart film 'Casablanca'. He had seen it years ago, and had always wanted to go there. Walking around the town centre he suddenly saw it, 'The Icon Bar', 'Rick's Bar'. They entered, it was packed with tourists, "Let's get a drink, and go outside with the camera and take some photographs." They found a fellow tourist who took their photopraphs!

Back on the ship, they decided to sit on the sundeck and get some rays, they had managed to find two sunbeds due to their early arrival back to the half-empty ship. Sunbathing had lost out to touring the shops. Being badgered by local dealers to buy their wares, pots, pans, fabrics, spices, shoes etc., wasn't to their liking and the flies were a constant pest. They could have gone on the tour bus, but it would have passed 'Rick's Bar' without stopping. So they just laid there holding hands, being lovey-dovey, so that anyone could see. The sun silhouetted the voice that said," Hello sir, can I get you something to drink?" She was a very pretty Asian girl.

"Yes," said Jon, "two large gin and tonics with ice and lemon, please." The drinks soon arrived, he signed the slip, no money changed hands on board except cash tips, which were gratefully received.

They spent the afternoon laying in the sun, and being together, Lorna squeezed Jon's hand, "I'm feeling very randy, would you like to accompany me back to our cabin, so that we can have a little sexual intercourse?" she almost begged.

"Yes," said Jon, feeling a movement in his swimming trunks! They both jumped up and walked quickly, very quickly, back to their cabin. For two hours they experienced the most amazing sexual activity! Jon woke up after an hours slumber, in a cold sweat, he'd had a bad dream, a very bad dream about Clarice. In his dream, she climbs back over the suite's balcony, still wearing her diamonds, and beckons him to join her down in the sea.

Lorna put her hand on his brow, and kissed his cheek, "Can I get you anything?" she asked.

"No, I'll be all right in a minute," Jon said.

At dinner Jon was his old self again, talking about 'Rick's Bar' and Casablanca. Zak and Sandra had done the bus tour, but complained about the heat and no air-conditioning, "It was like a sweat box," Sandra said.

"I wish we had just gone walk-about," Zak added.

"That's what we did, the locals and the flies were getting on our nerves, so we came back to the ship to do a spot of sunbathing."

"I wish we had done the same," they said in unison.

"Still, at least I can say that I bought these here!" and produced two plastic models of Humphrey Bogart and Ingrid Bergman, everybody laughed except the two pale honeymooners, who hadn't heard a word of the conversation. Now things had progressed to them feeding each other!

"C'mon you two, join in, you've got the rest of your lives to do that!" They took no notice, Zak's protest fell on deaf ears. David and Sangita just laughed and agreed in the right places, but didn't put much into the conversation. After dinner they all decided to go to the nightclub. Part of it was a long bar, sitting on one of the stools was a very attractive woman in her 40's wearing a dress with a side split that showed a very shapely leg. She smiled at Jon as they walked in, he thought, oh no, here we go again, but then thought to himself, one at a time ...... one at a time.

Lorna saw the woman, and steered Jon away from the bar, whispering "Don't even think about it," but there were no smiles or jokes, she was serious. She, somehow, found them, and sat at a table close to the four, and she was continuing to smile at Jon, adjusting her dress to show what was available. Lorna had had enough, she went over to the woman and said, "His name is Jon, he's quite rich, but unfortunately for you, he's mine. So cover up your thighs and keep your sexy looks to yourself, otherwise I'll smash your botoxed face in, okay," she turned and walked back to Jon, who just sat with his hand on his forehead, Zak and Sandra just watched in amazement. The woman stood up and walked out of the bar. This fracas had a double effect, it put another murder out of Jon's mind and sent the woman on her way. She possibly had had a lucky escape!

Zak and Sandra clapped their hands and Zak said, "Good on you, girl." Jon looked up, smiled and took Lorna's hand, pulling her down to sit beside him. They continued to be the close loving couple.

At breakfast, approaching Malaga after two days at sea, the news went around the ship that a woman's body had been washed up near Gibraltar, and the police were renewing their enquiries. Jon's heart sank at the revelation, but he was well away from it all, or was he?

As the ship docked at Malaga, Jon looked down and his brain started to go crazy, the police were waiting at the gangway, two plain clothes and two uniformed. He rushed back inside and told Lorna, "We'll stay on board today and sunbathe. Seen one Spanish town, and you've seen them all," he said. At 11pm the ship sailed and Jon heaved a sigh of relief, as did Lorna. The cruise continued and the couple spent most of the time on board ship, getting a good deep tan. Jon realised there was very little chance now of police investigation. It was up to the Spanish police to do any work on the murder case. Just another body washed up as far as they were concerned.

Chapter Two   Southampton

Jon looked down at the quayside, good, he thought, no coppers. Disembarkation went smoothly and quickly, the Golf was waiting for them after Jon handed in the parking permit and collected the keys. He had also retrieved 'the envelope' from the safe deposit box. They had been the only evidence that could have nailed him, but the police had missed it. They were soon on their way back to London and to a life of luxury with a quarter of a million pounds, at least. The diamonds wouldn't be on any stolen list as no theft could have been reported, but he decided to sell them piece by piece over a period of weeks in different parts of the country, starting in Hatton Garden, with the biggest piece.

His world fell apart when he entered a diamond dealer's shop, the bearded man behind the thick glass picked up the necklace, put in his eyeglass and put it down again, quickly, "I'll give you £120 for the gold weight, the stones are zircons, fake, of no value, I'm sorry." Jon walked out of the shop in a daze, he was numb. He had murdered for a load of junk. But he still had three rings and a watch, he hoped that they were real! He walked further down Hatton Garden, and went into another dealer's shop, he produced the watch through the security hatch.

The young bearded man put in his eyeglass and studied the piece carefully, "Very nice," he said, and put it down, "just a minute please," he said and went into his office, with a very obvious see-through mirror. Jon waited, but only for three or four minutes, "Okay," the dealer said, "how much did you want for the piece?" he asked.

"I really don't know, but I think it's worth ten thousand, after all it's a diamond Rolex."

"Well, yes," said the young man, "but first, if you don't mind, I have to check with the insurance computer. It'll only take a minute," he added. "Okay, everything's fine," he said, from his office door. He returned with ten packets of £50 notes, each containing a thousand pounds. "I need some details from you, name, address etc., just for my records," he said. Jon left the shop having given a false name and address. He felt better even though the necklace was worthless, and his forecast of wealth to Lorna was now much lower than the quarter of a million! He thought he would tell her over a nice dinner at her favourite bistro in Hampstead.

Over the said dinner, during the main course and after a large glass of Merlot, Jon reached into his pocket and brought out a tissue, in it was the necklace. He pushed it over to Lorna, she opened the bundle, "It's a fake," Jon said, "worth £120 for it's gold content, still that'll pay for this meal!" he added.

Lorna looked down at the necklace and mentally saw her sports car and handbags disappear, "Oh well," she said, "what you've never had you can't miss!"

"Oh, don't worry my darling, we've still got a lot of cash, and the rings, bracelet and anklet, they should bring in a few thousand so we are still well in the money. Tomorrow I'll go and cash them in and we'll see about changing our lives a little."

Hatton Garden was buzzing at 11 o'clock the next morning as Jon walked along the opposite side of the street to where he had sold the watch. He walked into a small shop, after pressing the entry button, "Good morning," the young woman said, with an air of authority. Jon produced the rings and the bracelet, passing them through the security slot in the thick glass window. She put her eyeglass to her eye, firstly the bracelet, and then the rings, "Do you want an advance or do you want to sell them?" she asked.

"I'd like to sell them," Jon said.

"I see," said the woman, "there are one or two checks I have to make, how much do you think they are worth?" she asked.

"I thought £20,000," he replied.

"Okay," she said, and disappeared into the back of the shop with the jewels. She re-appeared after 4 or 5 minutes and said, "I'll give you £18,000, that's my best offer, even though they are very nice, but this ring has quite a large flaw, that's a carbon piece," she added.

Jon thought for a short while and said, "Okay, it's a deal," as he looked into her beautiful brown eyes. She pushed a form and a pen through the glass gap for him to fill in his name, address and signature. He did this as she produced eighteen packets of £50 notes in thousands. Right, he thought, that's 28 grand.

He went to Lorna's agency, and said that he would pick her up at 5.30pm. She, although tanned, looked dreadful, she hadn't slept and her first day back at work had been hell. They discussed their position back at her small flat, "We've got over 40 grand," Jon said, "not enough, but we still have the anklet. But that's only about a grand, you may as well have that," he said.

"No, get rid of it," she said, shaking her head with a distasteful look on her face.

They ordered a Chinese takeaway, after which they went to bed, but no lovemaking, they just laid talking over their future. At midnight they had decided to do another 'run' as they called it, but where? They fell asleep, but Jon's sleep was again fitfull, the recurring dream that Clarice came back from the sea and demanded her diamonds back. He awoke and sat bolt upright cold, but sweating, finding it hard to breathe. He rushed to the window and threw it open, gulping in fresh air. Lorna woke and went to comfort him, calming down, he returned to bed and told her of his nightmare. He was still sweating but managed to finally go back to sleep. In the morning they decided that after Jon had collected Lorna from work, they would go to the West End for a meal and possibly see a show. They decided on an up-market steak house, and then managed to get late tickets for 'Les Mis'.

Leaving the theatre, they walked through busy streets back to the car. They had enjoyed the show and Jon was humming one of the songs. They arrived at Lorna's flat, where Jon surprised her by saying that he would be going on to his sister's for the night and to his flat in the morning for clothes etc. He said that he would pick her up after work, as he had to get back to work himself, he lied.

His sister answered the entry buzzer and activated the gates, Jon drove in and parked the Golf round the back of the house, then entered through the back door into the kitchen. She threw her arms around his shoulders and hugged him, "Where have you beeen since you got back?" she asked.

"Er, I've been here and there you know, I've met someone," he said.

"I know, I could smell her in my car, you naughty boy! I haven't done it in a car for years!" she laughed. Jon looked sheepishly down at the floor, smiling. "Will you be staying here tonight? Peter's in Paris, something to do with Bayer Pharmaceuticals and shagging his whore," she started to cry. "I'm going to divorce him, I've had enough, he's a bastard and I'm going to take him for every penny I can. The house, the cars, the villa in France, every fucking thing. Harley Street, ha! He'll finish up on skid row," she continued to sob. She poured herself a large glass of red wine.

"C'mon Vicks, that's not the answer," Jon said, putting his arm around her, "let's sit down, have you eaten?" he asked.

"No, I've no appetite, I'll take a sleeping pill and go to bed," she said.

"Is that wise?" Jon asked, "you've been drinking."

"Don't worry darling, I'm not contemplating suicide, I've got a lot of living to do, I'm only 39," she said, as she climbed the stairs to her bedroom, taking the bottle with her. Jon was worried and decided to stay the night. He laid awake for a long time before he fell into a fitful sleep. The same dream woke him, he gasped as he sat up, and rushed to the window, throwing it open for some fresh air. After a few minutes he felt better, the vision of Clarice beckoning him faded, and he went back to bed. But sleep didn't come, although the house was well built, he could hear Vicky sobbing.

Right, he said to himself the next morning as he walked into the kitchen, I'll get rid of the anklet today. Vicky was sitting at the breakfast bar drinking coffee and looking terrible, "How did you sleep?" Jon asked, knowing the answer.

"Lousy," came the reply, "there's coffee in the cafetiere, help yourself," she said.

They drank their coffee in silence, "Can I use the Golf?" he asked.

"You don't have to ask, take the bastard's Aston if you like, I don't care," she added.

"May I?" Jon asked.

"Sure," she replied.

He drove down into Holborn, with the hood down, feeling a lot better than the day before, what a car! he thought. A beautiful royal blue, with cream leather interior, £120,000 worth of sheer heaven. He parked the Aston outside a small diamond dealers in Hatton Garden. He pressed the security 'entry' button and was allowed in. "Good morning," said a middle-aged man with a beard and wearing a skull cap. He had seen Jon park the Aston and thought 'high class jewel thief', he was right!

"I'd like to sell this little piece," Jon said, as he passed it through the gap in the thick glass.

The man put in his eyeglass and studied it for quite some time, "How much did you want for it?" the dealer asked.

"Five thousand, the stones are quite big, and flawless."

"How about five thousand pence, it's a fake," he answered.

"Fake?" Jon almost shouted, as the man pushed it back through the gap.

"Good day to you," he said with a smile. Jon left the shop feeling down once again. The dealer thought, 'the car's probably a fake as well'!

Jon drove back to Lorna's office, and at a corner desk, he told her about the anklet, she didn't seem too worried and said, "Can we go again?"

"Yes," he answered, "we'll have to. What we've got won't last very long, but where?" As he said it, he noticed a small poster on the wall that announced 'New York Double. Cruise no fly, inc 3 day stop over. Shop and see the sights'. "How about that?" he said, pointing to the poster.

"It's very expensive, about £4,000 per head," Lorna advised.

"Well, it's a gamble anyway."

"Perhaps you should go alone," she added.

"I'll think about it," he said, "I'll pick you up at 5.30, bring some brochures, okay, see you then," and blew a kiss.

Back at Lorna's flat, after a Chinese takeaway, they went through the brochures. Jon said that he liked the idea of the 'poster' trip. "It's £4,000 basic, on the Queen of the Atlantic. It goes next Sunday, we've just enough time if we book it in the morning. Will that be both of us, or you on your own?" she enquired.

"No," Jon said, "I need you with me, hang the expense!"

Lorna booked the cruise, and Jon paid £8,000 in cash, "Well, at least I'll get commission on this!" Lorna laughed.

The familiar drive down to Southampton was uneventful,

he'd borrowed the Audi as he didn't want the Golf to get too easily recognised. Bloody cameras everywhere, he thought, especially at airports and docks. Embarkation was smooth and fast, the car was valet-parked and their luggage was whisked away to their stateroom on deck B. Jon looked down from the balcony, this was an amazing ship, five restaurants, seven bars, two casinos, two pools etc etc. But Jon was only interested in one thing, lonely rich women, and on this trip he had two chances, there and back! Sunday at 4pm, exactly on time with the Cunard band playing and hundreds of people waving, the ship, sounding it's departure, eased away from the quay. First night out dinner was a casual affair, and Lorna and Jon chose the London Carvery. The food, when chosen, was delivered to their table. Service was the order of the day, the fare was enormous, a menu would have been three feet long! roasts, salads, grills, seafood etc, and a host of desserts. They feasted and sat back in their seats feeeling absolutely bloated, "Let's check out the bars," Jon suggested as they left the restaurant. They looked at the ship's map and decided on the 'Palace Bar'. It was magnificent, furnishings denoted the splendour of Buckingham Palace, no American heiress could resist it! and sure enough there she was sitting in a velvet-lined booth looking a million dollars. About 40-ish, beautifully coiffured and wearing very expensive clothes, so Lorna said at a quick glance. Jon took a quick look and saw the double-row pearl necklace intertwined with diamonds, and the rings, about six of them all catching the light amazingly. Just before he took his gaze away, the woman smiled a long come-hither sort of smile. He returned it with a very quick one and then turned back to Lorna, and said," No lovey-dovey, you're my sister, okay?"

"Yes," she said, "I understand." She then stood up and said,"I'm very tired, I've got a headache too, see you in the morning," she added.

"Okay, sleep well," Jon said, hoping that Lorna's words were loud enough for the woman to hear. He sat back in the velvet luxury, and sipped gently at his drink.

"Been stood up?" an American accent asked.

Jon looked over the booth edge, and said, "Oh, no, my sister's had a hard day, what with the drive down here etc., " he explained.

"May I join you?" the woman enquired with good old American get-up-and-go.

"No," Jon said, smiling, "I'll join you. I've actually brought her away on this trip, she's going through a very messy divorce so I thought it would take her mind off of things," he added.

"Oh, I know what it's like," she said, laughing, "been there, done that, got the book!" she laughed again, "I hope she's taking the bastard for every penny, like I did. By the way, my name's Helen, Helen Smuthson, I've been doing Europe, fabulous! Paris, Rome, Venice, Naples, Sicily, oh and of course, London, wonderful London. I had three nights at the Ritz, wow! what a hotel," she enthused.

"I'm Jonathan Weston," he replied, "I sell very expensive cars to very rich people," and held out his hand. She took it and held on to it for longer than necessary, during which time he had a closer look at her diamond rings. Oh, lovely lady, if only you knew what was going on in my mind, he thought. The 'hand-holding' spoke volumes to Jon, she was just what he was looking for, and on the first night too! How lucky, he thought, it gave him two or three days to gain her confidence. But he couldn't be seen with her too often, he was so glad he had brought Lorna along, he would be seen mainly with her and had laid the foundations of the story to Helen, should things progress as he hoped they would.

They sat drinking and talking for most of the evening, until Helen said, "That's it for me, I'm bushed, I think I'll go to bed."

"I hope to see you again," Jon said as he stood.

"How about seeing a girl back to her cabin?" Helen said with a wicked smile.

"Of course," Jon said, "and then I must turn in as well, after I've checked on my sister," he added.

They reached her suite door, she took his hand and kissed him quite passionately, and said, "Goodnight, lovely man!" She opened the door, turned and blew him a kiss.

"Goodnight, Helen," he said, and walked down the corridor thinking that before he went for it with Helen, he'd see what else was available on board. After all, there were a lot of women on the ship, especially Americans, and it pays to shop around.

At breakfast he told Lorna all about the previous evening, she had been asleep when he got back to the cabin. "Just remember, no sitting close, no hand holding and no kissing, even though we want to, we are brother and sister. This is business, and let's hope it'll be very profitable," he expressed.

"Kiss me!" Lorna said.

"No, even though I want to!" he said, "Tonight we're in the casino after dinner, it's not a formal night, so no glad rags. I've got some extra cash, plus the on-board spend so we might be able to check out the players, it's where the 'ladies' go!" he said with a smile.

The casino was fairly busy with the roulette wheel spinning non-stop, with a full table of punters. Jon spotted Helen at one end of the table, feverishly placing chips on lots of numbers, but she must have been doing well as she had a large pile of chips in front of her. She spotted Lorna and Jon, and waved to them to join her, "Hi there, how are you two, hello Jon's sister, I'm sorry we've not been introduced," she said, all in one breath as the croupier pushed a pile of chips towards her.

"This is my sister, Lorna, and this lovely lady is Helen," he said. They touched hands. "You're doing well," Jon said.

"Yeah, I'm $3000 up, but the evening is young," she said. As she spoke, two chairs next to her became vacant as a couple of losers left. "There you go," Helen said, "sit down."

Jon reached into his pocket and took out a thousand dollars in 100's. The croupier gave him the same amount in chips, he passed 300 over to Lorna, who was surprised. "You can't sit at the table without playing," he said, laughing. Beneath the table she squeezed his thigh, which he moved quickly. Helen continued to win, and Jon also had a pile of chips amounting to $4000, but Lorna was down to her last $50. She looked very dejected, but she thought that Jon's winnings covered more than her loss. Helen yelped as she got a 'zero', which made her about $5000. In total she was $10,000 in front, the die was cast, she would be the one, Jon thought. But he would play the waiting game, after all she could lose the lot tomorrow night! He decided to play it very cool, until the time was right. Mid-Atlantic would be the time, three days to go he said to himself.

The next night was formal, Jon and Lorna were dressed

up, DJ for Jon and quite a cleavage-revealing dress for Lorna. Jon had said that the dress was too open at the top, Lorna said, "Darling, I'm your sister remember, I might get off with a nice man," she laughed, "they like tits!" she laughed again. Jon ignored her frivolity and guided her into the dining room. They were shown to a table where there was only one other couple, Tony and Georgie, Tony being the man. They introduced themselves as brother and sister. Tony had trouble keeping his eyes from Lorna's cleavage. They were joined by another couple, getting on in years, Victor and Linda, very boring Jon thought. They were only interested in the menu and wine list, no conversation.

When they finally joined in any conversation, Victor turned it to his hobby, buses! "Did you know," he said, "that a London Routemaster double decker was good for two million miles?" he enthused. "Obviously new parts were fitted over that time, but one would last 20 years."

"Yes," said Tony, "my mother had a broom like that!" They all laughed, but Victor turned red and fell silent as the obvious mickey-take was taken the wrong way, but it was only meant in fun.

After dinner, which seemed to take forever, they decided to go to the Crows Nest bar at the front of the ship, on the top deck. The view to the sea was magnificent, with a slight swell and rise and fall of the majestic bows. "Hi ya kids," came the greeting from behind, "may I join you, and buy you a drink?" she said, with her perfect $5000 smile.

Jon stood up, and pulled a chair over to the table and said, "Lovely to see you Helen, how's your day been?"

"I just love your English manners!" she said. The steward brought their drinks. "Doing the tables again tonight?" Helen asked.

"No, not tonight, we won't push our luck," Jon answered.

"Yeah, perhaps you're right," she replied, "I think I'll go down to the nightclub, to see what's happening." She finished her drink, "See you all later," she said smiling sexily at Jon, and winking.

Jon saw his chance, "You're not well, mal de mer, and you've gone to bed," he almost ordered, "remember, this is a business trip, you can watch a DVD while I go and lay the land with Helen," he added. He squeezed her knee under the table, "Don't worry, darling, this one's going to be big bucks," he assured her.

In the nightclub, Helen was dancing with an older man, when she saw Jon she excused herself, and walked over to him, "Hiya handsome, on your own?"

"Yes," Jon said, "Lorna's a bit sea-sick, poor girl, she's gone to bed."

"Poor girl," Helen said, " hope she fells better in the morning. Let's dance, come on, you can can't you?" she asked.

"Yes," he replied. They danced slow ones, fast ones and finally collapsed into a booth laughing and gasping for breath.

"My," she said, "you are quite a mover! Let's go back to my place and fuck," she suddenly offered.

"Okay," Jon heard himself say, looking at the four diamond rings, the watch and the bracelet, "you will be gentle with me!"

"Oh," she said, "I will be fantastic!"

So that they wouldn't be seen together, he suggested that he knock at her cabin in fifteen minutes, she agreed. He knocked on her door on time, it opened, she was wearing a negligee that left nothing to the imagination, what a gorgeous body she had. He entered the suite and she was immediately on him, her mouth sought his as she pulled him into the bedroom. Slowly she undressed him and when it came to his trousers, she lowered them with expertise that showed lots of experience, and when he was naked from the waist down she went down on her knees and took his penis in her mouth. The sensation he felt was fantastic, before his climax she said, "A blow job was always my forte!" After his ejaculation she disappeared into the bathroom. He looked around but couldn't see the jewellery, she wasn't wearing it, so where was it? The room safe, blast, he thought. Their love-making was magical, her orgasms were quite noisy, and his back suffered from her fingernails, no sunbathing for a day or two! he thought. His main thoughts were now the diamonds, but he had to get into that safe. She came out of the bathroom wrapped in just a towel, "Well?" she asked, "had enough? I could go again if you wish honey," she offered.

"Er, no, I'm sorry, you've drained me," he said.

She laughed out loud, "Yes, it's been said before, but you're good, very good, and now good night," she said, "I'll see you tomorrow, okay?" and kissed him on the cheek.

As Jon walked along the corridor he thought, 'I wonder if she's guessed it's the diamonds I'm after. No, she almost dragged me to her place, as she called it'. He told Lorna about the difficulty, she wasn't happy, but she knew that there was a crock of gold at the end of the rainbow and was willing to put up with Jon's activities.

Jon knocked on Helen's door at 9.30am, it opened, she looked amazing, there was an addition to the jewellery, a body chain. A diamond fantasy, at least 100 stones, he couldn't take his eyes from it. "It's beautiful, isn't it?" she said, "$60,000 worth of fine quality size-matched stones, and flawless. My late husband gave it to me for our 25th, just a year before he passed away," she added.

"Breakfast?" Jon asked.

"Yeah," she replied, "let's do it," and they walked down to the restaurant arm in arm.

Jon feigned a mobile phone call, he said it was from Lorna, he didn't want to be seen with Helen, "Look, I'm sorry, Lorna's not well, I'll just check with her and meet you in the restaurant," he said.

"Okay, honey," she said, and kissed his cheek, "see ya!" and she walked away.

He went back to his stateroom to check with Lorna, she wasn't there, oh well he thought, probably gone for a walk around the deck. He caught up with her in the restaurant, she was only having coffee and toast. As he walked in he waved to Helen, this was a good move, people would see him at breakfast with Lorna and not Helen. The day would be spent sunbathing, their tans were developing nicely, they finished breakfast and he waved to Helen as they left the restaurant.

"Tonight's the night," he told Lorna.

She looked shocked, and said, "It's not too soon, is it?"

"No," he said, "there's a room safe problem, and I've got to get to those diamonds before she locks them away."

"I see," Lorna said, but didn't look happy.

"Don't worry," he said, kissing her cheek, "it's going to be all right, those diamonds are fabulous," he added.

After a room service dinner, Jon went to the Crows Nest bar

alone. After about 30 minutes, he was tapped on the shoulder by Helen, "Hiya, handsome, how can a guy that looks like you be on his own?" she complimented. He stood up and took her hand, no cheek kissing, he didn't want to be seen being affectionate towards her. They ordered drinks, but Jon sat opposite her in the booth. "I'm getting vibes, don't you like little old me any more?"

"Yes, of course," he replied, "you're fabulous, but we will be going our separate ways in two or three days, and I don't want to get too intense," he confessed.

"Oh honey, it won't get intense, but we can have fun can't we?" she asked.

"Yes, of course," he said, smiling, "how about tonight, Lorna's met a friend and they will be doing their own thing."

"Good," she said, "the casino, and then bed!" she laughed.

The casino was quiet and they were greeted enthusiastically. They played for about an hour, but only came out even, so Helen tried her luck at blackjack, Jon just watched. She had some good luck, and won $2000. She then decided to go back to the roulette table and within another hour had amassed $12,000. She was euphoric, what with the cash and champagne cocktails, she was having a wonderful time. They almost fell into her suite at 1am, she wasn't drunk but very merry. She immediately went for the mini bar and pulled out a bottle of champagne and gave it to Jon to open, which he did with a nominally loud pop. He filled two flutes and she came close and, entwining her arm around his, said, "Here's to our fun and games!" Jon took a small sip, then put it down. She was wearing all her jewellery, he had felt the waist chain when he guided her through the door. He took his chance and grabbed her around the throat, pressing with all his strength on her windpipe, her eyes bulged, and she tried desperately to fight him off. But he was too strong, with the adrenalin making him stronger. She went limp, and her eyes were just staring and glazed ..... she was dead! He undressed her lovely body and put her clothes in a pile, including the glass he had used, the bottle etc., ready to throw overboard with the body. He removed all of the diamonds and put them in his pockets, including the body chain which had a special place in his inside jacket pocket, $160,000 he thought, fantastic. At

4 o'clock, after sitting and thinking of what he had done, did he have any decency in him? No, he thought, I am evil and a murdering bastard. Two gorgeous women dead because of my greed. He put his head in his hands and cried for a long time. Then, he lifted her over his shoulder, and with a tissue opened the balcony door, and tipping forward let her body fall. There was no audible splash, as the ship was going at a good rate of knots. He left the door open, but re-thought and put the champagne bottle back on the table with one flute. He washed the other one and put it back on the tray after washing the bottle. That could have been a mistake, but what's not there can't incriminate, he thought, he should have touched her fingers on the bottle, but it was too late now. He opened the door with a tissue, slowly looking up and down the corridor. He put a 'do not disturb' sign on the door knob, after wiping the shiny surface and the door handle. He saw nobody on his way back to his stateroom, and got into bed beside Lorna, who was asleep, quietly.

The Queen of the Atlantic, pride of Cunard, arrived in New York on schedule, with the usual fire boats sounding their horns and spouting huge amounts of water, with the ship also sounding it's horn.

Because he didn't want his name linked, Lorna had left the jewellery in a safe deposit at the reception. He didn't want to go through US Customs carrying them. They did the usual sights, Times Square, the Empire State Building, "Wow," they said, "we're nearly 1000 ft up." The East River looked like a little stream, Jon joked that if you looked up from the observation deck, you could see King Kong's claw marks! "Can you?" she said, looking up, then realised she had been had. "King Kong didn't have claws, he had fingernails!" she said. Jon burst his sides laughing, and then Lorna joined in when she realised it was a gag, and then playfully punched his shoulder. On the way down, Lorna asked, "Did it really knock that aeroplane out of the sky?" They started laughing again, to the amazement of the other people in the lift. They walked down 5th Avenue, or may be it was up, Jon laughed, he wasn't sure. They got back to the ship at 5.30pm after looking in at Macey's and Bloomingdales, fabulous stores, they said, but not as good as good old Selfridges, they laughed again.

Back in their stateroom, they showered and had wonderful sex, got dressed and went down for dinner, feeling marvellous, and now they could act like a couple with Helen out of the way. "Let's go to the nightclub," Lorna suggested.

"Okay, and then perhaps to the casino," he said, he wanted to be seen more and more with Lorna, so that from now on staff and crew would only remember him as being with her. They danced and drank at the club, making sure that they were noticed as an involved couple. In the casino, which was not very busy, the croupier had trouble keeping his eyes from Lorna's cleavage. Jon changed $200 into chips and was soon $500 up, this time Lorna was only a spectator but stayed close to Jon, showing affection. At 1 o'clock, Jon was about $2000 up and decided to cash in his chips.

The girl behind the pay desk said, "A different lady luck tonight?"

"Er, yes, but the other lady was only a fellow player, and has now found someone else. That's life!" he added, feeling a little worried that she had noticed and remembered. He took his winnings and left. They were soon in their stateroom, both very tired. They collapsed into bed, and slept soundly for eight hours.

Breakfast was taken in the coffee shop, latte's and Danish pastries, huge ones just like New Yorkers liked them. Central Park seemed like a good place to start their walking tour, "It's an enormous park," Lorna said.

"Yes," Jon replied, " a zoo, boating lake and enough muggers to sink our cruise ship," he said. They laughed and decided to take a horse and carriage ride around it. An hour and a half later they were back at Central Park's south gate and decided to have a drink in the Grand Bar of the Plaza Hotel, which was just across the street.

Up the steps, they were greeted by a liveried doorman, with an enormous white smile, "Welcome to the Plaza Hotel," he said, as he opened the door for them.

Jon slipped him a ten dollar bill and winked, saying, "This is New York ain't it?"

"It sure is!" the doorman said, "thank you, sir," and saluted Lorna with an extra flash of the teeth.

The bar was long, very long, and they sat at the park window end of it and ordered 'manhattans' at $15 a time! Once again, Lorna's cleavage attracted the barman's gaze, and he also gave her a whiter than white smile, and also an extra shot of whiskey. She said, "Thanks," to his name badge, Orlando, adding, "you're very kind."

He laughed, and said, "Your accent is beautiful, you're Brits right?"

"Right," said Jon, "just doing the sights."

"Right on," Orlando said, "go up to Harlem, it's fantastic!" he enthused.

"Yes," Jon replied, "we might well do that, thanks for the info," he added as he paid the bill with an extra $10.

"Thank yoo-o-o!" Orlando almost shouted as they left the bar.

"That was an expensive drink," Lorna said.

"The casino paid for it, and everything else on this trip, just go with it!" he said, putting his arm around her shoulder. He hailed a yellow cab and said," Take us back to the 'Queen of the Atlantic', Pier 90, please."

'Hi, this is Bruce Willis, whenever I'm in a cab I always put on my seat belt, it's not nice to die hard, I know. Bye now!' the recorded voice said, they laughed, but buckled up at the same time. Back at the ship, as they boarded, they saw two New York cops standing at the entrance. They took no notice of the returning couple, Jon took Lorna up to the reception desk and to his horror saw two NYPD detectives talking to the receptionist, and a ship's officer, who could have been the Captain. The trio then left, and disappeared into a lift. He watched the floor indicator and it stopped at B deck, where Helen had her suite. Soon afterwards a man appeared at the desk carrying a large metal case, forensic, Jon thought. His blood ran cold, but he thought, now Jon, don't panic, there's no way you can be linked to this. He watched as the forensic officer also went up to B deck. "Act normally," he told Lorna, "there was bound to be an investigation, especially for a US citizen," he explained.

"Jonathan Weston?" the suited American voice asked, "I'm Lieutenant Novak of the NYPD, can I ask you one or two questions?"

"Yes, certainly, but what about?" Jon replied.

"Helen Smithson."

"What about her? I only knew her as Helen," he said.

"She's disappeared, presumed dead and her body thrown overboard. That makes it homocide," he explained.

"Bloody hell," Jon exclaimed, "I didn't really know her, we had a drink and a dance in the nightclub and sat at the roulette wheel for a while, that's all I know about her. A woman like her, gregarious and friendly, could take up with a number of companions on a ship this size," he offered.

"Yeah I suppose so," the cop agreed, "Okay, we may have to talk again." As Novak walked away, he said to his partner, "That's our bastard, but how the fuck do we prove it?" he whispered.

Jon felt better as Novak left the ship, not realising that he was under suspicion. But the 'Queen of the Atlantic' was sailing the next day, so he was almost in the clear, or so he thought. His joyous thoughts were thwarted, when he heard over the ship's announcer, "Will Jonathan Weston come to the reception desk, please." He took his time getting there, fearing the worst. At the desk was Lt Novak with a uniformed cop, "Jonathan Weston, I'm arresting you on suspicion of the homocide of Helen Smithson, anything you say can be used in court when it comes to trial, you are not obliged to say anything."

"WHAT?" Jon shouted, "ARE YOU CRAZY?" he asked.

"If you'd like to come with us down town we'll get this sorted one way or the other."

"Can I call my partner?" he asked.

"No," said Novak, "the receptionist will tell her that you are at the 30th Precinct, Manhattan South," he added. The uniformed cop stepped forward and handcuffed Jon. He was led off the ship to a blue and white squad car, fellow passengers looked on in amazement.

Novak and a Captain Colletti, questioned Jon for 4 hours, but he was good, kept to his story and didn't fall for any of their interrogation tricks, such as "Did you think that she was rich because she had a suite?" "I didn't know know she had a suite."

At seven, Novak said, "Okay Jon, you're free to go. I'll get a squad car to take you back."

"No thanks, I'll get a cab," he replied. Novak followed him to the front desk, which was surrounded by cops, drunks and hookers. He finally received his envelope containing his belt, cash, watch and wallet.

"That's a lot of dough you're carrying, Jon."

"I won it in the casino on board, anyway you need it in this town, oh by the way, do I have to tip you?"

"No Jon, just think yourself lucky to be free," answered Novak, and walked away. "He's the one," Novak said as he walked into the Captain's office.

"No evidence," said Colletti, "there are 1800 passengers on the ship, it would take for ever to check them all."

"Yeah, but he was seen with her," he said.

"He was seen more with his girlfriend," Colletti said, "let's have a word with her on the ship in the morning, it doesn't sail 'til 4 o'clock in the afternoon, she may say something interesting, okay?" the Captain suggested.

At 10 o'clock in the morning the phone rang in Jon and Lorna's cabin, "I'm sorry to bother you Miss Harper, but there is a policeman at reception who would like a word with you."

"Okay," Lorna said, "I'll be there in 15 minutes."

She told Jon, who immediately started to panic, mentally, "Okay," he said, after calming down and starting to think properly, "just answer their questions very briefly, yes, no, I don't know, those sort of answers, believe me," he said, "they are clutching at straws, they know nothing, there's no evidence, have you got that?"

"Yes," she replied, and went down to the main desk area.

Standing there, was Novak alone, no cop, just him. He thanked her for her time, she found him very personable, he ushered her into a small 'business man's office' just close to the desk. He closed the door and showed her his ID badge, "I'm Lieutenant Novak of the NYPD, I just need you to confirm the movements of Jonathan Weston, your partner I believe."

"Okay," she said, trying not to display her nerves. Novak asked many questions about Jon and his movements since leaving England, but she was true to Jon's advice and answered the questions exactly as he had suggested. After about an hour, Novak thanked her for her time, opened the door for her and said goodbye, adding," I hope you have enjoyed New York City."

She returned to their stateroom, and her answers to his questions made him feel better. "Let's go to the coffee shop," Jon suggested, as he hugged her for a long time. She started crying as he shushed her to calm her down. She washed, and made up her face and once again she was lovely Lorna again. In the coffee shop Jon attracted one or two glances from passengers that had seen him arrested, but he held his head high as if nothing had ever happened. They thought a little on-board shopping was in order, so arm in arm they strolled slowly along the shopping deck, browsing in the gift shops and the boutiques. Prices were high, guided by the American tourists wallets. Jon received just one or two more glances, but ignored them.

"Mr Weston, would you please contact the main desk. As soon as possible please." the speakers asked. "Oh no, not again," he said to Lorna. They walked quickly to the source of the message, they were given a letter, Jon opened it. It was from the First Officer, 'Dear Mr Weston, Miss Harper and yourself are requested to leave the ship as you are now persona non grata. Please settle any accounts and go ashore no later than 3pm. You will be escorted to the gangway with your baggage.' Jon was not aware that the NYPD had requested this course of action. As they had the on-going murder enquiry, the Captain had no choice but to comply as the missing person was a US citizen, and the ship was on US territory. At exactly 3pm Jon and Lorna were at the reception desk with their baggage, the jewellery was retrieved from the safety deposit box and they were ready to go. The ship's Officers appeared, and a porter to carry their luggage, "Service to the very end," Jon said to Lorna. Down on the quayside they felt dreadful, but they soon cheered up when Jon said, "Don't worry Lorns, we're about 20 grand richer!" At that moment a cab pulled up and unloaded some Americans and their baggage. Lots and lots of it, Jon walked over to the cabbie and said, "Can you take us to a hotel, perhaps near Times Square?"

"Sure," the cabbie said, "thanks for the return fare," and started to load their luggage, "okay, let's go. My name's Cliff, 27 years pushing a hack around the greatest city in the world," he said, as he engaged the gear in the people-carrier type cab, "oh, by the way, it's $30 fixed fare, okay?" he explained. They stopped at a large tourist hotel just off Times Square in West 45th Street, Jon gave cliff $50, "Gee, thanks!" the cabbie said as he unloaded their bags from the back, "you have a good stay, okay?" he said, getting into the cab.

They were met by a porter who loaded their baggage on to a trolley and steered them through to the reception area. "Hi, how can I help?" the Hispanic girl asked.

"We'd like a double room, not too high, for a couple of nights please."

"Sure," the girl said, "may I have your credit card, please?" she asked.

"No," said Jon, "I'll pay cash."

"Sure, that'll be fine, two nights, double room, that'll be $600 please," she responded. Jon peeled off six $100 bills from his bundle, and passed it across the marble counter. "Would you fill in these registration cards please." They both filled them in, and passed them back to 'Clamenta', the name on her badge. As Jon had paid cash there was no need to check passports.

A porter took their bags up to the 10th floor, that was low in a 48 floor building! The room was fairly 'tourist' but comfortable, with a king size bed and a TV, air con: and a nice bathroom. Room 1009 should suit for the next two days, Jon now fixed his thinking to selling the diamonds. They were both hungry, Jon asked Clamenta to recommend a restaurant, "Yes," she said, "if you go out of the other entrance into the next street, you'll see a Chinese and an Italian, but be quick, they're fully booked soon by theatre goers."

"Thanks," Jon said.

"You're welcome," she replied, "enjoy your evening."

They managed to get a table for two at 'Gianni' Italian, it was packed with theatre people grabbing a meal before a show. At exactly 7.30pm the restaurant emptied, leaving just Jon and Lorna. The maitre'd looked at his watch and said, "Are you seeing a show, it'll soon be curtain time?"

"Er, no, we only arrived late afternoon."

"Oh, I see, you're English!" he said.

"Yes, we're here to shop and sight-see, er, perhaps you could help. I want to buy a diamond ring for my soon-to-become fiancee, where is the best place to go?" Jon enquired.

"Well," the maitre'd said, "if I were you I'd go down to China Town and the Jewish quarter, lots of dealers there, and by the way, congratulations!" and added, "have a drink with the house, what would you like?" Jon thanked him and paid the bill, the brandies went down very well. Back to the hotel, and they decided on an early night.

No breakfast included, thay went for a walk past the Italian restaurant and soon found a deli serving a full breakfast, which they ordered with coffee and extra toast, "$28 was a bit steep," Jon said, "but it was a hell of a breakfast." He saw a yellow cab at the corner of Madison Avenue, and hailed it, he said to the driver, "We want to go to China Town, please."

The driver looked strangely at him, he didn't hear 'please' often, "Canal and Mott is the centre, okay?" he said.

"Yes, whatever you say," Jon answered. The cab stopped at Canal and Mott, $16 on the meter, Jon gave him an extra $5, saying, "There was no seat belt message!"

"No," the driver said, "They get on people's nerves, especially Bruce Willis!" he said laughing, "and thanks, have a good day!" came out of the window, as he drove away. To the left, he saw shops and restaurants with Chinese signs and writing, to the right he saw Jewish signs, which way? he thought. "Lorna, let's flip a coin, chink or jew?" Jon asked. The coin spun, left heads, right tails, Jon caught it and looked, "Tails," he said, "so it's the Jew's." They crossed the street, and walked down through the Jewish quarter, he saw a sign saying 'Jewellery - Loans and Bought'. He pressed the security buzzer, and after a while was allowed in.

A bearded man wearing a skull cap, said, "Good morning."

"Good morning," Jon replied, "I'm from England and I want to sell this body chain, it's very valuable, could you tell me how much I can expect for it?" he asked.

The man, whose twin brother had the shop in Hatton Garden, placed his eye glass in his clip-on spectacles and studied the stones avidly. After a good ten minutes, he said, "You're right, it is very valuable, how much do you want for it?"

"$100,000," Jon replied.

"I see. I have to check on it, it will take about five minutes, take a seat," said the dealer. After three or four minutes another bearded man entered the shop and put a code into a side door, which allowed him into the rear office. Jon could hear voices, but they weren't speaking English, it sounded like German. The first man appeared and said, "I am going to share any purchase with my neighbour," he said, pointing to the second man, "we'll give you $80,000 for it, that's our only offer, we don't barter."

Jon sat, thinking for about two minutes, then said, "Okay, will that be cash?"

"Yes," the man said with a smile, "we only deal in cash." He went back into the little office with the obligatory see-through glass. He returned with eight plastic Bank of America packs, each containing $10,000, but before he handed over the money he pushed a form through the glass divider, "Please fill in your name and address etc." Jon gave a completely fictitious address in Bournemouth. They left the shop, but acting naturally, walked up the street arm in arm, not realising that they were on CCTV.

Lt Novak had spoken to the First Officer about Jonathan's departure, who told him about the taxi picking them up at the gangway. CCTV had picked up the Index no: of the cab and it was traced to Cliff, who remembered the nice Brits, and told Novak where he had dropped them off.

Clamenta looked at Novak's gold NYPD badge, "I'm Lt Novak, NYPD, do you have a Jonathan Weston staying here?" he questioned.

She checked her computer, "Yes, room 1009," she answered.

Novak nodded to his uniformed cop, they took the elevator to the 10th floor, Novak gave a knock of authority, "Police, open the door," he almost shouted. The door was opened by a scantily dressed Lorna, Novak feasted his eyes, what a pair of tits, he thought! "I'm Lt Novak, NYPD," he said, showing his ID, "I need to talk to Jonathan Weston," he announced. Jon appeared from behind the door, also in a state of undress, "Get dressed Mr Weston, I need to question you down town, you're not being arrested, but if you refuse you'll be cuffed and taken anyway," Novak barked.

Jon had thought this could happen and had put the bulk of the cash and the remaining diamonds in the hotel's safe. "I've told you everything I know, "Jon said, coolly, as he dressed.

"We just want to get a few more details, and for you to make a written ststement," Novak replied.

Jon was kept at Precinct 30 for six hours, but managed to keep to his story. Outside in the corridor Novak admitted to Colletti that there was, finally, no evidence to keep him in custody any longer. "Okay," the Captain said, "let him go," then added, "what about the girl, does she know anything?"

"No," Novak said, "I questioned her on the ship, if he murdered Mrs Smithson he did it alone. The girl was never present in the bar, nightclub or casino, according to witnesses."

When Jon got back to the hotel, Lorna was drunk and had been crying, the mini-bar had been well used. "Can we go home?" she slurred.

"Yes," Jon said," now we need to sleep." At 8am they awoke, Lorna had a hangover, but was still adamant that they left immediately. Jon agreed and said, "We'll pack, get some coffee and go to JFK to see if we can get a flight later today. BA is the best bet," he suggested. Jon and Lorna checked out, he retrieved the cash and the remaining diamonds.

Coveniently, there was a cab rank just outside the main entrance of the hotel, a cabby at the front got out of his cab when he saw the luggage, and opened the large boot of the yellow checker, "Where to?" he asked in a Brooklyn, gravelled accent.

"JFK, please, BA terminal," replied Jon, '$50 fixed fare' he was told. "Fine," said Jon, " let's go." They were soon across the Brooklyn Bridge and into Queens and JFK airport. The luggage unloaded, Jon gave the driver an extra $10.

"Have a good flight, and thanks," came the gutteral voice.

At the desk of BA they were booked in for the night flight to Heathrow, leaving at 7.30 pm. Jon paid for an upgrade, being over 6ft tall he wanted the leg room, the tourist class seats were too cramped. It was only when they were in their seats that Jon gave a sigh of relief. The six and a half hour flight went pleasantly, dinner was served at 8.30pm and they had time to get some sleep. Jon had given the jewellery to Lorna to wear. Necklace, three rings, and a bracelet, all of which were covered by clothing. This was just in case their luggage was searched at Heathrow.

"Lt Novak, there's something here I think you should see,"

the cop from the precinct office said.

"What is it?" Novak asked.

"It's a CCTV tape from the diamond district, I came across it yesterday when back-tracking on the screens," the officer said. They went into his office and the cop started the machine, it showed Jon and Lorna leaving Levin's shop and walking down the street.

"Fuck, fuck, fuck," he exploded. He remembered the croupier in the casino describing Mrs Smithson as, the 'diamond lady'. He grabbed a squad car and drove with blues and sirens, he was mad at himself for being so stupid.

He showed his badge through the door, after pressing the security buzzer. It immediately opened, the Jewish dealer said, "How can I help you, sir?"

"Did you buy any diamonds from a tall Englishman, yesterday?"

"Yes, I did," Levin replied.

"Let me see them," Novak demanded.

Mr Levin produced a velvet bag, and poured 100 stones on to a scales dish, "They were set on a white gold chain," the dealer said, "but I want to sell the stones seperately."

"Did you check the trade and insurance computer?" asked Novak.

"Sure, I wouldn't buy a bean without checking religiously," the dealer replied.

"Okay, thanks a lot, and good shabas," he added, it was late Friday.

"Thank you," Levin answered, "and good shabas to you," he smiled through his beard.

On his way back to the precinct house he thought, you schmuck, you let him slide through your fingers. What next, what next? went raging through his mind, extradition? not enough fucking evidence, the Brits wouldn't wear it. But there must be some way I can nail that murdering bastard. All these thoughts were going through his fuddled brain, this was going to be a long haul, but one day, Jonathan Weston, I will crucify you, he promised himself. Almost two years were to pass before he saw justice.

The 747 landed at Heathrow, exactly on time, they walked through customs without any hiccups, Lorna managed to keep her cool, wearing $100,000 worth of diamonds. They had to get to Southampton to retrieve the Golf, Jon approached the black cab booking desk, "How much to Southampton docks, please?" he asked the pleasant, grey-haired man.

"£140, fixed fare."

"Will the driver take US dollars?" Jon asked

"Just a moment, I'll ask him," the dispatcher said. "799" a voice crackled over the radio. "Gentleman and lady to go to Southampton docks, will you accept US dollars?" he asked. "Roger, $200, fixed rate," the cockney voice said. "Roger 799, ready to go."

They pushed their trolley out to the taxi pick-up point, a short cabbie jumped out of the black cab, and smiling, said, "Southampton?"

"Yes, please," Jon said.

The bags loaded, they set off towards the south coast. The journey on the M25 and M3 was slow, traffic was heavy, even for early Saturday morning. Road repairs, an accident, it all took time, but there was no real hurry. The ship hadn't arrived so the parking office girl was surprised to see them so early. Jon explained that they flew back from New York as Lorna had been very ill with sea-sickness. "I see," she said. Jon gave her his ticket, and she called on the radio for the Golf to be brought from the pound. Once they were on their way back to London they both felt better, and Jon reminded Lorna that they were richer by at least £200,000. They both yippee'd, but at the back of Jon's mind was the fact that two beautiful women were dead because of him.

They went directly to Vicky's house, she was out, no white Audi, but Jon did notice one thing, a 'For Sale' board at the front of the house. He called his sister to find out what was happening, "I'm on my way home, I'll be ten minutes and I'll explain everything."

"The bastards left me for his fucking receptionist, it's been going on for ages. The house is in his name, but I'll fight that, still the marriage is dead, I wouldn't want to stay here anyway. But I want half, plus a large maintenance cheque every month." Jon then introduced Lorna to Vicky, "Oh, I'm so sorry, and rude, it's a pleasure to meet you," she said.

"I need the Golf for a few more days," Jon said.

"Keep it," Vicky said, "it's a gift, I can only drive one at a time," she added.

"Thanks, thanks very much," and he kissed her cheek, "we'll see you again soon," he said, "get a good nights sleep and stay off the bottle!"

"You can stay here if you wish," she offered. They looked at each other and nodded agreement and thanked Vicky.

"I'll get the bags from the car," Jon said.

"Good, I could do with some company," Vicky replied.

The two women got on well, talking about fashion etc., and Lorna told Vicky about New York," Jon took me to the top of the Empire State Building and showed me Kong Kong's claw marks!" she said, with a wink.

"Yes," said Vicky, "our father got me with that one when I was a teenager, the trouble is, I believed it!" They laughed. Jon just sat with a drink, half listening and thinking about selling the rest of the diamonds. He left early the next morning, telling Lorna he'd be back at lunchtime. Driving down to Hatton Garden he put on a baseball cap so that no CCTV could see his face. He had already dirtied the number plates on the Golf. He went slowly along the street and picked out a large dealer, but kept his eye as to where the cameras were situated and was happy to see that the dealer was in a sort of blind spot. He removed his cap and pressed the buzzer, he was allowed in and went to the 'For Sale' window. "Good morning," a young bearded man said.

"Good morning," Jon said, "I have some jewellery for sale, they were my mother's. Could you assay them and make me an offer?" He passed the rings and the bracelet through the gap in thick glass window. In the car he had spread glue on his fingertips to spoil any prints, gladly it had dried quickly. The young man took the gems into a larger than normal office that had no two-way window, and looked at them through a large desk-mounted magnifying glass. He then started to check on the computer, this process took longer than usual, Jon started to worry, but this was unfounded.

"I've got good news, the stones, rings and bracelet are worth £100,000, I'm prepared to pay you £80,000, what do you say?"

Jon, not wanting to seem too eager, stood thinking for a

while, "Could you make it a bit more? mother owed that on a second mortgage," he lied.

"No, I'm sorry, that's my one and only offer," the young man said.

"Okay," said Jon, "it's a deal." He was passed the obligatory form through the window, he completed it and pushed it back through the glass.

"I won't be a minute," the young man said. He returned with eight plastic bags, each containing £10,000.

He donned his baseball cap, and walked back to the car feeling very wealthy indeed. As promised he got back to the house at lunchtime, he didn't bother to press the buzzer, he'd known the entry code for years! but now that Peter was off the plot, he felt free to use it. £150,000 in cash, tax free, he mused, now for some leisure and spending time. He sat in the bedroom with Lorna, after locking the door, and spread the money in it's entirety on the bed, every dollar and pound. The final sum was £320,000 after he had calculated rates of exchange. Jon had a re-think on a spending spree and told Lorna that they should act normally for six months, she should go back to work on Monday and continue as normal. He would stash the bulk of the cash in a safety deposit box, she agreed, in fact she thought it a good idea. "Just to let the dust settle," Jon said.

Lorna was troubled by a sense of foreboding, supposing he was to keep all the cash for himself, she hadn't killed anyone, she had only done what she was told. She wasn't in love with him as such, of course, she fancied him, and the sex was fantastic, he excited her like no man had done before. He was a murderer, a cold blooded killer and he frightened her. She didn't know what to do, may be she should write a letter to the police telling them everything and tell him that she had done so, and that the letter had been given to a friend for safe keeping, and the friend would give it to Scotland Yard if anything should happen to her, anything. At work she wrote to Scotland Yard, the letter would remain with her friend Zoe, whom Jon had never met or heard of. She then sent it to Zoe inside another envelope, with the instruction that it should only be sent upon her death. "Lorns, this is Zoe," the voice on her mobile said, "where have you been, it's four weeks since I last spoke to you, and what's this letter all about, what's going on?" she begged.

"I'll meet you for lunch, and tell you all about it," she arranged.

Over lunch in a wine bar close to Lorna's office, she gave Zoe only an outline, that she only thought that Jon was guilty. "Oh Lorns, you're imagining things," and that she was being silly.

" Okay, that's as may be, but just in case, hang on to the letter and send it if necessary. I hope you don't have to!" They parted and promised to keep in touch, she would never let Jon and Zoe meet.

"I've put the cash into the Marble Arch branch of Barclays Bank Safety Deposit Box, in both our names, here's your key," he said. He handed her a 2" thin brass key, "Don't take it all, will you," and laughed.

Lorna now felt terrible, but at the same time, safer and more confident, "Thank you," she said, kissing him on the cheek with a sigh of relief. She would never know that the key was a spare to an old garage tool box, but Jon thought that it would keep her on his side, and give her a false sense of security if things went pear-shaped. He, of course, had the only customer key and the box was in his name only.

The weeks floated by, and Jon and Lorna carried on as normal, Jon started buying and selling cars, mainly from high-class dealers, having them buffed up and then selling them in good trade magazines. He was doing well, and Lorna and him were living mainly at Vicky's house, but Vicky was happy with the arrangement. "We're having a dinner party tomorrow night, and I want you to meet my new man, I hope you're free," she said.

"Yes, that would be fabulous," Jon replied.

"Yes, fabulous," Lorna added.

"DJ and revealing dress, okay?" Vicky announced.

"I always do smart and posh," she laughed.

Lorna and Jon appeared down stairs for pre-dinner drinks at 7pm, looking absolutely fabulous. Vicky's new man buzzed the entry button, "Get that, will you Jon." He pressed the enter button and opened the door to see the latest Bentley coupe drive through the gates, wow! he thought, Vicky doesn't fuck about! He held the door open for a grey haired man, about 6ft tall in his mid 40's, "Good evening," Jon said, "I'm Vicky's brother, Jonathan."

"I'm David Mackenzie."

"Pleased to meet you," they said simultaneously.

Vicky appeared, "Darling, I'm so glad you came, you've met my brother Jon, and this young lady is Jon's partner, Lorna," said Vicky, introducing them, "Lorna, please meet Sir David Mackenzie, my special guest for this evening."

"No 'sirs', I'm just David, please let's be less formal," he said, looking at Lorna's cleavage.

Lorna felt that she should curtsey, but didn't, "Nice to meet you David," she said, gently shaking his tanned, well-manicured hand.

The buzzer sounded again, and Jon opened the gates and front door, this time it was an Aston Martin Vanquish, he held the door and two men came into the porch. Obviously a gay couple but very smart and refined in very smart DJ's, one white and one black. Vicky ran from the dining room, "Oliver, Grant, darlings, meet my brother Jon, he's staying for a few days with his partner Lorna," whom she introduced in the dining room, as the hired maid served champagne.

Then the buzzer sounded again, but after Grant and Oliver, Jon had left the front gates open. He opened the door to see the most beautiful girl, in her thirties, standing on the doorstep. Blonde, tall, quite Swedish looking, with green eyes. Vicky came into the hall from the dining area, "Asa darling, so lovely to see you, how are you?" They m'wah m'wah'd, and Vicky said, "Please meet my brother Jon, Asa is from Sweden, and a very clever heart specialist," she spouted, "drink for my lovely Asa, please," she said. Jon was thinking that Vicky had bashed the champers a little herself, she then introduced everybody to everybody else. Lorna saw Jon looking at Asa, and Asa looking at Lorna, inwardly he laughed, what a night this is going to be! He asked his sister if there would be any more guests, she said no, so he shut the front gates.

The dinner went very well, lots of very good food from the caterers and, of course, lots of wine. The guests were merry, it was a fantastic success that went on until 2am. Vicky said to Oliver and Grant, "You will stay the night won't you?" They agreed. Jon had noticed that Asa hadn't taken her eyes off of Lorna all evening, what a waste, a fucking dike, he thought. "Can you call Asa a cab, Jon," Vicky requested.

"I know what I'd like to call her!" he mumbled under his breath. "Of course," he replied. "Ten minutes," he shouted into the dining room for Asa to hear.

"Thankyou darling," Vicky said.

"Taxi," the voice announced over the gate intercom.

"Just coming," Jon said to the driver. Asa thanked him and took her beautiful self through the door, Jon watched until she was safely in the cab. As he walked back to the main door, I could give that some! he said to himself.

"Thank you darling," Vicky said, slightly slurring her speech, "David and I are going to bed," she giggled. "the caterers are just leaving, and Oliver and Grant have gone up to the guest room," she giggled again, "goodnight darlings," she slurred.

Jon and Lorna sat in the sumptuous lounge with two large brandies, "What was that Swedish bird all about, she couldn't take her eyes off you!"

Lorna laughed, and said, "Not to worry darling, she wasn't my type, let's go to bed and fuck." The sexual crescendo in the house would have breeched the Noise Abatement Laws!

At 10.30am Jon awoke, Lorna's side of the bed was empty. He put on his robe and went downstairs following the aroma of coffee. She was sitting with Sir David, who was admiring her cleavage through her very expensive Bloomingdales negligee. "Morning," Jon said.

David stood up, "Good morning, Jon," he said.

"Coffee, darling?" enquired Lorna.

"Oh yes, please," Jon said.

The two gays also appeared, having smelled the coffee, "Morning!" they said in unison, "what a fabulous evening!" They wore matching red pyjamas with black and red robes. Funny, Jon thought, they weren't carrying anything when they arrived, must keep them here for special evenings.

Vicky appeared, "Morning everybody," she said, as she kissed David's cheek," oh Lorna darling, please go and put your tits away under a robe, David's a randy sod, but he's my randy sod!" she said, they all laughed, and surprisingly so did Lorna, as she went to get the obligatory garment.

Grant and Oliver finished their coffee, "We both have consultations this afternoon, so we had better get going," Grant said.

"Two of the most eminent surgeons in the country, Oliver does brains and Grant does spines. They share a practice in Harley Street, rich people from all over the globe seek their services, and at £25,000 a procedure, at least, they do very well, very well indeed," Vicky related.

After a while they re-appeared looking immaculate in dark suits and carrying a Louis Vuitton valise, "Thank you for a fabulous evening, darling," they said, in unison at the front door, and both m'wah m'wah'd Vicky.

"Be in touch soon, won't you," she called as Grant started the Aston. They all waved as the Vanquish purred majestically through the iron gates. "I do some referrals to them, of wealthy English people, and they are very generous," she said as she closed the main door.

"What was that Swedish piece all about?" asked Jon, "what a waste of womanhood!"

"Poor Asa, she's a brilliant heart surgeon, up there with the best, she too has very rich clients and does extremely well. But she is looking for love, male or female, but he or she must match her pound for pound and must want to fuck every day. She is a complete sex addict, and she's yet to find 'the one'. She was married once, but it didn't last long, the poor guy couldn't satisfy her. I think that they are still actually married, but she lives alone in a lovely town house on the edge of Hampstead Heath."

A thought went through Jon's mind, but he dismissed it quickly, not on the doorstep, he said to himself, but with a smile on his face. But she was gorgeous, oh well, back to the holiday brochures!

<u>ANOTHER HOLIDAY</u>

It had been five months since they got back from New York, Jon was still comfortable, but he felt that he wanted to go on another 'special job' as he called it. The car business was going well, and he was making two to three thousand a week, sometimes more. They had found a luxurious apartment in a block in Belsize Park, close to where Vicky lived. He'd left the furnishings etc., to Lorna, her taste was very good and their new home looked marvellous. She was very happy. Baker Street Travel Agents beckoned to Jon one sunny morning, with a window display that announced a new luxury ship and a cruise to the Carribean, the 'Carribean Star' certainly looked luxurious. Three weeks to the West Indies from Southampton, £5,500 all included. He entered the shop and recieved a print-out and itinerary of the cruise, saying that he would show it to his partner, and think about it.

"Can you better this price?" Jon said, as he showed her the print-out.

She studied it, and her blood ran cold, "Jon, not again, please. Isn't the car business enough, you're doing well," she almost pleaded.

"Look, I don't want to be shlapping second-hand motors around for the rest of my life," he said, as he gently took her shoulders, "just one more run, and that'll be it," he begged.

"Okay, okay, but you'll have to go alone, I don't want to be there," she cried.

"Why?" he asked, "I need you there."

"No, no, no," she shouted, breaking free, "I've had enough, enough, enough," she shouted.

"Okay Lorns, I'll go on my own, all right, I'll go on my own," he repeated. This girl has got to go, he thought, but one thing at a time.

Lorna came back with a 20 per cent discounted price, "Okay," Jon said, "book it for me, I'll give you cash. I'm sorry you won't be coming, but perhaps it's for the best," he leaned forward and kissed her, "let's have a drink," he said, and took a bottle of Merlot from the rack. Pouring her a large glass, he said, "Oh by the way, I've found the car of your dreams, a Lexus 250 convertible, in white. They're quite rare I'm told."

Her face lit up, "Really?" she said, "when will I have it?" she asked, smiling.

"In two days, it's being showroomed as we speak."

"Oh, thank you Jon," she said, and kissed him hard on the mouth.

"Now, let's forget about all the business, and enjoy each other," he said. But he had further plans for Lorna. The car was delivered to her on time .... she loved it.

He loaded his cases into the Golf, which he still had as

a runabout, an airport car, a docks car, a station car, what a work-horse it was. He had bought, to trade on but fell in love with, a Mercedes Sports SLS 6.3 super car. He kept it in the garage at home, it was his piece of mechanical magic, his trophy, his metallic love. When he drove it, all the dreadful things that he had done melted into insignificance, he was in charge, tha main man, no one could ever take these feelings of superiority away. No Novak, who failed, not Scotland Yard, nobody. He probably knew by now that he was a homicidal maniac, who enjoyed killing women for their diamonds and wealth.

He arrived at the parking shed to begin his embarkation, exactly one hour before sailing, at 4 o'clock. Once again he boarded the devil's transport, he knew he would kill, he knew he would, once again, sell his soul to Satan for a handful of diamonds.

He found his stateroom, and his bags were soon brought in by 'Rikki', a short, skinny, but pleasant Asian boy with a perfect smile and teeth. He tipped him £5, and got the bowing and thanking treatment. He knew the programme well by now, the 'Carribean Star' was a very large liner, 90,000 tonnes, 3,000 passengers, 8 bars, 6 restaurants, 2 theatres, a shopping mall, 2 pools etc etc. He was sure that amongst all these people he would find what he was looking for, a huge killing, in more ways than one. He chose a blouson in navy, and a pair of white slacks, white shoes, no shirt. With the silk and cotton jacket unbuttoned to mid-chest, he went down to the shopping mall, just to have a look around. It was early, and the ship had only just sailed, the mall was almost empty but he felt that this would be the centre of his hunting ground. After all, women love shopping, he thought. He would spend many hours here, he looked for CCTV cameras, there were none, good he thought.

He was shown to a table in the 'Bahama' restaurant, only two people were there on a table for eight. He introduced himself, "Good evening, I'm Jonathan, from London," he announced.

A woman, obviously travelling alone, said, "Hello, I'm Amanda from Manchester," the uninteresting woman said.

The other person, a man, said, "Hello, I'm Michael from

Hove," and stood, holding out his hand, which Jon shook.

"Right, what's on the menu?" he said, as he looked at the first page of the comprehensive folder.

Amanda opened the ordering by asking for the wine waiter who, with a wave, came in about 30 seconds. She said, "I'll have a large gin and tonic, with ice and lemon, please."

Michael ordered a pint, and Jon a perrier with ice and a slice, "It's a bit early for alcohol," he said.

Another couple were seated at the table, and once again Michael stood up, held out his hand and introduced himself from Hove. This guy is a lonely bachelor, but he wore expensive clothes and a Rolex watch, possibly a 'cupboard queen', Jon guessed. The new arrivals at the table were Jim and Vera, from Essex, jovial and down-to-earth but working-class. "Hello, I'm Jonathan from London," he heard himself say. Fuck, he thought, you pratt, from now on no real names, tomorrow night a different restaurant, he thought again.

He spent the rest of the evening watching a DVD, but fell asleep before it had finished, waking at 2am in the morning. The machine had switched off, his room was in complete darkness except for moonlight through his balcony window. Was it his imagination that played tricks, or the light bouncing off the chrome balcony rails, or the fact that he was still half asleep? Perhaps it was all three, but there was Helen's face in an agonised grimace, staring open-mouthed at him. He rushed to pull the curtain and then sat on the bed, in a cold sweat. After about ten minutes he had a cold water face wash, went to the mini bar and had a large brandy. A bad dream made him sit up in bed at 6am, again in a cold sweat, 'now get a grip, you know why you're here, money, diamonds, a luxurious future with or without Lorna, but I'll worry about her later'. He decided to go for a walk on the Promenade deck, to clear his head. Land was in sight, he guessed it was either the Isle of Wight or southern Ireland, but he didn't really care. He was amazed at how many early morning joggers were pounding around the steel deck, 'can't be much good for their spines' he thought, ' they might one day be a patient of Oliver's, if they can afford him!' he mused. He went into the coffee shop for a light breakfast, a toasted bagel with smoked salmon and cream cheese, with black coffee. He left feeling much better, it's true what they say, 'a good breakfast perks you up', well at least it's what he thought they said! As he walked out of the coffee shop, he accidentally bumped into a woman, a very good looking woman, "Sorry," he said.

She replied, "That's all right," with an accent he couldn't quite place. Perhaps eastern Europe, no, Russian, yes definitely Russian.

"I hope I didn't bump you too hard," he added.

"No," she said, smiling a smile that would melt the hardest of hearts. True to his art, he looked at her hands, fucking hell he thought, look at those rocks! Had he found his prey? May be, but there were over 2,000 passengers on board, he may not see her again, but he sure would try.

As his super luck would have it, she was by the pool when Jon walked around to see the swimming area. 'What a terrific body she's got' he thought as she lay on a sun bed in a white bikini. She was wearing sunglasses, he couldn't see that she followed him with her eyes as he walked past pretending not to notice her among the other sun-bathers. The sun was high and fairly hot, about 78 or 79 degrees he reckoned. He looked good, he still had a tan from previous holidays which was set off by his white shorts and white T-shirt, and went and sat on the opposite side of the pool, near the bar. There was a rack of newspapers close, he chose one and sort of read it, while keeping an occasional eye on the girl. He looked across at her over the newspaper, and to his amazement, she waved. He waved back, but went back to his paper, 'play it cool, Jon, play it cool' he said to himself.

A shadow came across him, standing there was a steward, "Excuse me, sir, the lady on the other side of the pool would like you to join her for a drink." Jon thanked him, and nodded in agreement. As he did, the girl was already standing to walk towards him, it was more comfortable at the table. 'Am I going crazy, is this a dream?' he thought, and pinched himself, no it was no dream.

"Hello again," he said as he stood and held out his hand.

She took it and smiled, "No bump this time!" she laughed. Jon pulled a chair and held it for her to sit down. "I'm Katti," she said, "that's short for Kattinaya," she said, introducing herself.

"I'm Jon, short for Jonathan," he laughed.

"Are you cruising alone, Jon?" Katti asked.

"Yes," he replied, "are you?"

"Yes," she answered, "I'm celebrating my freedom, I've just divorced. I've already had a party at home in St Petersburg, now I want rest, sun and some fun," she enthused. Her accent was extremely sexy, her body gorgeous and her diamond rings very, very desirable. "I hope you didn't mind me sending the steward over to ask you for a drink, but I wanted to meet a friend so that I would enjoy the holiday to a greater extent, okay?"

"Er, yes," Jon agreed, "the same goes for me, but I'm not a divorcee." The drinks arrived, a large vodka and tonic for Katti, and a pint of lager for Jon. He had been observing Katti's rings, in total, nine good sized stones. He wondered what else she had, he had plenty of time to find out, 'the party had just begun' he thought. They sat talking in the warm sun for hours, her blonde hair catching the rays with a special light that framed her beautiful face. It was obvious that the attraction was very strong from both sides, and they arranged to meet and dine together, but first they would have cocktails in the Crows Nest bar at 7pm.

He chose a 'Boss' pale beige suit and a black silk shirt, black slip-on shoes and his recent gift to himself, a Rolex gold Oyster Perpetual. He checked himself in the full length morror, 'Wow' he thought, 'looking good, or what!' he said out loud, winking and smiling at his reflection, 'as I said young sir, the game is on' he added.

Katti arrived with a turn of heads from every red blooded male in the bar. Wearing a bright red trouser suit with split legs, showing enough thigh to be almost immoral, with the top button undone on the jacket at cleavage level. Jon gasped inwardly, especially when he saw the emerald and diamond necklace! The emerald settled neatly on her bosom, wow! he thought, a nice lump of cash there. He stood and took her hand, smiling, he kissed it. Now he had a problem, their togetherness had already become evident, he had to re-think how this would go. He would have some fun for a couple of weeks, then cool it so that she was seen with somebody else, after all there were plenty of men on board that would jump at the chance to escort the lovely Katti. Then wham! probably on the way back, about two or three days from home, yes he thought, that'll do it. Then back to London with the diamonds.

They managed to get a booth for two in the Bermuda restaurant, naturally it was shaped like a triangle as was the table and all the general decor, a sense of humour by the ship's designers. After dinner, "How about we check out one of the nightclubs, or may be all three, have a look in at the casino, the night is young," he spouted. They walked arm-in-arm along the inner promenade deck, past the chic shops. Heads turned to look at the attractive couple, Jon suddenly swerved to look in a shop window, a photographer was snapping couples as they walked along. This was a big no-no. He waited until the photographer went back into his shop, and then they walked quickly past.

"Is anything wrong?" Katti asked.

"No," said Jon. nonchalantly, "just looking." They arrived at the 'Ocean Spot', sort of nightclub, but it was not busy, so they turned around and walked on. Nowhere seemed to be busy, so they went to the casino, it was buzzing with would-be winners. Jon sidled over to the roulette table and watched, the house was doing well, Katti started talking to a be-jewelled middle aged woman in Russian. They were laughing, and the woman turned and looked Jon up and down and then smiled at him with a knowing smile. Jon wondered what Katti had said, he cast it aside as girl talk. A chair became vacant, so Jon took it, next to the Russian woman. He did this for two reasons, one of course, to play and the other, to take a closer look at her jewellery. Katti stood behind him with a hand on his shoulder, his first bet lost, but not much, he was mainly concentrating on his neighbour's diamonds. They were magnificent, rings, two bracelets, a necklace and a diamond Cartier watch. This trip could be double bubble for him if he was clever, and very careful. The chair next to him became vacant, he moved along one so that Katti could converse with her new found Russian friend. He gave her £100 in chips. The lady had quite a pile in front of her, and was winning steadily, Katti also was having a lucky run and had quadrupled the £100 quite quickly. After about 2 hours they said goodnight to the Russian lady, Jon in English and Katti in their own tongue.

The days rolled into one another, breakfast, sun-bathing

if the weather permitted, a light lunch, more sun, pool-side drinks, an hours siesta, shower, change then meet for dinner. Sex had not yet reared itself, but on this particular night, halfway across the Atlantic, Jon felt Katti's foot rubbing his leg, up until then it had just been a peck on the cheek at the door. He looked at her beautiful face smiling, with her sexy eyes smouldering. Tonight would be the night, but only for love-making, he had to stick to his plan. With dinner over they decided to walk around the promenade deck, on the outside. It was a warm evening with just a slight breeze generated by the ship's speed, about 18 knots Jon guessed. Katti steered him through doors that led to the lifts, she pressed the button for deck B, her deck. Still holding his hand she opened the door of B77, a very nice suite, that Jon had not entered yet. The door was closed and she unhooked her little black dress, it fell to the floor, apart from a tiny thong. No bra, she didn't need one. She then started to kiss Jon passionately while unzipping his flies, his penis was very erect as she started to stroke it slowly, then she knelt down and took it in her mouth, moving her lips gently to and fro. Jon had started to strip off his shirt, and then steered her into the bedroom after lifting her to her feet. They fell on to the bed by which time they were both naked, she then continued to take him into her mouth, moving her lips and tongue up and down. He reached an amazing climax. Katti went into the bathroom for only about a minute, "Now it's my turn, yes?" she laughed, climbing on to the bed and on top of him. She began to ride slowly at first, but then gained momentum until she grabbed his shoulders and began to yelp, but not loudly, and let out a huge sigh, her breasts bouncing, her nipples protruding proudly as her orgasm was complete. She lowered her mouth on to his, their tongues inter-twining, Jon climaxed again with a groan that was almost animalistic. Laying side by side Jon wondered where the jewels were, then he saw them spilling out of a jewel box on the dressing table, she still wore the rings. Now could be his chance, but no, too soon and too much forensic on the bed! Bide your time Jon, and it will happen, he thought.

"I'll order room service breakfast."

"No," said Jon, "I have to go back to my cabin to change," he said. They had made love twice more during the night and fell asleep at 2am. "I'll meet you at the coffee shop, let's say in 45 minutes," he said, looking at his watch, it was 9am.

The large coffee shop was busy, there was a queue but they didn't mind, they just stood talking very quietly about the night they had just spent together. They finally managed to find a table and started to enjoy their bagels and coffee. Katti looked fabulous in a see-through little flowered dress, but was wearing a blue bikini underneath. No jewels, just one single-stone ring on her marriage finger, the rest would be in the room safe in the jewel box, he guessed. After breakfast they walked towards the other pool area on top of the promenade deck, it was packed with children, their parents taking up all the sunbeds. "Oh no," said Jon, "let's find somwhere quieter, away from the maddening crowd." They climbed some steps to a small sundeck, through a little gate that had a sign saying 'Crew only'. Katti stopped, but Jon said, "C'mon, what can they do, make us walk the plank?" he laughed. It was deserted, with quite a few sun-loungers, he pulled two together with one of those small white tables, on the artificial grass. The sun was high and hot, about 80f, in a clear blue sky. The sea rolled very gently, what a terrific time this yob from Camden Town is having! he had dragged himself up to big money, but at what cost? Two innocent lives.

He cast the thoughts away and took Katti's hand across the little table and squeezed it. She turned and looked at him, saying, "You were terrific last night," she complimented.

He turned his head, "You were fabulous," he responded, then they both turned to the sun and dozed, it had been a hectic night!

"I'm sorry, this area is for crew only," the sun-blocking shadow said.

"Oh," said Jon, "it's just that the pool area is completely packed and we couldn't find anywhere to sit."

"Well, it does say so on the gate," the young jobsworth added.

"Well, why don't you go and ask the Captain or First Officer if we can stay here for a couple of hours, there's a good chap. As a special concession, please?" Jon laid down again as the shadow moved away. They had their 2+ hours before a tall, more senior person arrived and repeated what the first shadow had said. "Yes," Jon said, "we're just going." They stood up, smiled and thanked him. As they walked away the officer watched Katti's rear, and thought what a lucky bastard Jon was.

Chapter 3 St Lucia

The Carribean Star cruised slowly and majestically into the bay and headed towards the quay, it was lined with hundreds of brightly dressed locals selling souvenirs and home grown produce. A steel band played as streamers were thrown at the ship. The Russian woman suddenly joined them at the rail and started speaking in Russian. Jon noticed that she was wearing her rings, Cartier watch and a diamond bracelet. Jon took Katti aside and said, "I'd tell your friend to leave her jewellery on board, these islands are famous for their muggers and robbers, okay?"

"Thank you," she said, and related the words to the woman. Her face dropped and she put her hand to her neck, said something in Russian, and disappeared. Katti told Jon that 'Anna' said 'thanks for the advice'.

I don't want any other bastard to get those beauties, he thought, she'll be number 2 on this trip, he thought again. But where and when? mid-way on the way back should do it, yes, half way across the Atlantic on the return. The trouble was that he'd been seen with both of them. Well, that wasn't necessarily a bad thing inasmuch as he wouldn't leave any evidence, after all he'd done that with Novak and got away with it.

Katti suggested that Anna accompanied them on their excursion, "Yes, of course," he said, smiling. This way he would make a friend of her and gain her confidence, and when the time came it would be that much easier. They walked through the throng of locals pushing their wares into the trio's faces, fruit, clothing, even fake Rolex's. Jon bought one.

"$30," the guy said, claiming that it was genuine, "contrabando you know, man!" and putting his fingers to his lips.

"I'll give you $20," Jon said.

"$25, and it's yours," the man said. Jon gave him the $25 from a very small wad, best not to show a big roll of notes, the watch might last until he got back to England, but it looked good and he wouldn't lose much if he was robbed!

That night, back on the ship, Anna invited Katti and Jon to join her for drinks at 7pm. It was a formal night, DJ's and evening gowns. They met in the Kingston bar, which of course had the Jamaican theme, even the waiters and barman spoke with the lilt in their voices which Jon thought very attractive especially spoken by a woman. Anna had gone shopping-potty, and they had got back with gifts for her family and friends back in Moscow. Katti had done the haggling for her but she had still spent $500, she didn't seem to care, and would probably do the same in every port of call. She was wealthy, very wealthy indeed. Jon was shocked when she spoke English, "I vood like to tank you for the kindness thet you hef given me today," she said in her broken accent.

"You're very welcome," Jon said, as they raised their glasses.

"My English is bed," she said.

"No, no, it's good, much better than my Russian," Jon said. They all laughed.

"You are very hensom, Kattinaya is a very lucky gel."

"Thank you," Jon replied. They voted to go to the 'Americano' restaurant, which was advertised as having 'the best steaks in the world'. There was a $50 surcharge, but it turned out to be well worth it, a sort of 'a la carte' menu. Jon signed the dockets for the extras and the wine as they left, "Okay ladies, let's go to the roulette table." The casino was packed, but there was another one aft of the mall. They were pleased to see spare seats at the table, they sat. Anna put a thousand dollar bill across to the croupier for chips in 100's. Jon did the same and gave $500 to Katti. Anna was doing well and got a zero, twice, and at 35/1 that meant she raked in $7,000, but Jon and Katti were down to their last few chips.

Katti spoke to Anna in Russian, Anna said,"Niecht," with a smile.

"What did you say to Anna?" Jon asked.

"I told her that we were going to the night-club to dance and asked her if she wanted to come. She doesn't, I think she is having too much fun, and luck," Katti said.

Good, Jon thought, don't need to be too obvious. Katti suggested a walk on the promenade deck, that meant only one thing to Jon, sex. Once again she steered him to deck B, and to her stateroom. Was this another chance to do his 'job' as he called it? This time the seduction was different, she stripped naked and got into the shower, as she soaked herself she beckoned with her forefinger. A DJ etc had never been removed so quickly, when he saw her wet body shining and her breasts dripping water, his erection was complete. He joined her in the shower and she began rubbing soap over him, especially taking time around his erection and genitals, she even spread soap around his anus. This gave him a special sense of delight. He then did the same to her, and entered her, she moaned and said, "Please, don't stop." After their trip of ecstasy they rubbed each other down with large bath towels, then dropped on to the bed, laughing with their nakedness.

Barbados

More sophisticated, less crowded, the ship docked in Bridgetown in the small hours, after leaving St Lucia then a days cruising at sea, beautiful sun and sun-bathing together. Whilst doing so Jon made up his mind, Anna would be the first to go, he would check the itinerary and see which was the longest time at sea so that it would be a long time before her absence was noticed. He fixed on the days between Cuba and Miami, Florida. Gambling would be the key, Katti would get fed up with him going to the casino every night. Tonight in Bridgetown would be a good time to start. "How about going ashore and having dinner?" Jon suggested to Katti.

"Yes, that would be lovely," she said, "where is good food?"

"I think the best place is the Sandy Lane Hotel."

"Taxi," Jon shouted, and a white Mercedes cab stopped, "Sandy Lane Hotel, please driver." They both looked fantastic, Katti in a silver knee-length dress with a low cut front that showed her cleavage, and above all, the necklace with the emerald. Fabulous, he thought. Jon himself wore a white silk suit with a royal blue silk shirt. The taxi pulled up outside the hotel, walking into the restaurant the maitre'd asked them, after the greetings, if they had a reservation. "No," said Jon, "we're off the Caribbean Star cruise."

"Well, I'm sorry," he said, feasting his eyes on Katti's frontage, "we are fully booked."

Jon passed a $100 bill to him and said, "Surely you can find us a table for two."

"If you wait five minutes, I will see what I can do, sir," he said, pocketing the money.

A table was magically found and the couple turned a lot of heads as they were ushered to their table. Sandy Lane was well known to attract film stars, rock stars, and the famously rich. 'Who are they?' people were saying as they walked past.

They wined and dined beautifully, the finest food in the region. After settling the huge bill Jon said, "Let's dance!" when he saw the sign pointing to the night-club. Heads were still turning as they entered the room, the music was naturally West Indian but the band was good, and the female singer beautiful and had a very good voice. They danced until 2am, and then collapsed on to a long sofa, gasping and laughing at the same time. This would be the last time he would be cosying up to Katti, things would now be a lot cooler between them, but he would still be friendly towards Anna, probably in the casino, but at arms length. No drinks in the bar, just occasionally when playing at the roulette wheel. His plan was to follow her back to her suite, and do the deed, somewhere between Cuba and Florida.

At Katti's door he kissed her and said, "Tonight I must sleep. Until tomorrow then."

She smiled and said, "Yes, me too, goodnight," and kissed him.

He didn't go to the coffee shop the next morning, he ordered a room service breakfast and decided to spend the day sun-bathing on the balcony and thinking, yes, thinking, about Anna's diamonds, their value and exactly how he could get his hands on them. The next port of call was ....

Martinique

The ship docked at 3 o'clock the next day, not any real time to go ashore, so he took a walk through the shopping mall. In the men's boutique he bought a pair of white slacks and a bright red shirt, silk of course. The sales girl had trouble keeping her eyes off of him, gorgeous! she thought. She was a pretty young Hispanic girl with an olive skin and deep brown, almost black, eyes. "What time do you finish today?" Jon heard himself say. Through her olive skin, he could see her blushing.

"Ship's personnel are not allowed to date passengers," she answered sadly.

"Oh well," Jon said, "that's a great shame, you're beautiful."

She said, "Perhaps we could meet ashore, you know, by accident, that would be no problem," she almost begged, "I know this island, it's my home," she added, "my brother has a bar called 'Rodrigos', I finish at 4 o'clock."

"Good," Jon said, "shall we say 5 o'clock?"

Jon caught a cab at the quayside, "Rodrigos Bar please," he said to the driver whose driving skills left a lot to be desired! How many clutches must he go through in a year? he mused. Rodrigos Bar wasn't exactly 5*, but it was busy, and Jon recognised some cruising faces and made sure to smile or give a little wave to them, good he thought, they'll see me with another female. Anita was on time, and out of her work uniform. She was indeed beautiful, now her hair hung down to it's full length, almost blue-black. Her breasts fighting to break free of the gaily coloured fitted blouse she wore. Her long tanned legs well shown from a white mini skirt. Jon stood up from his bar stool and said, "You look fabulous, thank you for coming."

Her brother appeared from the other end of the bar, "Anita," they kissed cheeks across the wicker-work bar, and started speaking in Spanish. He looked at Jon and said, in Spanish, "Who is this man?"

Jon caught the gist of what was said, the word 'hombre' being the clue. "I'm Jon," he said, holding out his hand towards Rodrigo, " how do you do."

Anita intervened and said, "I'm sorry Jon, this is my brother

Rodrigo." They shook hands and continued speaking, but this time in English. Rodrigo looked at Jon's clothes and his Rolex watch and said something in Spanish and laughed. Anita smacked his hand playfully.

"What did Rodrigo say?" Jon asked.

"He said you are rich Englishman, he's very bold, I'm sorry," she added.

Jon laughed and said, "No, I'm a car salesman, from London."

"You have a Ferrari?" Rodrigo asked.

Jon laughed, "Just a small Lexus," he lied, not wanting to mention his Merc SLS.

Rodrigo had never heard of Lexus, and changed the subject. They drank cocktails, "On da house!" Rodrigo announced, they were called 'sex on the beach', fruit juice and rum.

Of all the bars in the West Indies, she had to walk into Rodrigo's, Katti was suddenly there carrying packages from her shopping trip. When she saw Jon with Anita, her face dropped but she rallied well, smiled and waved. Jon beckoned her over and introduced the two girls. The meeting was cool as they looked each other up and down. Jon, inwardly, was enjoying it! "Well, goodbye ladies," Jon said, "I've got to get back to the ship to do an email to London, business, sorry!" He hailed a scruffy cab outside, with a smile on his face.

Back on board he returned to his stateroom and laid on the bed. He had accomplished, with Katti's help, what he had set out to do, that was to take any suspicion away. But this was just the first of many to make a distance between himself and Katti, until she would be murdered, he would be forgotten by staff and crew as her escort. That night Jon went to the American burger bar, dressed in jeans and T-shirt, a casual evening on his own, he thought. After his burger dinner he decided to go to the large casino. As it was still early it wasn't busy, of course Anna was there and Jon sat next to her, saying "Hello Anna."

Her face lit up as she fingered the large pile of chips in front of her. He wondered how old she was, 50 - 55, but in decent shape. A good skin and well groomed greyish blondish hair, in fact she was quite attractive. "Hef you not being with Kattinaya tonight?" she asked.

"No," said Jon, "we're having a rest," he added, and winked. Anna smiled and winked back. He changed $500 into chips and thought he would follow Anna's bets. They started to attract a small crowd, Jon's $500 had grown into $5,000, Anna was almost hidden by her pile of chips.

Suddenly a large man in a DJ came over and said, "The management requests that you vacate your places and give other passengers a chance." He carried with him a large wooden box for Anna's chips, and they were escorted to the cashier's window, inwardly Jon was pleased, he'd had enough and Anna was showing signs of fatigue. She had won $22,000, and Jon had won $8,000.

"Shall ve celebrate with champagne and some caviar?" she suggested.

"Why not!" he said. They found a quiet corner in a 'quiet' room and ordered a bottle of Dom Perignon, and a dish of Beluga caviar. They chatted about travelling and holidays, and Jon learned that Anna's family ran a string of casinos in Russia, 'the new Russian rich', he thought. He never dreamed that one day he would meet her two brothers.

"You hef argue with Kattinaya?" Anna asked.

"No, no," said Jon, "she is a lovely girl, but we are just taking a break or we might get tired of each other," he said, smiling.

"Perhaps you vood like to escort me to dinner and dancing vun night?" she asked, with a wicked glint in her eye. That night came two days later when the ship had docked at Dominica.

Dominica

A very hot day, about 100f, the sundecks were crowded as were the pool areas. He saw Anna laying on a sunbed, he walked over to her, his shadow caused her to look up from her fashion magazine. She smiled and said, " Ello lovely man, you good today?"

"Yes," Jon replied, "and I can see you are very well," he added.

"Tenk you," came the answer to the compliment. Jon looked closely at her body, with great interest. Wearing a one-piece bathing costume, she was lovely, not quite Katti but fairly close. Long slender legs, slim waist and a pair of lovely firm-looking boobs. "Vill you sit with Anna ?" she asked.

"Yes, I'd love to," he replied.

"Tonight ve hef dining?" she asked.

"Of course," Jon said, "but I should have asked you!" he replied.

"Oh pfff, in Russia voman ask man to date, no western ideas!" she laughed. He pulled a chair close, there were no spare sunbeds. "Tonight, we will dance the night away."

"It's a formal night, DJ and party frock," he spouted.

"Goot," said Anna, "and then ve hef some love, yes?" Jon then did something he hadn't done for years, he blushed! "You don't fancy Anna?" she asked.

"Er, yes, but let's see how the night goes," he responded.

"Goot," she said, "I need a men, and in my country, ven a voman wants a men she, how you say, goes for him, okay?" she said, patting his hand.

Perhaps this will be more entertaining than he first thought, after all she is a damn good looking woman, he was quite looking forward to this evening, the 'Black and White Ball'.

Not many people ventured into the town, they probably thought the same as Jon 'seen one hispanic market place and you've seen the lot', the souvenirs, the vendors pushing their wares into your face, he didn't fancy it. He was concentrating on Anna and her diamonds, but he would stick to his plan and wait to get to get his hands on them. He would wait until their was a greater time at sea, on the way from Cuba to Miami, he mused, the 'Bermuda Triangle', people, planes and ships have been known to disappear there!

He didn't have a white DJ, but he had a white silk suit jacket, with a black silk shirt and black bow tie, he was sure to look good, and he did. He met Anna in the ballroom bar which was very luxurious. She looked amazing, did he think 50 - 55, she looked more like 35, beautiful. He bowed when he stood, as she walked in wearing a long low-cut black dress slashed up to the thigh, with a white zig-zag pattern across it. Fabulous, he thought, and of course, diamonds, lots of them, wow! there must be 200 grands worth there, he assessed.

"You are hensom tonight," Anna said, "I am lucky voman to be vith yoo," she added, "ve vill hef a goot time tonight, I think," she said, looking him up and down. They had dinner in the 'West Indies' restaurant and then went to the 'Jamaica Night Club'. "Ve are now goink to hef fun, yes?" she said to Jon, who was looking at her beautiful cleavage, and oof course, the diamond necklace.

"No gambling tonight?" Jon asked.

"No, I hef plenty of money, perhaps next veek, yes?" she answered.

"Yes," said Jon, thinking 'I'll soon have all that money from you' and wondering how much she had stashed in her suite, 50k, 60k ? He'd find out in a few days. His eyes lit up when he saw Katti enter the ballroom with a young man who was smart and good looking. Good, he thought, bloody good!

They didn't dance every dance, but almost, Anna stood up and took Jon's hand to lift him off of the comfortable settee, "Now ve hef more fun," and started to lead him out of the venue. He made sure that Katti saw them leave together. He looked over towards her and her escort, and waved, Katti gave a half-hearted smile and waved back. "Kattinaya is jealous thet she sees us together, yes?"

"I don't know, she has a man that's all she really cares about," he said.

Anna laughed out loud. They'd had some drinks, but they weren't drunk, Jon had purposely stuck mainly to Perrier water, he'd only had one large gin and tonic. Anna had a little more, but not much. They went into suite B220, and immediately she threw herself at Jon, kissing his mouth and face, he responded by doing similar and undid the zip at the back of her dress. To his surprise, she wasn't wearing a bra, her breasts were round and firm, it was the expensively made dress that created the cleavage. Then the penny dropped, she'd had surgery, but he didn't give any indication that he'd guessed until she herself said, "London last year, 'arley street men, £15,000, they are very goot, yes?"

"Beautiful," Jon said, 'deja vu' he thought, as she undid his trouser zip and fell to her knees taking his manhood into her mouth. This must be a Russian thing, but it was fantastic, he reached a climax quickly, with a groan. Anna went into the bathroom and re-appeared completely naked, but where were the diamonds?

They were both naked by now, on the kingsize bed, "Now we fuck, yes?" she said laughing. The sex was fantastic, she romped like a girl in her 20's, as many positions as the human body could manage, for three hours.

Jon was exhausted, but Anna still had energy, "I must sleep now," he said.

Anna laughed and said," I vill be beck for more in ze morning!" and laughed again as she put her head on his chest.

He excused himself to go to the bathroom, laying on the little side table was his quarry, all the jewellery, just casually slung with abandon! Her attitude made Jon feel easier about taking them, the uneasy part would be her disappearance.

They ordered breakfast from room service and sat up in bed, after which they had sex again. Then Jon went back to his stateroom to change, as he walked along the corridor he saw Katti's escort walking towards him, still dressed in dinner jacket. They nodded, it was obvious where he had been and what he'd been doing with Katti.

St Lucia

Jon and Anna watched as the ship docked at the quayside at St Lucia, the dock went a long way out to sea, probably there was not enough deep water. Buses were lined up to take sightseers into the main town. Anna said that she would like to go because she had heard that the town is beautiful. "Okay," Jon said, "get your stuff and we'll catch a bus, I'll wait at the gangway," he said.

"Five minoots I'll be," Anna said.

Another town, another island, but this could be different. He was escorting £200,000 and that was definite, until he had done the deed. They rode on the bus which was air-conditioned, it was too high and quite cold, Anna cuddled up to Jon, she was only wearing a thin silk voile blouse and skimpy shorts. 'Oh, those legs' he thought. When they stepped down on to the side walk the heat hit them, probably about 90f, and her nipples no longer protruded. As he guessed, the usual traders called to them and pushed their ornaments into their faces. It was only when Jon looked into an elaborate mirror, that he saw the reflection of Katti's escort from the previous night looking furtively behind him. Was he following them? he thought. His spine went cold, a fucking body-guard, of course. He was looking after Katti and Anna from a distance, they were very wealthy, Russian nouveau riche, loaded with diamonds. He had been hired to look after the girls, he hadn't spent the night with Katti, and when he saw him the next morning outside Anna's suite he was probably checking on her too. All this went through Jon's mind, and he decided to leave well alone. There's not a diamond in the world that's worth my life. But perhaps there was a way .... get rid of the bodyguard.

Anna and Jon found a quite nice cafe for lunch and feasted on lobster, but Jon could still see 'him' lurking at another table doing his best not to be seen behind a pillar. Whoops, Jon thought, may be Russian mafia, and I've got no fucking plan 'B'. Only one thing for it, the bodyguard had to go, now the follower would be followed, and at the right moment would go for a swim. Yes, thought Jon, and as soon as possible, he would soon be running out of time. That evening his plan would go into top gear, he made no date with Anna who accepted his reason of being tired and wanting an early night. He dressed in black, he didn't know why, but he thought it was applicable for what he hoped to do. He would stalk the 'bodyguard' once he had found him on the vast ship. Eventually he spotted him walking alone along the inner promenade deck. Walking in the opposite direction, they just nodded to each other, then Jon dived into the nearest shop. Unfortunately it was the men's boutique, and Anita was on duty, "Ola," she said, blushing.

"Ola," Jon answered in surprise, "how are you?"

"I'm fine," she replied, "I am very unhappy with you, you are very bad man when you leave me with that woman in my brother's bar."

"I'm sorry," Jon said, "but I had some business to attend to from London."

"Can we meet tonight?" she asked.

Jon thought quickly, "Yes," he replied, "I'd love to, shall we meet at the Crows Nest Bar?" she said.

"But you are ship's staff, and it is not allowed."

"Don't worry," she said, and produced a blonde wig from under the counter, she put it on and was immediately a different girl.

Jon laughed, and said, "Brilliant! shall we say 8 o'clock?"

"Yes," she said, and blushed. Jon thought, sex or murder? Sex won hands down.

At 8 o'clock Jon walked into the Crows Nest Bar and saw Anita sitting in a booth next to the bodyguard and Katti. He nodded and smiled, mouthing to her 'how are you?' Katti smiled and nodded and cheekily blew him a kiss. I'm still in there, he thought. Sitting next to a new blonde Anita, who looked stunning in a red silk low-cut top and a short black mini skirt, legs to die for, he thought, he kept his eye on Katti and her escort. "We go and dance now, please?" Anita said.

"Yes," he replied, as he took her hand to pull her to her feet. Entering the nightclub, Anita was already dancing as she walked in. Even though the lights were dimmed, heads turned at the sight of her, especially the men.

"Tonight we have a lot of fun, yes?" she asked Jon.

"Yes," he replied, as he saw Anna with Katti and the bodyguard sitting at an opposite table, they all nodded, the girls looking Anita up and down. Anita pulled Jon on to the dance floor and purposely danced close to their table, shaking her beautiful rear at the trio. The little minx, Jon thought, as he just stood there in admiration, just waving his arms about!

At about 2am they left the club, "Shall we have some love making?" Anita suggested.

Jon was slightly shocked, and said, "You are very naughty, but the answer is a big yes," as they stood and kissed. He thought, the woman's come on was a Russian thing, but then they were in this area once, he mused, and laughed to himself. Still, it would be nice to spend the night with a woman that you didn't intend to kill. Their love-making was different to what he had become used to. She started kissing his genitals, but didn't take his manhood into her mouth, perhaps Latin American girls didn't, but the effect was amazing. She guided his manhood to her and thrust herself upon it, she did most of the work and screamed when she orgasmed. Jon thought it was one of the best he'd ever had. Her scream must have been heard beyond the door. She left, and went back to her small cabin at 4.30am, luckily she didn't have to open her shop until 10.30 am, so she would be able to get some well needed sleep.

Jon now had to concentrate on the job at hand, get rid of that bloody bodyguard as soon as possible. Until early evening, he sunbathed on his balcony, then he dressed in a smart-casual outfit and went down to the shopping mall. He walked quickly past the men's boutique and didn't look in, he was on a mission, but he didn't quite know what. A West Indian souvenir shop had a magnificent display, then he saw it, a beautifully engraved knife with a leather sheath, perfect, he thought as he looked at it. "Careful, that baby is very sharp!" said a young Hispanic man.

"I'll take it," Jon said, paying in cash so there was no credit card record of the transaction. Now, how would he use it? He would have to play it by ear, once again he thought, the follower would be followed, but this time Jon would be carrying his new 8" steel, very sharp, friend. He had no romantic meetings for two nights, then just as the ship was approaching Puerto Rico his chance came. At about 2am, taking a slow walk around the promenade deck, he saw the bodyguard alone right up at the bow rail, as per the scene in the film 'Titanic'. Wearing soft soled shoes, he edged along the super-structure, he ran as fast as he could, knife in hand, and plunged it into his back, slightly right of the spine. His prey fell to the deck, grimacing in agony, Jon pushed the body through the rail with his foot, and then threw the knife and sheath into the sea. He looked up at the Crow's Nest, there was no one there to have witnessed the deed. He started to shake as he walked back to his stateroom, he needed a drink, a very large and very strong one. He sat on the balcony with what was a quad brandy, still shaking, I've killed three human beings he thought, three people have met gruesome deaths because of me. He poured himself another large brandy, another two brandies followed, until he collapsed in an alcoholic stupor on to the bed. Mid-day saw him open his eyes, then a knock on the door confirmed that he was awake. He struggled from the bed, wobbling on his almost lifeless legs, "Just a minute," he almost shouted. He put on a robe and opened the door.

"Sorry, sir," said the room cleaner, "I'll come back."

Without a word, Jon shut the door quietly, but it still sounded like a canon being fired in his head. I must get myself together, he thought as he stepped into the shower. He stayed there for at least 20 minutes, not even thinking, just wishing his head would stop throbbing. It did, but quite a long time after. He had walked around the promenade, he passed the bow, scene of the killing. He checked to see if there was any blood on the deck, there wasn't, the bodyguard's clothes must have soaked it up. By dinner time he was his old self again, no formal night, just smart casual, not even a tie. Just a silk blouson in navy, and a pair of white linen slacks, he walked into the aft 'Archipelago' restaurant. Good he thought, no one he knew. He sat alone just studying the menu, when he suddenly heard, "Hello Jon." He was surprised to see Katti standing there, looking fabulous. He stood and asked her to sit down, and offered her a drink, "Thank you," she said, and sat down.

"No bodyguard tonight?" Jon asked.

"Bodyguard?"

"Yes, the greying man with the Russian accent."

"Bodyguard! he's my father, after all I am only 23 and he is

44, my mother went off with a very wealthy ogliarch last year and he is still grieving his loss. She sends me $200,000 a month so we both live very well."

Jon's blood turned to ice water, what have I done? he thought, killed a man who was just looking after his beautiful daughter and had no real interest in Anna, it's just that she was always there with them. Oh my Lord, he thought again, and he's at the bottom of the Carribean Sea. He composed himself, and smiled at Katti saying, "Oh, I see, shall we eat? I'm starving," he added. He thought again, what will the poor girl do when she hears that her beloved father is missing, believed overboard? He ordered a small dinner as his appetite had diminished, and even then he just picked at it. All through an almost silent dinner he wished he could turn back the clock, just 24 hours. After dinner they went for a walk around the promenade deck, it was very busy, a warm balmy evening, moon shining on the water. With another frame of mind and a beautiful woman on his arm, he would feel good, but as they walked past the bow he shivered even though it was warm. Suddenly he saw himself plunging the knife into the man's back.

Katti felt that there was something wrong, and said, "You are not very happy, tell Katti what is wrong."

Jon shuddered again, and said, "I must have some sort of bug, I think I'll go to my cabin and go to bed."

"Would you like me to come with you, to keep you warm?" she asked.

He thought for a while, perhaps she would help to take things off of his mind, "Yes," he said, "but I don't think I'll be very good for sex," he admitted.

"That's okay, we just cuddle, yes ?"

"Yes," Jon said, "I'd like that." His stateroom wasn't quite Katti's suite, but it had a kingsize bed and was comfortable. They were soon in bed, naked but without passion. She didn't wear a lot of jewellery on casual nights, only two rings and the Cartier watch. Without the emerald necklace she was safe, that was the piece he really wanted.

In the morning they ordered a room service breakfast, Jon felt a lot better, and surprisingly, had slept well. Perhaps he was mentally exhausted or it was Katti's presence, or both.

Anyway, he must still continue with his quest. Anna would be first, he began to plan her demise.

Normally 48 hours would have to pass before anybody was considered 'missing', but Katti, after knocking at her father's door, started to worry. She had the reception desk put a call out for him, 'Will Mr Viktor Kalenko please contact the main reception desk as soon as possible'. The call went all over the ship, Katti waited, but there was no call from him. So she asked for an officer to open his stateroom to check if he hadn't been taken ill and was unconscious, he didn't drink so it wouldn't be that. The second officer opened the door with a pass key card, the room was empty, and the bed hadn't been slept in. The bathroom was tidy, but had been used, probably the previous night. Katti was now panicking, Jon put his arm around her shoulder, "I'm sure he'll turn up soon, after all he's still young and could be fast asleep in Anna's bed or some other woman he's met. there's plenty to choose from, and he is a handsome man," he said, comforting her. But his evil deeds were there and he felt worse being with Katti, his victim's daughter.

St Kitts

One of the smallest ports of call, tenders were lowered to transport passengers to the shore. The large liner had got as close as it could because of the lack of depth. Katti stayed in her suite, mainly crying and waiting for news of her father, sitting by the telephone. News of her father never came. Anna and Katti were questioned by the police as the islands were a British Protectorate. The Inspector was English and very thorough and, luckily, Jon wasn't approached. Done it again, you lucky bastard! he thought. Then he thought again, he had become two different men, easy going Jon, and an evil cold-blooded murderer, he shuddered at the thought, but it was too late now to save his soul.

The ship left St.Kitts after dinner so that the serving was easier for the stewards. At 9.30pm the Carribean Star pulled away from the quay amid the usual noise of locals shouting 'Come back soon' and the obligatory steel band. Obviously there had been no sign of Viktor. Katti stayed in her suite, Jon thought he would not contact her for a day or two, in which case he would concentrate on Anna. Yes, her diamonds are magnificent, unfortunately she would be next, but when? She undoubtedly would be in the casino, she was. Sitting with a high pile of chips on the table, he sat next to her. Her face lit up, "Ello hensom, it is beautiful to see you," her accent said, "are you playing tonight, yes?" she asked.

"Er, yes, I'll put a few dollars down," he said.

"Goot, then ve can hef some fun later," she added.

She looked fabulous with the collection on show, bloody hell he thought, there would be at least a thousand male suspects on board, beautiful woman, loaded and loved a fuck! The poor lady didn't know what was in store, Jon thought, this woman was really asking for it in more ways than one. Jon noticed an addition, the most exquisite diamond and ruby necklace. Was this woman crazy or just so rich she didn't care? he mused. But then he wondered if other passengers would think of them as being costume jewellery, but he knew the sparkle and therefore the difference between fake and genuine. He laughed inwardly as he put $100 on the red 23 block. '21 rouge' declared the croupier, whoops he thought, is Anna going to be lucky for me? After all the ups and downs of roulette they were breaking even at about midnight when they left to go to the Crow's Nest bar.

They sat in a booth and talked about Viktor, "It is a terrible mystery, yes?" Anna said.

Jon just shook his head looking sad. They chatted until 2am when Anna reached across the table and started to play with Jon's fingers, "We go to bed now?" she said.

"Yes, I think we should," he said. They reached Anna's suite, but Jon made the good old 'tired' excuse, kissed her on the cheek and said goodnight. She didn't show it, but she was very disappointed, and stood in the doorway watching him walk down the corridor.

Jon only had coffee and a croissant for breakfast, then went for a walk around the promenade deck. Wandering into the shopping mall his blood ran cold, walking towards him were the two St Kitts policemen, one in uniform. They nodded at him and he smiled nervously and nodded back at them. Of course, he thought, the Carribean Star was a British registered ship, they were on British territory they could stay on board until the mystery of Viktor was solved, until they got back to Southampton perhaps. But if he kept his cool he could ride the storm. People that had had contact or associated with Viktor were interviewed. Jon was called to reception and met Inspector Collins, "Thank you for your time sir," Collins said, "now we understand that you were with Mr Viktor Kalenko, in a group, is that correct?"

"Yes, for one evening, with two Russian ladies. I was escorting his daughter. Kattinaya. He was with Anna, I'm sorry I've forgotten her surname if I ever knew it, but he didn't speak much English and didn't say much. He was very dour, and obviously wasn't enjoying himself," he answered, "I'm sorry that's all I know, apart from the fact that I thought he was a Russian bodyguard for the ladies. But then Kattinaya told me that he was her father. That's it," he added.

"Thank you Mr Weston, you've been very helpful," Collins said.

Jon walked back to the prom deck with the words 'you've been very helpful' ringing in his ears, what did he mean by that? I said very little, he wouldn't have got much out of it. He cast the interview out of his mind, but the longer the cops were on board he would have to put everything on the back burner. His whole plan would now depend on the return journey, six days across the Atlantic at least, but was that enough distance and time to commit two gorgeous women to their watery graves? He hoped that the investigation team would have left the ship, but what would happen when the cruise finished at Southampton? Fucking police all over the place! Unless he killed them on the last day, yes, that was the answer, and they wouldn't be missed until disembarkation. The rest of the holiday until then, would be, well, just sunbathing and generally enjoying himself but not spending too much time with Katti or Anna, play it cool. Be a bit of a loner, or spend more time with Anita, after all she was good company and fantastic in bed. The next two days he spent sunbathing and some gentle drinking alone, and not going ashore. He had seen what he wanted to see of the West Indies, seen one island and you've seen them all! Anyway, the diamonds completely ruled his thoughts and needs. On the third day he had a full English breakfast, his batteries were now fully charged, he had cast previous self-damning thoughts out of his mind. He sauntered through the shopping mall and went into the men's boutique. Anita was serving, of all people, Anna, "Ello Jon," she said, "are you liking these silk ties for my brudder, yes?"

"Er, yes," replied Jon, "they are beautiful."

"Goot, I buy zem," she said. As she left she stroked his chest and said, winking, "See you later, yes?"

"Er, well, perhaps," Jon replied.

Anita said, "You have had sex with her, no? She is beautiful lady and very rich, no?"

"The answer to your very personal question is, no," he lied, "but we do meet sometimes on rare occasions, at the casino, she has brought me luck once or twice," he added.

"Will we be seeing each other tonight?" Anita asked

"Yes, that would be very nice, shall we say 7 o'clock in the Crow's Nest bar?" he responded.

"Fantastico," she almost shouted, and leaned forward and kissed his cheek, "later!" she said and brushed where she had caressed with the palm of her hand.

At 7 o'clock Jon entered the Crow's Nest bar and sat on the end stool, "A small scotch and lots of ice please, with a small jigger of water," he asked the young West Indian barman, whose name badge announced, Marlon. About ten minutes went by and Anita crept up behind him and put her hands over his eyes, "I wonder who that could be?" he said.

"It's me, you naughty boy !" Anita said.

"Who's me?" he asked.

"The best fuck on the ship!" she whispered into his ear. They laughed as she hitched up her skirt to sit on the bar stool. I don't know about the best fuck, but you've definitely got the best legs, Jon thought. "Pina colada for me, please," Anita asked, as she put her hand between Jon's thighs.

"That's naughty!" he said.

"I know," she replied, rubbing her tongue around her lips, "you want fuck with Anita tonight?" she said, very quietly.

"Oh yes," Jon said, "but first we eat. By the way, where's your wig?"

"Oi corrumba!" she said loudly, putting both hands to her head, "I will be back in ten minutes."

Jon laughed as she ran out of the bar. Twenty minutes passed and a completely different girl came back into the bar, she had even changed her outfit, which was just as sexy with a longer skirt that had a slit up to the hip. Jon hoped that she was wearing knickers! He found out later that a thong was the only thing covering her modesty! Luckily the barman didn't notice, he was too busy serving a rowdy group at the other end of the bar, but when he did return he had a slightly puzzled look on his face and must have thought that Jon had changed companions. They left the bar, smart-casual was accepted in the restaurants, Jon had only eaten in three of them and there were four large ones and numerous other eateries, like the Jamaican Deli. Anita saw it at the other end of the shopping mall, "The food is fantastic," she said, as they walked past her place of work shielding her face with her hand, even though she was also hidden by Jon. They sat in a booth and ordered, ribs and sweet potatoes with yams and spiced peppers. They both had rib sauce on their faces and looked like young children when they were being fed! But it was all delicious, they agreed. "I've never had the chance to stand right at the bow," Anita said, "can we go now, you can be Leonardo de Caprio and I will be Kate Winslett, oh please?" she almost begged.

"Er, no," Jon said, "I suffer from slight sea-sickness and after that meal it could make me throw up, I'm sorry," he said, putting his arm around her shoulder.

"Oh, I am sorry," she said, "I didn't know." They walked past her boutique again, and this time Jon shielded his face as the boy who had sold him the knife was standing in the doorway of his shop next door. "Why did you do that?" Anita asked.

"He is trying to sell me some souvenirs that I don't want," he said.

"That's unusual, he's a nice guy, never pushy."

"Oh, I don't know!" Jon said, changing the subject he suggested they go for another drink, this time at one of the other bars.

"No," said Anita, "let's go back to your stateroom for some fun!"

"Okay, yes," said Jon, hoping that her neighbour didn't mention the knife. No, he thought, he must have had dozens of customers since then, after all, it was a week ago.

His mind wasn't on sex, he found it difficult to retain an erection. "What's wrong?" Anita asked, "you don't want me tonight?"

"Yes," Jon said, "but I feel a little sick, I'm sorry."

"Oh, my darling, let's just cuddle and be together tonight," she said as she kissed him. They fell asleep in each other's arms.

The sun burst through the balcony window and woke them both at the same time, it was 7.30am. Jon got out of bed and went into the bathroom and showered. Anita joined him after a minute, and started to fondle his genitals and soon his erection was complete. They went to the bed dripping wet but didn't care, passion had taken over. their love-making was ferocious, with Anita being the dominant partner. They dressed in silence, Jon looked at her and laughed, "You can't walk through the ship like that!" he exclaimed. Anita looked at herself in the wardrobe mirror, she too started laughing. "Don't worry," he said, "I've got something here," and produced a pair of skimpy shorts and a t-shirt, "these should see you back to your cabin, you'll look like an early morning jogger, oh, and the stiletto heels will have to go, just carry them wrapped inside your dress, and go barefoot!" he added. They kissed goodbye, and she ran down the hallway back to her room.

Jon knew he wouldn't be able to 'do away' with Katti, oh well he thought, Anna's diamonds must be worth $200,000 at least, but not in London, there must be other towns and cities he could go to where he could sell them. As far as Katti was concerned perhaps he had found the last vestage of decency deep down inside himself. He may find another way of getting his hands on her jewellery without killing her. Perhaps he could get her drunk and feign a robbery with attempted murder, no, perhaps, perhaps. He cast the ideas out of his mind, Katti was safe, to live and keep her diamonds. Fuck, they are beautiful, he thought, regrettably. He showered again to get rid of the love-making sweat and aroma. Now wearing a pair of knee-length shorts and a t-shirt that was tight cut so as to show off his tanned arms, no socks and white deck shoes, he sought out a sunbed by the aft deck pool. It was quieter, no children screaming and peeing in the water. He saw Anna on a relaxer, and luckily there was a vacant sunbed next to her. His shadow made her look up from her fashion mag, "Ello hensom Jon," she said, "ow nice to see you, will you sit with Anna?" she said, patting the adjacent sunbed, "you hef seen Kattinaya, yes?" she asked.

"No," Jon said, "I thought I'd contact her tomorrow when we reach Jamaica."

"I hef telephoned her today, but she did not want to speak much to me," she said.

"I'll try tonight," Jon said.

Kingston, Jamaica

Jon had always wanted to visit Jamaica, he liked the laid-back way of life that the people enjoy. If needs must, in the future, the thought ran quickly through his mind to come here and stay. I'll go ashore alone, he thought, don't want to be seen with Anna too many times. As the ship sidled up to the quay the same welcome confronted them, he wondered if it was the same steel band that covered all the ports of call! he laughed at his silly thought. The bus into Kingston town looked too busy and clapped out, so he walked over to the taxi rank, "Yes, sir-r?" the young driver said, "cheapest taxi to Kingston town, only $20 yankee," he almost shouted. Jon got in the back of the ageing Ford, it smelled of stale food so he opened the window. "If you want air-r-r conditioning it's $5 yankee mor-r-r," he laughed, showing a set of brown teeth, which were probably caused by chewing sugar cane. After about 200 yards Jon wished he'd got the bus, this driver was a maniac! They must have broken all records for the journey, Jon gave him the exact fare. The only fast car he wanted to be in was one driven by himself!

Kingston was one big market, people trying to sell everything, and funnily, on one street corner a man was selling kitchen sinks! He sauntered around refusing offers, 'very cheap sir-r-r' the vendors said, 'no thanks' he said about a 100 times. Then when looking at some sort of antique stall what he saw in the reflection of an old mirror, made his blood turn to ice water, Inspector Collins lurking about 15 yards behind Jon. Now don't panic, he said to himself, he knows nothing, there's no evidence, so why the fuck is Collins following him? Perhaps he just wanted to see what company I kept, after all Jamaica had the highest crime in the West Indies, especially where drugs were concerned. Collins probably thought I was a dealer from London! Oh well, let him think what he likes, no evidence, no case. I'll lead him a merry dance, Jon thought. Wandering from stall to stall and shop to shop, he kept Collins on a leash of sorts.

"Ello hensom Jon, want to buy me a leetle drink, it's very hot here, yes?"

"Hello," he said to Anna thinking that at least Collins had seen them meet accidentally, good. Perhaps he'll give up and go back to the ship, but Jon had to be careful and would not bother with Anna while Collins was on board. Hopefully he would get off at the last port of call. Anita would be his entertainment until then, once again he thought, no evidence .... no case! Okay Inspector fucking Collins? and he had no intention of harming her, after all she had no diamonds, lucky girl!

They found a five star hotel in the town centre, 'The Grand', an oasis in the desert. The first floor terrace bar was beautiful with magnificent flowers and shrubs surrounding the bar area. Jon spotted Collins at a far table, he laughed inwardly and thought 'will your expenses cover these prices?' "Hef you buy anything here?" Anna asked.

"No, it's all rubbish!" he said.

"Yes, it's how you say, a load of craps!"

Jon laughed out loud, "Yes, a load of craps!" he repeated. The hotel was on the edge of the smarter side of Kingston, Jon and Anna stayed at the hotel bar for about two hours, surely Collins couldn't afford any more than iced water, which was free! Jon kept glimpsing the detective in a small piece of angled mirror on a bar pillar. He didn't let on that he knew he was following him. They left to return to the ship, just outside the hotel was a cab rank, oh no Jon thought, not him again was he the only bloody cab driver working in Kingston?

"Ello again sir-r-r," he smiled with his dentist's nightmare, "ar-r-r you going back to the ship?"

"Er, yes please," replied Jon, "but can we go a little slower this time?"

"Yeah sir-r-r," he replied. Anna threw a $50 note over to him, "Than kyew ma'am," the brown teeth smiled.

At least Insp Collins couldn't follow them, but he would know where they were going. They walked up the gangway and Jon turned to see if Collins was there, he was. Dammit, Jon said to himself. Two more ports of call, perhaps that will see the back of him.

"You come to sundeck vith Anna?" she asked.

"Er, no, I want to go gift shopping in the mall, I'll see you later, perhaps, okay?"

"Goot," Anna said, and tried to kiss him, but he turned away, Collins was watching.

No lunch today, but somehow he wasn't hungry, the drinks had filled his stomach, perhaps later in the mall he would grab something. "Ello sir-r, were you happy with your-r purchase?" the young fellow said as he stood in the doorway of the gift shop.

"Purchase? what purchase?" Jon asked.

"You know, the knife!" the boy said.

"I'm sorry, but you must have me confused with someone else, I don't own a knife," Jon lied, "so long," he said, and walked on in to the men's boutique to see Anita.

"Hello darlin'," the lovely face said, "can I help you with anythin', I mean anythin'?" she asked

Jon laughed, and said," Yes, you could help me enjoy my dinner tonight and perhaps a little something afterwards?" he suggested.

"Oh, yes please," Anita said, "I hope the 'afterwards' means a lot of fucking!"

"Shush," Jon said, looking around, "you'll give yourself a bad reputation," he said, smiling.

"I don't want reputation, I want yoo-o-o!" she almost shouted.

Jon turned towards the door again, and caught a glimpse of Collins lurking in the middle of the mall, pretending to window-shop, poor sod Jon thought, talk about 'flogging a dead horse!'

Jon was just applying some aftershave when there was a knock at his door, opening the door he was shocked to see Collins standing there with the biggest uniformed copper he had ever seen, 6'6"x5' and twice as nasty! "I have a warrant to search your stateroom," Collins said.

"Go ahead," Jon said, smiling, "by the way, what are you looking for?" he asked.

"We'll let you know when we find it," Collins answered sarcastically.

"Well, look, I've got a date, must go, you'll leave it as you found it won't you, I'll be in the Archipelago if you need me," he said smiling. He thought that Collins could possibly plant drugs or something, but then again he had the feeling that he was a straight, honest sort of copper who played it by the book. He never saw the Inspector again.

Cuba

Oh yes, Jon said to himself, as the ship approached the quay, this is the highlight of the cruise. Anita and he had enjoyed a fabulous lobster dinner, and the 'afterwards' was amazing, her yelping when having an orgasm compared with the ships horn, as it prepared to dock! He saw Anna down the queue, but he managed to get ashore quickly and grabbed a cab, a 1950's Chevrolet that had seen over 50 years of better days. Happily the driver remained silent after only saying, "Si signor," and drove slowly into Havana. Actually the cab suited the surroundings, Jon had been transported to the fifties, wonderful, he thought, considering he had been born in the eighties. The only 21st century signs were in fact, signs, KFC, McDonalds etc., otherwise it was the 1950's when Castro took over. Loud music played from speakers above a music shop, and youngsters were dancing on the sidewalk. He noticed that some of the young girls, as they swirled around, were not wearing knickers, as their skirts flared a young boy held out a hat to tourists for money. Jon obliged with some change from his pocket, "Gracias signor," the ten year old said. Not wanting to appear some sort of pervert, Jon walked on. Around a corner Jon saw a queue of classic American convertibles, for city tours. The first was a '57 Cadillac, fantastic he thought, and negotiated a price with the driver, for a one hour sightseeing trip.

The driver offered Jon a throw-away camera, "Ten dollar signor, yes?"

"Er, yes, thank you," he said giving the money to the young enterprising Cuban. The Cadi purred around the streets and down the tree-lined avenues as if it had just come off the assembly line almost 60 years ago. The hour went quickly, and back at the pick-up point Jon gave Luis (the name on his licence badge) a $10 tip. He had exhausted the 24 frames in the camera, snapping at old buildings, statues and of course, those of Castro and Che Guevara, he couldn't wait to see how they turned out. On board ship again, he went to the pharmacy to get them developed, "No rush," he said, after he had given his name and cabin number.

The Voyage Home

He felt a little sad leaving Cuba, it had been the best port of call of all, relaxing and entertaining. The snaps were very good, something to show Vicky and Lorna when he got home, 24 shots of Havana. Plans would now have to be made for Anna's demise, he was still in two minds about Katti. That emerald necklace was really something, and worth a lot of money, was there a way of getting it without doing away with her? He had six days to work that one out. He would keep away from Anna until the last day, he would be on his way back to London before she was reported missing. He could get Katti drunk, also on the last day, so that she passed out until leaving time. Yes, that would do it, a crew member finds her unconscious when everyone has gone, good he thought, I'll get both lots but only one will disappear.

At the NYPD Precinct, Lt Novak was mulling over the report of a female floater being washed up on the beach at Coney Island. The disappearance of Helen Smithson was still on file and had stuck in Novak's craw for months, and he knew that Jonathan Weston was the murderer, deep in his gut. "Get me the Coney Island coroner's office," he said to the station, "Novak, 30th Precinct," he said to the coroner, " do you have the body of the woman found on the beach?"

"Yeah," the coroner said, "it's not in very good condition, the fish have been at it. There's an arm missing and part of one leg," the voice said.

"I'm on my way down to have a look," Novak announced. He was shown into the examination room, the body laid on a table covered by a white sheet, the pathologist pulled back the cover. What met Novak's eyes, once a beautiful vivacious woman, was now a blob of rotting flesh, no eyes just a wisp of hair, one arm and only half of one leg, "Probably sharks," the pathologist said.

"Is it possible that any male sperm could remain in her vagina?" Novak asked.

"It's possible," came the reply, "but I doubt it," the patho said.

"Well, could you take a deep swab and analyse it to see if

there is any DNA, I want to try and get a match," Novak said.

"Sure, gimme 20 minutes and I'll get you a sample of what's there," came the answer. Twenty minutes later, exactly, Novak was given a plastic pack, "There was something there," the patho said, "I hope it's enough."

Back at his office, Novak contacted the police forensic laboratory, and told the technician what he was hoping to find on the sample swab. "It'll take a day or two," the tech said.

"Okay, there's no rush, I've waited a long time, a coupla days won't matter," Novak replied.

"Did you say the UK DNA data computer?" the tech asked.

"Yeah," answered Novak, "those Brits don't hurry, you know," came the reply.

"Okay," said the cop, "as soon as poss, thanks." A week went past before a loud, "GOT YOU, YOU MURDERING BASTARD," was heard from Novak's office when he opened the report from the forensic lab. "Now, I'm gonna get you back here," he read the report with relish.

The subject is:-

Jonathan Andrew Weston d.o.b 20.08.1986
Apartment 4, 26 Hampstead Road,
Chalk Farm, London, NW3
Time of sample on file :- 11.40pm 10.08.2008
Place:- Camden Town Police Station.

"YEAH, I'M GONNA GET YOU BACK HERE AND HAMMER YOUR BALLS, YOU MURDERING ASS-HOLE," he sang out loud.

The door burst open and the Captain said, "What the fuck's going on Novak?"

"I've got him, that cruise killer from England, look," he said as he showed the lab report to him.

The Captain read the report, "This only proves that he had sex with her, it doesn't prove that he killed the victim," the Capt said.

"I've got other evidence, he sold her jewellery in Jew town, that's on film and the dealer will swear to it," he announced, "no jury in the country will let him off by the time we're finished with him. That bastard is going down for life," he almost shouted.

"Okay, okay, okay," the Capt said, "but first you gotta get the Brits to agree to send him back."

"I'll go over to London and bring him back, once the extradition has been agreed," Novak stated, "but first a call to Scotland Yard."

The Extradition Treaty between the US and the UK had been in place for many years, and many criminals had crossed the Atlantic to meet their judges in both directions. But it wasn't a swift process, with a good lawyer it could be delayed for months and months. The worst case scenario was 5 years to bring back a homophobic killer, who was found 'not guilty' by a whisker thin margin, it cost the NYPD thousands of dollars. "You'd better be right on this, Novak, the department's down to it's last dime," his boss said.

Novak got through to Chief Inspector Lloyd at Scotland Yard, "Chief Inspector, sir," he said, "I am Lt Novak of the New York Police Department, we have an interest in one of your nationals, a Jonathan Andrew Weston. We have detected a positive match from a dead female body that was washed up at the Coney Island sea shore. She disappeared from a ship from England just before it came into American waters. She was an American citizen so we have to make a complete investigation on her death, which we think was murder, a murder committed by a British citizen. Would you be prepared to help us with our enquiries?"

"Yes, of course," Lloyd answered, "what would you like us to do exactly?"

"Weston's whereabouts in London, his address now. We have an address but an update would be of great help."

"I will put a man on to this as soon as possible, and will try to get back to you in 48 hours," Lloyd replied.

"Thank you, sir," Novak replied. Three days passed.

"Lt Novak?" the girl said on the office phone, "I've got Chief Inspector Lloyd of Scotland Yard."

"Okay, thanks, put him on," Novak said.

"Good morning," LLoyd said, "I'm sorry, but it's not the best of news, Weston is out of the country. One of our best men has been to his address and other addresses he has used, and he is not to be found. We will of course, continue with this enquiry," came the message.

"Thank you Chief Inspector, please keep in touch, this is a big one. Goodbye now, and thanks," Novak ended the call.

Lorna started to inwardly panic after the policeman left, the money, must get the money she thought. She'd told C.I. Lloyd that Jon was away on business, somewhere up north, looking for prestige high quality cars. She feigned trying to call him on his mobile but she knew it wouldn't answer because it was switched off in his bedside cabinet drawer. But she assured the C.I. that he would be back in 4-5 days. He thanked her and said it was just a routine question or two, nothing to worry about. Parking her car in a bay in Edgware Road, she walked quickly to Barclays Safety Deposit branch. Inside, she told the clerk that she wanted access to box no: 212, and showed him her key. "I'm sorry madam, but that is not a safety deposit box key," he said.

"But it's got 212 stamped on it," she almost shouted.

"Madam, that is probably the makers serial number, our numbers all start with an '0', I can assure you your key will not fit the box," he replied.

Without saying a word, she walked out of the bank. Standing outside on the pavement she said quietly, through gritted teeth, 'the bastard, the fucking bastard, but you won't get away with it Jon Weston, oh no!' In her rush, she had omitted to buy a one hour parking ticket and had been given a penalty ticket by a warden. She grabbed it and sat in the car, sobbing. When her anger had subsided she began to think clearly, perhaps he had given her the wrong key by mistake, perhaps! perhaps! perhaps! After all the flat was only rented, the furniture was on HP and the bloody Lexus was probably leased, these lies would mean nothing to him. He was an evil murdering thief, but then she had been his accomplice to the killings. Hell, she thought, I'm in a terrible mess, how could I face him again, let alone live with him? she started crying again.

The traffic warden tapped on her window, "Are you all right miss?" he asked.

"Yes, yes, I'm just going," she replied, and started the engine. He walked on as she pulled away from the kerb narrowly missing a shouting cyclist. She decided to go to Vicky with the whole sad story.

"You're not talking about my Jon," Vicky said, "I don't believe one word of this crap you're giving me, where is he anyway?" she asked.

"He's on his way back from a Carribean cruise, he's probably murdered some poor woman for her diamonds by now, as well," she added.

Vicky walked over to the drinks cabinet and poured herself a large glass of Merlot and downed half of it there and then, "So, how much is in the safety box?" Vicky asked.

"£320,000," Lorna answered as she showed Vicky the duff key.

She recognised it, and got her bunch of car keys. Producing a duplicate, she said "That's the key to my tool box in the garage!"

Once again Lorna's heart sank, "Could I have some of that wine?" she asked.

They finished the bottle and then opened another which was half empty after two large glasses. "You'd better stay here tonight," Vicky slurred, "you're in no fit state to drive home."

Novak telephoned C.I. Lloyd at Scotland Yard, "Hello sir," he said, respectfully, "has Jon Weston surfaced yet?" he requested.

"No, but I'll put a man down at Southampton docks to wait for the cruise ship to arrive, it's not due for another 3 days," Lloyd replied.

"Thank you," Novak said, "I'll await your call," and hung up.

The Last Murder

"Hello Katti, it's Jon," he said on the phone.

"Hello Jon," she answered.

"How about we meet tonight?" he asked.

"Yes, that would be nice," she replied.

"I'll knock on your door at 7 o'clock, okay?"

"Yes," she said, "that will be fine."

"See you then," Jon said, and hung up. his plan was to wine and dine her, but no sex, he would play the sympathetic friend tonight. His first priority was Anna, only three days left to deal with her, she would probably go overboard in the English Channel.

Promptly at 7 o'clock Jon knocked lightly on Katti's door, it opened, she looked lovely, perhaps a little heavy around the eyes, but lovely. They had a long quiet dinner and then went for a walk through the shopping mall, just looking in windows as the shops were all closed. Katti began to brighten up, but Jon still remained attentive and gentle. They sat on chairs on the promenade deck, suddenly Katti said, "Will you sleep with me tonight? I don't want to be alone." And that's all they did, after one or two night caps, they kissed goodnight and fell asleep in each other's arms. Jon wondered what she would do if she knew that she was in bed with her father's killer. The thought made him shudder. Two days to go, the Carribean Star was now on it's last leg, approaching Ireland's south western coast slightly ahead of schedule and had slowed down to about 10 knots for the night's sailing. The morning seemed to come quickly, Katti was still asleep. He got up from the warm bed and immediately knew that they were in British waters, the temperature had dropped overnight. Katti joined him at the balcony door.

Novak walked into the Precinct Captain's office and asked if he could go to London to 'nab' the murdering ass-hole, Jon Weston, and told him that he had enough evidence to convict, the DNA match, the Jewish diamond dealer and the CCTV footage. "Okay, okay, but you go tourist, NYPD is almost broke, and no eating at those fancy London hotels. Do they have McDonalds over there?" he said. They laughed.

"It's okay, I love burgers!" Novak replied. But it wouldn't be that easy, he would only be able to get Weston charged and taken into custody by the British Police, pending extradition.

Terminal 2 at JFK wasn't too busy when Lt Novak walked up to the check-in desk at British Airways. He showed his NYPD badge and said, "Is there any chance of a free upgrade, I'm 6'2" tall and need a little extra leg-room, please?"

"I'll see what I can do," the young British girl said, "if there is, I'll call your name over the public address to collect a new boarding card," she said.

"Thanks very much," he said. He sat in the departure lounge reading the 'New Yorker' magazine, looking up he saw BA 1008 to Heathrow - now boarding. Then he suddenly heard 'Will Martin Novak please come to the British Airways departure desk' the public address called. "There you are Lt Novak, your new boarding card, seat 6C BA World Travellers," she said.

"Gee thanks," he said, "thank you, if ever you get a parking ticket, let me know and I'll fix it!" he laughed.

"I'll hold you to that!" she said, laughing. He loved her accent and thought he would hear a lot more of it. He'd never been to England before, and was looking forward to the sights of London, if he had time.

Nabbing Weston was the main reason for him being here, the airport bus took him to Victoria Coach Station. He silently blessed the BA girl for his comfortable flight. Walking towards Buckingham Palace, according to the free street map he'd picked up at the bus station, he noticed a traditional English hotel 'The Reubens' almost next door to the Palace. He entered, walking under the US stars and stripes flag above the door, "Hi, I'd like a single room for a few days," he said to the receptionist.

"Could you be more precise please, sir?" she asked. He passed his platinum Bank of America card, which the receptionist put through a machine, then handed it back to him with a registration card. "That'll be £520, including breakfast," she said, "but it will not be charged until you ckeck out, I hope you enjoy your stay in London, sir," she added.

"Thank you," he said, as he passed back the registration card.

His wheeled case was taken to the lift by a young hall porter who smiled, and said, "Good morning, sir."

"Hi, how you doing?" Novak replied. His single room was spacious with a double bed, mmm he thought, could do some entertaining! Then laughed, not on my expenses! Looking out of the window to the street below, he took in the sight of the Palace wall, the black cabs and the double-decker red buses. So this is London, he thought, nothing like New York, it's quieter, and he was only on the fourth floor. Was it some sort of omen that he was directly above the stars and stripes flag? Mmm, he thought.

With just two days to go, Jon was getting fidgety about Anna, tonight would have to be her time, but it would have to be in the middle of the night, about 3am. But how would he get his hands on the gems? He could take Katti back to her suite at about midnight, and then go to the casino, Anna was bound to be there.

Katti's phone rang, "Hi, it's Jon," he said, "how are you?"

"Oh, not bad," she replied, "Jon, I hope you don't mind, but today I want to be on my own, perhaps we could meet for dinner?"

"Yes, that would be nice, I'll call for you at 7 o'clock," he answered.

"Thank you babushka," she said, and hung up.

He didn't know what 'babushka' meant, but it sounded nice, he was glad that she wasn't going to die. She would feel like death when she woke up to find that her diamonds had gone!

"I need to win some money, I feel lucky tonight," he told Katti after dinner, as they walked around the prom deck.

"I have money," she said.

"It's very kind of you babushka, but I have to get my own," he said. Katti laughed at his use of the word. "What's wrong? did I say a bad word?" he asked.

"No, no, it's a good word, it means 'darling' in Russian," she explained.

"Good," he said, and kissed her soft cheek as he looked at her necklace, thinking 'you'll be mine soon'. As planned, he said goodnight to Katti at about midnight, then went to the aft casino, Anna wasn't there. So he went up a deck to the midships casino, ah! he thought, there she is. No seats available, he said "Hello," and stood behind her. She was wearing most of her finery, the necklace, the bracelet, the watch and the rings.

Tapping her shoulder, she looked up, "Ello hensom Jon, vere hef you bin? Anna has bin lonely."

"I've been comforting Katti, she is feeling very bad after the death of her father," he answered.

"Hef you had sex with her?" she asked, almost in a whisper.

"No," he said, laughing, and for once in his life, telling the truth. He noticed that she had a nice big pile of high value chips in front of her, plus a pile of big bill dollars. Wow! he thought, tonight's going to be a big one. The chair next to her became vacant, and he sat down. Her hand went between his legs and she stroked his genitals, she smiled at him and winked, oh yes! he thought, tonight is the night! At 1.30am the casino thinned out, they were almost the only ones left. Anna gathered her chips and cash just before the croupier said ' Thank you ladies and gentlemen, the casino is now closing.' She collected $10,000 at the cashier window and promptly stuffed it into Jon's jacket pocket, "I can't take this," he protested.

"You are not takin' eet, you vill earn it!" she laughed loudly. They arrived at her stateroom, and she immediately went into the bathroom, "Five minoots," she said, "pour a drink, I'll have a big wodka plis, no ices." Jon sat on the ottoman-style settee, suddenly it was deja vu, she stood in the doorway completely naked, apart from all the diamonds. Oh, he thought, she is making this so easy! "Vot do you think hensom? do you like Anna like dis?"

Helen Smithson had done the exact same thing, "You are very beautiful," he said.

"Am I as beautiful as Katti?" she asked.

"Yes," said Jon, "but different."

"Now," she said, "you owe Anna $10,000 worth of fucking!" she almost demanded as she unzipped his flies. Her mouth soon found his manhood as he leaned against the wall, Russian women seemed to enjoy pleasing a man in this way, perhaps it was the Russian winters, they didn't want to get undressed but they could still please their lovers and husbands. His climax was noisy as he let out a loud groan. Anna went into the bathroom. Through the night, until 4.30am, they made amazing love, Anna was completely spent and laid on her back, she soon fell into a deep vodka and sex aided sleep. He lay and thought what he had touched, only the bottle of vodka and the two glasses. He slid very carefully and quietly out of bed so as not to disturb Anna yet. He dressed quickly and stood over Anna as she slept. Then the black mist came down, as if he had suddenly been possessed. He pounced, his hands had seemed to take on a super strength and her windpipe was soon crushed. She emitted no sound, but her eyes bulged and her legs kicked and her arms thrashed, but soon she was dead and just lay there, motionless.

Now to work, he said to himself, he wrapped her in the under-sheet which could contain traces of him. No, he thought, the whole lot goes overboard, the body, the bedding, the bottle and the glasses in a pillow case. At 20 second intervals each item was discarded over the balcony, the ship had speeded up and the body and the other items were soon gone, it was a very dark night, no moon so nothing would have been seen. He spent half an hour wiping where he may have touched, when satisfied he used a towel to turn the door handle and to wipe the 'Do not disturb' sign. Walking quickly back to his stateroom he saw nobody, which pleased him. He sat on the bed and started to shake violently, Jon Weston had returned from the devil's clutch, he started to sob uncontrollably. Four people had died at his hands, four innocent people killed for their possessions. He sobbed for a good fifteen minutes. Drying his face, he poured himself a very large brandy, he emptied his pockets and spread the diamonds on the bed. They were fantastic, the sparkle was caught from every source of light and reflection in the room. Another large brandy helped him sleep, his calculation of his night's haul was $250,000 including jewellery and cash.

Novak had a good steak dinner in the hotel restaurant. The hotel had a Scottish theme, the decor was mainly tartan, and Scots battle pictures were in profusion around the walls. The ground floor bar had a military decor, he sat with a scotch and ice for about an hour and a half just people-watching and listening to their different dialects of English. He then decided to go for a twilight walk down to the Palace with his new digital camera. Wow! he thought, the Captain didn't know what he was missing. The Palace was magnificent, it was beautifully lit and he took about 12 shots! The guards, the crowds, the police on the gold-tipped gates, and of course the huge statue of Queen Victoria in front of the Palace.

After a ham and eggs breakfast he went to the reception desk and asked the young lady," What's the best way to get to New Scotland Yard?"

"If you go around the corner to the left, into Victoria Street, then turn left again, it's about a ten minute walk, it's down on the left, you can't miss it."

"It's that close! gee thanks!" he said. Walking down Victoria St reminded him a little of 5th Avenue with the stores and shops, but he noted that the buses and cabs were all on the wrong side of the road! he laughed, crazy brits! He introduced himself to the reception officer at Scotland Yard (why is it called that when it's in London, England?) crazy brits! he thought again. He showed his badge and ID, "I'm here to see Chief Inspector Lloyd," he said.

"Yes, sir, I'll call his office . Hello sir, there is a Lt Novak from NYPD to see you, yes sir, I'll tell him," he said, " the Inspector is on his way down," he added. He was a very tall grey haired man, but old-school, old for a sargeant, Novak thought.

"Hello Lt Novak, welcome to London," Lloyd said, holding out his hand, Novak took it with a firm shake, he liked that. Lloyd was a shorter man than Novak, but broader than him, "C'mon up," Lloyd said. His office was spacious and comfortable, with winged leather chairs, not like the plastic rubbish at the 30th Precinct he was used to. "Well, let's see how far we've got with this Jonathan Weston. He's currently on his way back from a Carribean cruise, according to his girl friend. I'll put a man down at the gate quayside at Southampton to apprehend him when he disembarks. By then we will be down there to question him," Lloyd announced.

"Chief Inspector, that is music to my ears, I've got evidence here to nail that evil murdering bastard," Novak blurted as he patted his brief-case.

"Good," Lloyd said, "we'll get him back here as soon as

possible."

Jon wrapped the diamonds in a towel and packed them carefully in one of his two large cases and marked it near the handle with a cross scratched deeply with a knife into the leather trim. Then he put it near the door, for a fast exit!

Novak thought, twenty four hours and I'll nail him, take him back to New York and send him up the river for life. He laid back on his bed and watched 'Who wants to be a Millionaire', he thought it a good quiz show. He dozed off.

The dinner was terrific in the hotel restaurant, salmon salad, with ice cream in three colours, to follow and a large French brandy and coffee to finish. Fabulous! he thought, and good sized portions. His phone woke him, "Hello Novak, C I Lloyd here. Weston's ship docks at noon tomorrow, I'll pick you up at your hotel at 8.30am, is that all right?"

"Sure, Chief Inspector, as I said, music to my ears!" Novak replied.

Jon had the task of dealing with Katti, one he didn't relish, but then again he was only going to get her drunk and take her diamonds. She would be the only one to survive, and not go over the side of the ship .... like Anna! "Hello Katti, it's Jon," he said, "dinner tonight, yes?" he asked.

"Yes Jon, that will be very nice, thank you," she said.

"I'll pick you up at 7 o'clock," he replied, and hung up. "It's our last night," Jon said, "so we must make it special, champagne, dancing and possibly some special dessert!" he said, laughing as they walked towards the restaurant. After a sumptuous dinner which had started with champagne cocktails, Jon just took tiny sips of his to every full glass of Katti's, they went to the night club and danced almost every dance. Jon had a bottle of Dom Perignon brought over to the table, earlier he had ground up six paracetamol and had the powder in a small poly bag in his pocket. A lethal cocktail with alcohol. He chose his moment when she went to powder her nose, and emptied the powder into her topped-up glass.

She returned and laughing, said "I'm having a lot of fun tonight, thank you babushka, thank you!" She leaned over and kissed him on the mouth, then giggled.

Good, Jon thought, the champagne is having its effect, she'll be legless after the next drink, just right for me to lift those little beauties from her. He lifted his glass and said, "Cheers!" and made a big gesture of drinking the entire contents in one go, which was actually not very much.

She followed suit, and finished the glass in a few seconds, then laughed nervously, "Am I a naughty girl?" she asked.

"Yes, but it's good to see you enjoying yourself and happy." About ten minutes passed and she said she felt dizzy and she turned a very pale colour and suddenly slid down in her chair.

A crew member came over and asked if he could help. "Yes," he said, "just help me to get her back to her suite." She was just about able to stand. "It's quite a way to her suite," Jon said.

"Don't worry, sir," the well-built youngster said, "we'll get her there, she doesn't weigh much."

"Thanks a lot," Jon said, as he fumbled in her clutch bag for her key card.

"You're welcome, sir," said the helper, and walked smartly down the corridor.

Jon laid her as gently as he could, on to the bed. He lifted her eye-lid, she's gone he thought, for a long time! He started to remove her jewellery and wrapped them in a face flannel, putting it in his trouser pocket. For good measure, he mixed another cocktail with some whiskey spirit and another four paracetamol. Lifting her head, he said, "Drink this Katti, it'll help you sleep for a long time." She coughed and spluttered a little, but the lethal mix was swallowed and she just flopped back on the pillow. It was now 2.30am, the ship docked at 9am, he would pay his outstanding account as soon as he could, and be the first to disembark.

Happily, the ship arrived half an hour early, the half hour could be useful, he thought. He made a joke about leaving early, saying that he would be late for work! "Thank you, sir, I'm afraid it's a bit high, £2,035," she said.

"Okay, what's that in US dollars?"

She calculated it and said, "$3,050, at today's exchange rates," she said.

"Thanks," he said, and peeled off $3,100 and passed it

across the desk, "keep the change," he added as he walked away.

"But sir, I'm not allowed to accept gratuities."

"That's okay, I won't tell anyone," he laughed over his shoulder.

A porter came up to him with a trolley, "Can I take the bags, sir?"

"Er, yes, down to the gangway, please," Jon replied, and followed, keeping his eye on the case with the 'cross'. He was off the ship in ten minutes and had retrieved the Golf in twenty minutes. The M3 was easily accessed from the city and he was soon on his way. The Golf GTI was soon eating up the miles back to London. His bladder was somehow weak, it must be nerves, he thought. The matrix ahead announced 'Services - one mile', good he thought, I'm dying for a pee. He pulled into the car park and ran into the main building, making straight for the gents. Ooh I needed that, he said to himself. On the way out he noticed a set of public phones, he felt in his pocket for some English coins, there were none. He also noticed a 'Bureau de change', "I need some pounds," he said, passing $100 across the desk through the glass gap.

"It's $1.40 to the pound," the girl said, "okay?"

"Yes, that's fine, and I also need change for a phone call."

"Yes," she said, "is a pounds worth enough?" she asked.

"No, can you make it two pounds, please?"

"Yes, of course," she replied.

He collected his cash, thanked the girl and went to the phone. He dialled Vicky's number, "Hello, 8822," her voice said.

"Vicky, it's Jon."

"You keep away from here, you evil bastard, don't come anywhere near me. Lorna's told me everything, just keep away. The police are looking for you, I repeat, just get out of my life, forever," she said with a sob in her voice. The phone went dead. Panic went through his body like a streak of lightening, he sat in the car and tried to think logically. After ten minutes, he began to think clearly, right, I'll go back to London, keep away from the flat, get the Merc and go over to the Continent.

Detective Constable Davison was caught in traffic just north of the dock area in Southampton. When he arrived, passengers were already disembarked and carrying luggae hither and yon. He pushed his way up the gangway, showed his ID and went straight to the reception desk, "I'm looking for Jonathan Weston," he said.

"I'm sorry, but he left the ship about an hour ago," she replied.

"Oh hell," he said, and ran to the gangway. He asked if Jonathan Weston had disembarked.

The security girl checked the list and said, "Yes, he was one of the first to leave, at about 8.45am."

"Thanks," the DC said, and ran down the gangway through the passengers, "Sorry, sorry, sorry," he shouted as he barged through them. Down at the squad car he called C I Lloyd, "I'm sorry sir, the bastard's managed to slip past me, I was held up in traffic," he said.

"Don't talk to me about bloody traffic, there's been an accident here on the M3, at Cobham, we're at a complete standstill, even the eastbound lane to London is slow."

While this was going on Novak was fuming inside as he looked at the vehicles going the other way, slowly. Then what he saw made him shout, "Fuck, there he is, in that small silver car!" But by then the Golf had sped on and it's path was obscured by a coach. C I Lloyd immediately got on the radio to apprehend the driver of a small silver saloon going east on the M3. But as he said it, he realised the futility of his request. Fuck, fuck, fuck Novak said, under his breath, I've lost him.

Jon drove straight to his lock-up where he kept the beloved Merc, he left the Golf in a side street and just took the one important suitcase, and put it in the Merc's boot, it just about fitted in. He was soon going north on the M1 heading for Harwich, to get the ferry to Holland. Amsterdam was his destination. He had thought to go to the safety deposit box in London, but the old bill would be watching it for a while, so he would leave it for the time being. It would keep. Novak couldn't stay in England for much longer and C I Lloyd would be made busy with all the other crime in London. He already had enough money to stay away, no one knew the Merc, and the diamonds he had he would sell slowly in Holland and

Belgium. London was going to be a no-no for a long time.

Crew members were looking for Anna on the ship, her suite was searched. Novak and C I Lloyd got involved. After about an hour, they found Katti, still unconscious. "The evil bastard," Novak said to Lloyd, "we've got to get him, and get him soon, before he kills again."

Katti was finally interviewed, she screamed and cried when she realised her jewellery had gone, "My brother and his friends will get him, they are very powerful in Russia," she announced.

Novak looked at Lloyd and said, "This is going to get big, and very nasty."

"Yes, you could be right," he agreed.

"Novak?" the phone shouted. He recognised the Capt's voice, "What's going on?"

"Sorry boss, we lost him. The ship was early and the Southampton cop was late due to traffic."

"Fucking hell," said the Captain, "come back, the department can't afford for you to stay any longer, get back as soon as. The Brits will have to handle it." The phone went dead.

"Fuck you," he said, "how he got to be Capt I don't know! Well, goodbye lovely old London, it's been nice knowing you," he added. Still, he had dozens of snapshots to show the crew down at the 30th Precinct.

Jon came off the M1 at Luton and went on 'A' roads across Essex to Harwich. The queue for the ferry to Ostend was quite long, and he was almost the last to get on. Other motorists ogled his car, sitting in their Renaults and Fords! Once on board he was able to relax, he had rushed through passport control and payment, car registration etc., there was nothing to do now but enjoy the four and a half hour journey, 'here we go again, sailing the ocean waves, but this time , no killing.'

Arriving at Ostend on time, Jon finally drove down the ramp on to the quayside. Being at the back of the queue didn't help, but at least now he was on Belgian soil and able to roam freely without the fear of Novak and his cronies. Antwerp was about an hours drive away, well-known for it's diamond dealers, more or less a bigger Hatton Garden, he pulled up at a taxi rank, "Where's the best hotel?" he asked the first driver on the rank who couldn't take his eyes off of the Merc.

"Er, m'sieur, you go down zis street, turn left and it's the 'Excelsior' about 200 metres on the right."

"Thank you," Jon said, and passed him a $10 bill. He heard a loud 'sank you m'sieur, 'ave a nice day' as he gunned the V12 to his destination. The Excelsior was perfect, private car park and valet parking, "Take good care, please," he said to the car hop, and gave him $20.

"Sank you," the boy said, as he sat in the driver's seat with a huge smile on his face.

A porter took Jon's special case to the reception desk, and received $10 with a 'sank you, sir'.

"Good morning, Lt Novak," the voice on the phone said, "it's Lloyd, there's another woman missing, an Anna Borikova, from the Carribean Star, Weston's cruise ship. There's no sign of her, quite a wealthy Russian woman who wore lots of diamonds," he reported.

"Don't tell me, no diamonds found either," Novak said.

"No," Lloyd said, " no diamonds."

"Well, I'm afraid I've been called back to New York, sorry, NYPD can't let me spend any more time and money on this Jon Weston case."

"I see," said Lloyd," I'm sorry it went wrong, but it was a terrible mixture of circumstances, but don't worry we will get him sooner or later. I've got the police in five continental countries alerted, with all those diamonds we are concentrating on Holland and Belgium. The trouble is we don't know what he is driving, he abandoned the VW Golf in Camden Town, London, even left his luggage in it with the keys in the ignition. He probably hoped it would be stolen to confuse us. Sorry Novak, that's the best I can say at the moment," Lloyd announced.

"Okay, Chief Inspector, thanks for sll your help, goodbye and good luck," Novak said as he hung up the phone. Terminal 5 at Heathrow was buzzing, most of the passengers were fellow countrymen going home. In the queue to check in, he got talking to an attractive woman from Yonkers, in New York State. Luckily he was seated in tourist class across the aisle from Mary-Lou, his new friend. The man next to her, an English man, offered to change seats so that they could sit next together. 'Thankyou Lord', he offered up a silent prayer, she would make the journey much shorter! They had soft drinks from the trolley girl and chatted, and chatted, and chatted, and when she told him that she had been staying at the Reubens Hotel at Buckingham Palace, he laughed out loud and told her that he had stayed there! How did I miss this dish, he thought, what a shmuck! Oh well, that's life!

They landed at JFK New York, almost on time. Novak and Mary-Lou walked through the airport together, they had become very friendly and swapped phone numbers with promises to contact each other. There was obviously a mutual attraction, she is gorgeous, Novak thought.

"Well, that was a fucking waste of time and money," the Capt shouted when Novak walked into his office, "gimme your expenses sheet, and do I need to sit down?" he added. "Oh, I see, the Reubens at Buckingham Palace, how was the Queen? .... $2,850?" he almost shouted, "I hope your report can back this up, or did you spend most of your time sightseeing?"

"No Capt," Novak started, "I ...."

"Okay, okay, now let's get back to what's happening in good old New York City, eh," he said.

"Hello," Mary-Lou answered.

"Hi," Novak said, "it's Melvyn Novak, the guy you flew back from London with," he explained.

"Hi Melvyn," she said, "what a pleasant surprise, how are you, still jet-lagged?"

"No," he answered, "not after two weeks!" They laughed. "How about we meet up for dinner?" he asked, as his heart rate increased.

"Yes, I'd like that," she said.

"I'll drive up to Yonkers, how about Thursday night?" he suggested.

"Yes, that'll be fine," she said.

"Just give me your post zone number and I'll put it into my sat nav. Shall we say 7 o'clock?"

"Yes, fantastic," she said, and gave him directions. Mary-Lou Miller was a divorced, local Attorney, She'd been on her own for three years, and now felt it was time to meet someone. She thought Melvyn Novak was a very attractive man, gentle, kind, smart, with a good sense of humour. Shame he was a cop, but then you can't have everything, she needed some loving.

Novak left New York City in time to be in Yonkers, about 20 miles away, at 7 o'clock sharp or possibly a little earlier. As he drove into the pretty town which took him back to his childhood, the buildings, the narrow streets, the stores, a general store, the feed store even a horse storage and smithy's works, he saw a nice florist's and decided to buy Mary-Lou some roses. A beautiful bouquet, red, yellow, pink and white, a dozen in all. He straightened his tie, Italian bought in Harrods London, and knocked on the door of the very smart, one storey large house.

"Hi Melvyn," Mary-Lou said, as she opened the door, "you're right on time!" she added.

Novak produced the roses from behind his back, "For you," he said, smiling like a teenager on his first date.

"Come on in." she said, adding, "oh, they're beautiful, you shouldn't have!" she almost shouted, "thank you! Okay Melvyn Novak, what can I get you to drink?"

"Oh, call me Mel, all my friends, except the Capt, do," he said.

"Okay, big Mel, what's it to be?" she asked.

"As I'm driving I'll have something soft," he answered.

"No you're not," she said, and went over to a beautiful oak door and opened it.

From where Mel was standing he could see a fabulously laid table with candles and a central candelabra. His heart jumped or missed a couple of beats, he'd never been entertained like this before. "Wow," he said, "that looks gorgeous, but I had intended for us to go to the best restaurant in town," he spouted.

"This is the best restaurant in town," Mary-Lou laughed. Mel was in awe of this woman's personality, he thought, could this be love at first date? "So, how about your favourite tipple, scotch I bet, yes?"

"Er, yes," he said, "with ice please," he added. They tapped their glasses, and said 'cheers'.

Dinner was the best he had ever eaten. They laughed, talked about London, "What did you think of Buckingham Palace?" Mel asked.

"Fantastic," she replied, "it made the White House look like a hovel!" They laughed.

"Don't let Obama hear you say that!" Mel said, more laughter!

They rose from the table, and went into the beautifully furnished lounge area, "Brandy and coffee?" Mary-Lou asked.

"Er, coffee yes, but brandy no," he said, "I've got to drive back."

She went over to an antique drinks cabinet, and poured two very large balloons of brandy and brought one over to him, "You're not driving anywhere tonight!" she said, smiling.

Lt Melvyn Novak could not believe what was happening to him. Sure he had had a few successes with women over the years, but his job had dictated his private and public lives. But tonight would be one of his good nights, he was floating on a feeling of well-being.

"Tell me about the sort of cases you've been working on," she asked.

"Oh, I don't really want to talk shop, he said. He rose from his chair, and joined Mary-Lou on the velvet sofa. "I'm so glad we met on the way back from London," he said, and leaned forward and kissed her cheek. She turned her face, smiling, and cupped his face in her hands kissing him softly on his lips. Once again he started floating, as her hand went to his groin and gently rubbed his, now erect, penis. She stood, taking his hand to follow her in to the bedroom. they quickly undressed each other and fell gently on to the large silk covered bed. Their love making was both gentle and ferocious, neither of them had made love for a long time, and their orgasms were astounding and very vocal.

Ostend

Jon emerged from the hotel into the warm sunshine after a large breakfast, he lingered on the steps. The porter waited with him until the car hop brought his car to the door. He tipped both as he got into the Merc, "Antwerp here I come!" he said to no one as he patted the side jacket pocket containing Katti's diamonds. Anna's gems were well packed in his suitcase. It wasn't a long drive, through Ghent and then 20 minutes to Antwerp, the diamond capital of Europe. He accelerated on.

Chief Inspector Lloyd sat looking at the file that was now labelled 'The Weston Cruise Murders', he was scratching his balding head. The bastard has completely disappeared, nothing reported in England or on the Continent. He thought some speculative police work was in order, some good old detective work. He called a meeting with four of his best men, it was decided that they would go to Amsterdam and Antwerp. He would only go to those places to off-load the jewellery. "Hello, I'd like to speak to Lt Novak," Lloyd said.

"Hi, Chief Inspector," Novak said, "how you doing?"

"Fine thanks, I'm stepping up the search for Weston, in Europe, Holland and Belgium. We will get him, you mark my words my friend, mark my words Novak," Lloyd said, "we've got the police looking for him in the diamond districts of Antwerp and Amsterdam. We've also alerted the Dealers Association to report any Englishman trying to sell good high priced stones to dealers," he reported.

"Gee Chief Inspector, that sounds great, thanks," Novak said, "maybe I can talk my Captain into allowing me to come back to London, I'll try!" he added.

"I hope so," Lloyd said, "goodbye." The phone went dead.

Antwerp

Jon parked the Mercedes in the centre square on a two hour meter and walked over to a taxi rank, the driver started his diesel Mercedes as Jon got into the back, "Speak English?" he asked.

"Oh, yes," the cabbie said.

"I want to go to the jewellery district, oh and by the way, do you accept American dollars?"

"Oh, yes, one dollar is one and a half euros," he said.

"Okay, fine, let's go," Jon added.

"This is it," the driver said, making his calculation on the meter, "the fare is 15 dollars please."

"Thanks," Jon said, giving him a twenty as he got out. He started walking down a narrow, but well kept tree-lined street, just looking from shop to shop taking his time to choose the right one. He finally settled on a small smart looking corner jewellers. Looking in the well-dressed metal barred window, he saw the type of gems and prices he was hoping to sell. He pressed the security button, after a full minute he was allowed to enter. "Good morning," he said to the grey bearded stereotype man, "do you speak English?"

"Yes, of course."

"I've got some diamonds to sell," he pulled out a brown envelope, inside was a red handkerchief containing Anna's jewellery, he passed it across a normal counter without a glass partition. But the shop was very secure, with an armed guard standing in the corner.

The gem dealer unwrapped the red handkerchief and put the obligatory eye glass on to his glasses clip. "How much did you want for them?" the dealer asked, without taking his gaze from them.

"200,000 euros," Jon replied.

"I see, wait a few minutes please, I need to check them out on the computer." the Dealers Association hadn't got the news to Mr Manheim and he wasn't aware of anything being wrong. He returned to Jon, and said, "The best I will pay is 185,000 euros."

Jon went to a chair by a display counter and sat pretending

to think deeply, with his head bowed resting on his hands. After about three minutes he stood up and said to the dealer, "Okay, will that be in cash?"

"Yes," the bearded gent said, "a few minutes please," he added. He returned with poly bags with bank seals.

Jon counted the amounts after he had filled out the sale form, he gave his home address but used a false name. "Thank you," he said, as the guard opened the door for him. He didn't realise that he had been seen on eight different cameras, including the one in the shop, but at the moment they had no significance.

His cab stopped at the main square, near to where he had parked. He paid the same in dollars, "Sanku," the driver said, "hef a nice day, sir," he added. It was then he noticed two gendarmes looking at his SLS, were they just admiring it, or did they have a sinister interest? No, he thought, no radio usage and no note books, just looking and dreaming that they could one day own one like it he decided as he walked towards it. Another 180,000 euros, wow! that's half a million including what's in the bank, and about another 200,000 euros for Katti's lot and about $60,000 in my pocket! Bloody hell! nearly three quarters of a million! who said crime doesn't pay, and all tax free! He laughed, or was that the devil in him laughing, knowing that he would have his soul one day. He put his foot down on the 500 horses and watched as the three pointed badge rose and the rear tyres screeched round the square .... silly boy, one of the gendarmes took the English reg: plate and got on the radio to HQ for a name recognition. It was of no consequence to Jon, he'd never registered the Merc in his name. The supposed owner was a Tim Fuller of Hampstead, a fallen hedge fund banker who had sold the car in desperation when needing money. Jon had snapped it up for £65,000, an absolute bargain with only 10,000 miles on the clock.

Once out on the main road, to Holland and Amsterdam, to sell the rest of his haul.

Amsterdam

Once again he found himself asking a cabbie how to get to the diamond district. Looking at the Merc, the cabbie said, "It's very complicated from here mein herr, you will have to follow me."

"No, no," Jon said, "I'll park the car and you can take me there, okay?"

"Yes, sir," the cabbie said. After about ten minutes they were at a small square, "The area you want is down that street and you will be in the centre, okay?" He passed the cabbie a $20 bill, "Tenk you very much," the cabbie said, "for another ten I'll keep an eye on the Mercedes every time I pass, it's not busy in the afternoons sir!" he said.

Jon laughed and passed him another $20, laughing he said, "Keep two eyes on it!"

"Tenk you," came the reply.

He walked along the street to the gem centre, not realising he was on camera again. He saw a fairly large shop showing a good display of rings, watches, necklaces, bracelets etc., he pressed the entry button which immediately gave him entry. "Good afternoon," he said to the pretty young woman behind the metal grid. An armed guard stood in the corner.

"Good afternoon," she answered.

"I've some diamonds that belonged to my mother, to sell," the same red handkerchief was passed through the metal grille.

She had an enormous magnifying glass and studied the gems carefully, "How much were you wanting for them?" she asked.

"200,000 euros," he answered.

"I see," she said, "a few minutes please." She disappeared into a rear office, after about 5 minutes she returned, "170,000 euros is the best I can do," she said.

"I'll have to think just a minute," he said. He sat and feigned deep thought for two to three minutes, "Okay," he said, " will it be cash?"

"Yes, of course, would you fill in this form while I get the money."

He passed the form with its usual lies back to her, and she gave him the poly packs of euros. Once again he was on CCTV in the shop, but he walked back to the main street unaware that he had been photographed a total of 18 times since arriving from England. He was now wealthy, and walked as if he was on air. He was now heading for Germany, he thought it was time to get rid of his beloved SLS. Anything near £65,000 would do, and he'd buy a fast but nondesript car, to carry on his journey to who knows where. Perhaps to Italy, yes that sounded good, the Amalfi coast, beautiful, and he could live the life of luxury.

Germany

He would have to drive through the night on one of Europe's fastest roads to get to Stuttgart, where he thought was the best place to ditch the SLS. After all, it was the home of the Mercedes brand, the place was swimming in them! He certainly had the tool to get there quickly, 200kph in the fast lane would see him there in the early morning.

Arriving at 5.15am he toured around looking for a decent motel to get cleaned up and have some breakfast. He found the German equivalent of 'Premier Inns', parked the car near the entrance, grabbed his case and walked in. "Morgen," the middle aged man said, from behind the desk. He was obviously the night porter waiting to go off duty.

"Do you speak English?" Jon asked.

"Yes," said the man, smiling, "I used to live in Reading."

"Good," Jon said, "now, this is for you to put in your pocket, I want to shower, change and have some breakfast. Fill in the registration card for me with any name and sign it however you wish," Jon said as he passed the 100 euro note across the desk, "now, how much is the room?"

"30 euros," answered the night porter, "do you want anything else sir?" he asked.

"Just forget that you ever saw me, okay?"

"Yes, of course. Would you like the breakfast brought to your room?"

"Yes, thank you, that'll be very good," Jon added.

The room was adequate, he was just out of the shower when there was a knock on the door, he opened it, "Your breakfast, sir," the kindly man said, " and thank you very much, have a good day," he said, and went down the short corridor.

Leaving the motel feeling refreshed and clean, he drove around to find a car-wash, the Merc was filthy, fifteen minutes passed and he found a 24 hour autowash that also air-dried the car. He went through in about ten minutes and the SLS looked a lot better. Now to find a good second-hand car dealer, his intention was to acquire a less obtrusive model, grey or black, a car that didn't draw attention. By 10.30am he had done a deal for £55,000, which bought him a 3.5 litre diesel saloon in dark metallic grey and he received 1,500 euros change. He wasn't exactly over the moon with the deal, 'but needs must when the devil drives' he thought.

The young lady in the diamond dealers in Amsterdam looked at the computer screen in horror as she read an exact description and saw images , of what she had bought from the tall Englishman. She screamed, "Papa, papa, look! I have done a terrible thing."

Mr Hertzman rushed in to the office and looked at the screen at the updated Association 'stolen' list, which covered Europe. "Don't worry, there's nothing we can do about it now," he said, "I'll have to break the pieces down to their separate stones and distribute them around the trade. We'll lose some profit, but not much," he said, patting her head softly, "darling, don't worry, I'll start the breaking process now."

Jon found his new car powerful for it's engine size, and it quickly built up speed, it was very comfortable and had lots of 'whistles and bells'. He'd never had a diesel before, he was quite surprised at it's response and quietness, he'd always thought of them as truckish. He motored on towards Italy, down through Austria, it was a very long journey. He had got rid of the only thing that could incriminate him at the customs check-points at the borders. He was completely bona fide as a business man on his travels to find prestige cars to sell in England.

London

"Hello, can I speak to Lt Novak please?" There was no real answer, except he heard a female voice shout 'Mel, phone!'

"Yeah, Novak here," the voice said.

"Hello Lt, it's CI Lloyd speaking, from London."

"Oh, Chief Inspector, I'm sorry, it's like Armageddon here at the moment, eight killings last night, it's hell at the 30th Precinct."

"Well, I just called to tell you that Weston has disappeared again, a car he was using was sold under the name of Fowler in Stuttgart the day before yesterday. We spoke to Fowler and he said he put the car through a car auction for high-priced prestige cars, he doesn't know who bought it. The auction firm gave me a name and address, but it was false," he reported.

"Okay, chief Inspector," Novak said, "all I can say is, stick with it and good luck, thanks for the update, goodbye." The phone went dead.

"It's just come home to me," Vicky said to Lorna, "you were in on these murders, although I didn't believe it when you told me, you were hoping to get your hands on half of that money at the bank vault, weren't you?"

"No, no, you've got it wrong, I tried to stop Jon, but he was too strong for me. I thought that he was going to just rob those women," she pleaded.

"I want you out of my house, now," Vicky said.

"But I've nowhere to go," Lorna cried.

"Yes you have, to HELL," Vicky screamed.

Lorna packed in tears," how the hell did I get into this?" she said as she humped the case down the stairs. Her heart sank even lower when she saw two uniformed WPC's with a plain clothes detective, standing in the hall.

"Lorna Harper?" the detective said, "I have a warrant for your arrest on suspicion of complicity in the murders of two women on the cruise liners Ajaxia and Queen of the Atlantic on dates yet to be determined. You don't have to say anything, but what you do say you may rely on later in court." The WPC's moved forward, one with hand-cuffs and the other to pick up the case.

"Take that murdering slag away," Vicky shouted as they put her in to the unmarked police car. She was taken to West End Central police station, she was formally charged and put in a cell. Her wails of sorrow could be heard through two metal doors.

"Hi, honey," Mary-Lou's voice said, "how's my hunky cop?"

"Hi, Mary-Lou," Novak answered.

"Oh, Mel, you sound realy down, can I do anything to make it better?" she asked.

"I wish there was, I'm snowed under, eight murders in the city, rapes, muggings, the list is endless. I was still on duty at midnight, and that bastard Weston is still free-legging it in Europe."

"Oh, darling," she said, "I'm so lonely for you, can you find some time for little old me?" she almost begged.

"Yes, tonight. To hell with it, I'll tell the Capt I need this evening off and to hell with him!" he said, "I'll be over at 7.30pm, how's that?"

"Wonderful," she said, "everything will be ready for you, and I mean everything!" She laughed.

"Okay," he said, "I'll see you then," and put down the phone. On the way to Yonkers, his cell phone rang, it was the Captain's number, he switched it off and shouted at the windshield "I do have another fucking life, and that's where I'm going now!!" He started laughing. He stopped at his favourite florist that was just about to close, "The usual please," he said to the young lady.

"Of course!" she said, and made up his usual bouquet.

"Thanks very much," he said, passing her a $50 bill, "keep the change!" he added.

"Hello darling," Mary-Lou said, as she opened the door and kissed his lips passionately.

"Whoa, you'll have the neighbours talking!" he said.

"Aw shucks! They've been talking for weeks, who cares!" she said as she pulled him in to continue the passionate welcome. The roses were graciously accepted, as always, "Thank you," she said, and kissed his cheek.

The evening went well, with good food but not much to

drink, he had to be back at his desk by 8 o'clock in the morning. Although fairly short-lived, their lovemaking was amazing, they slept until six. Mel had spare clothes at the house and looked fresh when they said their goodbyes. Mary-Lou was hopelessly in love with Mel and had a plan for them to be together permanently, she would tell him of it on his next visit.

Italy

J on arrived in Italy a day and a half after leaving Stuttgart. Keeping up a steady pace, the diesel engine hummed along nicely at 150kph with the fuel gauge hardly moving, a damn good car, he thought, but not a match on his SLS. His journey had taken him through Austria and Slovenia, he'd slept in the car at car parks in service areas, breakfasting and washing in the main building. He'd done this so as not to be seen on his way to Italy by any motel cameras. He now thought of himself as the master of disappearance! Once across the Italian border, he set the sat nav for Venice, he would settle there for a couple of weeks, rest up and re-charge his batteries.

St Petersburg

The memorial service for Anna was attended by nearly 200 people at the Cathedral adjacent to the Hermitage Palace. Her family were in deep mourning, so much more than usual as there had been no funeral. To just disappear whilst on holiday was beyond belief, and her ex-husband and sons knew that she would have had her best jewellery with her. They had warned her against taking it, but she had insisted, "I want to look my very best," she had said as she went through the departure gate at the airport, on her way to Heathrow. After the service a group of ten black-suited men stood together discussing how they would investigate her demise. They would send special detectives to England, there would be no expense spared, no stone unturned until the murderer was caught and dealt with as only they knew how, it would be very slow and painful. Vasili Kashnosky, Anna's ex-husband, was the leader of the group, and pledged one million dollars to the cause, and said, "He must be found and punished, and suffer until he begs to be killed."

Venice

J on rented a villa away from the main city. It was a quiet area, mostly residential, his neighbours were mostly middle class, his car drew no attention, but he did. A young girl, about 25 years old living almost next door seemed to be there every time he went to his car or just went out for a walk to the mini market. She always smiled, and said, "Buongiorno," to which he replied in English, "Good morning."

"Oh, you are from England."

"Yes," Jon said, "taking a holiday."

"That's nice," she said, in almost perfect English, "my name is Monica Ambezi."

"Hello," Jon said, " my name is Chris Sutton," he lied.

"I work at the mini market which my father owns, if you wish I can deliver your provisions every day," she said.

"No, it's very kind of you, but I like to walk around to see all the Italian foods, perhaps in the future, yes?"

"Yes," she said, "it'll be my pleasure!" She walked off down the little hill, moving her rear sexily. Jon thought, that might be some fun, but it's a bit on the door-step, best left alone!

Jon's face was now being shown on television in England as a dangerous killer who preyed on wealthy women, the presenter on 'Crimewatch' said. 'He is wanted for at least two murders on cruise boats the Ajaxia, and the Queen of the Atlantic, and he steals the victim's jewellery before disposing of their bodies in the sea. The hunt for him will also be in mainland Europe as he is believed to have fled the country'. Jon had no idea of this broadcast, and carried on with his holiday. He hadn't noticed the satellite dish above the mini market. Monica was sitting at the cash desk during a quiet period, idly looking at the TV set, she grabbed the remote control and started to flick through the channels. As Jon's face appeared a woman came to the till, by the time she turned back to the TV the image had gone. Jon laid on his bed watching television idly, not understanding what he was watching. His blood turned to ice water when he saw his face on the screen, the text was in English, with subtitles, "Fucking hell," he shouted, "I've got to get out of here." He started packing, just throwing everything into one case and a bin bag. But one slightly lucky item on the TV said that the police were looking for a very distinctive Mercedes Sports car in white, FOW10R. His new car was dark grey and definitely not sporty, but he had to get going, and he had to disguise himself, hair colour, grow a beard and moustache. He called in at a pharmacy further on down the street from the mini market, Monica was sitting at the cash desk. "I thought you worked in the market," Jon said.

"Yes, my father owns this pharmacy as well!" Jon laughed, but only bought a tooth brush, best not to let her see that he bought hair dye. "Thank you," she said, "see you later, yes?"

"I hope so, just going to have a look at the canals and the Bridge of Sighs."

She sighed as he left the shop. Driving in to the city, he was able to pick up what he needed at a large supermarket, plus a large brimmed straw fedora hat to cover his face until his facial hair had grown. Fucking CCTV was everywhere, his intention was to go south, perhaps TV reception was different. He sped on down to Rimini on the coastal main road, only about three hours away at a steady pace. He rubbed his chin, 'come on you bastard, grow!' he shouted at the windscreen. He was fortunate to find a small hotel in this holiday resort where he could get lost! He went straight to his room, he kept his head down and wore his fedora low as he signed the register. Because of his passport he had to give his real name. He immediately switched on the TV to see if his face was broadcast, he watched a news programme for about half an hour, but nothing. Good, he thought, and went into the bathroom to change his hair colour to almost blond, and as soon as it grew he would give his beard the same treatment. He would lay very low and avoid any CCTV cameras, especially in the streets. He was lucky, Rimini didn't seem to have any, they were only used in expensive shops and stores which he avoided like the plague.

After nearly a week, his moustache and beard had grown to almost the required length for dyeing. He had spent very little time in the main area of the hotel, only sticking to his room and keeping his head down and his fedora covering his face. He could not believe his luck when he saw his old face on the TV with the name 'Giancola Westoni', thanks Italian TV, for being crap! he thought. He felt safe in Rimini, with beard and moustache growing longer by the day, he had the task of dyeing the extra growth, but that only took a few minutes.

New York

"Hi Chief Inspector, it's Mel Novak," the Lt said to C I Lloyd on the phone, "any news on Weston?"

"No, I'm afraid not," the C I replied, "as far as we know he's still in Holland somewhere, as soon as we're updated I'll call you immediately, but at the moment he has completely gone to ground. We really don't know where he is, sorry," he said.

"Okay, Chief Inspector, thanks anyway," Novak said, and hung up. With all his New York cases, Weston was still Novak's obsession.

St Petersburg

Vasili Kashnosky had set up quite a comprehensive web of agents to cover Holland, Belgium and Germany, with large cash bonuses. Belgium had only come up with the news that he had gone to Germany as his SLS Merc had been seen for sale in Stuttgart, and he was now driving a black 350 diesel saloon, but they didn't know where he was going. Germany, Austria France, they had no idea. Vasili upped the reward to 2 million dollars. "I want his balls in a dish, on my desk," he shouted, and banged the top of his Louis XIV desk, "and fucking SOON," he yelled.

Moscow

Katti's brothers Georki and Adriof were glad to have their sister home safe and sound. She and her mother bonded at the sumptuous villa in the best part of Moscow which housed all the billionaires in that part of Russia. The houses were high walled and security gated with 24hr armed guards and ferocious dogs. In Moscow you were very rich, or almost on the breadline so the rich had to protect themselves in the most stringent ways. It was common for a would-be burglar's body to be found in the street the next day having bled to death from dog mauling or gun shot wounds. The police did very little investigation as they knew that they would get nowhere, as the residents had the authorities where they wanted them, in their pockets, corruption was rife. Katti's brothers were also joining the race to catch Jonathan Weston. They also wanted his mutilated body on a slab and had sent their own agents to central Europe to find him. They were very powerful 'mafia' types, and had dozens of ruthless men in their employ. Her father's death was bad, her loss of diamonds was bad, but their loss of face and reputation was the main reason to catch him. To restore their place at the top of the tree of organised crime.

Rimini

Jon was enjoying his new identity and look, he now looked like a young blond Viking. His moustache was full, well across his upper lip, and his beard at least 4" long, it was a complete transformation. The old Jonathan Weston had gone, but now he had to get a new name and passport, how? he wondered. Rimini wasn't the place, he needed to be in a large city where the 'underworld' could be found. Rome was the place, he thought, after all the Romans were the most corrupt people ever, they almost invented corruption. He checked out of the hotel and started his long journey across Italy to Rome, two days at a steady pace should do it.

Rome

Driving in from the north, the other six hills were clearly visible, and in a strange way, majestic and beautiful. His route in to the city took him past the Coliseum which was smaller than he imagined, my lord, the things that went on there, he thought. Going through the inner busy part of the city, he started looking for a nondescript small hotel, and suddenly there it was, the 'Angelo'. Just right, he thought, with a small car park at the front, he manoeuvered the car so that it could hardly be seen from the thoroughfare. The unexpected happened when he tried to check in, he was asked for his passport. Thinking quickly, he said, "I don't have one, my car was stolen with my luggage in Rimini, but I will be paying cash," he explained, "Oh, by the way, this is for you," he passed the young man 50 euros, and winked.

The youngster's eyes lit up as he took the note, " Si signore, no problem!" he said, with a smile on his face, " grazie," he added and gave him the key to room 90.

Jon paid for the room four days in advance, 500 euros, room only. "Where can I do some shopping?" he asked Antonio.

"There is the market behind the hotel street, that's the nearest place," he explained.

He thanked the receptionist and went up to his room, he needed sleep and threw himself on to the double bed and almost immediately fell asleep. It was hot, three hours later he awoke in an extreme sweat. In his dreams he had re-lived the last few weeks, Helen, Viktor, Anna, Katti etc. Helen's face once again appeared above the ship's balcony rail and called for him to join her in the water. He rushed to the shower-only bathroom discarding his clothes quickly on the floor and was soon dousing himself in cold water. Out of the shower he wondered if he was still shown on television, he switched it on and laid back on the bed wondering if he was still news, on the 'wanted' list of Europe. He only had to wait about twenty minutes before the image appeared of his old persona, he looked nothing like the tele picture, he was pleased, and went to compare his now face to what he had seen, nothing fucking like it! he almost shouted at the mirror, nothing fucking like me! He rejoiced again, and danced around the room. He suddenly thought about money and he decided to have a 'roll call' of the cash that he had. $45,000 and 160,000 euros, in sterling that came to £182,000, he would have to tone down his spending a little. After 6 o'clock he ventured out to the car to retrieve his case from the boot, there was an older man on the reception desk who just nodded when Jon waved his room card on the way back in to the hotel with his large case. He hung his clothes in the wardrobe and caught sight of a bulge in his white linen jacket. Reaching in, he found $10,000 which he had forgotten as winnings at the casino, with Katti. 'Now there's a nice bonus' he said, 'very nice, and laughed. 'Bless you Katti!' Little knowing what her brothers had in store for him.

Yonkers - New York

"Sorry, sir," the young lady florist said, "I've run out of roses."

Novak said, "You've done what?" But he said it with a smile on his face, "what am I going to do?" He did a Groucho Marx walk around the shop, with his hand on his forehead, "Okay, okay," he said, laughing, "just do me a mixed bouquet." The girl laughed, thinking, he's nuts!

The door of Mary-Lou's house opened before he reached it, "Honee-e-e!" she said, and kissed him passionately, "don't stand there, the neighbours can see!"

"Oh, yes," he said, "they've got no idea that I visit here!" They laughed, and went inside to continue their passion.

"Are you staying tonight?" she asked.

"If you want me to I will," he answered.

"Is the President, Obama?" she almost shouted, and started fondling his genitals.

"Hey, not yet baby, I'm starving," he said, and started to explain the difference in the bouquet.

"They're beautiful," she said, and went to find a vase. After some very noisy love making, she suddenly blurted out, "I think we should get married."

Novak's eyes opened wide, staring at the ceiling, he said," So do I."

"I'm free tomorrow."

"Okay," he added, "thanks for asking!" They laughed, and sealed the proposal with more passion. Novak had thought about his position for a long time, the Captain was still reasonably young, it would be a long time before he would move upstairs. He made up his mind in a few seconds, he would ask for a transfer to a closer district to Yonkers, perhaps even Yonkers itself.

"Okay Novak," the Captain said, without looking up from his paperwork, "what do you want to see me about, eh?" he asked.

"I'm getting married and want a transfer to Yonkers, or close by," he said, quietly.

The Captain dropped his pen and looked up, open mouthed,

"You want what?" the Captain shouted. Mel repeated his request again. "Why, for pete's sake? you can be married and stay here," the captain said.

"I don't want to, my intended has got a beautiful house, and I live in a down-town pigeon coop. I want to get closer, it's nothing personal Captain, I just want to move on with my life."

"What about the Weston case?" the Captain asked.

"It's gone stale," Mel replied, "he's gone to ground somewhere in Europe. Chief Inspector Lloyd's intelligence have even found out that the Russian mafia are looking for him."

"Okay, okay," the Captain said, "put your request in writing and I'll put it to the Commissioner's office, but I don't hold out much hope," he added. He picked up his pen and went back to his paperwork.

Rome

Jon was settling into the Roman way of life, he had come to an arrangement with the hotel management to live there as a permanent guest at a very low rent per month. He had even found himself a girl friend, a Swedish student studying 'Roman art of the Caesars'. Tall blonde with blue eyes, a typical Swedish beauty, she had been attracted to his fair hair and beard, little did she know what lurked underneath the disguise. she was lucky, she had no diamonds and lived off of her parents and a student grant from the University of Stockholm.

Jon had thoughts of going to London, but first he must see about his passport. How would he find someone to get him one? He decided to go to St Peters Square, around the cafés he could probably find the person to help him. He chose a pavement cafe in a corner at the bottom of the square. Looking around, he was glad to see the lack of CCTV cameras, in fact, Rome didn't have many, just one or two near banks and important buildings. There weren't even any speed cameras on the main thoroughfares, good! he mused, Orwell's '1984' hadn't quite reached Rome, he thought again, but it will, one day! Sitting sipping his chianti he noticed two men lurking by a fountain, wearing black leather jackets. He guessed that they were Romanian possibly, and watched as they went up to a tourist with a map open, to ask him directions. As one kept him busy the other one easily picked his pocket very skilfully, he then passed the wallet on to a young girl who just walked on, not even faltering her pace. Bingo! he thought. The tourist walked on completely unaware that he had been robbed. Jon decided to follow the older looking map-man, who eventually sat on a low wall and mopped his brow with a dirty handkerchief. Jon sat on the wall about six feet away from him and said, "Do you speak any English?"

The man turned, and said nervously, "Yes, I used to live in Slough, but I was deported last year. Are you the police?" he asked.

"Good lord, no, I'm on your side, almost a fugitive," he added, "I need a passport," he confided, "do you know of a way I can get one?" he asked.

The man looked around, and said, "That could be expensive, do you have money?"

"Yes," Jon answered.

"Meet me at 6 o'clock, but not here, over at the last table at the far cafe on the square. I will be with a friend," the Romanian said.

When 6 o'clock came, Jon was seated at the table. He was suddenly confronted by three men, all obviously Roma's, "You wish for a passport?" one of them said. He was huge, over 6ft and almost as broad. "We hef Irish or German only, and they are 5,000 euros," he said, as they all sat down.

"Good," said Jon, "I'll go for Irish," he answered. The big man held out his hand as if for the money, "No, my friend, cash on delivery I'm afraid."

"Okay," the big Roma said. Obviously another deportee from Slough. "But I will need a photograph, and no dark glasses. We will be here again at noon, tomorrow," he said quietly, through his yellow teeth.

Jon was in the same seat at noon the next day and true to their word, the Roma's were on time. The large man produced an Irish Republic passport. "What name do you want on this?" Jon had thought about this and came up with the name 'Keiron Robert Pearce'. He wrote it on a small part of a wine list, and tore it off. "Okay, we will want the photograph today at 6 o'clock, here."

Jon walked around the shops outside the square until he found a pharmacy, and inside, at the back was a photographic booth. It took only ten minutes for the image to drop through the slot, good he thought, whatever happened to Jon Weston? he laughed. Six o'clock arrived and so did the big Roma, only. "Do you have the money?" he asked

"Yes," answered Jon.

"Give me the photograph, I will be back in 10 minutes," said the Roma.

Jon ordered some chianti, his drink had just arrived, as did the passport. The big Roma pushed the passport across the table, under his huge hand. It was then that Jon realised that the other two 'gentlemen' were standing behind him. Kieron Robert Pearce opened the passport and looked at the main page containing his image. Fucking hell! he thought, this is perfect! How do they do it?

"Now, my friend, the money," demanded the giant. Jon pointed to a magazine laying on the table. The Roma opened the pages to find 10 x 500 euro notes, he took the cash and put it his inside jacket pocket.

Offering his hand, Jon shook it and said, "It's been nice doing business with you."

"Goodbye," they said simultaneously.

It had been 3 or 4 weeks since the last bulletin showing his old persona as Europe's most wanted man, it seemed that it was old news and that he was yesterday's chip paper. So, he decided to book a flight to London.

London

Having been on remand pending investigations, Lorna Harper was finally called to trial at the Old Bailey. The evidence was not as solid as C I Lloyd had originally thought, her barrister was good, very good, and pointed out that she did not know what Jonathan Weston was doing, she didn't know that he had actually murdered the women in question. She thought that he had only robbed them. The trial lasted three days, and Lorna was found 'not guilty', she left court. She was broke, homeless and jobless, really just another victim of Jonathan Weston. Of course, she had perjured herself, and would have to live with that for the rest of her life. After all she hadn't the power to stop him, and the thought of a wealthy life-style appealed to her bad side, and anyway she was a looker and would easily climb the ladder of well-being again. She phoned her sister in Brighton and told he that she had been found innocent, "I know," her sister said, "it was on TV news."

"Can I stay with you for a while, I've got nowhere to go, plee-e-ez?"

"Okay, but you must find a job and flat as soon as," her sister said, "Jack likes his privacy and the flat isn't that big."

"Bless you," Lorna almost shouted, "I'll be down about tea time," she added. "How much to Hove?" she said to the cab driver at Brighton station.

"What street?" the driver asked.

"Wordsworth street," she replied.

"About £7.50, depending on the traffic," he answered.

"Okay, yes please," she replied. The cabbie put her roller case in the boot.

Rome

Jon went to the nearest travel shop to find out about dates and fares. Via Dublin looked good, any official eyes might not be looking at any passengers landing in London from there. He booked through Ryanair, who seemed to be the cheapest. Of course, he could afford schedule flights, but this way he thought he was safer. It had been many months since he had been to London, and hoped his trail was completely cold. Landing at Dublin airport, this would be the first real test of his new passport. He walked through passport control with no problems, the desk officer hardly looked at it, but his bag, only one, went through the x-ray machine. One bag was all he needed, he wanted to travel light. He crossed the concourse to book to Gatwick, also with Ryanair. His flight was in one hour's time, just long enough to have a sandwich and a beer. His flight was on time at Gatwick, through passport control, on English soil, made his heart pound in his chest, but there again the desk controller hardly looked at it. He did notice a police presence at the customs 'out' door In to the main concourse, but they may or may not be looking for him. Jonathan Weston, definitely not Keiron Pearce, a blond man with a beard.

The next part of his visit would be tricky, the safety deposit box. He looked at the key in his hand and turned it over and over, £320,000 in there, just waiting for him! It's just opening time at Barclays branch at Marble Arch, oh well! Shit or bust, he thought and crossed the street to enter through the automatic doors. Walking across to the safety box counter, he said to the desk clerk, "I'd like to access my box please," he held up the key.

"Yes, sir," the young man said, "please follow me." He was led through a glass door, down a short corridor and shown in to the large heavy-doored room containing hundreds of boxes, all in numerical order. He soon found 0771 and pulled out the box from the aperture. He opened the box and there it was, 320 grand in euros and dollars. He loaded the lot into his bag, pushed the box back and locked it again. Walking out, he sighed a huge sigh of relief and thanked the desk clerk, handing him the key, "I won't be needing it again," he said and walked out. He hailed a cab and said, "Gatwick airport please, oh, and do you take US dollars?"

"Yes, sir," came the reply, "it's a fixed fare, $120."

"Okay," Jon said, "let's go." Arriving at the north terminal, he passed $150 to the driver.

"Thank you, sir," he said, after hearing the magical phrase 'keep the change'.

His cab journey from London had been a little fraught, traffic was thick but it was a comfortable trip. He sat back in the seat and watched the rolling hills of Surrey, were they called the North Downs? He thought it would be a long time before he would see them again. A very long time. Jon sat in the main hall thinking about his next move, should he fly direct to Rome, or go via Dublin again? No, it's probably better to go direct, he thought, I'll be well out of the area in a few hours.

Rome

His Ryanair flight landed on time at Rome airport, he had gone through passport control and customs without a hitch. Leaving the airport, he hailed a cab back to his hotel. He was greeted by Gretta with a passionate kiss. They went up to Jon's room and did what Romans had been doing for centuries .... "Fuck, fuck, fuck, fuck," she almost shouted as she reached her orgasm.

They wandered from the hotel, hand in hand, down to the small shopping area and found a bistro, typically Italian, and sat at a corner table. They ordered canneloni and a bottle of chianti.

Yonkers - New York

The wedding was to take place at the Town Hall Registery office, Mel being Jewish and Mary-Lou being Christian, a religious service would not be possible in the time allotted. Either one would have to go through changing their religion and they felt that that wasn't necessary. There were about 50 guests including Mel's widowed mother who did nothing but cry! still, she enjoyed it! Mel had managed to get a transfer to New Rochelle, just a 30 minute drive away. His new life and bride had turned him into a new man, completely, "Thank you Lord," he said quietly as the newly married couple walked past their family and friends outside the civic office and were covered in rice and confetti. Unfortunately, being the new boy on the job, and Mary-Lou being snowed under with law work, their honeymoon would have to wait, but that didn't matter, they were well engulfed with what newly-weds do, anyway!

St Petersburg

Vasili sat at his huge desk with six of his 'agents' almost standing to attention in front of him, (in Russian) "What the fuck is going on? Do you not care that my Anna has been killed, why have you not found this animal yet, and presented him to me to deal with? Does any of you know where he is?" They looked at each other nervously.

"WELL?" he screamed.

A brave young one said, "He was last seen in Stuttgart, where he changed his car, but has not been seen since."

Vasili thought, if he went from Amsterdam to Stuttgart, he must have travelled south. "Okay," he said, "I want that you should concentrate on Austria and through to Italy, get more agents on the trail, AND FIND THE WHORESON," he screamed.

Vasili and his colleagues were well used to 'dealing' with people, many had suffered at their hands. A quick bullet in the head wasn't their way, garrotting with piano wire and the use of blow torches were only some of the deaths that Jon could expect after being castrated, had his tongue torn out and his eyes and teeth removed.

London

C hief Inspector Lloyd received a call from Barclays Safety Deposit branch, telling him that the box of Jonathan Weston had been emptied and that they were sorry the police were not informed at the time because the young man on the desk was covering for the usual operative who had phoned in sick. "Wasn't the instruction spread to all bank staff?" Lloyd asked.

"Yes," said the bank man, "but the bank has a policy of rotating staff every four months and the meeting with the instruction hadn't happened at that time." The instruction being that Jon's request was 'stalled' on an excuse, and the police called, but it all went wrong.

Lloyd put down the phone and held his head in his hands and said to no one, "I don't believe it, I just don't believe it. We had him and let him go! DAMN" he shouted, and banged the leather-topped desk.

His door flew open and Sgt Bryant asked, "Are you all right, sir?"

"Yes, I'm fine," he said, "just pissed off, we missed Weston by a whisker. Oh he's clever, very clever, but the fucker's going to get caught one day and I hope it's soon," he added.

Rome

Was the devil working on Jon again, he had feelings of restlessness. Lounging around in Rome was boring him, he had a wicked thought, a cruise, not necessarily to murder a rich woman for her jewellery but his thoughts were going that way. He would have to give that one a lot of consideration. He had found an apartment not far from the hotel, it had all mod cons, was cheaper than living at the hotel and Gretta was able to move in with him and give up the bedsit-sized flat she was living in.

The shopping centre included a travel shop, deja vu kicked in as he looked at the window display, 'CRUISES' the large poster said and listed lots of examples, including pictures of the cruise ships. Mmm he thought, ' I wonder' he said to himself, smiling. Had the devil taken up residence again? One of the ships was enormous, 14 storeys or decks high, he counted, it went to the Greek Islands, Greece, Cyprus, the Holy Land and Egypt, for three weeks than back to Orbetello, the nearest deep port to Rome. The ship boasted large staterooms with balconies, 'luxury on the waves' it said. He walked in and said, " Inglese?" to the young man at the desk.

"Yes, signore," he replied.

"Good, I'd like to book the cruise advertised in the window. What's the price for a mid-ship, half-way up, stateroom?"

The young advisor referred to the brochure and his computer, "Okay, sir," he said, "6,000 euros including 150 euros on-board spending."

Jon laughed and said, "Can I put the 150 euros spend on the red, in the casino?"

"Yes, of course, and I hope you win!" said the youngster, also laughing.

"Okay, let's go for it, I need to get out of the city and get some fresh air in my lungs."

"Magnifico!" said the salesman, and started to fill out the booking form. He showed Jon the graphic of the ship and pointed to the exact stateroom.

"Perfect," Jon said. The 6,000 euros was passed over the desk, he received a copy of the booking which was also his receipt. The cruise would leave in two weeks time, good he thought, 3,000 passengers, at least half of them women.

He left it for another week before he told Gretta that he had to go on a business trip to Ireland. His family house in Dublin had been sold and he had to see to the sale of the contents and other assets to do with the property. "Why are you taking your dinner jacket?"

Thinking very quickly on his feet, "My family is having a big celebration because of the sale, at a posh hotel in Dublin, but as you aren't coming I will buy you something very very special," he promised, and kissed her cheek.

"That would be very nice," she said smiling, and kissed him passionately.

A simple soul, he thought. He left with his luggage on the morning of the sailing which was timed for 3pm, which gave him three hours to get to the ship and check in, and to park the car etc. His case and suit carrier was taken and his car was parked. Terrific he thought, that's what I call service. His stateroom aboard the 'Cesaro Roma' was luxurious to say the least, absolutely terrific!

London

Chief Inspector Lloyd lay in bed unable to sleep, how did that cheeky, audacious, murdering bastard get away with getting his hands on the 320 grand at the safety deposit bank? he said to himself. Then it hit him, "Disguise," he said out loud, waking his wife.

"What did you say?" she asked, "you've been mumbling in your sleep for hours, now please shut up and go to sleep!" He did.

"Bryant," he called loudly to his DS, "we're going over to Barclays Bank, have a plain car brought round."

"Yes, sir," the officer said.

They walked into the bank and up to the deposit desk, "I'm Chief Insp. Lloyd, Scotland Yard," he said, showing his warrant card, "I'd like to see your CCTV recording of Wednesday the 8th of July." It took about 15 minutes to find the recording, they were ushered in to a small rear office where the play-back equipment had been set up on a desk. "Right," he said to the clerk, "please could we see from opening time?" The clerk ran the tape, after about ten minutes the image of a tall blond bearded man walked in and up to the desk. "Was that the man with the deposit key 0771?"

"I don't know sir," said the clerk, "I was off sick on that day."

"I see," said Lloyd, "can you get the chap who was on duty, please?"

"Yes, sir, I think it was Andrew Backley," and disappeared.

He soon came back with the young clerk whose face was ashen and wide-eyed. Lloyd showed him the stilled image of Jon, "Is that the man who entered box 0771 last Wednesday?"

"Yes, sir," he said with a wobble in his voice.

"Did you not know of the instruction that we were to be informed when he turned up?"

"No, sir, I was a temp on the desk that day," he added.

"Okay," Lloyd said, "you can go now, both of you," he grunted. He sat studying the image, "Bryant, take this down, blond hair, blond moustache and beard, 6ft 1" or 2". Now all we've got to do is to get this new description circulated on every TV station in Europe. He's probably using an alias, but the image is the main thing," he declared.

They walked out of the bank past the two clerks who said, "Goodbye gentlemen."

Lloyd waved half-heartedly, and said sarcastically, "Should be serving burgers."

The ship was almost an hour late due to the tardy arrival of a group of American tourists, which was music to Jon's ears. He laid back on his king-size bed, and started to watch TV. The news came on and after about two minutes he saw himself on the screen, "Fucking hell!" he said loudly, "those poxy bank cameras." There he was, almost full faced, at the deposit desk. But in his favour was the fact that he could discard the facial hair. He went immediately into the bathroom to shave. there was nothing he could do about his hair, but just wear his fedora hat.

He went for a walk around the main deck of the enormous ship and decided to count the number of blond men who were about his height. The TV description had said 6ft+, slim, blond hair, moustache and beard. He checked his reflection in a window, nothing like the TV look-alike, even with his hat off. He had counted 38 men on the ship so far, that would answer to that image, probably from Scandinavia, they loved the Mediterranean. If he was challenged at a passport control he would merely say that he shaved off his beard because of the hot climate, job done! The Russians, Scotland Yard and even NYPD had the bearded face on record now. Would his one step ahead all the time one day come to a halt? Perhaps South America would get him away from the furore? He had all the money with him, mostly in the ship's safe, which was in larger notes that he had changed at the 'Bank Roma' before he left.

Rome

Sitting watching TV with a salad dinner, Cecila Moretzi recognised the face of the man who changed 200,000 euros into notes of 1,000 euros. She had thought it a little strange and had sought permission from the manager who came out of his office and asked for identification. Jon showed him his Irish passport, and said that he was in Italy to buy second-hand Ferrari's or Maseratti's. The manager's face lit up and praised the fact that he wanted the best that the Italian motor industry could offer, 'Yes,' he said to the girl teller, 'it's okay. Molte grazie,' he said, going back into his office.

"Hello (in Italian), is that the police?"

"Yes," said the deep male voice.

"I have to report the sighting of a wanted murderer who was pictured on TV news, I work in the 'Bank Roma' and this man came in to change some large amounts of money that totalled 200,000 euros."

"What was his name?" the policeman asked.

"I don't know but he showed his Irish passport to the manager."

"Okay," he said, "we'll come to the bank in the morning, first thing, thank you for the call," he said, and hung up.

The captain of the local Polizia showed Cecila the photo tele image of Jonathan Weston, "Is this the man?" he asked.

"Yes," she said.

"Was he using the name on the photo?" he asked.

"I don't know, the manager looked at the passport." They were joined by him but he couldn't remember the name. He apologised and could only confirm the face and that it was an Irish/European one.

As he walked out, he said to himself, "Should be serving pizzas!" He laughed.

St Petersburg

"He's been seen in Rome," he said to ten of his agents, "GO AND GET HIM OR DON'T FUCKING WELL COME BACK," he screamed. Vasili Kashnosky normally meant what he said. The men were on large bonuses but their lives were their main concern, and they went about the business with brute force to anybody that stood in their way.

Two private jets were waiting to take them to Rome and closer to Jonathan Weston, but where would they start? The underworld of Rome might be a good place. They started asking questions in St Peter's Square, the Romas were targetted. "Have you seen this man?" he asked one, who knew immediately who they were and his blood chilled a little.

"No, but you see that man sitting at the end table of the cafe, he might be able to help."

Once again the Russian asked, "Have you seen this man?" as he showed him the photograph.

"Yes," the Roma said, "I sold him an Irish passport three days ago," he replied. He too knew who they were, and shivered slightly.

"What name was the passport?" he demanded. The Roma took a piece of paper from his pocket and gave it to the Russian. "Keiron Robert Pearce, good, if you are right you will be rewarded," he said, and walked away.

The Roma wondered what would happen if he was wrong, perhaps the industrial cattle carcass grinder that he had heard they use, he shivered again, more violently.

The Cesaro Roma

The first port of call was Naples, to go to Pompeii. At this sight-seeing point Jon (Keiron) could see any likely candidates. The buses were lined up for the journey to the ancient site, among the passengers he spotted a woman about 40 years old. What attracted him was the diamond encrusted Rolex and a twin row diamond bracelet with a necklace to match. Nice, he thought, I wonder what else she had? He looked at her hands for rings, none, but that didn't mean she didn't have any. He kept reasonably close as they wandered around the ruins, what she was wearing was about 80 thousand quids worth, he guessed, still plenty of time to find out! With about 3,000 people on the ship, if all went well with any future plans, no one person would be missed for a long time. But first he would have to get to know her, his luck kicked in when she stumbled on some loose ground and almost fell. However, she did drop her camera which Jon retrieved from the grey dust and wiped with his red handkerchief, after steadying her to her feet. "Why, thank you," her American accent said with a smile. "Do you speak English?" she suddenly asked.

"Yes, I am from that part of the world," he answered, putting on a very slight Irish accent.

"Ireland, right?" she almost shouted, smiling.

"Yes, Dublin," he lied.

"I've never been to Ireland," she said, "I hear it's beautiful."

"Oh yes," he said, although he'd never been there either! They seemed to keep together for the whole sight-seeing trip, but Jon kept out of the sight of vision whenever she took photographs. Towards the end of the trip she put her arm in his, she definitely fancied him, he thought. Back on the bus they sat together, and once aboard the ship again they agreed to meet at 7 o'clock in the Palermo bar. It was an informal night, Jon (Keiron) wore white slacks, white shoes, no socks and a navy silk shirt. It would be the first time she would see his blond hair, and as a woman she would know that it was dyed. A fedora hat would look wrong.

"Hi Kieron," Liz from New York said. Jon stood and suggested that they take a corner table. Good old American straight talking kicked in when Liz asked, "Why do you dye your hair?"

He laughed, "I'm an actor."

"An actor!" she said loudly.

"Yes, I've been doing part of a James Bond movie at Cinicenta, in Rome, but I'm finished there now, until shooting resumes in, wait for it, New York! I play the part of a Swedish villain's henchman," he lied.

"Wow!" she exclaimed, "I've got me a James Bond villain."

"Shush!" he said, looking around and laughing, "can we keep it under wraps?"

"Sorry," she said, "Oh, by the way, I'll have a champagne cocktail please, shaken not stirred!" she burst into uncontrollable laughter. Jon ordered her drink and a scotch on the rocks for himself. She, apart from the necklace, bracelet and Rolex, was now wearing a ring on her opposing marriage finger, the right hand. It was an exquisite single stone surrounded by sapphires, big ones, in all about 9 carats adding up to at least 150 grand. Very nice, he thought, and started to wonder how he could get his hand on them, but first gain her confidence. Wine her and dine her, and if she wants, sleep with her.

They thought the 'Ionian' restaurant would be nice for dinner, Jon found it difficult to keep up the Irish brogue, but after three champagne cocktails she didn't notice any change in his speech. Dinner was typically Italian and very good, the service impeccable. Jon insisted on signing the bill for everything and then realised that the dinner was inclusive. She reached across the table and asked quietly, "Is my little James Bond having a good time?" as she took his hand and rubbed his fingers in a very suggestive way.

"Yes," he said, forgetting his Irish brogue, "he's having a very good time!" He had learned that she was a divorcee from Yonkers, New York State, but also had an apartment in Manhattan. Her poor ex-husband had borne the expensive brunt of the divorce through his philandering.

"Good," she said, "let's hope it gets even better!" she laughed and winked. He thought, was this woman a re-incarnation of Helen Smithson, returned to haunt him?

Three large casinos, quite a choice, four night clubs and bars, amazing he thought. "What deck are you on?" Jon asked.

"I'm one below the promenade deck," she replied, "nice and quiet."

Good, Jon thought, not too far to drop. The devil was rising within him and he couldn't help it, diamonds had a very evil effect on him. They sauntered through the atrium and through the shopping mall, still buzzing with shoppers, and walked into one of the night clubs. The 'Ionian Nights' was super luxury, lovely waitresses wearing very short skirts and skimpy tops, thighs and tits abundant he thought, and laughed inwardly. "Okay, handsome Irishman," she said, "I want you to help me boogaloo until I can booga no more," she laughed. She was amazingly attractive, a cross between Doris Day and Grace Kelly with the figure to match, almost as tall as Jon, in heels, gorgeous he thought, and was very happy for her to be on his arm. Heads turned as they took a table in the corner, as far away as possible from the gyrating bodies. Above the loud music, Jon ordered a champagne cocktail, "No, no," she cried, "a bottle of the best French champagne," she insisted with a wicked smile. Tonight she was wearing the necklace, the bracelet, the watch plus the ring, the very expensive beautiful sapphire ring, and another single diamond, about 4 carats. Her dollar tally had gone up to about $200,000 plus any cash she may have. He thought, the devil's ride was gaining momentum! There was quite a long time to go, but he had perfected a plan in his mind. He would wait until the last port of call before doing the evil deed and be off the ship and away before she was missed. He wasn't too bothered about being seen with her because he had now counted 110 tall blond men on board, and whenever he spotted CCTV he was either wearing his fedora or he covered his face with his hand as if he was coughing. He thought of his hat, but he had seen a lot of them on the ship.

"Okay honey," Liz said, "let's make some moves James Bond baby, my booga needs some looing!" she laughed after at least two flutes of Dom Perignon. She stood, took his hand and pulled him on to the dance floor. At one o'clock Liz fell on to the seat at their table, "That's it," she said, "I'm bushed. More champagne!" she said, and poured the last two glasses that were left in the bottle. A waitress came, bending over to clear the table, she smiled at Jon and displayed the most beautiful pair of bosoms. Jon smiled and passed her 10 euros, Liz grabbed the bill for the champagne and signed it, "My turn to pay," she said.

"Do you gamble?" Jon asked Liz.

"No, not really, but I seem to be lucky at roulette," she replied, "my ex showed me how to go red black and double your bet each time. It certainly worked in Monte Carlo, but that may have been just beginner's luck. We won $10,000, he kept it of course!" she replied, and laughed, "but I got it back with interest," she added and this time laughed uncontrollably. This was all music to Jon's ears, cash would also be very desirable, but his eye was on her very expensive jewellery. They went into the large casino on what was called the 'pleasure deck'. Two casinos to choose from but the big one seemed busier, with Americans and Russians placing large bets. Fuck me, he thought, just look at that lot, he saw the most amazing diamond collection on a huge woman sitting on the other side of the table. The diamond necklace with a huge emerald resting between her enormous cleavage, plus three or four diamond rings, a diamond bracelet and a square, diamond encrusted, Cartier watch. She must have been 18 stone, and 70 years old, but to Jon she was the most desirable woman in the room! The black mist started to descend as he ogled the gems, he would murder Liz and the fat lady, or just rob the obese one. Plenty of time to reach a decision, romancing the second female would be out of the question. She must have been wearing half a million quids worth, and the way they caught the light told him that they were the 'Real McCoy'. He smiled at her, she ignored him and just tidied and counted her huge pile of high-value chips, at least 20,000 euros he mentally calculated. Diamonds and cash, he started to salivate, the evil one was working inside him.

Liz's red and black system didn't work, they both lost. Leaving at about 2.30 am, Jon walked Liz to her suite on deck B. They stopped at her door, "Thank you for a fabulous evening, honey," she said, "call me at about 10 o'clock." She pecked his cheek and went into her room, she wasn't as gushing or as keen as his previous 'ladies' had been, but there was plenty of time, plenty of time indeed! She would succumb sooner or later, he said to himself.

Jon called Liz at 10 am, "Hi honey, is it ten already, I've not had a good night, strange vibes and dreams, must have been too much champagne!" She said, "see you in the Mall coffee shop in an hour." the phone went quiet.

They spent most of the afternoon on the sundeck, after a salad bar lunch. "Do you like sex in the afternoon?" Liz asked.

Jon almost choked as he said, "Sorry, what did you say?"

"I said, do you like sex in the afternoon?" she repeated, putting down her book.

"Er, yes," he said, "but it's been a long time," he said.

"It's been a long time for me, morning, noon or night!" she laughed. She stood up from her sunbed, picked up her bag, book and towel and said, "c'mon honey, it's party time," she said, and pulled him up by his hand. Stripping off her black bikini quickly, once inside the suite, she went into the shower and after about a minute he heard, "C'mon in baby, the water's lovely." They soaped each other and kissed passionately, she spent a long time rubbing suds into his groin which had the desired effect. His erection was almost immediate and she fondled it slowly while he gently held her breasts and slowly rubbed them with soap. Without drying, they fell on to the bed and began their supreme fornication. Unlike his previous conquests, her orgasm was only a very long sigh. They lay panting for about five minutes, "You know when I said do you like sex in the afternoon, I meant the cocktail!" she laughed, "but that was better! But now we will have an afternoon cocktail," and in her nakedness went over to her mini bar and took out a bottle of Moet and poured two glasses. Lifting her glass and chinking Jon's, "It's five o'clock somewhere!" she shouted, laughing. They finished the bottle and once again fell on to the bed and fell into a drowsy embrace and were soon asleep. At 9 o'clock they woke and decided they would order a room service dinner, they had time to dress and make themselves respectable before there was a knock at the door. Their food was wheeled in on a trolley, the steward set up the table and served dinner from silver service beautifully, and received 20 euros. He thanked Jon after he signed the bill. After a good dinner they sat on the balcony watching the stars and the full moon. Liz had poured two large balloons of brandy, and they enjoyed the silence, just the quiet lapping of the waves against the ship broke the ambience. They didn't speak, just gently sipped the cognac. Jon stayed the night.

The sun shone with piercing fingers on to their bed, both were naked, the night had been very warm and they needed no bed clothes. Nine o'clock was ablaze on the digital alarm clock, which happily had not been set! Jon stirred, and doing so awakened Liz who smiled and said, "I really am a Bond girl now!" They laughed, and she jumped out of bed and went into the bathroom. Once again they ordered room service for breakfast and sat on the balcony, watching as an island floated past, or so it seemed to! not far away.

"I must go to my stateroom to shave and change," he said. They kissed lightly and he said he would call her in 40 minutes or so. He hadn't stopped planning his murderous moves, would it be Liz first or the big woman? but it would have to be the last day of the cruise. He had moved on Liz, but how would he get to the fat lady, perhaps through gambling, yes that's it he thought, a bit of joviality, every woman, no matter who, loves the attention of a young man, he would visit the main casino. Calling Liz, they arranged another days tanning, after all he wanted to go home looking good, the darker he got the better, but he would have to top up the blond hair colour. He would do this in the late afternoon instead of sex. It took at least two hours to get the Scandinavian look again, he would use this as an excuse to Liz so as to go back to his stateroom.

Dinner was informal, they opted for seafood salads in the speciality bar in the Mall. "I was watching satellite TV news earlier," she said, "and they showed a guy that slightly reminded me of you, with a beard. He's wanted for something, but then the screen went hazy, and it was in Italian anyway, but his name was Jon Weston from London, a mad English serial killer, you're not a serial murderer, are you Keiron?"

He laughed, and said, "No, I haven't hurt a fly since I was 5 years old," he replied.

"Well, you certainly didn't hurt me last night!" she said, smiling a wicked smile, and winking.

Whoops he thought, I'm a TV personality again, but Liz was the only one who had got close to him, and there were over a hundred men that looked like him, blond, tall etc., on board, and the TV face was bearded. "I thought I might try my luck at the casino, to see if I can get my money back," he told Liz.

"Okay, honey, I'm gonna have an early night with a book," she said.

After a drink in the 'Da Vinci' bar, Jon wandered through to the larger casino, no large lady, he then walked up a deck to the upper atrium casino, there she is, perhaps she likes to try her luck at all the tables. Luckily there was an empty chair to her left, he sat down and smiled, she nodded and smiled back, at the same time tidying her medium sized pile of chips. This was obviously a nervous habit when playing roulette. Jon placed a thousand euros on the table to be changed into chips, which were pushed over to him. The woman glanced at this handsome young man and smiled again. "Good evening," he said.

"Good evening," she replied.

"How's your luck?" he asked.

"Oh, so so, not as good as last night," she added.

He thought he heard a Scottish accent, "My name is Keiron Pearce, from Dublin," he said, putting on more of an Irish accent and extending his hand.

"Hello," she said, "I'm Molly McKern from the Isle of Hoy in Scotland, but I now live on the Cote d'Azure, in France. I had 45 years of snow, gales and zero temperatures, so when they found 18 billion cubic feet of natural gas beneath my farm, I vowed to go and live somewhere warm," she smiled with a slight giggle.

"Good choice!" Jon agreed. She picked up her winning chips and added them to her pile, Jon had not yet placed a bet and decided to copy his neighbour's choices and won a quick 500 euros. Molly had doubled that amount, they turned towards each other and 'high fived', Jon now felt that he had well and truly broken the ice. He, all through their conversing, had been admiring her jewellery, but she hadn't noticed as she had the knack of talking, keeping her eyes on the roulette wheel and placing her bets all at the same time! Jon followed her bets once again and they lost, but only a small amount in his case, Molly however had broken almost even apart from 50 euros on red, it was then that he decided to go for Liz's system. He put 200 euros on red, "Just for fun," he said to Molly, who didn't bet. "That's lucky, it won." He continued to win with the formula, red, black, double up. It wasn't fool-proof but it seemed to get near the house odds. At 1.30am Molly was very tired, she said and was going to 'her wee bed.' "Yes, me too," he said, "maybe I'll see you tomorrow, goodnight," he said.

"Goodnight," she replied, and walked the slow wobbling walk that fat people do.

How would he get his hands on those beautiful gems? His inner demon would soon help him with his quest. He checked the casinos, but didn't see Molly for two nights, but on the third day, while cruising the Adriatic towards Corfu, he spotted her on the sundeck. He walked over to her table. "Hello my handsome friend, how are you?" she asked.

"I'm fine," he said, "like a leprachaun at dawn! Where have you been, dear lady?" he asked.

"Oh, I wasn't quite myself and had to rest, I had a wee angina attack. The doctors say I need a bypass, but I'm frightened to go under the knife, they open your chest you know," she shook her head and grimaced at the thought.

"Don't worry," Jon said, "I'll look after you, when possible," he added.

She giggled a girlish laugh, and said, "I'll hold you to that!" The devil had spoken! "Will you be having a wee flutter tonight?" Molly asked.

"No," he said, "I'm having dinner with a friend."

"Oh well, not to worry, but you'll be sadly missed," and held his hand warmly.

This is definitely in the bag, or rather, her jewellery is, he thought. The devil was coming to the forefront more often, the black mist descended again. But how, he thought, tipping 18 stone of dead weight over a balcony would be almost impossible, he would have to give that one a lot of consideration. "Hi Liz, it's J.. er Keiron," he said, that was nearly a stupid slip of the tongue.

"Keiron, what's happening my man?" she said in her Manhattan vernacular, "by the way, who's J?" she asked.

"Oh, I was about to say to the steward, just a second, he's delivering my lunch," he lied, this boy is a quick thinker!

"How about we meet up this afternoon and enjoy some ray-catching?" she suggested.

"Yes, that'll be terrific, I'll meet you at reception, shall we say 2.30pm?"

"Yep, that's great, see you then," she replied.

He watched TV news to see if his former face was being shown, after almost twenty minutes ... nothing. He hoped he had become old news. Did Liz want sunbathing or sex in the afternoon, he wondered. He hoped it was sunbathing, it was nearing 40 degrees centigrade, too hot for passion even with air conditioning and tepid showers. Perhaps later, when the sun went down, that way he could satisfy both Liz, and meet Molly in the casino later. Being a formal night Liz and Jon donned their finest dresswear. He went to Liz's suite to escort her to dinner, the door opened to reveal one of the loveliest feminine visions he had seen. "My, oh my, just look at my James Bond, you look amazing. Is that jacket silk?" she asked.

"Er, yes," he said.

"It is gorgeous," she added.

"I don't even come anywhere to the way you look!" he complimented.

"Is that the blarney coming out?"

"No, no," he said, " you are absolutely stunning."

"Okay, let's close the mutual admiration society and go and eat, I'm starving," she said, putting her arm through his. He noted that she was wearing the entire collection, fabulous he thought, absolutely fabulous! Dinner was a fairly sedate one, although the red wine with the fillet steaks did flow freely, but this was contrived by Jon. He sipped his slowly, while topping up Liz very generously when she wasn't looking and pretending to top himself up at the same time.

"I'd better order another bottle," he said, "it's only 9 o'clock, the night is very young."

"Yes," Liz said, "this French merlot is so good with steak, or is the steak so good with the merlot?" They laughed. A second bottle was emptied with Liz having downed the lion share. She stood to go and 'powder her nose', but was unsteady on her feet.

"I'll see you to the door," he said, "and wait outside, of course."

"Yes, honey," she said, "I think you'd better do that!" It was agreed that she should go to her suite to lay down, "I'm sorry 'James', for spoiling your evening," she said.

"No, no, don't worry, I just want you to be comfortable, and feel better." He helped her on to the bed and she went into an alcoholic sleep almost there and then! Right, he thought, I'll go back to the restaurant, act normal, finish dinner, sign the bill and go and find Molly. The large casino was packed but Molly wasn't there. He was finally lucky when he saw her sitting in the lesser used, smallest one. "Hello Molly, me darlin', how are you feeling tonight?"

"Hello Keiron," she said, "I'm not too bad, a little breathless so I brought my angina pump," she said, showing him the small cartridge, "this little apparatus could be a life saver to me," she added. Jon made a mental note of that.

They sat together for about two hours, not winning but only losing a very small amount, Jon noticed that Molly had trouble breathing and kept rubbing the top of her chest. She didn't wear much make-up so her grey colour was easily visible. "Molly," he said, "I think you'd better call it a night, me darlin', you don't look well, I'll see you to your suite," he said.

"Oh, thank you," she said, "you are a good man." He walked her slowly to the room, opened the door, and led her to the bed carefully but as he did she dropped to her knees gasping and holding her chest. She fell backwards on to the floor and went into unconsciousness. He looked through her bag and found the heart pump, not knowing what to do with it, he just left it on the dressing table. He felt for a pulse through her fat wrist, nothing. He then quickly removed all of her diamonds, and pressed the emergency button on the bedside phone.

The First Officer and doctor were soon there, Jon put on an act of panic as they ran in to the room, "How long has she been like this?" the ship's doctor asked.

"About five or six minutes," Jon replied. The doctor started pumping her chest, but to no avail, Molly was dead. Jon feigned sorrow, sitting on a chair with his head in his hands, "She was such a nice lady, only a little while ago we became gambling buddies," he said with his Irish accent, "but I didn't really know her."

"I'm sorry," they said, "there's nothing we can do now. I'll need to speak to you later, er Mr?"

"Er, Pearce, Keiron Pearce, stateroom 314C," he answered, looking sadly down at the body, but inwardly laughing. The black mist was present again, but this time he had committed no crime, well, apart from robbing a corpse, anyway she didn't need the diampnds any more.

"We'll be back with a couple of porters and a stretcher, er, are you all right to stay with her, sir?" the First Officer said.

"Er, yes, I'm fine," he said, "as long as it's not too long," he added. When they had gone he looked through her handbag, "Just what I was looking for," he said, as he found a folded piece of paper with her room safe four digit number on it. Inside the safe he found £30,000 in euros and sterling, "Bingo!" he said, and stuffed the cash into his pocket, but he did leave £200 and credit cards in the box so it did not look like burglary. Slamming the safe door, he threw the piece of paper over the balcony. To look upset, he went just outside the door and waited for the stretcher bearers.

Her body was taken away and the door sealed by the First Officer, "Thank you Mr Pearce, I'll contact you some time tomorrow morning." He (Jon) had wiped the safe door free of prints. He walked back to his stateroom, patting his pockets and saying to himself 'mission accomplished'. Spreading the haul on his bed, he reckoned that he had won about £200,000 tonight, in cash and jewellery. Nice, he thought, and no one can possibly think badly of me. I didn't kill Molly, it was a heart attack.

St Petersburg

Vasili paced up and down his office, his reputation as all powerful would be tainted if Jon Weston wasn't caught and dealt with. There had been no news, sightings or word from his henchmen, he was furious. Perhaps he should go to Rome and direct operations himself, yes he thought, I'll go. "Stephan, I'm going to Rome as soon as possible, make all the travel arrangements," he barked into the phone. An executive jet waited for him on the edge of the airport. Stephan was a trusted, good servant, he used to be an enforcer back in the '90's but arthritis had become his enforcer. He packed the wardrobe on the Lockheed with light-weight suits, mohair and silk made in Paris and linen, voile and silk shirts, all freshly laundered and cleaned. "Thank you Stephan," Vasili said. Apart from family, he was the only one to hear please and thank you or the word 'tavarich'. He would gladly die for Vasili who had rescued him and his family from a Siberian Gulag in the late 70's. He gave Stephan a thousand ruble note and said, "Take your lovely wife to dinner."

"Thank you, Vasili," Stephan said.

Rome

The private jet landed, Vasili walked over to the black-windowed Mercedes limousine. The car went directly to the penthouse apartment he kept above an exclusive building on the edge of St Peter's Square. He went out on to the balcony and looked down at the crowds of tourists and sightseers, and said, "Are you down there Jon Weston? I will catch you and you will suffer the most painful death you can possibly imagine, believe me!"

The Cesaro Roma

"Yes, yes, yes!" Liz almost shouted as she reached yet another orgasm. She and Jon were spending the afternoon in bed at the request of Liz. After a light lunch and finding the sun too hot for sunbathing, it had sent most of the sun worshippers to find shade. But it was still about 100F and most of the sunbeds were vacant. All the bars were busy dispensing cold drinks. Liz and Jon showered and opted for some shopping at the mall. They sauntered in and out of the shops and said that they would meet at the end of the mall by the casino, if they missed each other. About an hour went by and they met as arranged, both carrying packages, "Look what I bought for you," Liz said to Jon, and produced a New York City baseball cap.

"I'm sorry Liz," he said, "but I couldn't wear that, it's what yobs wear in the UK."

"Yobs?" she said, "What's a yob?"

"A yob, my darling, is a young backward boy who hangs around street corners and mugs old people," he answered.

"Oh, I'm sorry," she said, "I'll take it back and change it."

He sat on a long bench while she was gone, he counted 29 tall blond men in just fifteen minutes, good he thought, I am not alone! Liz returned and sat next to him, she opened a small jewel box to show him a New York City tie slide, yuk he thought, but lied when he said, "That's nice," and kissed her cheek, "now it's my turn," he said, and opened a package to reveal a silk pashmina in purple and pink.

Yuk, she thought, and lied when she said," Oh, that's gorgeous." I'll give it to somebody for Christmas she said to herself.

They were crossing the Ionian Sea to the next port of call, Cephalonia, a beautiful Greek Island sitting in the bluest clearest water in that part of the world. Famous for it's exotic fish and sea-life, trips in glass bottom boats were a favourite of tourists.

Cephalonia

A flotilla of tenders ferried passengers to and from the ship which had to anchor in deeper water about a kilometre from the quayside. Jon and Liz were amongst quite a few who opted to stay on board. The ship was there for two days, they would go ashore tomorrow and probably take a trip on a glass bottom boat to see through the clear water, if the fish didn't get in the way! he joked to Liz. She looked blank and bemused, "Never mind!" he said, and laughed.

"Was that an Irish joke?" she asked, "I thought that it was the fish we wanted to see!" He laughed again. Liz softly punched his arm. They lay sunbathing on the , almost empty, forward sundeck. But at noon the sun had peaked and it was very hot, about 110F, even with factor 40 they felt as if they were burning. They almost ran into the air-conditioned, covered upper deck and sat panting on a long sofa. "I'm glad I didn't go topless," she laughed.

"I'm not!" Jon said, "but maybe I'll have a peek at them later!" he laughed.

"Okay," said Liz, "but I'm too hot for sex at the moment!"

Moscow

Katti and her brothers were still mourning the death of their father, they had no proof that Jon had killed him, but they were sure he had when Katti told them that he thought Viktor was her bodyguard, and that her diamonds had disappeared at the same time. With political contacts in the government they were able to alert agents attached to the Russian embassies in all the European countries. His photograph was forwarded to them but not as a blond Kieron Pearce, only the original dark Jonathan Weston, which was useless.

New Rochelle - New York

Mary-Lou and Mel had settled very well into married life, Mel's job was a lot easier in New Rochelle, burglaries were the main crimes on his desk. There had only been one murder since his arrival at the Sherrif's office and that had been quickly solved and the guilty one sent away for life. The area was full of wealthy retired people, large houses with well cared for front lawns with miulti-coloured flowers and shrubs. Expensive cars, mostly from abroad, sat in the drive ways, the local car-valeter had a very lucrative round calling once a week to wash, vacuum and polish the Mercedes, BMW, Lexus and Bentleys, "Morning Mr Lewison," he said when the door opened to reveal a short man with a grey toupee.

"Hiya Ben," he said as he handed him the key to his Lexus. Having lost most of his family in the holocaust, he refused to buy German products, the Lexus being Japanese, "oh, you'd better clean the wife's Volvo as well," he added.

"Thanks Mr Lewison, will do. Oh, by the way, that nice lady from the big house up at the corner, is off to Europe for about two months, she's asked me to keep an eye on the house while she's gone even though it has a police contact top-of-the-market alarm. She even gave me the code so that I could go in and feed the fish and water her indoor plants," he said.

Mr Lewison looked around, and put his finger to his lips, "I didn't hear you tell me that," he said. "Schmuck," he said quietly to himself, "he's going to be cleaning cars for a long time."

Yonkers

"How about September for our holiday, honeymoon?" Mary-Lou said to Mel.

"Yeah," he said, "I'll arrange it with the office, just let me know when, and book it. Where do you want to go?"

"I thought Europe, and possibly cruise around the Mediterranean to one or two romantic places, Rome, Naples, Capri," she said.

"Shall we go back to London?"Mel said.

"Yes, of course honey, that would be great, I only ever went on that business trip, and I was alone!"

"Let's do it!" Mel said loudly, "let's do it!" and grabbed his bride for a passionate kiss.

The Cesar Roma

The time was getting close for Liz, little did she know she only had two days to live. "Hi honey, are we meeting up tonight?" she asked Jon.

"Yes, of course, I'll knock at your door at 7, okay?"

"Fine," she said. The phone went dead. It was the last formal night of the cruise, Jon tapped on the door at exactly 7 o'clock, the door opened to reveal a vision of beauty and sexiness that made his knees go slightly weak, "Hi Mr Bond," she said, framing herself in the doorway with one hand on her hip and her left thigh protruding through the high split in her gorgeous navy and silver dress with shoes and handbag to match. She looked fabulous, but to top it all, she was wearing the entire collection, rings, bracelet, watch and the fabulous necklace. He thought he might bring 'the job' forward a day, while all the jewellery was readily available and not locked in her suite safe.

First it was drinks in the 'Venus Bar', which had the huge statue of the Roman goddess in the centre. They found a corner booth and sat side by side, her dress fell open to reveal her lovely legs, almost to the hip. He thought, if it was tonight there would be no sex, no DNA and no fingerprints, as soon as they were inside the suite, he would do the deed. He would make sure she had plenty to drink. They sat chatting for about an hour, Liz was plied with champagne cocktails, while Jon sipped only one and made the second last a long time, until they went into the 'Diana' restaurant for dinner. They ordered a la carte, lobster, shelled and langoustine salad, with champagne sauce, at extra cost, "What the hell, I can afford it," he smiled to himself.

"What's funny?" Liz asked.

"Here I am eating the best food, sipping the best wine, on a beautiful ship, with the loveliest woman aboard, I'm happy, that makes me smile," he romanced.

She reached across the table, showing her cleavage, and took hold of his hand doing suggestive things to his fingers, "Are we going to fuck tonight?" she almost implored.

He laughed, "Yes, I think there's every chance, if I'm in the mood!"

She slapped the back of his hand, "I thought James Bond was always in the mood!" She laughed, "You'd better be, 'cause I'm feeling hot tonight, or as you say this side of the pond, randy!"

After taking an hour to lose $200, they walked back to Liz's suite slowly, he needed to psych himself up for what he was about to do. She put her key card into the slot and opened the door, he followed her in and shut the door with his elbow and a slight slam. She turned towards him just in time to receive his hands around her throat, his thumbs dug deep into her windpipe which immediately crushed. She tried to say something that sounded like 'Jon', her eyes bulged and her body went limp, he let it fall to the floor before testing her pulses through a tissue. She was undoubtedly dead, he bent down and closed her beautiful, staring, sightless eyes with a tissue. He now had to wait until 3am at the earliest to commit her body to the sea. He opened the sliding door to her balcony and heard voices, someone was having a nightcap, he daren't go out in case he was seen. He started to remove her jewels carefully, having smeared soap on his finger tips just in case he touched something he forgot to wipe later. Three o'clock was a long time coming, when it did he went to the balcony doors to listen, 'fuck' he said to himself as he heard a man laugh to the left. He would have to wait longer, at 4 o'clock he went to the balcony again but this time could hear nothing. He lifted her, fireman style, up on to his shoulder and carried the body to the balcony and tipped it over the rail. He quickly returned to the suite and stood gasping, the black mist had lifted. He sat on the bed and started sobbing, after ten minutes he went over to the mini bar and poured himself a very large cognac, it went down in one gulp. He wiped the bottle and washed the glass, being careful to handle both with a tissue as well, which he put in his pocket. He opened the door, again with the help of a tissue, wiping the 'do not disturb' sign, he placed it on the handle, closed the door and walked quickly down the hallway. Back in his stateroom he poured another very large brandy which was swiftly followed by another. The effect worked and he soon fell on to his bed and into a deep sleep. Jon was awakened by a room operative to service the stateroom, he looked at the brandy bottle, apologised and said that he would come back later. Jon looked at his watch, it was noon, it had been over 8 hours since Liz's body had gone overboard. He emptied his pockets and spread the diamonds on the bed, beautiful he thought, there's 200 grand there, he said to himself, not a bad night's work!

Yonkers - New York

Packing for Mel and Mary-Lou Novak was not easy, a month 'doing' Europe needed a lot of outfits for Mrs Novak, not so many for Mel. Their flight from JFK was at 6pm to London, Heathrow. Mel knew that they were well overweight on luggage allowance for American Airlines, but "that's life!" Mel said. They would be spending three days in London, Mel had called the Reubens Hotel at Buckingham Palace and booked the same room above the stars and stripes. Their flight was on schedule at both ends, they caught the shuttle bus to Victoria coach station, as Mel had, and then hailed a cab, the luggage being the main reason. As it was only a short trip, Mel gave the cabbie an extra $10. "Hello again, little room," Mel said as they walked into their home for the next three days.

"Is the Queen at home in there?" Mary-Lou asked, pointing at Buckingham Palace.

"Probably," Mel answered, "we'll find out in the morning."

"How?" she asked.

"If the main gates at the front are open, with police guards then she is not in residence, if the gates are closed and the British flag is at full mast, then she is at home," he said.

"We'll go there in the morning and take lots of pictures!" she enthused.

"Sure honey," Mel said, drawing her close and kissing her lightly, "but after a good full English breakfast, we may be doing quite a bit of walking," he added.

"Good, you need to lose a few pounds!" she said.

"I know," he replied," it's the good cooking you give me, happiness and contentment!" he agreed. They had a light, 2 course only, dinner in the hotel restaurant, then they sat in the bar with coffee and cognac before going to bed. Their London love-making was quite audible, the Queen could possibly have heard Mary-Lou's orgasm!

After their full English breakfast Mary-Lou said, "We really need to walk that off!"

"We sure do," Mel answered as they turned right out of the hotel to walk to the front of the Palace to see it in all it's glory.

"Look at that," Mary-Lou said, as they turned the corner off of the main thoroughfare, "it's beautiful." She was awed by the Palace guards in their 'bushy' hats!

"No, honey, it's called a busby," Mel corrected.

"Whatever!" she said, "they're cute." Mary-Lou snapped away with her camera for about an hour and then they decided to walk across Green Park to Piccadilly and to see Berkeley Square, Mel was planning the route with his map of the west end of London. "This is so beautiful," Mary-Lou said, as she stood in the middle of Berkeley Square with the trees in multi shades of green. Mel took many photographs including one of a Rolls Royce convertible, in the showroom. "Why did you snap that car?" Mary-Lou asked.

"Oh, it's just beautiful, and we never see them in our neck of the woods," he replied, "I may have it enlarged and framed when we get back home! Who knows I might even buy one one day, it's only $250,000!" he laughed.

After three fabulous days in London taking in all the sights, it was packing time again. Their next rendez-vous was Paris, but this time by Eurostar, under the English Channel. They took a cab to Waterloo train terminus, direct to Paris, no airport, mich easier. Plus they would see some French countryside albeit at 125mph! "Fabulous!" Mary-Lou said.

Paris

A taxi took them to a family-owned hotel on Montparnasse, a lovely part of Paris. The Aviatic Hotel was small but very comfortable and the service excellent. It wasn't until they checked into the hotel that Mel realised that Mary-Lou spoke perfect French. She had let Mel show the taxi driver the brochure with the hotel's address. "Where did you learn to speak French like that?"

"My mother was from Quebec, my original christian name was Marie-Louise and my first language was French, until we came to America when I was 4 years old."

Mel sat down on the bed looking puzzled, he wished he hadn't asked, and just said, "Oh, I see."

"Tomorrow," Mary-Lou said, "it's the Eiffel Tower, the Champs Elysee, the Elysee Palace and Notre Dame."

"Whoa," Mel said, "that's about three days rolled in to one, I'll need an extra pair of feet!"

"And the next day, a cruise down the Seine in one of those glass topped boats," she said.

"And the day after that, you bury me!" Mel said.

"Don't talk like that," she said, "at least give me a few months of married life!" They laughed.

"Oh, you've got me for a lot longer than that," he said, pulling her down on to the bed.

"Has Paris had some sort of an effect on you?" she asked.

"No, I feel like this anywhere when I'm with you," Mel said. IT happened.

VENICE

Mary-Lou had booked the Orient Express from Paris to Venice, what a fabulous train journey, gourmet food, wonderful silver service and beautiful scenery. Through the Alps to Italy then across to Venice, neither of them had been there before. They arrived at midday, on what was one of the hottest days of the year, 105f. Their taxi took them to the Adelphi Grand Hotel, "It's beautiful," Mary-Lou said.

"Wow," Mel said, as he gazed at the 150 year old facade. As their cab stopped at the front, a porter stepped forward, pushing a luggage trolley, to take their bags into reception.

They were already booked 'on-line' by Mary-Lou before they left home, in fact she had booked everything 'on-line'. "I don't know how you do it," Mel said when she showed him all the tickets and paper-work for the entire trip.

"Easy," she replied, "I'll show you how, one day!"

"Buongiorno," the receptionist said, "Signore and Signora Novak, yes?"

"How did he know that?" Mel asked.

"We're the only yanks arriving with Orient Express labels on their luggage," she answered, "are you really a detective?" She laughed.

"I thought I was," he said, "until now!"

Rome (Cesaro Roma)

Just a few hours and the cruise would come to an end, Jon had packed and was ready to go ashore, and as soon as possible. He would be the first at the gangway after settling his bill. "That's £1,800," the cashier said, "or $2,380," she added.

"Fine," he said, "don't need a receipt," and gave her $2,500, "keep the change," he said over his shoulder as he grabbed his bags and put them on a porter's trolley. At the top of the gangway his blood went cold when he saw three leather-jacketed big men, standing by a black Mercedes. He also saw a taxi a few yards in front of their car. He walked slowly down the gangway wishing he had mingled with a group, but it was too late, he ran to the cab, dived in and told the driver, "Avanti! avanti!." The driver was good, and was away from the quayside before the Russians had realised, they jumped into their Merc and were soon chasing the taxi, but Jon had chosen the right cabbie for the job! Up side streets, down side streets, even through alley ways just wide enough for the Fiat cab, soon he was at his apartment, he gave the cab driver $100, who wanted to kiss him!

Gretta wasn't at home, good he thought, and then saw a note pinned to the TV screen. It read 'Hello Jonathan Weston', that's all. He grabbed one case and went down to the street, it took a while to get a taxi, but he was soon on his way back to the port. Walking around the quayside he was able, after about half an hour, to find a fishing boat. "Could you take me to Capri?" he asked.

"Are you crazy?" the young fisherman said.

"No, but I will pay you well," Jon said.

"How much?" the boy asked.

" $1,000."

"Let me see it," Jon was asked.

"When we get half way there," he said.

The lad looked at Jon's clothes, his watch and his leather case, and said," Okay."

150 miles straight down the Tyrrhenian Sea, staying fairly close to the Italian coast, it would take between 2 and 3 days, depending on tides and weather. How did Gretta know his

true identity, he wondered. But she was obviously scared and moved out with all her belongings, but at least there were no police waiting for him. He also wondered if she took the car, shame he thought, it was a nice one, not to worry it's only a lump of metal! One item of jewellery in his pocket will pay for another one.

They lived on freshly caught fish during their journey and drank a strong red wine from a huge bulbous container, but not too much! They both needed their wits about them. Capri came into view at the end of the third day, Jon had given Guido $500 with the promise of the rest when they landed. Under cover of nightfall the boat heaved to at the very end of the long quay leading to the outskirts of the main town. It was quite a long walk, about a kilometre, and his case was getting heavier, he was dirty and reeked of fish, but he was alive and had all his money and jewellery. Guido became a friend and was pleased to have earned more in six days than in a normal month. It was 6pm and the sun was going down rapidly and he needed to find a hotel. Up a back street hill he suddenly found himself on the main drag, and opposite was a nice looking 4* hotel. He crossed the narrow, but dual, carriageway road at a crossing that drivers ignored! Walking up to the reception desk, a couple passed and held their noses when they had gone by. "I'd like a double room for a week, please," he said as he put his passport and a wad of cash on the surface.

"Si, signore," the young girl said, "but our only double is being cleaned at the moment, it will be about 30 minutes," she said, trying to avert her nose.

"That's fine, I'll do the business then have a drink, oh and by the way, when you next see me I will look and smell a lot better!" he said, smiling.

"Si, signore," she said, trying to smile. He ordered a large brandy to be served in the foyer, he didn't want to offend any bar users with his fishy odour!

8pm saw a smart shiny and sweet smelling Jon walk into the ground floor bar 'Americano', in fact he turned one or two female heads as he took a seat at the end of the bar. Yes, he thought, I can chill out here quite nicely for at least a week, I can afford it, might even have a bit of female fun, who knows! The restaurant was nice but the food not quite what he was used to, never mind, he felt relaxed and safe here, he was hundreds of miles from his pursuers and therefore his enemies, who would see him destroyed in the most horrendous ways.

Rome

The honeymooners had arrived from Venice having done the whole of the tourist journies including the 'Bridge of Sighs' and the Grand Canal tour in a gondola, which they thought was enormously expensive, it was obviously a price for American tourists, but "You only do it once," Mel said.

"If he starts singing 'O sole mio' I'll push him overboard!" Mary-Lou said. They laughed.

The journey across Italy by train had been comfortable and the scenery amazing, through the mountains. The train went between two of the 'Seven Hills' and passed close to the Colliseum, "Wow, that is something," Mary-Lou said, "how old is it?" she asked Mel.

"Oh, about 3,000 years old," Mel answered.

"Really?" she said, "why is it in ruins?" she asked again.

"Mainly earthquakes over the centuries," he replied with a smug look on his face.

"Well, they've had enough time to repair it!" she laughed.

The search for Liz Fenner had reached fever pitch, but after 4 days it was concluded that she had gone overboard. Her belongings were taken to the police station.

They were booked in at the 'Fantasia' 5* hotel, just off St Marks Square. It seemed out of place in the area, all stainless steel and tinted glass, but it had everything for the tourist, and some. Their suite was sumptuous, gold bathroom fittings and a huge balcony that cornered on St Peters Square, fabulous, they thought. Mel stood on the balcony and watched two men do the 'map' routine on an unsuspecting tourist. He called down to the tourist, "Look out!" As he spun round the thief dropped his wallet and ran off. The Roma trio disappeared very quickly, they'd be somewhere else in a few minutes. The tourist looked up and shouted, "Danke!" German, Mel thought, and wished he hadn't bothered.

Sitting in the space-age bar, Mel casually picked up a newspaper, he read the headlines, with a picture of an attractive woman. He could only make out 'American Tourist', he showed it to Mary-Lou, "Hell," she said, "that's Elizabeth Fenner, I was on her divorce case a few years ago," she said, and jumped up to go over to the bar, "What do these headlines say?" she asked.

The barman looked and said, "AMERICAN TOURIST missing from cruise liner, believed to have drowned overboard."

When Mel heard this, his blood ran cold and hot at the same time, the murdering bastard's here in Rome, or was, but there was nothing he could do, no jursdiction, and anyway he was on a very expensive holiday and didn't have a hope in hell of actually catching Jon Weston. "Honey?" Mary-Lou said, "what's wrong?"

"Oh, I just hate hearing about US citizens dying like that, it sounds dirty."

"She was a lovely woman," Mary-Lou said, "full of life and very wealthy after her divorce, about 12 million dollars, plus that big house on the top of Summer Hill, it's beautiful," she enthused. Mel's hands were tied, but he thought that he would visit the local police and tell them what he knew about Jonathan Weston. They probably didn't even know that he was in Italy, or that he was a prime suspect.

"Oh, honey," Mary-Lou said, "we're on honeymoon, please don't be there too long."

"I won't hon, you can go shopping, but be careful of young dark girls, and men in leather jackets and jeans, with maps!"

Mel took a taxi to police headquarters, and with him a copy of the newspaper plus his identification and badge. He waited in a very ornate and large outer office for about 10 minutes, then he was ushered into the police Commissario's office, " Buongiorno," he said.

"Lieutenant Novak."

"Nice to meet you," he said. Mel showed his ID and badge. "Why are the New York state police interested in this case?" the chief asked.

"I used to be with the New York State police department, and about 15 months ago I was assigned to a case where an American woman disappeared from a ship bound for New York. About 4 months later her body, minus certain parts, was washed up on a beach near New York City. Her name was Helen Smithson, from Oklahoma, but we got very lucky, we found DNA samples from semen in her vagina, it belonged to Jonathan Weston, from London, England."

"That doesn't prove that he killed her," he said.

"No," Mel agreed, then told him adbout her jewellery being sold in New York a day after the ship had docked. "He was with a Lorna Harper, who was sent to trial for taking her part in the crimes," Mel told the chief.

"I see, so you want us to make all the efforts to find this man in Italy."

"Yes," said Mel, "there's another woman gone missing from an Italian cruise boat only yesterday. He is definitely in your country. It has been highlighted on your TV news with his picture, and description."

"Lieutenant Novak," the chief said, " our tourist industry is very important to us so we will search high and wide for this evil man. We will extend the TV coverage and instruct areas where he has been seen to dig deeper and turn over even the smallest stone."

"Thank you, sir, I will keep in touch although I am here on holiday with my wife," Mel said.

"You go and enjoy our beautiful country," the chief said, "and thank you for coming to see me," he added.

Mel got back to the hotel and called their room, there was no answer. As he put the phone down Mary-Lou struggled through the main door helped by the doorman. "Is there anything left in Rome? Do we have any money left?" he asked.

"Yes and no!" she laughed, "how did you get on with the poice chief?" she asked.

"Fine, he's a nice guy, and he's going to help as much as possible with the Liz Fenner case."

"Good," she said, "now, can we get on with our honeymoon please, there's nothing you can do to help the poor lady now."

"You're right," he said, "okay, let's get this lot up to the room." He walked over to the doorman and gave him $10, "Grazie signore!" the boy said.

Up in the room there were shirts, ties, socks, shoes, dresses, trousers etc., spread all over the room, "Have you forgotten luggage flight charges?" Mel asked.

"No," Mary-Lou said, "there are a few things we are going to leave behind, like those trousers," she said, pointing to his chinos.

"Hey, I like these pants with extra pockets!" he said.

She opened a package and produced another pair in cream, instead of the grey/brown colour of his present pair, "With extra pockets! Tah dah!" she laughed.

"Gee thanks honey," Mel said.

"You are 34" x 32" aren't you?" she asked.

"Er, yes, I think so!" he replied.

Capri

Jon was enjoying life on the 'Island of Romance', he had found himself a pretty young Italian waitress he had picked up at a coffee shop that he frequented every day at 10.30am. Today was no different, he chatted to Carla when she wasn't serving customers. They were mainly tourists with quite a few being young honeymooners, walking hand-in-hand. He heard American voices, English, German, Scandinavian, Capri was probably the most visited place in Italy, apart from Rome. Jon met Carla most nights at 7 o'clock when she finished work, and took her to their favourite bistro in a side street not far from the harbour, but tonight would be different. "It's my birthday today," she said, "and I'm inviting you to a little party with my family, at my home, please say you'll come?"

"Er, yes, I'd love to," he said.

There wasn't an enormous gathering at Carla's house, a moderate dwelling at the top of a picturesque cobble-stoned hill, but very homely. "Welcome," her father said.

"Thank you," Jon replied

"I'm sorry," Carla's father said, "there is no signora, my wife died when Carla was born, 25 years ago to the day," he said looking to the sky, and crossing himself.

"I'm sorry to hear that."

"Oh, non c'e problema, it's many years and I have my Carla," he added, putting his arm around her shoulder and kissing her head, "and I have my Bruno, her elder brother, he's with the polizia, a detective sargeant."

The tall good-looking man of about thirty smiled and shook Jon's hand,"Nice to meet you," he said as he stared into Jon's face. Jon suddenly became uneasy and broke into a cold sweat, a fucking copper, he thought.

The evening was jolly, with friends and neighbours joining in until about midnight, but it was ruined for Jon by Bruno's constant sideways glances at him, fuck he thought, somehow he has recognised me. He even tried the old trick of calling him 'Jon', but it was ignored and after that he gave up. He stopped calling at the coffee shop and told Carla that he was now doing 'Estate Business' and could only see her once or twice a week. A copper's sister, he thought, no thanks. He decided he needed a car, hiring's the best bet, something small and unobtrusive. Near the hotel was 'Nuova Auto Rental', he took, for a month, a small grey Fiat Cinquecento, just about enough leg-room for him, but nippy and as common as muck on the island, lovely, he thought!

Naples

The train journey down from Rome was hot and very uncomfortable, and took longer than the three and a half hours predicted by the official at the train station. No air-conditioning, and rolling stock left over from the second world war, Mel said, and no refreshment carriage, just a boy with a trolley selling soft drinks at grossly inflated prices. "Five bucks for a warm coke," Mel almost shouted.

"Don't worry, hon," Mary-Lou said, "you can have an ice cold beer at the hotel, soon!"

The Hotel Royal more than made up for the train journey, about 400 years old, very ornate with 'da Vinci' style paintings everywhere. Their large double was a very large double, probably was once the bedroom of a nobleman, the Doge of Naples. "We've just gone back 400 years," Mary-Lou said, looking at the high ceilings.

"I bet these walls could tell some stories," Mel said. With all that, the hotel had all the mod cons. The Cafe Nero, the bars and the restaurants were magnificent, but expensive, "Oh, well," Mel said again," we are only here once."

"Don't worry, honey, you can do some extra shifts!" she said, patting his hand as they sat in the bar.

"Ten bucks for a beer," Mel said, "let's find a licquor store and bring some in."

"The hotel will charge us if they find out," Mary-Lou said.

"I'll take the chance, we can take the empties out with us!"

"Will you shut up for a few dollars, you'd probably drop them half-way across the lobby anyway!" she laughed as her mind's eye pictured Mel picking up the pieces.

"Okay, okay, but we cut down on champagne," he said with a grin.

Naples was beautiful, unless you strayed off of the tourist tracks, down by the harbour the hovel dwellings with dirty children, garbage all over the streets and the stray dogs, the smell was terrible, the honeymooners found out the hard way when they took a wrong turn off of a main street because Mel mis-read the map!

St Petersburg

Vasili had returned from Rome without success, there had been no news apart from old TV images, and his men were shaking in their shoes because they had missed 'Keiron' at the quayside and lost him in the car chase. They had scoured the area but with no luck, hotels, coffee shops, bars, restaurants were all checked for days. Romas were questioned, but apart from the Irish passport lead, nothing, just a dead end. Vasili's younger brother, Mikhail, had the idea of checking the docks to find out if 'Keiron' had taken a yacht or some sort of boat to somewhere. He walked along by the small yachts and fishing boats asking what people were there, if they had seen the man in the photograph. He had no luck until he came to almost the last fishing boat, "Have you seen this man?" he asked the young fisherman.

"Who are you, foreign police?"

"Yes," the Russian answered.

"You have no power here," the boy said. The Russian opened his jacket to reveal his pistol, and at the same time he took a wad of dollars out of his pocket.

The boy looked wide-eyed at the pistol and the money, "I took him to Capri about two weeks ago," he said, at that moment he didn't know whether he would receive some dollars or a bullet.

Mikhail peeled off a thousand dollar bill and gave it to the trembling fisher, "If you have lied to me, I will be back with this," the Russian said, tapping his pistol.

"It's the truth, I swear," the boy cried.

"Okay, good," said Mikail and tapped him on the cheek.

Vasili soon heard the news and ordered a jet to take him to Capri as soon as possible. He didn't own a private jet, but he did own the company that leased them. Eight Lockheeds worth half a billion dollars, about an eighth of his entire wealth. Nobody got the better of him, he killed, tortured, maimed or at least bribed, but that wasn't very often, pain, punishment and death were his main methods, and Jonathan Weston was at the top of his list for the worst punishment conceivable. Arriving at the private park place, he was met by Mikhail and six 'agents', "Well done, my brother," he said to Mikhail, "you see, it took my family's brain power to find this animal. Now, spread out and find him and FUCKING SOON," he screamed.

Jon didn't know about the new visitors to the island, would he be caught by the Italian police? it would be better for him if he was, far better. The gang would find it easier on such a small island, even though it was crowded with tourists of all nationalities. The Russians spread out as Vasili had ordered, two of them even walked past his little Fiat when he was in it, his blood ran cold, he knew who they were, he had to get off the island. Inside he was panicking, he was aware of what these people would do to him, he shivered. Right, think Jon, think, he said to himself. Deep breaths, deep breaths, he repeated inwardly. He sat there for ten minutes and then drove to the hotel, he packed a few clothing essentials into a backpack and left the rest behind, he nonchalantly walked over to his car and drove up into the hills until nightfall. A fishing boat would be the answer, he drove down to the harbour. At the entrance he couldn't believe his eyes, four of the Russian bastards walking along the quayside, easily recognisable, perhaps it was the way they walked, but it was very obvious who and what they were, death on legs. He turnrd the little car around and left the harbour area, if they had no luck tonight, which they wouldn't, he would come back early next morning. He drove back to spend the night in the hills, in the cramped Fiat, but it was worth it, he thought. The sun woke him as it came over the brow of the hill, cars and trucks were beginning to trundle up the steep incline. The smell of wild plants and flowers flowed in as he opened the windows, he ached in places he'd never ached before! "Right Jon," he said, "how do you get out of this one?" He put on his fedora and drove down the hill in to town, he needed a coffee desperately. At the bottom of the hill, on the outskirts of town where the shops began, he found a small cafe, 'perfect' he said to himself, 'this will put some life into me'. It even had a convenience where he was able to wash, paper towels only, but it was better than nothing. He gave the girl behind the counter 10 euros for the coffee and the facilities. As he left his picture appeared on the TV on the wall shelf, her mouth dropped open, and she immediately phoned the poice with his description and that of the car plus the direction in which he was going. About half a mile down the road, it was blocked with police cars and heavily armed police. He skidded to a halt, but it was too late ...... 'this is it' he said to himself, 'this is it, finally.' He couldn't believe it when the police walked right past him to a similar car about five behind him. It suddenly dawned on him as he looked at the little bonnet, the sun shining on the paintwork made it look silver, the girl in the cafe had seen him drive off in a mid-grey car that, in the blazing sun, made it look silver! A policeman waved him on whilst his colleagues pulled the other driver out of his silver Fiat!

He drove on down to the town and approached his hotel from a rear street, he went in through the tradesmans entrance to the surprise of the kitchen staff. He climbed the rear stairs to the second floor, in his room he took everything out of the safe. His case was quickly packed and he disappeared down the rear stairs and was soon driving through the back streets down to the docks. He parked between two warehouses and looked up and down the quayside, no sign of the Russians, 'good' he thought and walked over to a fishing trawler at the quayside. Working on the deck was an old man of the sea, "Do you speak any English?" 'Keiron' asked.

"A little, from Americans during the war. Got any gum?" he laughed through an almost toothless mouth.

Jon pulled out a small wad of dollar bills, the old boy looked at the money, "Can you take me to Sicily?"

"Sicilia?" the man almost screamed.

"Yes," said Jon.

"You are rich?" the fisher asked.

"No, but I can pay you well, in American dollars," he said.

"$4,000," the old man said.

"Okay," Jon agreed, "$2,000 now, $2,000 when we get to Palermo. When will we go?" he asked.

"When my son arrives in one hour, we must fish on the way."

Guiseppe, the son, arrived and looked very suspiciously at 'Keiron', "Who's he?" he said in Italian, and the father explained. "No, no," the boy said, "cinque mille, cinque mille euros, no dollars," he was shouting and waving his arms about. He walked over to Jon, "Inglese?" he asked.

"Yes," Jon said.

"The price is 5,000 euros, and that is if we have a good catch on the way," he explained, "and we won't tell the police that we took you there."

"Okay, you drive a hard bargain, but it will still have to be dollars, I haven't any euros."

"Okay, I'll work it out in dollars," the shrewd little bastard said, knowing full well that Jon was on the run, he'd seen his face on a bar's TV earlier that day. His father and he spoke Italian all the time, which worried Jon, he didn't trust them but he had no choice, he had to get away from the police and the Russians quickly, in fact, immediately.

The trawler left within 30 minutes, Guiseppe refused to cast off until he had received$3,000. Jon was shown where he could sleep, a small locker room behind the wheel-house. He found a large gutting knife in there, he slipped it down his trousers. He was told that food would be a hundred extra, and the journey would take 7 or 8 days. He spent most days just sitting in the stern end just sunbathing, apart from 2 days when there was very welcome rain, quite heavy, and he used it as a shower. He had soap and a towel in his case and was able to shave and change his clothes. Laying in the sun on the fourth day his thoughts turned to things evil, the black mist was descending. The two fisherman were going over the side after he'd killed them, he would turn the trawler north into the open sea and set the throttle on 'full ahead'. His escape would be by an inflatable boat with an outboard engine that was on quick release clamps on the port side, just in front of the net dragging boards. They hadn't done any fishing by trawl and had only been using throw nets over the starboard side. Guiseppe came to Jon and said they couldn't go into Palermo harbour as it is for liners and tourist craft only, no fishing boats. They had to go a long way to Trappani and it would cost another 1,000 euros, Jon was angry, but said that he had no choice. Sicily came into sight, tonight would be the night. As night fell he readied himself for the evil deed, the old man was at the wheel and manoeuvered closer to the land, Jon crept up behind him and slit his throat in one smooth and easy stroke. His son was near the stern, folding the throw nets, the engine went quiet and Guiseppe turned to see why and walked forward to the wheelhouse. As he passed Jon he received the kniife deep into his heart, he was dead as he hit the deck. Jon retrieved his money from the father's pockets. He rigged up a rope from the throttle lever and threw it over the side near the inflatable, after which he released the clamps, it fell into the flat sea, but was held by a single rope. He then jumped the 5 or 6 feet into it, following his case. Grabbing the throttle rope he pulled it gently and heard the satisfying sound of the big diesel engine revving, and the boat went north, accelerating all the time, into the gloom. He watched it disappear into the moonlit night, "nobody takes my money," he said to the sea, "and lives," he added, laughing. He revved the outboard and steered to the lights of Palermo, about one and a half miles to the harbour. As he got closer there was a loud explosion behind, out to sea, he guessed that the engine of the trawler had blown up, oh well he thought, all the evidence had gone, he'd even thrown the knife over the side. The harbour lights were getting closer as police and rescue boats rushed past him at very high speed with sirens screaming, good he thought, they won't notice little me creeping into port. They didn't, he looked back to see flames leaping into the air for about 100 feet. He tied up the boat at the very end of a jetty and walked towards the bright lights, police and ambulances were lined up on the other side of the quay, as he walked quickly in the gloomy shadows, up some steps into a side street and further on to a main road brightly lit by hotels and shops. He found a nice medium sized 4* hotel just off the main drag, the 'Mediterranean Palace' suited his purpose, lots of tourists wandering about.

Naples

"Hey, you bum, yeah I'm torkin' to you, you wanna meet the godfather!" Mary-Lou said, laughing, as she showed Mel the next port of call. "Sicily, the home of the Mafia, are you ready? It's a three and a half day luxury cruise to Palermo, across the calmest sea in the world with the bluest water," she said, showing him the brochure, "the boat leaves tomorrow at 5 o'clock, so be on it, punk!" she said, making a gun from two fingers and digging them into his ribs. 'It' happened!

The 'Sicilian Princess' wasn't a huge boat, but it had all the facilities of the very big ocean liners. Their large outside cabin was quite luxurious, they unpacked just what they were going to need for the short journey. There were no formal nights so the tuxedo and the long dress stayed packed, just smart-casual, even at dinner time. Mel and Mary-Lou went on to their balcony and sat with pre-dinner drinks. Dinner was typically Italian, but very good, later in the bar Mel once again saw Jonathan Weston's image on News TV, reporting his sighting on the Isle of Capri. Fuck, thought Mel, he's just one step ahead all the time, one day my man, one day, he thought. That day would be sooner than he thought, five days in fact, in a chance meeting.

Palermo

The trawler had been hit by a cruise liner while speeding on it's un-manned course, it had exploded and burst into flames as was evident from the shore. Lifeboats had reached the area in 15 minutes along with rescue and fire boats. The liner only suffered superficial damage with a few minor injuries to passengers. The fishing boat, according to an eye witness, had been struck amid ships by the liner's bow as it cut across the cruiser's course. The witness also said that he thought he saw someone laying on the deck near the wheelhouse, but he wasn't sure. The trawler had continued about 30 metres before it exploded and took only a few minutes to sink, taking any evidence of murder with it. Once again the devil had taken care of his ward.

Jon made himself comfortable in his room, a large double overlooking the interior gardens and pool. He sat on the balcony with an ice cold lager from the mini bar. He had managed to do a 'package holiday maker' deal with the hotel by paying for two weeks in advance, in US dollars, nice, he thought, free passage though not exactly 5* travel, but nice! He was enjoying life. Being on the island that's known for it's criminal activity, he wondered about Molly's and Liz's diamonds, he was sitting on nearly half a million dollars. He would start making enquiries in the morning after hiring another little grey Fiat, his lucky car!

No Jewish dealers on Sicily, they didn't exactly get on with the Cosa-Nostra, and preferred mainland Europe, and no Romas, they would not be welcome here. Anyway, Romas would steal the gems, not buy them. He was here for as long as he liked, barring problems, he would take his time finding the right dealer.

The Sicilian Princess

The honeymooners were enjoying their sea voyage, neither had done a sea cruise before in such beautiful surroundings. The wonderful calm and azure sea, the luxury of the liner, everything was perfect for their holiday of a lifetime, as Mel said, "We won't be able to do this again," as he rubbed his fingers together denoting 'money'.

"Oh, will you shut up, you old grouch, we are on our special, once in a lifetime honeymoon, and if you don't stop it I will withdraw my favours, or I may charge for them, okay Mr Novak?" Mary-Lou said.

"Okay, okay," Mel said, and threw $5 across the table, "that's for tonight!" he said.

"Five bucks!" Mary-Lou shouted as she snatched the note and tore it into small pieces, "you're on the couch tonight!" she said, laughing as Mel tried to salvage the $5 bill.

"Okay, okay," Mel said, "$10, but it's cash on delivery," he added.

"That's more like it," Mary-Lou replied. 'It' happened, Mel left $10 on the table.

Palermo

Jon (Keiron) mingled among the down-town crowd looking for clues as to how to approach the Sicilian Mafia about the sale of the diamonds, it was proving very difficult. 'Omerta' was the rule, 'silence at all times', nobody was willing to impart any information, not even the child beggars in the street. His second way of finding a buyer was to wander around the back streets of down-town Palermo, and then it struck him, nothing opens a mouth like the sight of a wad of American dollars. Bribery was probably high on the agenda of running this town. He walked into a junk type, antique sort of shop and showed the middle-aged man his least valuable ring, "Inglese?"

"Si signore."

The man looked at the ring that Jon offered, saying, "I want to sell this ring."

The Sicilian took a magnifying glass out of the drawer in his desk and scrutinised the jewel. He gave it back to Jon and said, "No signore, it's not for me, it's beyond my money."

"Who would buy it from me?" Jon asked.

"I don't know signore, goodbye," he said and stood staring into Jon's eyes with a cold glare that sent a sort of shiver down his spine.

No luck there, these people seem to be under a cloud of extreme fear. He walked out of the shop thinking that perhaps Sicily wasn't the place for plying his trade, but not to worry, he thought, I've got plenty of money, about a quarter of a million he reckoned. The diamonds will be my pension, he hoped, but would they? The devil had the answer.

The Sicilian Princess

The cruise liner docked at the quayside at Palermo an hour ahead of schedule, at 8 o'clock on Sunday morning. Breakfast was served at a leisurely pace and the honeymooners had time to do some last minute packing and have a last stroll around the promenade deck. "So, how have you enjoyed our honeymoon so far?" Mary-Lou asked Mel.

"It's been fabulous," he said and kissed her cheek, "but," he added, " we've still got another ten days to go before we fly home."

"Yeah," Mary-Lou replied, "and it will be fabulous, hey, look," she said, looking out of the balcony window, there's a cruise boat just sitting at anchor," she said.

Mel went to have a look, "It's bows are damaged," he said, "it's been in some kind of collision." There were salvage boats and tugs around the bow of the ship checking the damage. Hundreds of passengers on deck were enjoying the extra day at sea in the sunshine, watching the action. A TV news boat was also on the scene.

Keiron (Jon) sat in the hotel bar watching the commentary knowing full well that he'd been the instigator of an event that would cost somebody millions of euros. He kept watching to see if he was still front page news, he wasn't, but then again this was Sicily TV. Good, he thought, the mainland stations might be different, but he was in Palermo. Had he become yesterday's news? He hoped so.

The Novak's cruise liner docked at midday, the hotel's bus was waiting to take them to the 5* 'Majestic Hotel', it had a new facade but the actual building was art deco, "Beautiful!" Mary-Lou said. Their baggage was taken from the bus to reception by a young man that "should be in the movies!" so Mary-Lou said.

"Yeah," Mel said, "so was Lassie and the Three Stooges!" They laughed.

"But he is very dishy," she added. He gave the 'movie star' $10 for taking the bags to their double room which faced the sea, and being on a hill he could see the stricken cruise liner almost on the horizon.

Little did Mel know that he was only 300 metres away from Jon Weston, the closest he had been for almost two years. His hotel was in the next block. Would their paths cross?

Capri

Mikhail and his men had turned the island upside down, no stone had been un-turned, no bribe un-bribed and no threat un-threatened, but Keiron had once again, been one step ahead. Satan, his mentor, was working well for him.

"Mikhail," Vasili screamed into the phone, "come back, you are fucking useless." He had contacted some 'friends' in Sicily and the Italian mainland that owed him one or two favours, "And tell those idiots with you that they will suffer for their stupidity," he added, "I have made other arrangements with people down there that know what they're doing, they'll find the bastard and deliver him to me. I don't care how long it takes or how much it costs," he continued screaming, then the phone went dead.

Palermo

Sightseeing was the order of the day for the honeymooners. The main road led to the town centre, about a ten minute stroll, they admired the architecture above the ground floors that had been converted to shops and restaurants. The small statues and gargoyles added a strange quality that they hadn't seen before, on a corner property above a coffee shop there were three small gargoyles, "There you are," Mel said, "the Three Stooges, Larry, Mo and Shep!" he pointed out to Mary-Lou.

"You are crazy," she replied, but they still laughed.

The square in the centre was beautiful, with lots of amazingly coloured flowers everywhere and a huge central fountain. Over in one corner was an enormous spread of tables and chairs belonging to 'La Casanova Ristorante' with a huge statue of the 18th century lothario as a centre piece. Many people were seated at tables and at one, sat Jon, just surveying the overall scene. The last time he had seen Mel Novak the Lieutenant was wearing a tie and dark suit, so he didn't recognise the American tourist wearing a light shirt, small brimmed sun hat and cream chino-style trousers. Neither did Mel Novak recognise the blond Scandinavian looking guy sitting at a table not two metres away. As Mel and Mary-Lou sat down, one of the many aproned waiters wiped their table, and said, "Si signora and signore, can I help you?"

"Two cappuccinos, please," Mary-Lou said.

"Si, signora," said the waiter, and scooted off to get their order. They just chatted about the ambiance and beauty of the surroundings.

Jon (Keiron) put his arm in the air denoting to a waiter that he wanted to pay his bill, but the waiter virtually ignored him, "I don't know," he said in Mel's direction, "he doesn't seem to want my money," he laughed.

Mel's spine went rigid, and his blood ran cold. "You've gone a funny colour," his wife said.

"Shush," Mel said, "er, sorry, but I need to hear that guy speak again." He turned away from 'Keiron' so as not to raise his suspicions.

The waiter finally came over to 'Keiron's' table, "Sorry, signore, we are very busy today, there are lots of tourists off of the cruise boat that came in yesterday."

"Oh, really," Keiron said.

"Si, signore, mostly Americanos."

"Yes," Keiron said, "they certainly like to see the world," he added, smiling at Mary-Lou. He stood up and walked away towards the main square, Mel still had the grey colour even through his suntan.

"Honey, what's wrong?" Mary-Lou asked.

"Oh, it's nothing, it's just that I thought I recognised that guy from the case I was on in London, before we met," he explained. He called over the waiter and asked, "The man that was sitting at that table, does he come here every day?" as he asked he put 10 euros in his hand.

"Si signore, every day at 11 o'clock and sits for about an hour with two mocha coffees," the waiter answered.

"Thank you," Mel said. He now had to explain to Mary-Lou what it was all about. They sat for an hour with more cappuccinos and Italian liqueurs. After he had told her the whole story she sat there wide-eyed and with her mouth open.

"You mean to tell me that the guy sitting just six feet away, was a murderer of women on cruise ships for their jewellery and then just casually threw their bodies overboard?" she asked.

"That's about it," Mel replied, "I need to find the nearest police station."

"Yeah," Mary-Lou said, "let's get that bastard behind bars."

Across the square they saw a policeman just wandering around on walk-about patrol. "Do you speak English?" Mel asked the tall young cop.

"Si, signore, I am tourist corps of the Polizia," he replied.

"Good," Mel said, "where is your headquarters?"

"It's just over at the end of the square to the left, as it meets the main road," he answered.

"Thank you," Mel said, "thank you very much," leaving the policeman looking puzzled and scratching the back of his neck. They walked up the marble steps through the large open wooden doors up to the reception officer, a short stout man with a chubby face. "Do you speak English?" Mel asked.

"Si signore, this is a tourist area," he responded.

Mel showed his ID and badge, "I am Lieutenant Novak of the New York State police, is it possible to speak to your Chief Inspector?" Mel asked.

"Si, signore," the man said and picked up the telephone, he spoke Italian for about a minute then put down the phone, "he will be here in a minute or so, please take a seat," he said.

He was a silver haired man of about 55, fairly tall and smartly dressed, "Lt Novak," he said, "welcome to Sicily, how can I help you?" Mel explained the whole case to the Chief Inspector. "Are you sure he's the same man, this person in the square today?"

"Oh yes," Mel said, "I interrogated him for hours in New York, it's him, definitely."

"Well," the CI said, "be here at 10 o'clock in the morning."

Mel didn't sleep well, on his mind was how they would capture Jon Weston, would he be surrounded at the table by armed police, or would the Police Chief give Mel a gun to perform the arrest? He and Mary-Lou just cuddled, 'it' didn't happen.

Breakfast was in silence, Mary-Lou could see that Mel was on the planet justice, it was one of the reasons she had fallen for him, his ardent sense of right and wrong. Today could be the culmination of a lot of hard work by the NYPD and Scotland Yard, Mel hoped. At ten on the dot, the Novaks walked into Police Headquarters to meet the Chief Inspector. They waited for about 20 minutes before the Chief arrived, "I'm sorry, but the operation's been cancelled, orders from the Commissario, something to do with the safety of the public. He may be carrying a gun himself, I will try to arrange something soon, how long are you here for?" he asked.

"For as long as it takes, we have an open ticket back to London," Mel replied.

"Good," the Chief Inspector said, and arranged to contact them at the hotel in a day or two.

"He's been primed by the local 'gentry'," Mel said, "I'll put next months salary on that."

"Yes," his wife agreed, "fancy a cappuccino?"

They walked to the huge al fresco cafe in the corner of the square, and sat, but not as close to Jon's corner table, in fact they were about 20 metres away. Thirty minutes passed before Jon turned up, as he passed their table he nodded to Mary-Lou but ignored Mel. He sat at his usual spot, the waiter having seen him arrive was on on the ball and delivered his coffee and liqueur almost immediately. A few minutes went by and a young man walked past carrying a package. He went into the cafe for about a minute then walked out, as he did a powerful motor bike came into the square, the young man climbed on to the pillion, the bike did a 360 turn, as it went past Jon's table the package was opened to reveal an automatic pistol which splattered Jon's chest with at least four shots. He fell to the ground clutching his chest, with blood oozing through his shirt and blouson. The motor cycle did a wheelie of triumph as it left the square, locals dispersed very quickly, leaving only tourists to stand open-mouthed, like statues. An ambulance immediately arrived, and Jon was taken away. Mel's trained powers of observation noticed that one of the ambulance men was also the pillion passenger, fuck he thought, where had they taken him?

Mary-Lou just sat open-mouthed, and then said, "Are we on a set of a James Bond movie, or did all that really happen?"

"It really happened," Mel said, "but I don't believe it."

"What happens now?" his wife asked.

"I don't know, I just don't know, the only thing we can do is ask at the local hospital," he added.

"Whoa," Mary-Lou said, "I think we should just let it go."

"I can't," Mel said, "he's a murdering evil bastard, and I want him, if he lives."

"Honey, they're the rulers of Sicily, we don't stand a chance, please don't take this any further," she begged.

"Okay, okay," Mel said, "but we must contact NYPD and Scotland Yard and inform them."

Back at the hotel bar, the couple watched the latest news on the huge screen, it appeared that 'Keiron Pearce' was still alive, but in a critical state in the local hospital. The 'assassins' had used small calibre and small load bullets, almost blanks, but enough to do a fair amount of damage but not so much as to kill. They wanted him to survive, this was the Russian directive! After a sort of recovery he was to be crated up and flown to Russia. But satan had a different idea!

Four days passed and 'Keiron' was moved to a day ward, having progressed well, but he was still unwell, with dressings from his waist to his neck. But he felt a lot better and just wanted to get out of the hospital as soon as possible. He remembered the inflatable boat down at the end of the quay, and planned his escape. He would go further down the coast and steal a yacht or some sort of boat, to get away from his enemies.

Mel and Mary-Lou had only five days left before they would have to fly back to London, and then home.

Jon found his clothes and his back-pack, that went everywhere with him, it contained his future. All of his cash and jewellery were in tact and where they should be. Honest Sicilian hospital staff, who would have thought, hundreds of thousands, untouched! Satan was working for him again.

St Petersburg

Vasili heard the news of 'Keiron's' shooting, and sent two of his trusted men , his brother Mikhail and nephew Peter, to see to the transfer to Russia. They would fly there in one of the Lockheads and the crate with 'Keiron' in a seated position tied and drugged, would be brought back to be 'dealt' with, as Vasili put it. At least that was the plan, but Keiron's mentor was in charge once again.

Palermo

Jon dressed slowly behind his drawn curtain at midnight, and waited until it was quiet. At 1 am, and painfully, he left by the stairs at the rear of the building, which also served as the fire escape, and led to the staff car park. Making sure that the coast was clear, he walked uncomfortably out on to the road and slowly down the hill towards the quayside where he hoped his inflatable would be. The wonderful thing about Sicily was that theft crime was low, as would-be thieves were worried as to who the property belonged to! There it was, including the outboard motor, wonderful! Satan was again at his side. He had no strength to pull the starter cord, his chest and upper arms were weak and painful, so he tried by wrapping it around his ankle and pulling sharply. It started on the 4th attempt, in the bottom, under the seat, was a twenty litre can of fuel, it was full. Good, he thought, that'll get me well down the coast. At the first sign of dawn's light, he re-started the outboard and cast off towards the open sea. The 200hp engine was fast and he was pleased to see the bow lift, he thanked the fisherman silently for providing him with the means to escape. He had no maps but he knew he was heading east, and keeping fairly close to the shore with lights in his sight. He kept going for about two hours, following the coast wasn't easy as it was not a straight coastline, he had to turn in to the shore quite a few times. He was feeling cold and weak and very hungry. There was a deep bay with a village at the deepest point, he made for the dimly lit, small harbour and tied up on a metal, well rusted, ring that protruded from the ancient quayside wall. He sat, feeling un-well, he must find some food and sleep. With no shelter in the boat, he began to get colder. He managed to climb up the low wall on to the quayside, with a lot of pain. He noticed that his blouson had the blood stained bullet holes across the chest, he had to find something to warm him him and cover the holes. He wandered through the small hilly streets, and once again, Satan was with him. A fishermen's sweater hung on a washing line, he just walked into the small cottage's frontage and took it off the line, it was clean and dry! Who would steal a sweater on Sicily? he thought, and laughed.

He now needed food, he was weak and in pain, but Satan was at hand to help. Even though his ward was carrying nearly half a million dollars in cash and diamonds he was almost a vagrant in a small fishing village on a secondary island in the Med, how did it come to this? he thought. But then the alternative was frightening, living off of his sister, slumming about in Camden Town, no, this would only be temporary. Two or three days at the most, he would rest up to get his strength back. He wandered down a narrow street and suddenly saw a sign 'Appartamento' in the window of a medium-sized house. He knocked on the door which opened quickly, "Si?"

"Appartamento, per favore?" Jon said. The woman looked him up and down, and started to close the door without saying a word. "American dollars," he said.

She looked at the wad of dollars that he showed her, "Avanti," she said, opening the door wider. She took him up a flight of stairs to two rooms which were comfortably furnished with furniture from the fifties, but it was very clean and would suit him for a week or so.

"Si," he said, "quanto costa questa?"

"You are English?" she asked.

"Yes," Jon said.

"I speak some English, for one week $100," she announced.

"Okay," said Jon, and peeled off two fifty dollar bills and gave it to the woman.

"Grazie," she said, and showed him the shower room etc.

"Thank you," Jon said "I need some clothes, you see my boat sank and I lost everything."

"Si," the woman replied, "I have clothes from my son who has gone to the Army on mainland at Salerno Training Camp, I will bring for you," and she finally smiled.

"Thank you again," Jon said, and thought, this is a piece of luck! I can stay here until I'm fit and well again. The clothes fitted him quite well and he gave the landlady $100 for them, which she declined, but he forced her to take the money.

"Molte grazie!" she said.

Over the next few days Jon was treated like his landlady's long gone son, food, more clothes were supplied. He feigned gratitude, because when he left he would not be able to carry them. It suddenly occurred to him that he didn't know where he was! "What is the name of this village?" he asked his landlady.

"It is called Trepani," she answered, "a very old fishing village from the days of the Romans," she enthused, "but we have no tourists," she said with her arms raised, "only fish. We don't even have television, because of the hills," she added. This was good news for Jon, at least he could walk around without being recognised.

Walking through the village was like going back hundreds of years, apart from the odd twenty year old tiny Fiat or Lambretta scooter. Shops were very rare apart from a grocer-come-delicatessen store that also sold licquor. He went in and pointed to a bottle of Italian brandy for 20 euros, the young girl had to stand on a chair to reach the bottle, her skirt, which was already short, rose to almost show her nicely rounded buttocks, and she knew it! As she turned, she smiled as she got down from the chair, "Si signore," she said, flashing her eyes, "venti euros per favore."

"How much for the arse show?" he laughed. He passed a 50 euro note, as she took the money she looked sexily into Jon's eyes.

She was about 18-20, and very, very pretty, she gave him his change and said, "The arse show is free!" in almost perfect English.

"You speak English?" Jon said, feeling embarrassed.

"I am here on holiday from the Sussex University in Brighton, do you know it?"

"No," he said, "but I've heard of it."

"This is my parents shop, and I can't wait to get back to civilisation, but that won't be for another month. Do you want to take me out one night, you are very handsome?" she said, cheekily.

Jon laughed a very nervous laugh, and said, "Er, yes, but where is there to go?" he asked, he had to stand aside while two customers were served.

"There is a club down at Marsala where some tourists go, I have a Lambretta, it takes about 20-25 minutes, we could go there," she said, once again flashing her eyes.

"When had you in mind?" he asked.

"Tomorrow night, perhaps?" she suggested, "Where are you staying?"

"At Signora Mantini's house. My boat sank four days ago while I was out on a pleasure cruise from further down the coast. I lost everything because I had my suitcase in the boat to go to Tunis. Luckily, my back-pack with my passport and money survived, they were wrapped in plastic," he lied. "These clothes belong to Mrs Mantini's son," he said.

"I thought I recognised that shirt," she said, "he's in the army now, in Salerno," she said.

"Yes, his mother told me."

He'd never ridden pillion on a scooter, it was a new frantic experience for him, especially on the mountain roads! But Naomi, as he now knew her, was a good and careful rider, she'd even provided Jon with a crash helmet, and went very slowly around the hairpin bends. It took exactly 30 minutes to get to the 'Vegas Club', they stopped outside then Naomi did something very unusual, she started to get undressed. She removed her jeans to reveal a little blue dress, then removed her leather blouson to complete a very sexy and attractive look. "Okay," she said, as she locked her clothes in the under-seat locker.

"Is that safe?" Jon asked, "this is Sicily."

"Believe me, it's safe," she answered as she took his arm and they walked in to the club. She paraded Jon around so that friends and acquaintances could see her with a handsome man. Fair enough, he thought, and started to enjoy the evening, he felt safe and stronger, the pains in his chest and arms had abated.

At about 1 o'clock, after lots of dancing, they had started to kiss while on the dance floor. Naomi was very willing to get passionate and Jon could feel it in the way she pressed herself against him. They left on the scooter after Naomi got dressed at the road-side. When they arrived back at her home she put the Lambretta at the back of the shop and then took his hand and led him to a door at the side of the building, this led to a small self-contained apartment with a very comfortable looking double bed. She was naked in less than a minute, and started to kiss Jon passionately as her hands undid buttons and zips to undress him. He winced as she pulled his shirt off to reveal the bandage around his chest, "Oh, I'm sorry, did I hurt you?"

"No, I just cracked a couple of ribs when the boat sank," he lied. He pulled her towards him, her skin was like silk, fresh, and smelled of a very exotic bath oil, it made his erection stronger and more rampant. Their lovemaking continued for at least two hours and they fell asleep in each others arms.

A distant rooster announced the dawn, Naomi awoke and immediately started to fondle 'Keiron's' genitals. He woke and smiled at his gorgeous little lover. She rolled over to be on top of him, "I'm going to ride you, be the dominant one!" She gently lowered her straddled body on to his erection, and the lovemaking was something that 'Keiron' had not experienced for a long time. Her orgasm broke the sound barrier! Naomi's parents were away on holiday on the mainland, visiting relatives in Naples. "I have to open the shop," she said, "but I will make breakfast first." She kissed him and then went into the shower.

Palermo

"How in the Lord's name, did he manage to escape?" the Chief Inspector shouted.

"He went to relieve himself and when he returned the curtain was still drawn so he thought all was well," Sgt Gambrelli replied.

"Okay," the CI said, "check the airport and the harbour, I want him back here, SOON!" he screamed, his well-being depended on it. The 'gentry' had warned him that his safety was in question, not to mention a large cash inducement! He distributed photographs of Jon (Keiron) to every officer in the city and it was decided to put his picture on television news, but that was of no consequence in Trepani as it was a TV-free area.

Trepani

Jon still didn't feel safe on Sicily, he would try to find a boat to take him to Tunis, the nearest point of the African coast, may be he would go down to the quay-side to see if any large trawlers were in. Walking down the hill he could see his inflatable boat bobbing about gently on a very slight swell. There weren't any boats in the small harbour, but in the distance he could see a large boat, it was an ocean-going trawler. He waited, sitting on the wall, until the trawler came to the quay-side, it was big and to his surprise, had Arabic writing above the name 'L'Ariana'. Satan was still helping. He waited until a crew mwmber had tied up at both ends and was leaning against the wall with a cigarette, "Buongiorno," he said, "do you speak English?"

"Si, a little," he said.

"Do you go to Tunis?" Jon asked.

"We are going tomorrow, it is our home country."

Jon couldn't believe his luck, "Could I pay you to take me with you?"

"I will ask my brother, he owns the boat." He jumped aboard and went to the wheelhouse and spoke to a grey haired, brawny man who looked down at Jon and said something to the younger brother. His luck was in as the boy said, "Yes, it will cost 1,000 euros."

Jon pretended to think hard about it, then said, "Yes, what time are you leaving tomorrow?"

"Six o'clock," the boy said.

"I'll be here," Jon said.

He went to see Naomi at the shop, she ran around the counter, threw her arms around his neck and kissed him saying 'Would you like an arse show?' and before he could say yes or no she'd run back and was climbing the step ladder, this time however, she wore no knickers! She looked back at him, smiling and said, "How's that?"

"Very nice," he said, "now come down, I have something to tell you."

Her smile disappeared, "What is it?" she asked.

"I'm leaving in the morning," he said.

Naomi's face dropped, and her eyes moistened, "Where are you going?" she asked

"I'm going back to the mainland, probably Rome," he lied.

She started crying but soon composed herself when a lady customer came into the shop. Jon took the opportunity, and left the shop quickly, and as far as Naomi was concerned, was gone forever.

Jon left Mrs Mantini's very quietly, leaving a 100 euro note on his bed. he took the minimum amount of clothing in his back-pack including his money and the diamonds, arriving at the quay at 5.30am. There was a single light on in the wheelhouse, but there was movement and the boy came to the side of the boat and lit a cigarette. Seeing Jon, he beckoned him aboard. He climbed on to the flat deck and went to the wheelhouse, "Do you have the money?" the boy said. He gave the lad a 500 euro note. "My brother said 1,000 euros."

"Yes, I know, 500 now and 500 when we get there, okay?" Jon said.

"I'll see what my brother says," and went below deck. Jon waited, he had taken a large stout kitchen knife from the signora's kitchen and had it inside his shirt, wrapped in a tea towel so as not to cut himself.

The fishing boat left at 7am, being a powerful ocean-goer Jon was pleased with the rate of knots that it made out of the harbour and in to the open sea, beautiful blue and flat. He looked at the sun and calculated that they were heading SW, good he thought. He asked the young fisherman how long the trip would take, "Two days," he replied, "and my brother now wants 1,200 euros for keeping him waiting for the rest of the money, and food," he announced.

"Okay," said Jon, "when we get there," he added. I hope they live to collect it, he thought with an evil smile, as he patted the package inside his shirt.

They did some fishing and the catches looked very good, a load with each trawl, Jon even helped to bring up the nets as best he could, he was now a lot fitter and stronger. The fish were dropped into steel-lined bins, still writhing and flapping around, then something happened that Jon didn't expect, two dark Arabic girls came up to the deck and started to gut the catch. They worked at a furious rate, throwing the entrails overboard. From out of a clear blue sky, a huge flock of seagulls fell upon the flotsam of fish remains. The girls didn't seem to notice Jon, they probably just thought he was a hired hand for the trip.

Russia

Both in St Petersburg and Moscow, the dogs had been called off, with high rewards being offered for Jon's capture, but they were concentrating on Europe, they hadn't thought of anywhere further afield, but that was to come. Jon Weston would always be top of their 'wanted' list and they had very long arms and informants everywhere. In every Russian Embassy there was someone on their payroll, ready to tell them any news of a sighting. It was a long way off, but he would have his day of reckoning, but who would it be, the NYPD, the UK Police or the Russians?

Palermo

M ary-Lou and Mel Novak were packing and almost ready to have their luggage collected and taken down to reception, "Well," said Mary-Lou, "now the long haul home," she said, sadly.

"Yep," Mel agreed, "still it's been wonderful hasn't it, hon?" he said, pulling her close and kissing her head. Their flight would take them back to London to take a flight to New York.

"Yes," Mary-Lou said, "and exciting."

"Yeah," said Mel looking down, "I wish I'd had the jurisdiction to nail that evil bastard, but he's gonna get what's coming to him one day, and I want a front row seat."

He heard that Jon had escaped from the hospital after speaking to the Asst Chief Inspector, "He is very clever," the ACI had said, " he has the devil on his side."

"Yes," Mel had agreed, "in fact I think the devil is driving him."

They arrived at the airport with time to spare, he had somehow become obsessed by every tall blond man, looking at their faces, he even ran over to the check-in desk and grabbed the arm of a man and spun him round to get a better look at his face. "I'm sorry," he said, I thought you were a friend of mine." The young fellow was Norwegian and didn't understand a word of what Mel had said.

"Honey, will you stop it, you're making a fool of yourself, if you don't there's gonna be trouble, big trouble," Mary-Lou almost shouted.

"I'm sorry, you're right," he said.

Tunisia

Midday on the second day, they sailed past a headland and into calmer waters and followed the coast line on the port side. Ice containers were brought up to the deck from the freezer below, and the freshly gutted fish were sorted and packed ready for the fish market. "How long before we reach land?" Jon asked the younger brother.

"Five or six hours," he replied.

I couldn't kill all four of them, Jon thought, I'll have to pay up, after all I didn't pay for the trip to Palermo. He smiled a wicked smile. He now had the task of selling the diamonds, were there any dealers in Tunis? May be there was a Jewish quarter, after all Arabs and Jews lived side by side in Israel, especially Jerusalem.

Being a fairly busy tourist destination the hotels were very modern and luxurious, three or four star would do if he could get into one. His first attempt drew a blank, fully booked the young man said, sniffing at Jon's fishy smell. The same answer came from the next four tries, and then he saw a sign 'Holiday Apartments' flashing neon. He walked up the few steps through a glass door to a counter manned by a middle-aged woman. She looked Jon up and down and sniffed. "Do you speak English?" Jon asked.

"Yes, of course, this is an area of tourism, are you a fisherman?"

"No," Jon said, "my boat sank and I was picked up by a fishing boat. I'm sorry if you can smell it, but I have plenty of money to pay for accomodation." He pulled out a wad of US dollars. "How much for a week in a double apartment?"

"$500," she replied, "in advance."

"Okay," he said.

"Passport please," she said. She looked at it and gave it back to him, "thank you," her attitude had changed when she saw his wedge of money. She also passed him a form to complete, it took 2-3 minutes to fill in, she then passed him an old fashioned key on a label, "apartment 110 on the first floor, front," she said, smiling for the first time as she took the five $100 bills.

He climbed the stairs to the first floor and soon found the door to Appt 110, it faced south, it was well appointed and very clean and comfortable, and it had a TV. Good, he said to himself, and immediately switched it on. He watched as he looked around, opening doors and drawers. Looking in the wardrobe, he was reminded that he needed to buy some new clothes. He would first have to get clean and wash what he was wearing. He took everything into the bathroom and ran a bath, nice and hot, he said to himself. He left the clothes to soak after rubbing it all with toilet soap to get rid of the smell of fish. He laid naked on the bed, after taking a shower, watching TV, there was no news or image of him, good he thought, I'm not notorious in North Africa! From here he could travel freely, but he had to sell the jewellery first. His cash balance was still very healthy but he wanted to get rid of the diamonds and turn them in to cash, preferably dollars. He went for a walk, the reason mainly to buy some clothes. In the main tourist trap shopping area, there were some familiar names in fashion. He chose an Yves St Laurent outlet and spent $!,800 on smart casuals, including shoes. He tried to pay in euros but they wouldn't accept them. Having changed in to one of his outfits in the store, he asked the assistant to get rid of his old stuff and gave him an extra $10, saying "Keep the change!" The young trendy man bowed and thanked him. Further down the street there was a taxi rank, now if anyone knows where I can sell jewellery, the cabbies will. "Do you speak English?" he asked the first driver.

"Yes, sir-r-r," the portly man replied, "we have to learn for our licence, and for the tourists."

"Good," said Jon, "I want to find the area for buying and selling jewellery?"

"Oh, yes sir-r-r, the Jews in El-Macabi Street, I will take you," he said, opening the door of his bright green and white Toyota estate car.

Jon knew he was being ripped off because the meter remained 'off' and they had passed the same buildings and statues, twice! But he smiled and thought he'd haggle for a bit of fun when they reached his destination. Turning down a narrow street, he recognised signs in Hebraic writing that he had seen in New York and Antwerp. The cab stopped and the cabbie said, loudly, "El-Macabi Street sir-r-r, $30 plizz."

"No," Jon said, "$20, you went past the large soldier statue twice and you didn't use the meter, $20 or I report you to the police," he added.

"Okay, okay," came the reply.

Jon gave him $25 and said, "I suppose that's what you call free enterprise!" and walked away laughing.

"Go home yank!" the driver shouted.

"I'm not a yank, I'm Irish," Jon said, laughing loudly again. He looked carefully for CCTV cameras, there were none. Good, Tunis is lagging behind in catching felons, but woe betide them when they do, Arabic jails are very nasty, he thought. Walking down one side of the street and then up the other, pretending to be a window shopper, he was accosted by shop owners inviting him in to look at their goods. But he declined their offers with a smile and a 'no, thank you', until he was invited into a large well-appointed emporium by a young man wearing the traditional skull cap and prayer tassles hanging below his shirt. "Do you speak English?" he asked.

"Yes," came the reply, "I went to school in Golders Green, in London."

Two miles from where I lived, Jon thought, but pretended not to know it, "I'm fom Ireland, and I have some diamonds to sell, do you buy jewellery?"

"Yes, may I see them?" the young man said as he went behind a thick glass secure partition. Jon took out his red handkerchief to reveal Molly's gems, the necklace, the bracelet, the three rings and the watch, and passed them through the slot. The dealer took at least 20 minutes to eyeglass them. "How much do you want for the lot?" he asked Jon.

"$200,000," Jon answered.

"Mmm." The man thought, "I'll have to call in other dealers, I do not make such large purchases, but I have fellow dealers close by that will be very interested in buying part of the lot. It will take about an hour, is that all right?"

"Yes," Jon said, and sat on a comfortable chair. Three older dealers entered the shop similarly dressed, with skull caps and prayer tassles. They all went in to a back room. The hour became an hour and a half during which Jon heard the Germanic language spoken fairly loudly.

"We will give you $180,000," the younger dealer said.

Jon sat and pretended to think deeply for a few minutes, stood and said, "$190,000, let's split the difference, they're top quality gems, especially the necklace." The man went back to his colleagues but returned with a $185,000 offer, "Will that be dollars, cash?"

"Yes, of course," the man replied. The three other dealers came out, looked at Jon, nodded and smiled. They spoke to the shop's manager in the foreign tongue. "They will return soon," the younger man said. After receiving the money, he thanked the dealers and left the shop. He still had Liz Fenner's diamonds but he would hang on to them as some sort of nest egg!

Tunis was a very vibrant city, more tourists than he had seen anywhere else, no wonder the taxis were all new, latest models, including Mercedes and BMW's. Fuels were about half the price of Europe but the taxi drivers were all descendants of Ali Baba's friends and preyed on tourists like vultures, charging exhorbitant prices to go just short distamces. He thought he would extend his stay at the apartment for at least another week, after all he could well afford it, if not better, but it was comfortable, cellular and very private.

Yonkers & New Rochelle

The town was still smarting over the disappearance of Liz Fenner. Ben Schwartz, the car cleaner, walked into the Sherrif's office and handed in the key to Liz Fenner's house. The junior officer called Mel Novak to the front desk, "Will you be able to attend the coroner's inquest? as there is no body he just wants to establish, by witnesses, who exactly Liz Fenner was."

"Yes, sure," said Ben. Being a law student, this would be of the utmost interest to him.

"Mrs Fenner's family, what there is of it, will be there, okay?" Mel said, "oh, and by the way, you're the only one now that knows the gate entry code, what is it please?"

"6969," Ben replied, not knowing why Mel smiled.

"Thanks Mr Schwartz, we'll be in touch." As he walked out Mel and the junior officer laughed loudly, "6969," they almost shouted, "Hey, shut up," Mel said, " the poor lady is dead."

The Inquest

L iz Fenner's sister Paula was present, but her only interest was the will that Liz may have left. She had flown in from Los Angeles after being informed by the NYPD which had taken a lot of trouble placing national newspaper ads. She had contacted Capt Colletti and learned about the inquest. She was introduced to Mel Novak by the coroner's assistant, "Well," she said, "have you got anywhere in finding her murderer?"

"No," Mel replied, "but he is being sought all over Europe, TV images, newspaper pictures etc., he was recently shot by the Sicilian mafia in Palermo, but escaped from the hospital. No one knows where he is now."

"I see," she said, "Who is Elizabeth's attorney?" she asked.

"Rackman Davis of Manhattan," Mel replied, "There will be a representative at the inquest. But I must tell you that there will be a statutory waiting period of two years before her will can be implemented, because there wasn't a body."

"WHAT?" she shouted, "that's ridiculous."

"It's the law," Mel answered.

"I WANT THE ADDRESS OF THIS RACKMAN DAVIS," she shouted.

"I'm a policeman, lady, I'm not allowed to give out such information," he lied, as he didn't like the woman or her attitude.

"I'M GOING TO SEE YOUR SUPERIOR AT NYPD," she shouted again

"That's your privilege," Mel said and turned away from her and left the building. He could have helped her a lot more as his wife, Mary-Lou, ran the local office of Rackman Davis.

Over dinner at home, he told Mary-Lou about Liz Fenner's sister, "It'll probably come home to roost at my office," she said, "your superior in New York City will tell her the same," she added.

"And then she'll probably go to see the Governor at State Capital," he laughed, " she's only interested in getting her manicured hands on Liz's fortune," he said.

The proceedings were short-lived and only lasted about 30 minutes, Liz's sister was present with an attorney who tried to get some sort of injunction to have the will reading brought forward, but the coroner ruled against it and quoted the law.

"I WANT TO LODGE AN APPEAL," she stood up and shouted. Her attorney urged her to sit down and told her that an appeal could cost her up to $100,000, win or lose. She went quiet and started to cry silently. This lady was desperate, but nobody knew why. But the truth was that she was the lover of Liz's husband before he married her, and she was convinced that the legacy should be hers. She needed it badly, when she heard that Liz was missing, believed dead, she inwardly rejoiced and had dollar signs in her minds eye. Her younger lover had left her, taking half the assets of their boutique's business and gone off with a younger woman ..... and she was heading for bankruptcy.

Tunis

Satan's protegee felt the black mist descending as he sat watching passengers from a cruise ship walking towards the main town. He noticed one in particular, tall, elegant and very well dressed, he would follow this woman and get to know her if he could. She had a nice way of walking, perhaps she was an ex-model. She did some window shopping and waved off shop keepers who invited her into their shops. She eventually went into a small square and sat at a table in the corner of a coffee shop. A waitress asked her what her choice was, she ordered. Jon sat at a table about 10 metres away and pretended to just watch passers-by, he did, however, notice her looking his way and he gave her a cheeky smile and she smiled back. After about ten minutes he stood and walked over to her table and introduced himself, "Hello, I'm Keiron Pearce," he said.

"Hello, I'm Agneta Garner, from Sweden, and you're from Ireland, right?" she said.

"That's right, from Dublin, how could you tell?" They both laughed, her smile lit up the sombre sun-less corner they were in. "Why don't we go over to another table that's in the sun?" he suggested.

"I'm afraid I can't at the moment, this is my day of shade as I call it, I've had too much sun in the last few days, best to be careful," she explained.

"Oh, I see, er yes, the rays in this part of the world are very powerful," he answered as he sat down, "how long is your ship in Tunis for?"

"Three days," she replied, "I'm hoping to buy some leather goods, I've heard it's very good here and not too expensive. In Sweden it's outrageously costly, and I want to possibly set up a source of supply for my shops in Stockholm and Malmo," she said.

"Well then, perhaps I can help you carry your bags?" he laughed.

"Yes," she said, "that would be nice, and helpful!"

"And you'll need me to deal with taxi drivers, they're outrageously expensive too, to tourists," he added.

"Are you a gigolo?" Agneta asked with a saucy giggle.

"Jesus, bless you!" he said, wanting to sound very Irish, "No! I'm a car dealer from London taking a long holiday in southern Europe and north Africa," he said, "do I appear to be a gigolo?" he laughed.

"Yes, you're tall, smart and very handsome. I will be happy for you to accompany me and help me with my shopping," she smiled a 'perfect teeth' smile.

Jon paid the bill and they walked off to where the main shopping area was. Leather shops were abundant, and shopkeepers were busy trying to get them inside their emporiums, 'yes beautiful lady, we have the best leather garments in Tunis' seemed to be the chat up line, but Jon smiled and said 'not today, thank you' while Agneta felt the quality of the goods hanging outside.

"The soft quality is very good," she said, "and about a third of the price of Sweden. I will buy about 5 or 6 jackets and trousers to take home, they are very trendy now and make good profits. But to make big money I need a constant supply," she said, "I hope to get a big stock for the winter." She found a shop and manufacturer, she presented her card and asked if he spoke English.

"Yes, of course, we have to for the tourists, also French and German," he said.

"Good, I want some samples of your make to take back to Sweden, but I want very good prices," she almost demanded. A deal was struck, and Agneta now had her source of supply at agreed prices, she would confirm the agreement by email as soon as she got back home. "We will now go back to the ship and I will buy you lunch," she said.

"No," Jon said, "I won't be allowed to board the boat."

"Oh, I see," she said, "is that because you might stow away?"

"Possibly, I don't know," he admitted, "let's find a restaurant and have a lunch of local food," he said. A very nice looking restaurant was in the square where they first met. Agneta was a lucky lady, no jewellery, her attraction was her beauty and personality plus a lot of sexuality.

After their lunch they took a slow walk back to the ship, when they reached the gangway with all the packages,

Agneta showed her wristband and keycard, "Can my friend come aboard?" she asked.

"No, I'm sorry, it's company policy about non-cruisers boarding the ship," the huge security guard said.

"Don't worry," Jon said, "perhaps we can meet later for dinner, Tunis is full of good eateries," he added.

"Yes, that'll be nice, shall we say, here at 7 o'clock?"

"Yes, that'll be terrific." Jon moved quickly, he booked out of his apartment, bought a suitcase and booked in to the 5* Tunisian Palace Hotel. His plan was to take her there for dinner, and then seduce her.

Seven o'clock soon came round, Jon had booked a double luxury room overlooking some beautiful gardens, the scent of the plants and flowers would add to the seduction scene. When she walked down the gangway Jon's chest started to pump, she looked fabulous in a yellow and black knee-length dress with a discreet split up the right thigh. She was also wearing a beautiful pearl and diamond necklace, if real, about $50,000 worth, plus diamond rings with fair-sized stones, and a diamond encrusted watch. Oh dear, he thought, as the black mist started to descend. "Hey," she said (Hello in Swedish) as she looked at him in his YSL jacket and slacks, "you look very handsome," she said, and kissed him on both cheeks but being careful not to spoil her lipgloss!

He hailed a taxi that was waiting at the rank, "The Tunisian Palace Hotel," he said to the driver.

"Yes sir-r-r," the cabbie replied.

"Is that where you are staying?" she asked.

"Yes," he said, "but I only moved in today. Before I had a self-catering apartment, but I realised I prefer the finer things in life, with some good service." Good lord, he thought, I'm telling the truth for once! "I've heard the restaurant is excellent," he added.

They arrived at the venue and walked in through the auto doors into the Arab-influenced foyer. It was busy as Jon guided Agneta to the Carthagian bar. They were greeted by a young girl in belly dancer's costume and was shown to a table. She then produced an enormous wine list, bowed and walked away with a wiggle. "Shall we celebrate your successful business day with some champagne?" Jon suggested.

"Yes please," Agneta said, "I love it!"

Jon ordered a bottle of Chrystal '99, he didn't know, but the price said that it was a good vintage! "Cheers, and good trading with your leather boutiques," Jon said as he raised his glass and chinked Agneta's glass.

"Thank you," she said, and blew him a kiss, "why does your accent change sometimes?" she asked.

"Oh, it's because I've spent so much time in London talking to cockney car dealers," he felt himself blushing, "my sister, in Dublin says the same!" he lied.

"What's cockney?"

Jon laughed, "It's the accent of London, especially among car dealers, they have their own language. For instance, a car is a 'jam jar'," he explained.

She laughed, "Does that mean that my Mercedes is a German jam jar?"

"Yes!" said Jon, and they both laughed loudly. She is wonderful, Jon was thinking, absolutely fabulous, I could settle down with her, but that was a crazy thought. "Do you need to do any more shopping?" he asked.

"Yes, shoes!" she replied, "but you won't want to be with me when I go shopping for them," she said.

"Oh, I don't mind, it'll be nice just being with you," he said, very smoothly.

She reached across the table and held his hand and didn't let go, then she said something that really rocked his world, "As you're not allowed on the ship, we can go up to your room."

Jon felt sand-blasted, amazed, shocked and happy at the same time but played it cool and gathered his breath. He took time to fill her glass again, he hoped it wasn't the champagne talking, but she'd only had one glass. She meant what she said, he thought.

Their dinner was exotic and a little spicy, but delicious, the service couldn't be better. In the distance they could hear music, Jon hadn't looked around the hotel, but he guessed there was a nightclub near by. They left the restaurant having had a marvellous dinner, a bottle of exquisite champagne and two balloons of Napoleon brandy. They walked towards the melodic sound, a doorman dressed in Aladdin garb opened the very ornate double doors for them, "Good evening," he said, as they entered a dimly lit, but not too dark, venue. It was quite busy with Aladdins and belly dancers serving drinks to lots of customers. The music was supplied by a group of five, playing modern western songs. They found a table for two and ordered two cocktails. Sipping the drinks, Agneta gazed into Jon's eyes with a smouldering look, and Jon ogled her jewellery first, and then looked into her eyes. The magical sex spell was set. They danced closely to slow songs for about an hour and a half, at midnight they decided to go up to Jon's room on the first floor. He opened the door and ushered Agneta inside, almost immediately she put her arms around his neck and found his mouth with hers. The kiss lingered for quite a while as they began to undress each other, zips, buttons and buckles were quickly dealt with until they were both naked. They fell on to the bed with arms and legs entwining, moaning in ecstasy.

She turned on to her stomach and said, "Like dogs do it, from behind," she added. Jon had only heard of the position but had never indulged, it was fantastic and their orgasms were amazing and simultaneous. They laid side by side gasping, and laughing nervously.

Jon rose from the bed and went over to the mini bar and found two miniature cognacs, he poured them into ordinary wine glasses and they sat on the bed sipping the nectar. "Get dressed and I'll call you a taxi," he said.

"No you won't," she almost shouted, "I'm staying the night, I haven't finished with you yet!" she laughed loudly.

"What about your 'check in' back on the boat?" Jon asked.

"I'll phone them, I have the number in my bag," she said.

The phone call only took five minutes and she settled back on to the king-size bed, she was still wearing her diamonds. The black mist started to descend once again, but Jon pushed it to the back of his mind and joined her on the bed. Still sipping her brandy with one hand, she fondled his genitals and kissed him passionately. His ardour returned and they made love again during which she rolled on top of him. The diamond and pearl necklace dangled in his face, they gleamed and sparkled in a tantalizing way and once again the black mist descended .... but it didn't affect their orgasms. She screamed and said something in Swedish, she then started laughing. "What did you say?" Jon asked.

"I called myself the 'bejewelled fucker'," they laughed loudly.

More brandy from the mini bar was poured, Jon went into the en suite and ran the hot tap to freshen up. As the steam rose on to the mirror words appeared on the glass 'U.O.ME' and underneath was the letter 'S' as some sort of signature. Jon's mouth dropped as he looked at the demonic message, he broke into a cold sweat, no, he thought as he wiped the mirror, it must be the brandy, I'm seeing things. When he returned to the bedroom Agneta was asleep, the empty brandy glass was on his pillow, he was still in a sweat over the 'message'. On the bed beside his 'bejewelled fucker' he laid looking at the ceiling and feeling scared, very scared. He fell into a troubled slumber as Agneta snored very slightly and quietly.

Agneta ordered a room service breakfast, coffee, toast and scrambled eggs. She gently shook Jon who woke with a start, shouting, "I'm sorry, I'm sorry." Agneta jumped back as Jon sat upright wiping the sweat from his forehead. "Bad dream about a car accident I had in London," he lied, thinking quickly.

"Oh I see," she said, as she put his tray on the bed and kissed his hot forehead. They showered and dressed after breakfast, Agneta looked at herself in the long mirror, and laughed, "I can't go out dressed like this," she said.

Jon also laughed, and said, "What size are you?"

"I can get away with size ten trousers and a 34 top with size 5 shoes," she replied.

"Okay," he said, "I'll be back in twenty minutes," and left the room.

True to his word, he was back as said, with a pair of white trousers, a navy striped silk top and a pair of flat white casual walking shoes. "Where did you get these?" she asked.

"In a little boutique opposite the hotel," he answered.

"They're fabulous," she said, and went in to the bathroom to shower, she had left all her jewellery on the dressing table. The temptation for him was enormous, but he resisted it, this one would be different. He put the mirror message to the back of his mind, he put it down to the alcohol. She came out of the shower wrapped in a white robe and couldn't wait to try on the new casual outfit. She oohed and aahed when she saw the finished image in the mirror. "It's perfect," she said, "thank you, how much do I owe you?"

"No, no,"Jon said, "call it a gift to a bejewelled fucker!" he said, and they laughed.

Having just one day left of the Tunis stop-over, they spent it shopping for gifts for all her family, including her sister Gretta. Gretta he thought, no, that's impossible, there must be thousands of Grettas in Sweden, he put the daft thought to the back of his brain. Her ship was due to sail at 6 o'clock so they had a room service late lunch and sex at his hotel. At 4.30pm a taxi was hailed and they went to the boat with all her packages. Jon was allowed to go on to the cruiser, but only as far as the entrance lobby, with a security person standing by. They exchanged loving words and promises to meet again (sooner than Agneta thought) She gave him her card, saying, "Please don't leave it too long." With moist eyes she kissed him. He watched as she walked into the body of the boat, she looked back and blew him a kiss.

He asked the security person what their next port of call was. "Palermo, then Rome," came the answer. Fuck, he thought, Rome, that sounds dodgy. He would leave it for a couple of weeks and then phone her to see what her reaction was when she heard his voice.

New Rochelle (New York)

Liz Fenner's memorial service was very well attended, her sister made a drama of mourning. She was comforted by a young good-looking man who kept his arm around her shoulder throughout the service. (A nice bit of Hollywood, Mel thought.) After the service the young man asked Mel when he thought the will would be read. "Two years," Mel said, and walked away from him, how many times did these people have to be fucking-well told?

"We had a visit at the office from Liz Fenner's sister this afternoon," Mary-Lou told Mel over dinner, "she wanted the keys to Liz's Manhattan apartment. I told her that it was impossible until the will is read in two years time," she said, "I nearly called 911 when she started to go berserk, kicking chairs and screaming obscenities, but the man with her calmed her down, as she left she shouted 'it'll all be mine, just you wait and see'," Mary-Lou told Mel. He asked if there were any other relatives. "There's an adopted son and daughter, and her mother-in-law whom she was strangely close to," she told Mel, then, "I haven't told you that, okay?"

"Yeah, it's forgotten," he said, "so it looks as if it won't be 'all her sister's'."

"You said you'd forget it!" Mary-Lou said.

"Yeah, sorry, oh, just one more thing, would Mr Fenner her ex-husband, have a claim, after all it all came from him originally?"

"No," she said, "divorce in New York State is complete severance unless specified in her will, which I doubt," she answered, "now, please get on with your dinner!"

Tunis

The message on the mirror was still on Jon's mind, I fancy a short cruise, he said to himself. May be along the north African coast, calling in to Casablanca and Gibraltar, perhaps. 'Tunis Travarama' was on the Avenue Afrique, the middle aged woman smiled, and in perfect English said, "Can I help you?"

"Yes," said Jon, "I would like to take a cruise, about ten days, possibly calling at Casablanca and also Gibraltar, for some duty-free!" he said.

"Yes, of course," the lady said with a nice smile. "We have exactly what you want, leaving in two days time, is that too soon?" she asked.

"No, that's fantastic," he replied, "how much for an outside stateroom with balcony, preferably midship?"

"I'll check the computer," she said. Sitting at her desk, she typed away at the keyboard, then smiled, "Yes, we're in luck," she said, "cabin 330, deck 3, midship, and it is priced at $2,850 or 2,200 euros," she answered.

"That sounds perfect, let's do it, I'll do the business now," he said with a broad smile.

"Any visa charges will be collected if you go ashore, when you're on board."

He paid in dollars and received all the paperwork. On his way back to the hotel he called in at the Yves St Laurent boutique and bought some 'Going Cruising?' clothes. Suit, white shorts, shirts, deck shoes and a very nice tuxedo with all the dress accessories to go with it. Once again, the young man received a very nice 'keep the change' tip, bowed and said 'thank you sir-r-r'. He was $1500 poorer but ready for the trip. Back at the hotel he hung his purchases in the wardrobe. He would pack and be at the cruise reception area at the quayside, in two days time.

The Afrique Queen

Not a huge cruise liner, it's passenger capacity was 2,000, but big enough and very luxurious with a Franco Moorish decor. He found his stateroom, with his luggage already delivered. He poured a large whiskey and soda and said 'it's five o'clock somewhere' dropped in a cube of ice saying, 'cheers' as he took a large gulp. He walked out on to the balcony and sat at the small circular table, he was suddenly aware of a woman standing at the rail, "Good afternoon," he said.

"Oh, hello," she said, smiling with almost perfect teeth, "are you taking the afternoon air?"

"Er, yes, and a nice libation!" he answered, raising his glass and saying, "happy cruising!"

"Where are you from?" she asked.

"Originally from Ireland, but I've spent a lot of time in London, I buy and sell expensive cars."

"Oh, a second-hand car dealer, eh!" she laughed.

"Well, no, they're mostly brand new imports," he lied.

"Oh, I'm sorry," she said.

"Oh, no apology needed!" he smiled. "What do you do?" he asked, and then said, "I'm so rude and sorry, I'm Keiron Pearce, originally from Dublin but now a resident of old London town. Camden Town to be exact," he said.

"And I'm Hannah Golding from Hove in Sussex, getting away from the hustle and bustle of business and work. I manufacture denim jeans and skirts, quite successfully. In fact, trade is very good, even during this damn recession," she added.

He noticed quite a large diamond ring on her right hand, obviously not an engagement ring, at least not a current one. He looked again and reckoned it to be about 4 carats, if it was real, it's sparkle and light colour changing suggested that it was. "Well, if you will excuse me, I must unpack," Jon said, adding, "I hope to see you later."

"So do I," she said with a very nice smile.

He showered and changed into a new white blouson and black trousers. As he was leaving his stateroom Hannah came out of hers, "Oh, hello again!" they said simultaneously, and laughed. "How about we take a walk around the deck, have a nice cocktail and go in to dinner together?" he asked.

"I was hoping you'd say that," she said. They walked about half way around the ship then went in to the main body to the 'Bar Americain'. It had a jazz art deco theme of decor, all chrome and black. They sat at the end of the bar on chrome tubular stools.

"How about some champagne to set the mood for the evening?" he suggested.

"Oh, yes please," she laughed, "what a wonderful way to start my holiday!" she enthused.

Jon took a good look at her, she wasn't beautiful, but very attractive with a very comely figure and a lovely cleavage. It was at this point that he saw the multi-diamond two tiered necklace, about twenty good sized stones and of very good colour and quality. The bottle of 'Chrystal' arrived and the barman poured two flutes of the golden bubbly, "Cheers! Happy cruising!" he said as they chinked glasses. She looked at him with a wanton smile as she sipped the'Chrystal nectar'. With the bottle empty they decided to go in to dinner, as they walked out of the bar and on to the concourse, she took his arm, whoops he thought, the old charm is still working! Just a short walk to the stern, was the 'Casablanca Restaurant' with large pictures of Humphrey Bogart and Ingrid Bergman illuminated with blue spotlights. A little 20th century they thought but the food was the most important thing, which was very good, especially Jon's fillet steak. Hannah's sea bass was not only very big, but delicious. After dinner they just sat talking about their lives, she had been married to a gambler but she hadn't known until his fashion business folded and the bailiffs moved in on the bank's behest. The house and the cars went, luckily there were no children involved. She'd started her business in a little shop in Brighton, with just two machinists and working 14 hours a day, 7 days a week. But now she had an industrial workshop and employed 30 people. Nice, Jon thought, very nice.

"What make of cars do you import?" she asked.

"Mercedes, Audi, Maseratti, Lexus and occasionally Ferrari," he said.

"What about Rolls, Bentley and Jaguar?" she asked.

"I don't have to," he said with a smile, "they're made in England!"

"Oh, yes of course," she giggled, covering her full-lipped mouth.

"Who's looking after your business while you're on holiday?" he asked.

"My brother Monty, he's brilliant, an absolute brick. Do you gamble?" Hannah asked.

"No, it's a mugs game, the odds are always in the house's favour, the ordinary punter stands no chance," he said.

"Well, I wouldn't mind a little 'spiel' in the casino," she announced.

"Okay," Jon said, "I don't mind watching."

They found a chair at the black-jack table, "Hit me!" she said to the dealer as she was holding 16, "Wow!" she said, "a 5, that's 21, dealer pays black-jack." Hannah played for about an hour and finished winning $200. But Jon had had his attention taken by a good looking woman on the roulette table, wearing a veritable array of jewellery. Necklace, two diamond bracelets, a watch and three diamond rings. Wow he thought, that's my kind of girl! But oh no, two possibilities on one trip, how am I goig to see to both in ten days, or can I? he pondered. He decided not to get too involved with Hannah for now, but at the same time get to know this roulette woman, if he could. But softly, softly, catchy monkey! he thought.

"Well, how did you do?" he asked Hannah.

"I won a few bucks," she said, smiling.

At one o'clock Jon feigned tiredness and walked Hannah back to her stateroom, as she opened her door, he opened his, he kissed her on both cheeks. They exchanged pleasantries and she went in and closed the door, he didn't, he stayed outside and closed the door loudly, but he switched on the interior lights so that they could be seen from her balcony. He scooted down the corridor and made his way to the casino, she of the diamonds was still sitting there with a decent pile of high value chips in front of her. The diamonds, if real, were to die for, they caught the light beautifully, with many exquisite hues and colours. 'They're genuine all right' he said to himself, 'the real McCoy'. He stood opposite where she was seated, just watching the action, she's good, he thought, six straight winning bets, he decided to bet off-table and copy her. After about 7 or 8 bets she realised what he was doing and smiled while wagging her forefinger at him. He smiled and gave her the thumbs up. After a while he realised he'd won about $1500. Suddenly the casino manager tapped him on the shoulder, he had been watching them and decided that they had some sort of scam going on, he didn't know how but he was sure that somehow they were working together. "I'm sorry sir, but the table is now closed for you, the lady can stay."

"Why?" Jon asked, "I don't even know her."

"I'm sorry sir, it's the casino's decision," the man said, "you are of course free to play everywhere else in the room."

The woman watched what was occurring, then stood, collected her chips and went to the cash grille to collect her winnings. Jon was watching the black-jack when he received another tap on the shoulder, "You kept very calm with that heavy guy," she said in a New York accent.

"Oh, I don't worry about people like him unless they have more to accuse me of. I'm not really a gambler, I just like a flutter now and then. I won a little but it won't change my life," he laughed.

"I like you," she said, "you've got a good slant on life, my name's Rosa, Rosa Mitchum. I'm Robert Mitchum's niece, do you know him?"

"Oh yes," said Jon, "Cape Fear, Danger Road and many, many war films, a wonderful film actor."

"Yuh, that's right, but I didn't really know him, he was on the other side of the family if you know what I mean, but he was a generous man and spread his legacy fortune right across the family," she shook her bracelets, "know what I mean?" she said.

"My name's Keiron Pearce, from Dublin and London, hence my crazy confused accent!" he admitted.

"I thought I could hear some Irish," she said, "what do you do?"

"I import cars from mainland Europe, only expensive ones, and sell them to wealthy people in England."

"Could you sell me a Bentley?" Rosa asked.

"No," he said, "because there is a Bentley showroom on

Fifth Avenue, I'm guessing that's in your neighbourhood?"

"Yeah," she said, "Manhattan, although originally Brooklyn, I lived in the same street as Barbra Streisand, in fact my grandmother and her mother were at the same school," she enthused.

"Really," Jon said, looking at the gems and not giving a hoot about Barbra Streisand or her mother. "Would you like to go into the bar for a night-cap?"

"I thought you'd never ask!" she replied. They went in to the 'Bar Americain' and Jon ordered two brandy cocktails, as they sat at the bar on corner-shaped stools they talked for well over an hour and downed more cocktails. Rosa more than Jon, she was showing signs of being slightly drunk, but she held it well, it only showed in her slightly slurred speech.

Jon looked at his watch, it was 2.30am, "I think we should climb the slumber hill," he said.

"Yes," Rosa agreed. They walked arm in arm back to her suite on the prestige deck (nice, he thought, this lady is wealthy). They parted with a kiss on each cheek and said that they would meet again tomorrow.

Jon went to sleep with only one thing on his mind, diamonds, and he meant to get his hands on them by hook or by crook. In a dream he was walking through a black mist into a cave full of jewels, and sitting at the end was Satan smiling and saying 'these are all yours Jon, to have for eternity, you know what I want, you owe me!'..... 'Yes' Jon said, 'but I must fulfill my quota of kills.' He woke in a cold sweat and went into the bathroom to have a cold shower, it was 5 o'clock and the sun was rising. He stood with just a towel around his waist, looking out to sea, thinking what would his future be, he knew it would only be a short one so he was going to live it to the full "starting today" he said to the world loudly, at the balcony door.

He went out on to the balcony and was surprised by Hannah sitting at her little table with coffee, "Hi," she said, with just a bath towel wrapped around her, "I had room service bring me a pot of coffee, would you like some?" she asked.

"Yes, please," he said.

"Climb over," she said, "we don't need two balconies to drink coffee!" she laughed. He climbed over the rail and as he did his towel slipped to reveal all, he quickly pulled up the coverage! "Don't be shy," she said, "I've seen it all before," she giggled.

He changed the subject by saying, "I'll have mine black please." It's said that a lot of women are 'morning people' sexually, and Hannah certainly was. She stood to pour his coffee then bent and kissed him, a long lingering and passionate kiss that he felt down to his toes. She reached down inside the towel and felt his erection building, she got down on her knees and took his manhood in her mouth and gently moved her lips up and down on it. His orgasm was immense, even Hannah almost shouted "Wow, that must have been the second coming!" as she ran into the bathroom.

He sat waiting for her to return, then suddenly heard, "Keiron, in here, now," she demanded. It was obvious to Jon that Hannah had not had sex for quite some time, she enjoyed three orgasms, each one louder than the last. "You are amazing," she shouted on her last thrustings. They laid side by side gasping, even though they were at sea it was hot, even at seven in the morning.

They showered together, then rubbed each other down with towels, Hannah didn't stop kissing Jon, but he only half enjoyed it. In fact, he'd had enough sex, he stood and said, "I must get dressed, shall we meet down at the pool?"

"May be later, I want to do a little shopping in the ship's mall," she answered.

As he climbed over the rail a male passenger on the neighbouring balcony smiled and winked, touching his nose, "Morning," he said, still smiling a knowing smile. Jon just smiled and nodded, all he could think of were the diamonds, but there was something not quite right about her story. Would a woman who was building up a business spend about £150,000 on jewellery, may be £50,000, he would have to take a closer look at them, but how? could they be fake? he wondered. Jon walked down to the coffee shop and had a light breakfast of coffee and toast. The pool area was not yet too crowded, he bought a novel in the gift shop, something to do with the surrender of Singapore, a WW11 story. He had a choice of sunbeds and selected one that was, for the time being, in the shade. Settling down, he opened the book and was soon getting in to the story. The sun came around the super-structure of the ship and bathed him in heat. Applying some high factor cream, a shadow crossed him and stopped, he looked up to see Rosa Mitchum standing at his feet, "Hi good looking, how you doing?" she asked with a beautiful smile.

"I'm fine," he said, jumping to his feet, "are you staying, or just passing through?"

"I'll stay if I may," she said.

"Please, dear lady," he said with a little blarney, and pulled a sunbed closer to his and a little table for her bits and pieces. "How is your holiday so far?"

"Oh, it's fine, but I've been a little lonely, I'm a 'people' person, can't stand being alone," she admitted, looking deep into his eyes, sexily.

Whoops, he thought, as the black mist started to descend. After about an hour and a half the sun was beginning to burn, so they decided to bring over a parasol on a stand. The waiter helped to set it up, "Would you like a drink sir-r-r?" the young man asked.

"Yes, good idea," Jon said, "Rosa, what is your pleasure?"

"I'll have a large manhattan, with lots of ice," she said.

"I'll have a cold beer, nice and tall please," he asked.

"Yes sir-r-r," said the waiter.

"It's five o'clock somewhere," Rosa laughed as she chinked her glass against Jon's.

"It must be," he said, "round about India I'd say!" they laughed

"Well, here's to India!" Rosa laughed.

Another round of drinks and they decided to go for some lunch, he saw Hannah walking around the deck above carrying quite a few packages, luckily she didn't see him with Rosa, but he had made no promises after their sexual encounter and no arrangement to meet, just a loose 'see you later'. They had a lobster salad with it shelled, with a fruit salad to follow, and coffe and cognac. "What shall we do this afternoon?" Rosa asked

"Well, perhaps we could go back to the pool deck, and just chill," he said.

"Yeah, and then we could go back to my suite and fuck!" Jon was shocked, and laughed nervously. "Does that idea not appeal to you?" she asked

"Er, yes, but the way you said it was a sudden, wow!" he replied, "Let's meet later and have dinner and see what happens," he suggested.

"Okay," she said, "but I still want sex!" she giggled.

"Well, perhaps you might be lucky later, who knows!" He'd never been propositioned in this un-subtle way before, but he would like to see her jewellery again, he was sure hers was the real thing.

He didn't know how Rosa obtained his phone number, she must have asked at reception, "Hi honey, it's sexy Rosa, dinner is being served in my suite at 7 o'clock, sharp. No need to dress, in fact, don't wear anything!" she giggled.

"Okay," Jon said, "but what will people think when I walk along the corridors?"

"They'll think, wow!" she shouted, and hung up.

He arrived at her suite at exactly 7 o'clock, but was dressed in white slacks and a navy silk shirt. He knocked on the door which was ajar, and just opened slowly, he walked in and gasped at the sight that confronted him. Rosa was sitting naked at the table, apart from every piece of jewellery she owned, and a smile, "C'm in and undress!" she said.

He sat down and undressed but only to his 'skimpies', it was then that he noticed that Rosa was wearing a thong. "Well, at least we are partially dressed for dinner!" he said.

Her breasts were firm and proud, and the natural cleavage contained the necklace beautifully. Rosa lifted the covers on the dishes, lobster, caviar and a well tossed bowl of salad, and of course, strawberries and cream with two bottles of Chrystal champagne. The toast was to 'cruising' and they chinked glasses. The food was fantastic and they sat back in their chairs very, very well fed, and burst into laughter. "Have you ever done this before?" Rosa asked.

"Yes, dozens of times," Jon replied, "in my dreams!"

Rosa giggled, the Crystal was going to her head, she stood and poured two brandies from a nearby table, "Now, let's just relax and gather our strength for some very serious sex, okay?" Their sexual session lasted until midnight when the food and alcohol took it's toll on their stamina and Rosa fell asleep. Jon could have done the evil deed there and then, but the timing was wrong, it would have to be nearer the end of the cruise. He looked at the gems, but strangely the black mist didn't descend. He was sure that these diamonds were genuine and beautiful and he would soon have them. Oh yes, he thought, $150,000 worth, he couldn't let them slip through his fingers, he would now work out how to do it without being suspected or caught. The next port of call was Algiers, which would be at midday today, good, he could spend some time with Hannah and possibly find out the provenance of her jewellery.

Algiers

A beautiful Moorish city, over-populated and very, very busy. The ship docked at ten o'clock in the morning with most of the passengers eager to disembark and go into the souks and casbahs to snap up souvenirs that after two weeks at home, would finish up in a cupboard and be forgotten. He saw Hannah in the queue to go ashore, but luckily she didn't see him, today he wanted to be alone and not go ashore. After all, he lived in an Arab city and knew what going ashore would mean, 'very cheap today for you sir-r-r', 'feel the quality sir-r-r', 'come into my shop and see my wonderful bargains sir-r-r'. No thank you, he thought, he was on the cruise for one reason and one reason only, diamonds, and to kill if need be. Every morning he had woken with diamonds on his mind, and the black mist descended. Only a few days to go and Rosa's would be his.

Tangier

Another Arab/Moorish city and the same old souvenirs, statuettes, spices, outrageous shirts and other soon-to-be-forgotten garments, no thanks he thought, I'll stay on board and enjoy some peaceful relaxation. He called Hannah and conveyed his thoughts to her.

"I've had enough sun for the time being," she said, "and I feel the same about going ashore, let's see what a half-empty ship has got to offer, see you for a coffee at eleven-ish in the coffee shop, okay?" she suggested. At the rendez-vous, Jon would take a good look at the large single stone rings, those babies must be real, he thought, this could be a double event!

Jon went into the shower in a very good mood, he was even singing. Afterwards he moved over to the wash basin, and on the steamed up mirror was the word 'SOON'. His blood ran cold, he looked again and the glass was clear. His mood immediately changed, he dressed slowly, feeling inwardly sick, but he was too far down the road of damnation. There was no return and no repentance, he was the devil's property now, only what was left of his life could be a consolation of wealth and luxury. He had no alternative but to carrry on killing and robbing, he would never be rid of this black mist and his hunger for diamonds and money and the devil.

He met Hannah as arranged, she looked marvellous, wearing a white silk self-patterned top and navy shorts, her slender legs were shapely and tanned, "Hi babe, why the long face?" she asked.

"Oh, nothing, I think the heat must be getting to me, now that the ship is half empty I may go for a swim in the pool later."

"I'll join you," she said, "I feel the same, even 10 minutes after a cool shower, the humidity must be bursting the barometer." They drank their coffee in silence, with Jon just staring at her rings, "They're gorgeous aren't they," she said.

"Yes," he said, "to die for!"

"2.9 carat matching stones that I bought from a dealer in Hatton Garden a few months ago and had them made into rings," she told him. He smiled and thought perhaps he would be getting some of his old merchandise back! "40 grands worth," she said, "I thought, I owe them to myself after all the hard work I've put in to the business. The necklace, the watch and the bracelet were what I managed to hang on to after the divorce, if my ex knew, he'd blow a gasket! He could spend many happy hours in a West End casino with a blonde bimbo with what they're worth."

Jon laughed, "He sounds like a bad man," he said.

"Only when it came to gambling and young blondes with big tits and short skirts. He was very good looking, very charismatic, he could sell ice to the Eskimos, and I probably still love him, but as there were no children involved I decided enough was enough and severed all connections with him. Since he heard I've done well he wants us to get back together, no way, NO WAY!" she said, loudly, " he'd only fritter it away. That's enough of my life, tell me more about you."

(Into Kieron mode) "I was born in Dublin and lived there until I was 20 and then came to London to seek my fortune. I lived with my sister, a successful private doctor, but then I started dealing in expensive cars thanks to a loan from her, and now I have a turnover of about two million a year," he lied.

"What sort of expensive car?" she asked.

"Oh, the usual, Mercedes, BMW, Lexus, top range Range Rovers even the odd Bentley, in other words, anything over 30 grand," he said, "I advertise them in good trade mags and papers."

"A cut above a second hand car dealer then," Hannah said.

"Yes, I suppose," Jon agreed, "but no Fords, Toyotas, Renaults, Citroens etc., too cheap!"

"I've got a Renault Espace," she said, with a serious look on her face, and then laughed, "it's a very useful vehicle!"

"I'm sure it is," he said, "but not for my customers!"

"Fuck off, you snob," she laughed. That was the first time he had heard her swear. "Is the casino open during the day?" she asked.

"Let's go and see," he replied. They walked from the coffee shop through the mall to the casino, and to their surprise not only was it open, but there were quite a few midday punters. They managed to find two seats at the roulette table, Jon changed a $100 bill in to chips, Hannah changed 100 euros.

"I think I'll go red and even block," she said, putting 40

euros on the table.

"It's going to be black and the odd block for me," Jon said.

"Red, 24," the croupier said.

"Yes!" Hannah said, quite loudly, as her winnings were pushed on to the table and Jon's chips were taken.

"Oh well," he said, "I'll try again." He did and this time he won, not much but he would try and build up a pile. After about three hours they were running about level in their winnings, nearing $1000 each, "Not a bad afternoon's work," Jon said, as they cashed in their chips.

"We missed out on lunch," Hannah said, "let's go and eat, but only a sandwich or something, don't want to spoil dinner." Their next port of call was Gibraltar.

Gibraltar

Being British territory, Jon realised he had to be careful, and wore his wide brimmed fedora when he went ashore. It was well pulled down over his eyes, CCTV was probably used here because of the electronic, booze and jewellery stores. But one dire problem would be British TV possibly showing his face as being wanted for murder. Hannah and Jon walked into a 'Brit' pub for a well-earned cool drink, he spotted the TV set up on the wall above the bar, and positioned himself facing it and therefore barring Hannah's view. He watched the screen intently, but thankfully he was now old news and his picture didn't appear. "You don't need your hat in here," she said.

"Oh, sorry, I didn't realise I was still wearing it, it's so lightweight," he lied.

"Shall we stay ashore for dinner?" she suggested.

"Good idea," Jon said.

"By the time we go back to the ship and change etc, we'll be starving, we can spend some winnings in the best restaurant in Gib."

"Sounds good to me," Jon said. He stopped a taxi, "What's the best eating place in Gib?" he asked the driver.

"The Rock Hotel," came the reply.

"Okay, let's go," Jon said, and they got into the taxi. Anywhere in Gibraltar is 15 minutes, the Rock Hotel was about half way to the top of the rock. The building was actually built into the granite and a beautiful colonial mansion facade fronted the large venue.

St Petersburg

Vasili's reputation and power had waned amongst his peers in the underworld and the brotherhood. The word had gone out that he'd been made to climb down from catching the man who'd killed one of his family and robbed them of thousands of dollars. In short, he'd been made to look a fool, and he would have to do something about it. To make things worse, a rival gang had robbed one of his gambling outlets and burnt out one of his Lear jets.

He summoned Mikhail and five of his best men, "Go and find me a substitute for this Jon Weston, and we will bring him back here and make a big show of killing him, IN FUCKING PUBLIC," he shouted. "He must be English, and look like Weston," he demanded.

It was a very warm day down by the Hermitage, tourists by the hundred from all over the world, "What does an English tourist look like?" He parked the Mercedes opposite the queue, Mikhail needed to get back into his brother's good books. Over $500,000 had been spent looking for Jon Weston, he read the description and studied the photograph.

James Sumner, an accountant from London, with the obligatory large lens camera over his shoulder, walked along the snaking file of people to enter the museum to see its treasures. The Mercedes crawled slowly along the road and then the rear door opened and two henchmen got out and grabbed the Londoner, pulling him into the large car. His camera fell in the gutter as the horrified queue watched. The car screamed away at break-neck speed, Mikhail turned around in the front passenger seat and said, "English?"

"Yes, yes, what's going on?" he shouted, "let me out, I'm a British citizen."

The Russians laughed, "But you are in Russia now," Mikhail said.

"What do you want, money? I'll give you money," he cried, and tried to reach into his pocket for his wallet. One of the men grabbed his wrist with an iron grip.

"No, we don't want money, we've got plenty," Mikhail said, "we want English lessons or perhaps we want to teach the

English a lesson." He laughed.

James was pushed in to Vasili's office, Vasili stood and looked him up and down, walked around him and then read the description while he looked at Jon Weston's photograph. "Very good, Mikhail, you and your men have done very well. Sit down Mr Weston," Vasili said.

"My name is James Sumner, I'm an accountant from London," James answered.

"NO, you are Jonathan Weston from London and you killed a member of my family, stole her jewellery and threw her body into the sea."

"No, no, I can prove I'm James Sumner, here, here, look I have my passport," he cried as he offered it to Vasili who slapped it out of his hand and then slapped James across the face sending his spectacles across the marble floor. One of his henchmen stood on them, smashing them to pieces.

"Put the word out that we have brought Jon Weston back. Tell London, New York and Rome, and we will bring him to justice. Find me the best make-up artist to make this man look more like Weston and then take his photograph with a copy of the day's newspaper above his head, " he said calmly, but with menace.

James was shaking, sweating and crying at the same time, "You've got the wrong man," he shouted. He received a heavy slap across the face again that almost rendered him unconscious. Mikhail walked towards him with a hypodermic syringe and plunged it into his neck, blackness descended, James Sumner was as good as dead.

The word was soon spreading around the world's TV networks, the web and all other media, announcing that the 'Cruise' killer was in custody in Russia and would be put on trial there.

Yonkers - New York State

Mel Novak threw his newspaper into the air and shouted, "The Russians have got him!"

Mary-Lou rushed in from the kitchen, "I don't believe it, I presume you are talking about Jon Weston?" she asked.

"Yes, but I don't know how they did it," he said.

"A very tenacious people, the Russians, and they've got friends everywhere," she said.

Mel looked at the picture of Jon Weston, it had been a long time since he last saw him, but it definitely looked like him, or did it? Mel thought, but now it was way beyond his tenure, and after all, he had, allegedly, murdered a Russian citizen.

In Los Angeles, Liz Fenner's sister had been made bankrupt and had tried to convince a bank that she was the beneficiary of a large fortune, with forged documents, in cash and property, by mis-representation. She had been charged with attempted fraud, found guilty, and imprisoned in the state women's penitentiary for two years, with a twelve month parole order. Mary-Lou said, "She'll only do 6 months, otherwise she'll go crazy in there, I know, I've been to these places on client visits, they are the pits!"

St Petersburg

Vasili had put out an edict to punish the raiders of his casino's and the arsonists that burned his jet. Four lesser members of a rival family were brought to him and paraded before his ornate Louis XIV desk. "You know what to do," he said to Mikhail. The four unfortunates were taken to an enormous basement area, two video cameras had been set up to record what was about to happen. They were suspended upside down, naked, above industrial cattle carcass grinders. When these were switched on the screams were blood-curdling.

Mikhail shouted, in Russian, "You will soon be fertilizer," and the victims were lowered into the machinery, screaming, which soon stopped as they were devoured by the spinning knives. The cameras had recorded the whole event, with sound, which made it more horrific.

"I WANT A COPY OF THE DVD SENT TO EVERYONE IN ST PETERSBURG," shouted Vasili, and when Weston goes in, he goes feet first." They laughed. "And I want recordings sent to Scotland Yard to show them how to treat murderers of women," he added. James Sumner was dragged from his cell-like room still in a drugged state, then suspended by his arms. He was lowered, feet first, into the grinder. His screams stopped at about his midriff, it was all recorded, sound and vision, in colour.

New Scotland Yard (London)

Chief Inspector Lloyd opened the stiff envelope and pulled out the disc, the note attached read 'Jonathan Weston's justice'. He put it in his DVD player and what he saw made him feel sick, he'd seen a lot of horrific things in his long career, but this was the worst. "Get me NYPD, I want to speak to Captain Colletti at the 30th Precinct," he said to the operator. "Hello sir, I'll get straight to the point, I've just seen the most disgusting DVD of the execution of Jonathan Weston by the Russians. I won't go into detail, but it was completely barbaric, strictly from the dark ages of the tzars. Perhaps you'd like to pass on the information to Lt Novak."

"Okay, Chief Inspector, I'll do that, thanks for calling." The Captain hung up. I'll send it to him, he thought.

Yonkers - New York State

"The Russian mafia have executed Jonathan Weston," Mel told Mary-Lou, "in the most horrific way. But he had no trial, just captured and executed, they don't waste any time, those bastards, do they?"

"I think sometimes that's better than keeping them on death row for years," Mary-Lou said.

"Yeah, may be you're right," Mel said, "it's a shame we couldn't have brought him to good old American justice," he added.

"Yeah, and he would be a VIP on death row for 10 years and then have his sentence reduced and be paroled in two years to go cruising again!" she said.

"Wow!" Mel said, "you are very radical and I didn't know it!"

"When it comes to murderers of innocent women for their jewellery, I am," she answered.

Mel could only agree, "Yeah, he was an evil murdering bastard," he said.

The Afrique Queen

Jon could not believe his eyes watching the CNN news in his stateroom, it announced the execution of himself by the Russians. The British Foreign Office had lodged a complaint and the Russian Ambassador had been called to be seen by the Home Secretary to explain his countries' policy of a no trial execution of a British subject. It came to nothing and was just put on file to be brought up at the next International Conference ..... end of. A formal notice would be sent to Moscow to be filed somewhere, but no one would ever find it again either in Moscow or London.

Jon was definitely now, Kieron Robert Pearce, an Irish citizen, a free man of the world, or was he? He was still in debt to Satan, who had undoubtedly arranged the fiendish episode in Russia, also his finger prints and DNA were Jon Weston's and there was very little he could do about it but hope that the reason to check them would never arise.

Just two days cruising left, and Keiron had to deal with two women and get their diamonds, but hang on a minute, he might go to Brighton and strike Hannah there, and that would leave only Rosa to worry about. "Rosa, it's Keiron, what's happening?" he asked on the phone.

"Nothing, I was waiting for you to call, you bad boy, I'm lonely and need some company, come to my stateroom for coffee and doughnuts on the balcony, and we'll talk about today," she said.

"Okay, I'll be ten minutes," he said. It was time to concentrate on the job in hand, he knocked on Rosa's door.

"C'm in," she said as she opened it, "good to see you, handsome, sit down."

As she poured the coffee, he looked around and noticed a jewel case partially open with part of the necklace hanging out of the lower drawer. The black mist descended, but it was too early in the day, it would have to be much later because of cabin cleaners, plus he didn't want to sit with her dead body for the rest of the day, until about 3am the next morning. As previously, he would wine and dine his victim until the early hours, and when the time was right he would kill her, and her jewellery would be his. They spent the day together. After an early lunch they laid on the sundeck, but it was too hot, 90+ even in the shade. They kept the bar staff busy, but with soft drinks, Keiron wanted to keep his head clear for later, he said the same to Rosa with a wink, and Rosa agreed but she had a different reason!

It was a formal night, a 'black and white ball' with a special menu in all three restaurants, and a grand dance in the magnificent central ballroom. At 6.30pm Keiron knocked on Rosa's door which opened almost immediately, "Wow!" she said, "you look fabulous."

He wore a white silk DJ with a black silk shirt and bow tie, with black mohair and silk trousers. "And you look out of this world!" he enthused. She was in a black dress, knee length, with a white squared pattern, low cut to reveal her beautiful cleavage, and of course, the necklace to which Keiron's eyes were magnetically drawn, "You, my darling girl, look absolutely beautiful and I will be so proud to escort you tonight," he blarnied.

"Thank you, kind sir," she said. He also ogled the watch, bracelet and rings. It wasn't the black mist that descended, but he was filled with a strange warmth and almost started to salivate like some sort of beast of prey. He managed to control himself and took her hand as they started to walk to the bar for pre-dinner drinks. "Good lord," she said, "your hand is very hot!"

"I'm sorry, I've been hot all day, being with you," he said, they laughed.

But she felt a little uncomfortable and took his arm instead, the warmth came through his sleeve, but he wasn't sweating, 'weird' she thought, but let it slide. They walked in to the 'Casablanca' restaurant and turned many heads, they were shown to a table on the central, raised part of the venue. "Keiron," Rosa said, "let's have a bottle of champagne, I am in the mood," she added.

"You bet," he agreed and gestured to the wine waitress, "a bottle of Chrystal, please," he said. It was soon brought in a bucket of ice on a stand and served with a flurry and a bang from the cork. "Here's to you my darlin'," Keiron said.

"And here's to us having a 'special' night," she said, with a wink.

Keiron picked up his champagne flute and saw the word 'soon' etched in the mist on the glass. Caviar to start was ordered, beluga of course, followed by lobster in champagne sauce. They ordered another bottle of champagne, Keiron made sure that Rosa's glass was brimmed and his was only a third full. "It's time to go dancing," Rosa said, as they finished their coffee and cognac. Just a little unsteadily Rosa took Keiron's arm which she said had 'cooled down'.

"Good," he said, "it must have been the cold champagne!" The six piece western style band were very good, and Rosa and Keiron went straight on to the floor and danced to 'Love me do' by the Beatles. They danced to three or four Beatle hits, then fell in to a booth and ordered large cognacs, and sat looking at each other in a lecherous way, but Keiron's sights were on the gems, not Rosa, although he managed to catch her sexy gaze. "He looked at his watch, it was 1.15am, the time was getting close.

"Let's go, my lovely Irish boy, I am feeling very naughty," Rosa said.

"Okay," Keiron said, "so am I." But he meant it in a more sinister way.

"Another brandy?" Rosa said as they entered her stateroom.

"Yes, why not, it'll finish the evening off nicely," he said.

"Oh no, I've got something else in mind to finish the evening off!" she giggled. She poured two large Remy Martin cognacs into balloon glasses and they sat on the balcony listening to the waves lapping against the side of the ship.

Sipping their drinks, looking at the gems that Rosa was wearing, he began once again to feel the inner warmth and the black mist started to descend. He jumped to his feet and took her by the throat and at the same time dragging her back into the room, all the time pressing with enormous satanic strength on her windpipe which was soon crushed. She stopped breathing and her eyes bulged, she was dead and he laid her on the bed and started to strip her of her diamonds, he also removed her dress etc. He'd taken the precaution of washing the glass, he hadn't actually touched anything, the door, anything on the balcony or in the bathroom. Rosa had handled the bottle, there were none of his prints on anything.

He waited until 3am before he lifted her off of the bed, carried her, fireman style, and let her body drop into the sea. A man on a lower deck turned to go back into his stateroom just as she fell past his balcony, he heard the splash but thought nothing of it through his alcohol-filled haze. Once again, Jon wiped the 'Do not disturb' sign as he hung it on the outside of the door and went back to his stateroom. He thought, she would be missing for one day, even if a room attendant went in all they would do is clean after finding no one there, and remove the sign. Rosa would not be seriously missed until disembarking time, and by then he would be gone and away with her jewellery. He patted his pocket containing the diamonds and once again the inner warmth started to engulf him, but he went straight into a cool shower. But even with very cool water, the mirror began to steam up and the words 'U O ME MORE, S' appeared, still wet he poured himself a very large brandy and sat on the bed. He woke at 6.30 and went into the bathroom, the mirror was clear, he ran the hot tap so that steam would cover the mirror, but nothing appeared. He thought it could have been the alcohol or the fact that he could have dreamed it.

Tunis

B ack at the home port, Keiron found Hannah in the reception area, "Hi," she said, "not really a holiday romance was it! You must come over to England some time and come and see me in Brighton," she suggested, as she gave him her card.

He looked at it, and said, "Hollingbury, that sounds nice, and very rural."

"It's an industrial estate," she said, laughing, "but please come over soon, I've enjoyed our 'dalliance' even though it was only for a few days," she kissed his cheek and whispered, "soon!".

Keiron thought, yes I've an idea it will be! He checked back into his hotel for another two weeks and was able to do a tourist deal for cash in advance with a double de luxe sea-facing room. He laid on his king size bed and watched European news, an item about Jon Weston's death in Russia, and that the government had made a protest to the Russians. Keiron thought 'well, that's the end of me', he laughed and went over to his mini bar and poured himself a large scotch and added lots of ice, 'here's to Keiron Pearce' and raised his glass.

Brighton

Keiron landed at Gatwick airport at 5pm, at the north terminal, he went through passport control without any problems even though he was carrying a huge amount of cash. If he'd been stopped he'd have shown his newly printed business card in his new name, but the occasion had not arisen. His haul of diamonds and the bulk of his cash was in a safety deposit box in the Bank of Tunisia. He walked out of the terminal straight into a taxi, "Brighton, please," he said to the Asian driver who said 'it'a a fixed fare of £60, sa', "okay, fine let's go, and to the best hotel on the seafront, I think it's the 'Grand'."

They arrived at the hotel about an hour later, having hit road works, and rush hour traffic, "Here we are, sa," the driver said, as he jumped out of the cab to get Keiron's luggage from the boot. A doorman took the bags to reception. Keiron gave the cabbie £70, "Thank you, sa," he said as he got back into the cab.

"I'd like a double facing the sea, if possible, I'm sorry I don't have a reservation," he said.

"That all right, sir, I think we can accomodate you," Rebecca said, "I've a double on the second floor, but it won't be ready until 7 o'clock, perhaps you woud like a drink, complimentary of course, in the bar," and gave him a blue card with 'bar token' written on it.

"Thank you," he said, and walked into the bar which was just a few yards away. He paid for three days in advance, in cash, always cash, credit cards were too traceable. The Grand's dollar rate wasn't good, but he had no choice having left his euros in Tunis. A porter approached him and told him that his room was now ready and apologised for the delay. In the room, he walked over to the balcony doors and opened them and looked out to sea. This will be the last one, he thought, Hannah's diamonds would set him up, his plan was to go back to car dealing, but not in London, his face was too well known. Unless of course, he had a bit of facial surgery, he pondered, but first things first.

"Hiya Hannah, it's Kieron," he said on the phone, "how are

you?"

"Hi darling, this is an unexpected call, where are you?"

"At the Grand Hotel, in Brighton," he replied.

"WHAT? I don't believe it, when did you get here?" she asked.

"Last night," he answered.

"When can we get together?" she almost begged.

"How about tonight, grab a cab and we can have dinner here," he suggested, "let's say about 7.30, okay?"

"That'll be very nice," she said, excitedly.

He hoped she would wear her jewellery, but tonight would be too soon, it would be the build up to the final act. He sat in the bar at 7.30pm as arranged, and waited ten minutes before Hannah arrived, "Hello gorgeous," she said, and kissed his cheek, "how fabulous to see you so soon, don't tell me I'm the only reason you're here," she enquired.

"No, I'm to buy a Bentley for a Tunisian business man," he lied.

"You come all this way to buy one car?" she questioned.

"Yes, it's quite special, £150,000 worth," he lied again.

"Wow!" she said, "you don't mess with Renaults do you," she laughed.

"No, I'm sorry," he said, "only cars that make top dollar, but my expenses are high as you can imagine," he said.

Hannah changed the subject by asking, "Has your room got a double or kingsize bed?" she giggled.

"Kingsize," he replied with a huge smile. He ordered a bottle of Dom Perignon at a table in the conservatory. They watched the seafront traffic and sipped their nectar just looking at each other as well. "Dinner?" Keiron suddenly said, "Shall we go and eat?"

"But first finish the bottle!" Hannah said.

Unless you go to Claridges, the Savoy Grill or the Ritz, hotel food, even 5*, around the country, is the same, it always tastes as if it was cooked yesterday. This was the opinion of Hannah and Keiron as they sipped their cognacs in the bar conservatory. At 11.30pm they took the lift to his room, the door had only just closed and they were undressing each other and in passionate embraces. Their love-making exceeded all boundaries and they collapsed on to both sides of the kingsize bed, completely spent. They started laughing as Keiron jumped off the bed and said, "Another nightcap, I think," and poured two large brandies. Hannah laying naked on the bed, wearing her necklace, made him start to heat up from the inside, a sip of his drink and he went for a shower, but only tepid. Out of the shower he turned the water to hot, after a few seconds the word 'soon' appeared, but only for a short while, then disappeared. He returned to the bedroom thinking, I could do it now, but he would miss out on the bracelet and watch, only getting the necklace. He wanted the whole lot!

"Shall I stay tonight?"

"Yes," Keiron said, "I'll be lonely if you don't," he blarnied.

"Good," Hannah said, "cos I'm not moving from here!" and laughrd.

"Well, you'd better be a good girl during the night," Keiron said, smiling a wicked smile.

"Oh, I'll be marvellous," she answered. They slept until 7 am and Hannah was in the mood 'for a little of what she fancied' as she put it, "And this is where I stop being a good girl!" she giggled, and put her hand down between Keiron's legs. They made love again, then collapsed across the bed. They showered together and ordered breakfast from room service. "Wow, look at the time," she said, "I must go to work, can we call a cab, please. Shall we meet for dinner tomorrow night? I've got some late work to do tonight."

"Yes," Keiron said, "but this time we'll go to a restaurant."

"Yes, I know a good Chinese in the Lanes." They kissed goodbye as she said, "I'll call you tomorrow at 6 ish." The cab pulled away as she waved from the window, Keiron looked out to sea from the hotel steps, the ocean, he thought, my friend the sea, I may need you again very soon, very soon indeed.

"Put on all your glad rags, honey," he said to Hannah over the phone the next day, "there's a summer ball at the hotel tonight, I'll have to hire a DJ etc., but we will look fantastic, I've got tickets."

"Fabulous," she said, "I will look like a million dollars!"

$200 will do, he thought with a wicked smile, "Grab a cab and get here at about 7 o'clock." He hired a white DJ with all the accessories from a good store in the town centre.

Heads turned as they walked arm-in-arm into the special

banqueting suite of the hotel, a string quartet played near the entrance as Keiron handed the tickets to the doorman. The six course dinner was very good and Keiron ordered a bottle of Bollinger, the best that was available. He had declined the table that they were shown to and asked for a table for two near the dance floor, the waiter had said 'no' until he received £20 in his hand and then his attitude suddenly changed with a smile and a 'thank you, sir'. He ran off to move tables and chairs to make room for a table for two. They received the best of service, perhaps the waiter expected another £20, but he didn't get it. They danced fast ones, medium ones and smoochy ones, the band was terrific, with the female singer smiling at Keiron a lot of the time.

Hannah noticed, and said, "Silly tart, can't she see you're with the best looking woman in the room!" Keiron laughed, and the most be-jewelled, he thought. Once again the black mist started to fall, the deed will be tonight, but how? he wondered. Could he take her for a walk along the beach, it was a warm balmy night and they could kick off their shoes and go for a paddle, and then WHAM!

At 1am the venue started to empty as weary revellers left to go home, he suggested a walk along the shore, "Okay," she said, "is there any sand?" They found that the tide was out a long way and they walked barefoot on the soft sand that felt fantastic between their toes. It had become pitch black, there was only the start of a new moon. They walked to the ruined pier, and as they did Keiron put on a pair of latex gloves and manoeuvred Hannah towards some shingle then pushed her to the stones and put his hands around her throat pressing with all his strength on her windpipe, which was soon crushed. Her arms and legs thrashed about for a few minutes, then stopped, she was dead. He dragged her body to an up-turned rowing/fishing boat and in it's shadow removed her diamonds, then lifting the boat, he rolled her body under it and let it entomb her. Putting his shoes and socks on and brushing himself down, he walked westward, away from the boat and up the steps to the main promenade. A drunk man asked him for some change, he ignored him. "Tosser," the man said loudly. But Keiron didn't want any confrontation and therefore recognition. He crossed the road and then turned towards his hotel, he walked through reception and went up to his room and started to pack. He would leave at 6 am, get a taxi to Gatwick and then back to Tunis.

He booked a cab for 5.45am and had an alarm call for 5am and was ready at reception, on time, paid his bill and waited at the front door. Suddenly he thought about the DJ kit which was in his luggage, oh well nothing I can do about it now, anyway it would have his DNA, perhaps a happy mistake! At Gatwick he checked in at BA and the Air Tunisia desks for the first flight out. BA had one going at 11.30am, that'll do nicely, he thought as he walked to the sales desk. He paid for his ticket and received his boarding card and then went straight through to air-side, keeping his head down away from the CCTV cameras. He wandered around the shops, still keeping his head down. His flight number came up on the screen 'boarding gate 25', he walked slowly with his head down, reading a newspaper and sat in the waiting area, still reading. He had spread the jewellery around, the necklace wrapped in a handkerchief in his large suitcase, he wore the rings on his little finger with the stones turned inwards and the bracelet and watch were wrapped in clothes in his smaller case. His luggage went through without a hitch and so did he. He had passed a shop window in the air-side shopping area and he saw, in the condensation, the words 'I'm here', his blood ran cold and the inner heat built up. He sat with his head down, being a scheduled flight and a first class ticket holder, he turned left at the plane's doorway.

Tunis

Tunis customs were very relaxed, in fact the x-ray machines were switched off and the two officials were standing just chatting and smoking as they waved passengers through to the luggage carousel area. He collected his cases and went outside to get a taxi, at the hotel he paid for a further week in the same double room. They were glad to see him back and afforded him the graciousness a regular customer would expect, in fact in his absence the room had been decorated and the furniture renewed even two shirts and a pair of slacks had been laundered and were hanging in the wardrobe with his freshly valeted dinner suit, of which he now had two! He unpacked and wrapped the gems in the red handkerchief and put them in a large envelope and took it down to the hotel's safe, but padded it with newspaper to disguise the feel of jewellery.

Brighton

Hannah's brother Monty reported her missing 24 hours after her failure to arrive at the factory. She had never missed a day without calling him first, whether sick or any other reason. The police learned that she had been seen at the dinner and ball after a taxi driver saw her face in the local paper and told them that he had taken her there at about 7pm the night before last. Police searchers covered the beach and a young WPC suddenly shouted in horror, "Over here." As she and two PC's lifted the boat Hannah lay there staring skyward, with dark bruises on her throat. She was taken to the mortuary where the pathologist began his examination.

"Straight forward strangling," he said to Detective Inspector Wickes of Sussex police.

"Yes," he said, "are those scratches on her neck, as well as the bruises?"

"It looks like a chain or necklace has been removed in a hurry."

"Thank you," DI Wickes said, "I'll go to the Grand and ask who, if anyone, she was with."

They found the name of the waiter that had attended them, "He's not on duty until 6pm."

"Get him here now, this is a murder enquiry," Wickes demanded.

"He'll be a while, he lives in Worthing."

"I'll wait," he said. David Markham looked very worried and flustered when he met DI Wickes. "Right," Wickes said as they sat in the conservatory, "what did her companion look like?"

"Tall, very smart, suave, you know, Rolex watch, suntan, good looking and spoke with a slight Irish accent," he said.

"Irish eh, that's interesting. How was the lady dressed?" he asked.

"Oh, she was lovely, beautiful jewellery, and lots of it. He was a good tipper, I got the impression he was some sort of gigolo, we get them here all the time."

"I would like you to come to the police station to do a photofit comparison, okay?"

"Yes, of course," David said, "I'll clear it with the boss."

"That's all right, you'll be back by six."

At the police station, the photofit technician made an almost perfect face of Jonathan Weston, but they didn't know that, and DI Wickes took a copy of the photofit with the intention of putting it on websites all over the world, for him to be caught. He hoped it would be soon, airports and ports were checked but to no avail, Wickes thought, and hoped that he was still in the country, but Jon Weston was at least a thousand miles away. Once again Satan had helped him to disappear.

Now he wanted to sell the diamonds, but he would have to go to another country in North Africa, Algeria perhaps, just a short flight from Tunis, he could be there and back in one day. With just a small brief case he went to the travel agent and booked a flight to Algiers. Two hours was the flight time across the Med, to avoid landing air traffic overland. He had in mind that he would have no trouble selling the gems and hoped there was a 'diamond quarter', they paid the best prices because they recognised quality diamonds. He went through customs with the usual lackadaisical attitude of the officers. They were just looking for guns and other armaments, and drugs. Outside the airport he found a cab and said, as it was their second language, in French, "Place de diamond, si'l vous plait." This area was small, with a square with a Moorish tiled fountain in the centre. In one corner he saw just what he was looking for, a large double fronted shop with signs in Arabic, French and English. He pressed the security buzzer which opened the door almost immediately, a grey haired bearded man stood behind a thick glass partition with a microphone on each side. "Do you speak English?" Keiron asked.

"Yes, we cater for all nationalities."

"I have some diamonds to sell that belonged to my mother."

"Why have you come to Algiers to sell them?" the dealer asked.

"I'm here on holiday and didn't want to leave them in my London flat for safety reasons."

"May I see them?" the man said. Keiron took the envelope from his pocket and passed it through the opening in the glass. "I'll have to check them on the world list computer," he said, "I'll be ten minutes." He returned from the rear office and pushed the rings and the bracelet back through the partition, "I'm sorry," he said, "but these pieces are zircons, but I'll offer you 60,000 euros for the necklace and the watch and that is a very good price as there is a stone missing from the watch band," he pointed to the gap where the stone had been. Keiron sat down in a customer's chair, fucking fakes he thought, fucking fakes! "I'll give you 200 euros for the metal content of the rings and the bracelet," the man added.

Keiron thought, 60 grand is 60 grand, he stood and said, "Okay, I'll accept your offer." The dealer pushed the obligatory form through the glass, he filled it in with some lies and just one or two truths. He came out of the shop angrily thinking that he had killed a beautiful woman for just 60,000 euros. He suddenly stopped, he had just fallen for the oldest trick in the jewellery dealer's book. He went back to the shop, pressed the buzzer and was let in , "Hello again, as you have only bought the metal of the rings could I have the fake stones?" he asked.

"No, Mr Weston you cannot. Now, if you don't leave my shop I will call the police, your face has been on satellite TV for two days, so I suggest you go quickly," the dealer threatened.

He left the shop smarting from the thought that he had just been had, still, he thought, I was lucky to get the 60,000 euros, he could have kept the lot and called the police. New problems were upon him now, fucking satellite TV was showing him around the Middle East. Where can I go now? South Africa, South America? Is my picture all over the world? Inwardly he started to panic, back at the hotel he walked in with his hat on and his head down. Up in his room he dyed his hair blond once more, and laid on the bed to contemplate his future. Plastic surgery might be an option but a lengthy process and very expensive if the surgeon recognised him. He took a tepid shower to get rid of the sweat of the day, even though the water was barely warm the mirror had steamed up, in the steam just two letters appeared 'UK'. Of course, he thought, that's the last place they'll look for me!

New Rochelle (New York State)

"Chief Inspector Lloyd of Scotland Yard."

"Mel," shouted the lady phone operator at the sheriff's office, "he wants to talk to you."

"Jon Weston is still alive," came the message on the phone, " he's been seen in Tunisia and Algiers."

"WHAT?" said Mel, "have these sightings been confirmed?" he asked.

"Yes, and we think he may have killed a woman here down on the south coast, in Brighton. We've got him on CCTV at the Grand Hotel and at Gatwick boarding a flight for Tunis," he reported.

"Well I'll be," Mel said, "this guy would survive a nuclear holocaust, so who did the Russians kill?" he asked.

"Some poor tourist that looked like him," he replied, "they do that sort of thing to save face and put it out on the internet for all to see, he died a terrible death."

"Yeah, I know, I saw the DVD," Mel said, "what can we do about it?"

"Nothing at the moment, unless he comes to England."

"Okay, Chief Inspector," Mel said, "thanks for the call." The phone went dead.

London

"**I** want airports and ports covered 24/7," he told his 2nd in command, "we're going to get this murdering bastard, we've been trying for two years," he stated.

The response was amazingly quick, the next day Jon Weston was seen at Gatwick's north terminal. He was going through customs in the queue and he suddenly looked up at the screen. DI Wickes was sitting watching the screens in the control office when he saw him, "That's him," he shouted, "stop him getting through," he called over his police radio to two armed PC's on the floor. "Grab him, the one in the sun hat." The two officers ran to the area and Jon Andrew Weston was grabbed.

"What's going on?" he yelled as DI Wickes came running up.

"Jonathan Andrew Weston, I'm arresting you for the murder of Hannah Golding on or about the 20th of July this year, in the town of Brighton, East Sussex." He then read him his rights. He was marched through to the luggage carousel where an officer picked up his cases, they might contain valuable evidence. The drive to Scotland Yard took about an hour and a half, Jon was taken into the main police station and then formally charged with Hannah Golding's murder.

"My name is Keiron Pearce, my passport is in my jacket pocket." His pockets were emptied, the passport was found and sent down to forensics for verification as to it's authenticity.

In the interview room Jon protested his innocence in his Irish accent, Wickes banged the desk and said, "You're about as Irish as I am, you're Jonathan Andrew Weston from Camden Town, London, and when the report on your passport comes back perhaps we'll get to the truth," he said. "We've got you on CCTV at the Grand Hotel in Brighton, arm-in-arm with Hannah Golding."

"That proves nothing," Jon said.

"We'll see about that as soon as the report comes back, we'll take a step in the right direction." The passport report was decisive, "Well," the DI said, " it appears that the number of the passport belongs to Kevin O'Leary of Waterford, who unfortunately died two years ago, what do you say to that eh? Jon Weston of London?" Jon buried his head in his hands. "Oh, there is a lot more evidence we are going to show you, you will probably appear in front of the magistrates in the morning."

Bow Street Magistrates Court

"Jonathan Andrew Weston, you are charged that you did unlawfully kill Hannah Riva Golding on the 20th of July this year 2012, how do you plead? Guilty or not guilty?"

"I am Keiron Pearce of Dublin and I plead NOT FUCKING GUILTY," he reverted to his Irish accent.

The magistrate opposed bail, "Take the prisoner into remand," he said. He was taken down to remain on remand until his trial at the central criminal court, the Old Bailey.

St Petersburg

Vasili's phone rang, "Hello," he said.

"They've caught Jonathan Weston in England, the real one with an Irish passport, he came in on a flight to Gatwick from Tunisia," Mikhail said, "that's all Georki knew, he's a good agent."

"I'll send him a reward," Vasili said, and put down the phone.

Two men were sent to London, they took up residence in a flat owned by Vasili, in Kensington Gardens. Peter, the older one, was an expert marksman and assassin, his father had been one of Stalin's heroes and had taught him everything he knew about poison darts, firearms, bombs etc. If anyone could get to Jonathan Weston, he could. He spoke four languages including perfect English. Every day they went to the Old Bailey disguised as paparazzi with long lens cameras, every morning the accused would arrive in a white dark windowed prison van. Cameras flashed through the little blackened windows hoping to get a shot of the serial killer, as it was alleged in all the daily's and red-tops. Peter thought that a bomb would be the answer, as they went over a piece of road en route, BANG! Peter chose the corner just before the van turned in to the entrance. At two in the morning he put up an emergency board in the middle of the street with the warning 'Gas leak - no smoking or naked lights'. He and his colleague dug up the cobble stones and dug to a depth of 18 inches, they then laid 4 kilos of semtex, very high explosive. When buried, the power became as much as 50lbs of gelignite, the van and everybody in it would be blown to pieces. The bomb would be activated by remote control, with a mobile phone, all he had to do was press the 'call' button. A beat constable suddenly appeared, saying, "Gas problems?"

"Yes, officer, but we've managed to solve the problem, thanks for your concern," Peter said. The policeman walked on at a slow pace. They packed all the equipment into their little van and sped off, they would be back in the morning.

At 6am a Swedish tourist made a phone call to Stockholm, as he pressed his 'call' button in a nearby tourist hotel there was an enormous explosion just down the street from the Old

Bailey. At first it was thought to be a gas main, the patrolling PC had reported workmen at this location to his desk sergeant as he went off duty. The police checked with the gas authority who said that no such work had been authorised. A red alert was called 'Terrorists'. The devastation in the close-built area was huge, not a window within a quarter of a square mile survived. The 'Pen and Wig' pub/restaurant close to the courts was badly damaged, even the doors were blown off. The fire brigade and police were there in 6 minutes, there was only one casualty, a cleaner on his way to work, but his injuries were superfluous, just cuts and bruises, he was very lucky and only spent one day in hospital. The Old Bailey was put on terrorist alert, the whole area was cordoned off to the public and traffic, news cameras and even a TV news helicopter hovered above the scene.

Jon Weston was kept in his cell, he asked the warder the time, who said, "Don't know." Jon's Rolex had been retained as possible evidence. Hot water, for a wash and shave he thought. The single sealed razor was in the prisoner's special pack, the blade, if tampered with, would disintegrate (for possible suicides). He had to wait for the water to flow, it wasn't switched on until 6am, but at least he knew now what time it was. As the small mirror steamed up after running the hot water, the words 'OUT SOON' appeared on the glass.

The Old Bailey - The Trial December 15Th 2012

"**P**risoner at the bar," the Clerk of the Court said, " are you Jonathan Andrew Weston, also known as Keiron Robert Pearce, residing at 12D Albert Street, Camden Town, London?"

"No, I am Keiron Robert Pearce of 90, McCoyle Road, Dublin," he lied.

The Clerk referred to the Judge who called the prosecution QC to the bench and was told about the false passport and fake identity. "Prisoner at the bar, you will be tried for murder in the name of Jonathan Andrew Weston, the jury will adhere to that ruling," the Judge said.

"I AM KEIRON PEARCE!" came the shout.

"The accused will remain silent or be taken down to the cells and be tried in his absence," said His Lordship.

"Is he going for some sort of insanity plea?" asked the prosecutor's colleague.

"I hope so, the trial could go on for weeks while his sanity is verified, or not," he answered with a knowing smile. Jon remained quiet sitting behind the thick glazed dock between two policemen, and handcuffed to one.

"You are charged that on the 20th of July of this year, 2012, you did unlawfully kill by strangulation Ms Hannah Goldring. Do you plead guilty or not guilty?" the Clerk said.

"Not guilty," came the reply.

The prosecution QC stood to address the jury, "Members of the jury, I will introduce you to a man that has covered two oceans with horrible crimes of pre-meditated murder. He has killed four women on the high seas for their jewellery, callously throwing their bodies overboard after seducing them and stealing their diamonds," he said. "But here today, we are only concerned with the murder of Hannah Riva Golding, who was strangled on Brighton beach on the 20th of July of this year, 2012, and her body callously put beneath an upturned fishing boat. He was then caught on CCTV boarding a flight the next day, to Tunisia. He subsequently returned on the 22nd of July when he was arrested and taken into custody. A trail of vicious killings will be unfurled during this trial."

"Objection m'lord," said the defence barrister, "the accused is only on trial in the case of Hannah Riva Goldring, and no other."

"Objection sustained," his Lordship said.

"Thank you m'lud," came the reply from the defence barrister.

"Why did Jonathan Weston change his appearance by dying his hair and growing facial hair, why did he buy a fake passport in the name of Keiron Robert Pearce, and where did he amass $580,000 and 300,000 euros in cash? Only from the sale of ill-gotten gains. These amounts of money were found in his luggage together with about £50,000 worth of jewellery that he has yet been unable to sell. So, members of the jury, I can only ask you to return a verdict of guilty. The prosecution will show how the accused befriended and seduced Hannah Golding on a cruise holiday in the Mediterranean. He then followed her to Brighton two weeks after their liaison on the 'Afrique Queen' cruise ship and booked into the 'Grand Hotel' in Brighton. There is CCTV evidence and booking paperwork to substantiate this. He then accompanied her to a 'Grand Ball' on the 20th of July, after which he took her to the beach opposite the hotel and did strangle her until she was dead. He then robbed her of her jewellery and hid her body under an up-turned rowing/fishing boat that was conveniently on the beach. The next morning he took a taxi to Gatwick airport and flew back to Tunis with her diamonds. For some reason he decided, after three days, to return to England, possibly to sell te gems. He was arrested upon returning to Gatwick, on suspicion of the crime. There is CCTV evidence of him escorting his victim to the ball, and a waiter's testimony that they spent the evening together, and left the venue at 1.15am, leaving the hotel arm-in-arm. Thirty six hours later her body, minus her jewellery, was found under a fishing boat. Meanwhile, the accused went to Gatwick early in the morning by taxi and boarded a flight for Tunisia, arriving some three and a half hours later. As previously stated, he returned to England and was then taken into custody, it can only be surmised that he came back to England to turn his ill-gottten gains into cash. I now call David Markham." The waiter from the hotel entered the witness box and was sworn in. "Are you David Markham of 27, Richmond Road, Worthing, West Sussex?" the lawyer asked.

"Yes," replied Markham.

"Do you recognise the prisoner at the bar?"

"Yes," he replied.

"When did you last see him?" he asked.

"At the Grand dinner and ball, on the 20th of July."

"Who was he with?" he was asked.

"He was with a very attractive dark haired lady who wore lots of diamonds on her neck and on her hands."

"At this juncture m'lud I will state that no such jewellery was found on Hannah Goldring's body," the QC said.

"Carry on Mr Marks."

"Yes, m'lud," came the reply.

The trial lasted 3 days, no other victims of Jon Weston's were brought into question, although there was an investigation as to the cash that was found in his luggage. On the last day of the trial, Jon Weston stood in the dock as the jury were recalled. The Clerk of the Court stood and addressed the foreman, "Members of the jury, have you reached a decision?"

"Yes, sir," he said.

"Do you find the defendant guilty or not guilty of murder, and is it a majority verdict?"

"It is, sir," he said.

"And the verdict is?" the Clerk asked.

"Guilty," he answered. There was a strange silence in the court as the verdict was announced, it lasted until the Judge stated that the prisoner would be sentenced on January the 10th, 2013. He was taken down to a holding cell to await transport back to Belmarsh remand wing. The van arrived, and in handcuffs and with a head covering, he was led to the van just a few feet away. The van pulled out into the main street, travelled 20 metres when there was an enormous explosion directly below the van. For the second time in one year the Russians had tried their vengeance, the van was blown to pieces with the police motor cyclists and the squad car escorts killed. The van driver and his mate's bodies were spread all over the area, but out of the wreckage walked Jon Weston. He started running and running and running, even his handcuffs had gone. He ran up small streets, along main roads, until his lungs were almost bursting. He came to a small side street and parked there was the old VW Golf, he looked inside, the keys were in the ignition just as he had left it all that time ago. He jumped in and drove off, the fuel gauge registered 'full', he drove into the countryside and turned into a wooded area and stopped. His breathing had calmed down. Opening the boot of the VW there still was his suitcase, but on top was a red envelope. He opened it to find a Saudi Arabian passport in the name of Suliman Mouhammed Hussain, but the photograph was not Jon Weston, that is until he caught his reflection in the rear window! He now had dark skin and thick black hair and a moustache, exactly like the photo in the passport. He opened the suitcase, it contained three new, high quality suits, six very good shirts, underwear, silk socks and three pairs of good hand-made shoes, toiletries etc., plus all of his cash and a small piece of red paper with the word 'MORE' written on it. He started the car and logged in Heathrow airport on the sat nav, it would take about an hour to get there. He kept glancing at himself in the rear view mirror. About one mile into the journey he suddenly realised that he was no longer driving the VW Golf, it was now his beloved Mercedes SLS. The heat overtook his body as he sped along the M4 to the airport, his transformation was now complete. He said goodbye to Jonathan Weston and Keiron Pearce, but he thought that they had served him well and he had enjoyed them, after all they had made him a fortune, and with his new persona he could continue. Perhaps he would now dance to his master's tune in Dubai, lots of wealthy gorgeous women there, and his new passport could now take him anywhere in the world to ply his trade. Standing at the desk of Saudi Arabian Airways, he heard the stewardess speak in Arabic and he understood every word and when he faced her to buy a ticket to Dubai, he spoke the language perfectly.

How wrong he was, the women in Dubai were mostly covered in religious black garb. He booked in to the 'Burj-al-. Arab Hotel', it seemed to be the most luxurious hotel he had ever seen. His luggage was taken to his single suite, which was a double de-luxe in Europe. Being on the 20th floor he could even see the Royal Palace about a mile away, it was a magnificent edifice with minarets rising majestically above the rest of the city. He unpacked, showered and decided to go down to the reception area just to look around. He asked the girl at the tourist desk if the hotel had a bar, "Tourists only," she said with a beautiful smile. He went back up to his suite and found his passport, 'damn' he said loudly, 'it's a Saudi passport.' Well, there might be another way around this, he said to himself. He rang for room service, it took just 2 minutes before there was a knock on the door. He said, enter, in Arabic. The boy came in and bowed. "Does this suite have a mini bar?" he asked, holding up a $50 bill. The waiter took a key from his pocket and walked over to a panel in the wall, he inserted the key and pulled out a fixture of shelves containing a host of spirits, bottled beers, wines and champagnes. The bottom shelf held glasses and an ice box.

He gave the money to the boy, who then gave him the key and an envelope containing another key, "Your car has been delivered, sir," he said.

"My car?"

"Yes sir, it is in the basement garage." The boy then bowed and left.

Jon poured himself a very large single malt whiskey and almost downed it in one. He then went down to the basement garage, so many super cars, the best marques in the world, Bugatti, McLaren, Ferrari, Maseratti, Rolls Royce, Bentley, Lamborghini, he pressed the tiny button on the ignition key so that he could see the flash of his immobiliser light. There it was, way down on the right hand side, he almost ran to it. He got in and then realised it had suddenly become a left-hand drive car. On the seat was a red envelope, he opened it, it was a name, Baroness Nina Mescotti. Who was Baroness Nina Mescotti, he thought. Only one way to find out, he said to himself. He went to reception and said to the young girl "I'm meeting Baroness Mescotti, has she arrived yet?"

"No, she is due in at 7pm," she replied.

"The thing is, the meeting was arranged over the phone," he confessed, "and I don't know what she looks like."

"Oh, you can't miss her, she arrives with an entourage of at least six aides and a mountain of luggage, just be here at 7pm and you will meet her. She is a very, very beautiful and rich woman. They say that two of her entourage are millionaire ex husbands."

At exactly 7 o'clock a Rolls Royce limousine pulled up at the front of the hotel, followed by an estate car. Porters started to unload both the boot of the Rolls and the estate car, cases, trunks and hanging dress covers. A chair was put about 6ft from the reception desk, and the Baroness made her grand entrance. Looking straight ahead, not looking left or right, she sat down on the chair provided, while her entourage saw to everything. She was beautiful, probably the most beautiful woman Suliman (Jon) had ever seen, a goddess. Obviously of Mediterranean descent, Italian perhaps. He sat to the left of the reception desk with a newspaper. He especially wore one of the new silk Armani suits, cream with a burgundy silk shirt and brown lattice shoes, but no socks as was the Muslim way. She started to look around while waiting for the bookng of the whole second floor to be completed. Her eyes stopped for a few seconds on him, he smiled and went back to his newspaper. The Baroness and her followers disappeared, he continued to sit, just thinking and people-watching, when suddenly a middle-aged well dressed man came over to him and said, " Baroness Mescotti would like to invite you to her drinks party in her suites on the second floor, at eight. Shall I tell her that you will be there?" he asked.

"Yes," Jon replied, "it will be my pleasure. The man bowed, took one step back and then walked to the lift.

At 8.05pm he pressed the lift button to the second floor, he had changed into a black suit and white silk shirt, the lift door opened and standing there was the man who had invited him. He smiled and ushered Jon into the main suite, she was sitting on a purple velvet chair. When the Baroness saw Jon she stood and walked towards him holding out her hand, "Welcome," she said, "how nice of you to accept my invitation at such short notice," she said with the most fascinating smile.

"It's my privileged pleasure," he said as he kissed her hand very lightly. As they spoke, more guests were arriving, and a waiter started to mingle with a tray of champagne. Jon had done his best to keep his eyes off of her fabulous necklace, it was the finest he had ever seen, large diamonds and rubies set in platinum, he was completely enthralled. He didn't even notice the rings and the bracelets, they were all magnificent, about $2 million worth. Her dress of purple and white silk was a beautiful cover to her very gorgeous body, although she wouldn't see 40 again, she was very beautiful, and he wanted her and her jewellery. Finally there were about 20 guests, mainly middle-aged, but obviously wealthy people, one or two young ones made up the number but they left at about nine, leaving the older ones to finish the canapes and chrystal champagne. Jon just sat watching and the Baroness was watching him. She came over and sat next to him, she asked "What is your name?"

"I'm Suliman Mouhammed Hussain," he replied.

"And I am Nina Mescotti," she said, "where are you from?"

"Saudi," he answered, "Riyadh, actually."

"Are you a Prince, are you very rich?" she asked, smiling cheekily.

"Yes," he replied.

She laughed, "I'm sorry," she said, "I'm very naughty."

"Yes, I'm a Saudi Prince," he lied.

"Oh, how nice, my first boyfriend was a Saudi Prince, but he only wanted me to join his large harem," she laughed, "do you have a harem?" she questioned.

"No, I like to have one beautiful woman on my arm," he said.

"That's nice, very nice, would you like to have me on your arm?" she asked with a cheeky smile.

"Oh yes," he said, "it would be a pleasure that I could only dream of," he said, kissing her hand.

"Come," she said, "let's drive into the desert and make love under the beautiful moon and stars." She phoned someone called Guido and said, "I am alone tonight, I will want to be undisturbed until 9am." She hung up, her orders were understood, they had been heard many times before when she had taken a new lover. They stood at the hotel entrance waiting for the Mercedes to be brought round for them. When the Baroness saw it she said, "It's too small, take it away and bring me my Rolls Royce," she demanded. Five minutes later the Rolls was in attendance, "There you see, it's got a lot of room, especially in the back," she laughed cheekily. They drove for about half an hour into the desert with the Baroness sitting in the back. With audio talk through, they were able to hold a sexy conversation, she suddenly said, "STOP." He pulled off the road and drove behind an old monumental ruin. He got out of the car and opened the rear door, what he saw took his breath away, she was sitting completely naked except for her jewellery, and a beautiful smile. He climbed in and before he knew what had happened she had undressed him and was caressing his erection. Their lovemaking knew no boundaries, it lasted until 4am when they both sank back against the luxurious upholstery, gasping for air. "You are fantastic," she said, "you must have left many broken hearts along the way," she added.

"You could say that," he replied, thinking, and a few broken necks! This opportunity was perfect, but the car and the timing was wrong. The windows were steamed up and the word 'soon' was written on the driver's partition glass, it disappeared in about 10 seconds, only he saw it. They arrived back at the hotel and the car was taken away for valeting and re-parking. He returned to his suite and the Baroness returned to hers with a satisfied smile. He slept until midday, having had a recurring dream of the Baroness's diamonds, he had to have them, but how? he thought. Perhaps another drive into the desert and only he would come back. He went down to the ground floor reception area and almost went into shock. Baroness Mescotti's luggage was being loaded into the estate wagon and he just caught a glimpse of her as the Rolls sped away. He had missed his chance to get half a million dollars worth of diamonds, women like her move on quickly to their next adventure, he had already passed from her mind, luckily for her and her jewellery!

A waiter approached him with a package, "The Baroness Mescotti wished that you would receive this."

"Thank you," he said. He walked over to a corner table and opened the parcel, it contained a diamond encrusted Rolex and a note that read ' I hope we meet again, thank you, you were fabulous!' He sniffed the note which was impregnated with possibly the most expensive perfume. He looked at the exquisite time-piece, about $50,000 at least, he thought. Well, at least I got something, it might just cover my hotel bill.

Two days later, at midday, he presented himself to check out and asked for the bill, "It's been paid, sir," the receptionist said, "Baroness Mescotti settled it before she left, in fact there is an over payment of $1500."

"Spread it amongst the staff, including yourself," he said.

"Thank you very much," the receptionist said.

He ordered his car to be brought from the car park, in minutes it arrived and his luggage was put in the boot. "I've left your gratuity at the desk," he told the boy.

"Thank you sir," he said, smiling.

He drove his beloved Merc into the desert towards Abu Dhabi, a journey of about 150 miles or two hours in his super car. The Emirates were very peaceful and calm, the capital being very modern and westernised, and it was a port of call for cruise liners that were known for their rich cruisers, American, Russian and European especially Germans. Yes, he thought, blonde blue eyed arian women with lots of cash and lots of jewellery. He drove into the centre of the city, he found a beautiful edifice, the 'Emirate Palace Hotel', all stainless steel and tinted glass. He stopped at the cab rank and asked the first driver, "Is this the best hotel in the city?"

"This is the best hotel in the world!" the driver laughed.

"Thank you," he said, and drove to the main entrance, up the slight ramp. A young man came to greet him and ask him if he was to be a guest. "Yes," said Jon. He handed him the key and the luggage was taken to reception and the car taken to the car park. At the desk he asked for a single suite, not too high, overlooking the pool, at the same time showing a wad of American dollars.

"Suite 333 is available, that will be $1500 per night, how many nights will you be staying?" the girl asked.

"I don't know," he replied, "let's say 7 nights," he said.

"That will be $10,500," she said, "I'm afraid it's in advance unless you leave your credit card," she added.

"I don't have credit cards," he said, "I always pay cash," and gave her eleven $1000 bills. "Put the change on credit for my in-house spends," he said.

"Yes, sir," she said, smiling.

Wow! he thought, as he entered the suite, if this is a single, the doubles must be amazing, definitely the best that he'd seen and the most expensive, but worth it. He looked down from the balcony to the pool, there were people swimming but no one sun bathing, all the sunbeds were vacant, it must have been 100f out there. He took a shower and whilst admiring himself in the full length mirrored wall the word 'soon' appeared. His blood ran cold, yet there was an intense heat inside him that took his breath and gave him palpitations. He lay on the enormous bed trying to breathe. Sinking into a troubled slumber, he began to dream terrible dreams of hell and purgatory. He woke in a cold sweat and took another shower but this time very cold. Shivering, he went on to the balcony to lay in the hot sun with just a towel covering his lower body. He lay there for about 20 minutes and suddenly heard "Hello." Opening his eyes at the sound of the soft female voice, he saw a beautiful blonde woman aged about 35, wearing a blue bikini top and sarong. She was standing on the neighbouring balcony, "It's very hot," she said with a western European accent, possibly German or Dutch.

"Yes," he said, "I was just testing the sun, I think even for me it is too much."

"My name is Gudren, how do you do," she said, she made a hand shaking motion, he did the same, "it's too far to reach!" she laughed.

"My name is Suliman, but my friends call me Solly, please do," he said with a smile, "how about we meet for drinks in the main bar at 7 o'clock," he suggested.

"Vunderbar," she replied, with a beautiful white smile.

She's definitely German, he thought, laughing at himself. As arranged, they met in the bar at seven, she looked fabulous in a long cream dress that clung to her and showed every contour of her fabulous figure, her long legs, her slender waist and proud breasts. They kissed cheeks, "I always like to start the evening with champagne!" she said.

"Of course," he answered, and ordered a bottle of Dom Perignon as they sat at a table near a panoramic window that over-looked the well sculptured gardens. The waiter poured the champagne into their glasses after popping the cork with a professional flurry.

"Cheers!" she said, "here's to us!"

"Cheers!" Solly said, wondering what she meant by 'us'. She is being very forward and fast, he thought, but then forgot the thought.

"So, you must tell me about yourself," she said.

"Well," he said, "I was born in Riyahd, in Saudi, the son of a brother of the King, oh yes, I am a genuine royal Prince, but I prefer not to advertise it! I was sent to England when I was 12 years old to be educated at Eton which I hated, every damn minute of it! But at the age of 16 I came back home and became a precocious horrible young man, until one day , when I was 20, I decided I wanted to see more of the world. Money was no object and I went to America, New York to be precise, where I had the time of my life. I stayed for ten years, living in Manhattan," he lied, "I am now 38, and still single, the family are begging me to take a wife, but I am not ready."

"I bet there are hundreds of princesses at home that would jump at the chance," she said, laughing.

"There were one or two candidates," he said, "but I wasn't interested," he lied.

"So," she said, "I will tell you about me, it's not much really, my name is Gudren Voigter from Stuttgart, I am 32 years old and I too was educated in England, at Roedean which I loved. It is a beautiful school in Sussex on the south coast. I haven't travelled an awful lot apart from the usual, you know, skiing in Switzerland, Gstaad, the Riviera, Marbella, the hotspots. I'd love to go to America, especially Los Angeles and Hollywood. My father is a director of Mercedes Benz and soon will retire after 40 years with the company, but he will still be a big shareholder as his pension."

A major share-holder in Mercedes Benz, wow! he thought, this lady is very wealthy, but why no jewellery he asked himself. He decided to invite her to the Gala Party in the grand ballroom the next night to see if she wore any diamonds. The Gala Party was indeed an enormously splendid affair, a western orchestra of yesteryear playing Gershwin, Goodman and Glenn Miller, then there was a Beatles tribute group that were superb and a Queen tribute band with a Freddie Mercury incarnate who really set the room alight. What a night! "The best," Gudren said as she thanked Solly, giving him a full blown kiss with a beautiful soft mouth on his. His body tingled, not because of the kiss, but because of the huge emerald on a diamond studded chain around her neck which had been partially hidden by her high necked dress. The black mist came down as he realised that he was looking at a million dollars worth, at least, of the most exquisite stone he had ever seen ...... he had to have it, but how? Already a plan was formulating in his mind, we'll take a ride into the desert in my SLS, she'll like that, and then I will go to work and that wonderful emerald will be mine. He suggested that they have a nightcap and take a ride into the desert, she readily agreed and finished her drink quickly. He ordered his car to be brought up from the car park, when she saw it she said, "How wonderful, I have one of these but mine is black, how beautiful it is in white," she said, "let's go!" and got into the passenger seat. He drove slowly from the hotel and then on to the road that led to the desert highway, then he put his foot hard down on the gas pedal and wham! the V12 engine went crazy and they were soon doing 120mph in just a few seconds. With nothing on the road the miles slipped by, he stopped at a ruined temple and drove off the road and behind a high wall, Gudren sat smiling provocatively, "What is going to happen now?" she asked as she hitched up her dress to reveal a beautiful pair of legs. "With this dress I don't wear any lingerie," she said, giggling sexily, "do you want to make love to me?" she asked.

"Yes, of course!" he said, and leaned over and kissed her beautiful mouth, at the same time his hand caressed her thighs and vagina. She started to moan with pleasure, she was very moist and warm and she reached for his erect penis. He opened the door and they fell on to the soft sand, her orgasmic screams could only be heard by the desert creatures and the stars. His plan was now complete in his mind, it was very chancy but with his mentor in charge he was confident that it would work. As she lay there he took her head in his arm, she smiled as he twisted it through 90 degrees and her neck snapped. It was quick, she just laid there staring at the night sky, he removed the necklace, loaded her back into the passenger seat, then drove further up the highway for about two miles. Then, spinning the car around, he drove back towards the ruins, 100 - 120 - 140 - 150 mph and as soon as he was almost level with the ruins he put the car into a sideways slide, it hit the wall with tremendous force that threw him out of the car on to the sand at the side of the tarmac. He lay there for about 20 minutes before he gained the strength to stand up, he walked over to what was left of his beautiful car, the headlights were still shining and the engine was running, where she had been sitting was completely crushed and her body squashed into a space of about 12 inches. He started to walk away from the wreck, when there was a sudden gust of wind and in the sand at his feet appeared the word 'NOW'. He looked back, and sitting in the driver's seat was Jonathan Andrew Weston just staring into the night, with dead eyes. The emerald necklace was again around Gudren's broken neck. He walked on for about three metres and then realised his footsteps left no prints in the sand. A sudden gust of wind, and Jonathan, Keiron and Suliman .... were gone.

THE END

EPILOGUE

After being married for just four years, the Novaks divorced, the reasons being that their careers had made them grow apart. His police work and her working evenings meant that they saw very little of each other. Mel settled for $250,000 and just went back to New York City PD. Luckily, Colletti had just retired and he was made Precinct Captain.

....

Ben, the car valeter, passed all his exams and set up his practice as an attorney in New York. Every week his young nephew would come to valet his Jaguar, Ben's pride and joy.

....

Vasili and Mikhail were killed when their Jetstream jet exploded at 30,000 feet over Siberia on their way to Vladivostok. A rival family had bribed a mechanic to plant a bomb aboard, he was caught and put through the carcass grinder. The rival family eventually took over the St Petersburg operation.

....

Lorna Harper became manageress of a very up-market boutique in Brighton and married the owner.

....

Vicky Weston continued in her private practice, but dumped David when she found him in bed with a young boy at her house. She had returned early from a medical conference in Paris.

....

What happened to Jonathan Weston .... is your guess !!!